THE PHANTOM
of PEMBERLEY

THE PHANTOM
of PEMBERLEY

A PRIDE *and* PREJUDICE
MURDER MYSTERY

REGINA JEFFERS

Ulysses Press

30661 7158

R

Published in the United States by
Ulysses Press
P.O. Box 3440
Berkeley, CA 94703
www.ulyssespress.com

ISBN: 978-1-56975-845-8
Library of Congress Catalog Number 2010925863

Acquisitions Editor: Kelly Reed
Managing Editor: Claire Chun
Editor: Kathy Kaiser
Editorial Associates: Lauren Harrison, Alice Riegert
Production: Judith Metzener
Cover design: TG Design
Cover photo: © Compassionate Eye Foundation/Katie Huisman
    (gettyimages.com)

Printed in Canada by Webcom

10 9 8 7 6 5 4 3 2 1

Distributed by Publishers Group West

CHAPTER 1

~ ~ ~

"WE SHOULD TURN BACK," Fitzwilliam Darcy cautioned as they pulled their horses even and walked them side-by-side along the hedgerow. They explored the farthest boundary of the Pemberley estate, near what the locals called the White Peak.

"Must we?" Elizabeth Darcy gave her husband an expectant look. "I so enjoy being alone with you—away from the responsibilities of Pemberley."

Darcy took in her countenance. Hers was a face he had once described as being one of the handsomest of his acquaintance, but now he considered that compliment a slight to the woman. Her auburn hair, her fine sea-green eyes, her pale skin, her delicate features, and her heart-shaped face made her a classic beauty, and Darcy thought himself the luckiest of men. "For a woman who once shunned riding for the pleasure of a long walk, you certainly have taken to the saddle," he taunted.

"I have never said that I prefer riding to walking. Most would think me an excellent walker," she insisted. "It is just that when I sit atop Pandora's back and gallop across an open field, I feel such power—as if Pandora and I were one and the same."

Darcy chuckled. "Do you call how you ride 'galloping,' my Love?"

"And what would you call it, Fitzwilliam?" Even after fourteen months of marriage, he could still stir her ire, though she now understood his love for twisting the King's English and his dry sense of humor. It had not always been so. Elizabeth had told her friend

7

Charlotte Lucas that she could easily forgive Fitzwilliam Darcy his pride if he had not mortified hers. And Elizabeth's mother, Mrs. Bennet, had once described Fitzwilliam Darcy as "a most disagreeable, horrid man, not at all worth pleasing."

Darcy's eyebrow shot up in amusement: He recognized that tone. They had certainly challenged each other often enough. Actually, shortly after their official engagement, Elizabeth declared it within her province to find occasions for teasing and quarreling with him as often as may be. She had playfully asked him to account for his having ever fallen in love with her. The scene played in his mind as if it were yesterday.

"How could you begin?" said she. "I can comprehend your going on charmingly, when you had once made a beginning, but what could set you off in the first place?"

It was a time for honesty between them, so he told her, "I cannot fix on the hour, or the spot, or the look, or the words, which laid the foundation. It is too long ago. I was in the middle before I knew that I had begun." He laced his fingers through hers.

"My beauty you had early withstood." She teased him by running her hand up his jacket's sleeve, and Darcy could think of nothing but the natural ease of her touch. "And as for my manners," Elizabeth continued, "my behavior to you was at least bordering on the uncivil, and I never spoke to you without rather wishing to give you pain than not. Now, be sincere, did you admire me for my impertinence?"

"For the liveliness of your mind, I did," he said diplomatically. He did not—could not—admit to her his dreams of making love to her.

"You may as well call it impertinence at once; it was very little less." In retrospect, Darcy silently agreed. He often found himself lost in his fantasies of her; so much so that he did not recognize Elizabeth's challenge as impertinence, but more of flirtation. *"The fact is, that you were sick of civility, of deference, of officious attention. You were disgusted with the women who were always speaking and looking, and thinking for your approbation alone. I roused and interested you because I was so unlike them. You thoroughly despised the persons who so assiduously courted you."* Startled by

this revelation, Darcy had to admit that Elizabeth was correct. She caught his attention because she was his complete opposite, although she perfectly complemented his nature. With her, he had become freer. And he had come to think less poorly of the world.

Elizabeth cleared her throat, signaling Darcy that she awaited his response. "I believe, my dearest, loveliest Elizabeth," he said as he winked at her, "that I must call it a breakneck ride from hell."

Elizabeth glared at him for but a split second, and then she burst into laughter. "You know me too well, my Husband. Of course, you must take the blame. It was you who taught me to ride to the hound."

"Why is it, Mrs. Darcy, that all your bad habits came from my influence?"

"It is the way of the world, Fitzwilliam. Because God created Eve from Adam's rib and breathed life into her form, a woman is a vessel for her husband's generosity, but also his depravity."

"Depravity?" He barked out a laugh. "I will show you depravity, Mrs. Darcy." He reached for her arm, threatening to pull her from Pandora's back to his lap.

However, Elizabeth anticipated his move, and she kicked her horse's flanks, bolting away, across the open field toward the tree line. She lay forward along the horse's neck, cooing encouragement in her mount's ear. Her laughter tinkled in the crisp morning air, drifting back to where Darcy turned his horse to give chase.

He flicked Demon's reins to send his stallion barreling after Elizabeth. Although Pandora was as fine a mare as he had ever seen, Elizabeth's horse stood no chance of beating Demon in an out-and-out race. As he closed in on her, Darcy admired how she handled her animal—how she gave Pandora her head, but still knew when to exercise control over the horse. Elizabeth was a natural, as athletic as the animal she rode.

Darcy pressed Demon a bit harder, and the distance between them shortened. As he accepted his success as inevitable, horror struck. From nowhere and from everywhere at once, sound exploded around him. Pandora bucked and then stood upright, pawing the air. Elizabeth's scream filled him, as her horse threw Elizabeth forward. His wife nearly slid over the horse's neck, and then she slipped from the saddle, smacking her backside hard against the frozen ground. From the tree line, the screech of an eagle taking flight set Darcy's hair on end as he raced to her side.

Sliding from his horse's back, he was on the ground and running to her. "Elizabeth," he pleaded, "tell me you are well." He brushed her hair from her face as he tilted her head backward.

She groaned but moved with only a few awkward movements. "I am most properly bruised." She brushed the dirt from her sleeve. "And I fear my pride is permanently damaged."

Darcy kissed her forehead, relief filling his chest, as he helped her to stand. "Are you sure you can make it on your own?" He steadied her first few steps.

Elizabeth walked gingerly, but with determination. "Did you see him?" she asked cautiously.

"See who?" Darcy looked automatically toward the tree line. "I saw no one, Elizabeth; I concentrated on you."

"The man…I swear, Fitzwilliam, there was a man…there by the opening between the two trees." She pointed to a row of pin oaks. "A man wearing a cloak and carrying a hat."

"Stay here," Darcy ordered as he walked toward the copse, reaching for the pocket pistol he carried under his jacket.

Elizabeth watched him move warily to inspect where she had indicated. "Be careful, Fitzwilliam," she cautioned as he disappeared into the thicket.

Nervously watching for his return, Elizabeth caught Pandora's reins as her horse nibbled on tufts of wild grass. After securing her horse's bridle, she led Pandora to where Demon waited. "Easy, Boy," she said softly as she took Demon's reins, but she never took her eyes from where Darcy had vanished into the shadows.

After several long moments, he emerged from behind an evergreen tree, and Elizabeth let out an audible sigh of relief. As he approached, Darcy gestured toward where he had searched. "I am sorry, Elizabeth. I found nothing—not a footprint or any other kind of track. Nothing unusual."

"Are you sure, Fitzwilliam?" Still somewhat disoriented, she anxiously looked about her. "It seemed so real."

"Let me take you home." He moved to help her mount.

"Might I ride with you, Fitzwilliam? I would feel safer in your arms. Plus, I do not think my backside cares to meet Pandora's saddle right now."

Darcy's smile turned up the corners of his mouth. "You cannot resist me, can you, Mrs. Darcy?"

"It is not within my power, my Husband." Despite her nervousness, her eyes sparkled

Darcy slid his arms around her and brushed his lips over hers.

Elizabeth's arms encircled his neck. She lifted her chin to welcome his kiss. "You are indeed irresistible, my Love."

"I was simply uncomfortable," Elizabeth told Mrs. Reynolds, Pemberley's long-time housekeeper. They sat at the kitchen's butcher-block table; they had spent the past hour going over the coming week's menus and now shared cups of tea.

"Ye be seein' one of the shadow people, Mistress," Mrs. Jennings, the estate cook, remarked although she had not been part of the initial conversation.

Elizabeth hid her smile behind her teacup; but her voice betrayed her skepticism. "Shadow people, Mrs. Jennings?"

"Yes, Mistress." The woman wiped her floured hands on her apron. "People be seein' shadow ghosts 'round here for years. It be a man. Am I correct, Mrs. Darcy?"

"Yes, I believe that it was a man, although Mr. Darcy thinks it might have been some sort of animal—maybe even a bear."

Mrs. Reynolds tried to downplay Mrs. Jennings' fear of the supernatural, a fear shared by many Derby residents. "I am sure it was a bear, Mrs. Darcy. Mr. Darcy would not minimize your concerns by placating to you."

"Of course, you are correct, Mrs. Reynolds. Mr. Darcy would never ignore a possible danger to anyone at Pemberley."

Mrs. Reynolds chimed in, "Mr. Darcy is the best landlord and the best master that ever lived. There is not one of his tenants or servants but what will give him a good name. If I were to go through the world, I could not meet with a better."

The very man of whom they spoke strolled through the doorway. "There you are, Elizabeth."

Elizabeth offered up a bright smile: Her husband's masculine appearance always made her heart catch in her throat. Broad shoulders—slim waist—muscular chest and back—well defined legs and buttocks—no extra padding found on the man. And Elizabeth relished the idea that he chose her. "I apologize, Fitzwilliam; I was unaware that you sought me out."

Darcy's steel gray eyes caught hers. "I thought we might spend some time in the conservatory; the temperature turns bitter. We are in for a spell of bad weather."

"Really?" Elizabeth stood to join him. "My first winter in Derbyshire was quite mild. Should I expect lots of snow? We normally received some snow in Hertfordshire, but I was sadly disappointed with Derby last season. I had hoped for sledding and skating."

"Well, Mrs. Darcy, I do believe you will receive your wish." He placed her on his arm and led her away from the kitchen and toward the main part of the house.

However, when he turned to the main staircase and their private quarters, Elizabeth leaned into his shoulder. "I thought we were to enjoy the conservatory, Mr. Darcy," she reminded him.

Darcy tilted his head in her direction to speak to her privately. "Do you object to a change in our destination, my Love?"

"Not even in the least, Fitzwilliam." A blush betrayed her anticipation.

"I enjoy the flush of color on your cheeks, Sweetling." He brought her hand to his lips. From the beginning, she had driven him crazy—creating a powerful yearning he controlled only with great determination.

Elizabeth tightened her hold on his arm, but she could not respond. Darcy had that effect on her. Even when she had thought that she despised him, in reality, she sought *his* attention—*his* regard—*his* approval. They made the perfect pair. Darcy gave her the freedom to have her own thoughts and opinions, something she treasured; and Elizabeth showed him how insufficient were all his pretensions to please a woman worthy of being pleased. She truly esteemed her husband, looked up to him as a superior. Yet, theirs was a marriage of equals in all the essentials, those that made people happy. He was exactly the man who, in disposition and talents, most suited her. "I love you, Fitzwilliam," she whispered.

"And I love you, Elizabeth."

"Did you hear that?" Elizabeth sat up suddenly in the bed.

"Hear what?" Darcy groggily sat up and looked around for something out of place.

Elizabeth clutched the sheet to her. "I do not know. It was a click—like a latch or a lock being engaged."

Darcy pulled on his breeches and began to check the room. They had locked the door when they entered their shared chambers, and it remained secure so he checked the windows and the folding screens, but found nothing.

Elizabeth's eyes followed his progress.

Darcy released the door lock. Peering out, he nodded to someone in the hall and then closed the door again. Sliding the bolt in place, he turned toward the bed. "Murray is changing the candles in the hall sconces. Perhaps that is what you heard."

"Perhaps," she mumbled as she relaxed against the pillows. "It just sounded closer—as if it were in the room, not out in the hallway."

Darcy returned to the bed and followed her down. "I believe your fright earlier today with Pandora has colored your thoughts." He kissed Elizabeth behind her ear and down her neck to the spot where he could easily feel her pulse throbbing under her skin. "Let me give you something else upon which to dwell."

Her moan signaled her agreement. Lost to his ministrations, neither of them heard the second click echo softly through the room.

Seventeen-year-old Lydia Bennet Wickham traveled by public conveyance to her sister Elizabeth's Derbyshire home. It was her first trip to Pemberley, which even her husband reported to be one of the finest estates. She would rather this visit included her husband, Lieutenant George Wickham, but as Elizabeth's husband, Mr. Darcy, refused to accept Wickham in his home, that was not possible. The men had a long-standing disagreement, of which Lydia generally made no acknowledgment. In Lydia's estimation, Mr. Darcy should do as the Good Book says and forgive. However, men were stubborn creatures who neither forgave nor forgot, and Mr. Darcy and her husband continued their feud.

Lydia found the whole situation disheartening. Even Elizabeth had taken offense at her congratulatory letter, although Lydia did not know why. She had spoken the truth, and she had lowered herself to ask for Elizabeth's help. All that she had asked was a place at court for Wickham and three to four hundred a year to make ends meet. She had even told her older sister not to mention it to Mr. Darcy if Elizabeth thought it might upset him.

To Elizabeth and Mr. Darcy, it seemed that Mr. Wickham held out some hope that Darcy might be prevailed on to make his fortune; and in Lydia's mind, this all made perfect sense. Darcy had the means to help Wickham. She hoped on this visit to soften Mr. Darcy's feelings about her husband. Lydia recognized her strength: She could charm any man. Of course, she hated wasting her talents on such a prideful and conceited man as Fitzwilliam Darcy, but she would prevail on him in order to help her husband. Maybe then, their marriage might be saved. Wickham would stop thinking her such a poor choice if somehow she could sway the great Fitzwilliam Darcy.

Not many young women—married or not—traveled alone. But

Wickham had bought her the ticket to visit Elizabeth because he had been ordered to Bath for the following month. He had seen her to Nottingham before they parted. Now, she traveled unaccompanied.

"What is a fine young lady such as yourself doing traveling alone?" A man in his thirties, who smelled of stale cigars and boiled turnips, leered at Lydia. He glanced quickly at the matronly woman riding beside her. The woman's eyes remained closed, and she breathed deeply.

Lydia recognized the man's intentions, and although she would never consider such an alliance, she welcomed the conversation. Sitting quietly for long periods was not part of her makeup. Most acquaintances thought her chatty—boisterous even. Her husband often ordered her silence, claiming that she *chattered on like a magpie*. "I am going to visit my sister, who is near Lambton."

"I know Lambton well, Miss. Your sister is well placed, I assume." He noted Lydia's stylish traveling frock, one of three new pieces she had insisted she needed for this trip, despite her husband's declaration that they could not afford the additional expense.

"Very well placed." Lydia puffed up with his notice. "Do you know Pemberley?"

The man's initial tone changed immediately. "Pemberley? Everyone for miles around knows Pemberley," he asserted. "Might your sister be associated with such a great estate?"

His words brought satisfaction to Lydia; she liked the idea of people admiring her, even if by association. In that way, she and Wickham were very much alike. Sometimes she dreamed of what it might be to have her own home—her own estate. And sometimes she regretted having not set her sights on Mr. Darcy herself, although Lydia supposed the man preferred Elizabeth because her older sister devoured books—just like their father. Lydia preferred fashion to Faust and society to Shakespeare. In all considerations, Elizabeth definitely better suited the man. If Mr. Darcy treated everyone as he did her Wickham, she would disdain his company in a heartbeat. "My sister is Mrs. Darcy; she is the mistress of Pemberley."

"The mistress of Pemberley?" The man let out a low whistle. "I am duly impressed."

"Mrs. Darcy is one of my older sisters," Lydia babbled, "but my eldest is Mrs. Bingley of Hertfordshire. Charles Bingley counts Mr. Darcy as his best friend. My husband, Lieutenant George Wickham, grew to adulthood on Pemberley. We three sisters remain connected, even though we find ourselves scattered about England. My dear Wickham serves his country: We reside in Newcastle."

The man tried not to betray his amusement at the situation's irony but there was a glint of laughter in his eyes at the folly of this pretty, voluptuous, empty-headed girl marrying George Wickham. The girl offered nothing: no substance upon which a man might really build a relationship. "I know of George Wickham," he mused. "Even in Cheshire, your husband has female admirers." He chuckled. "It will break many hearts when I spread the story of your marriage, Mrs. Wickham. Are you newly wed?"

"Lord, no. In fact, I was the first of my sisters to marry, although I am the youngest of five. Mr. Wickham and I have been married nearly two years."

"Two years?" The man looked amused again. He said, "I suppose it too late then to offer my best wishes?" His eyebrows waggled teasingly; yet, he thought, *I cannot imagine the George Wickham I know tolerating such an immature girl, nor would he practice fidelity.*

Lydia swatted at his chest with her fan. "I am an old married woman, sir."

Knowing she expected a compliment, he murmured, "You may be married, ma'am, but you most certainly are not old nor are you the picture of matronliness." He nodded in the direction of the sleeping woman and then winked at Lydia.

Lydia giggled, suddenly aware of the privacy of their conversation. She turned her attention to the coach's window. "I certainly do not enjoy traveling in winter. The roads in the North were abhorrent—so many ruts and holes. Passengers could barely keep their seats. Thankfully, my husband kept me safe, but a lady we left in Lincolnshire tumbled most unceremoniously to the floor."

The man's eyes followed hers. "The farmers at home—in Cheshire—would probably say we are in for some bad weather. See how the line of dark clouds hug the horizon." He pointed off to a distance. "I simply hope we make it to Cheshire before the storm hits. I prefer not being upon the road when Winter blasts us with her best." He leaned back and closed his eyes. "We will stay in Matlock this evening. You should be in Lambton by mid-afternoon tomorrow."

"I will be pleased to be away from this coach," Lydia murmured as she settled into the well-worn cushions.

As the man drifted off to sleep, he managed to say, "You will have the best that money can buy at Pemberley."

"Fitzwilliam," Elizabeth said. She had found her husband in his study. "Georgiana and I plan to call on some of the cottagers today." She stood before his desk, looking down at the stack of ledgers piled five high. "I thought you might care to join us, but I see that you are busy."

"I am afraid this business cannot be postponed." He gestured to the many letters lying open before him.

Elizabeth moved to stand behind him. She snaked her arms over the chair back and around Darcy's neck. She kissed his ear and then his cheek. "You will miss me, Mr. Darcy?" she inquired, her breath warm against his neck as she continued to kiss along his chin line. Unable to ever resist her, Darcy reached up to catch her arm. In one smooth motion, he shoved his chair away from the desk, making room for her on his lap, and pulled Elizabeth to him. She rested on his legs before sliding her arms around his neck. "I love you, my Husband." She laid her head against his shoulder.

Darcy used his finger to tilt her chin upward so he might kiss her lips. "So nice," he murmured. He deepened the kiss. "I could drown in your love," he whispered to her ear.

"You are so not what the world expects." Elizabeth ran her fingers through his hair.

Darcy chuckled, "I am exactly what the world expects: I serve this estate well and my sister well." Elizabeth envied his confidence and the deep respect he inspired in the community.

"And me well." Elizabeth moaned as his lips found the point where her neck met her shoulder.

Darcy pulled her closer. "That is what is unexpected—how much I love you—how I can give myself over to you so completely."

"You have no regrets about aligning yourself with a woman without family, connections, or fortunes?" It was a question she asked often, although his answer remained the same each time.

It amazed Darcy that she could continue to doubt his loyalty—his love. "Elizabeth, you possess me body and soul. Do you not know how much I need you in my life?"

"I know," she admitted. "It is just that I need to hear it regularly. I realize it is foolish of me, but it is my weakness, I fear."

"Then I will resolve to tell you more often, my Love." He kissed her tenderly.

Elizabeth scrambled from his lap when she heard the servants outside the door. "I am sure Georgiana waits for me by now. We will return in a few hours."

"Do not go far, my Love. The winter weather looms; we are in for a bad spell."

"Listen to you, Mr. Darcy," Elizabeth joked as she headed toward the door. "You sound like one of the old hags who claim they can tell the weather from their rheumatism."

Darcy cleared his throat, stopping her exit. "Elizabeth, I have lived my whole life in Derbyshire. I understand the harshness of the winters. Trust me, my Love."

She stopped in her tracks. "If you are serious, Fitzwilliam, I will follow your lead," she assured him.

"I think only of you and Georgiana."

"Do you suppose Lydia will arrive before this weather changes?" Elizabeth now expressed the same concern as he.

Darcy stood and came to where she waited. "A rider brought me some papers from Liverpool today, and he said that the weather turned bad quickly. If he is correct, the storm is at least a day out, but it is likely to be here by early in the day tomorrow. Mrs. Wickham's coach will be driving into the storm. Your sister may have some uncomfortable hours, but I am relatively certain she will arrive safely."

"You will go with me to Lambton—I mean to bring Lydia to Pemberley?" Elizabeth inquired.

"I will not leave you to your own devices." Darcy kissed her fingers. "Have a good visit with the tenants."

"Mrs. Hudson needs someone to repair her window," Elizabeth reminded him as she prepared to leave.

Darcy followed her to the door. "I will see to it immediately."

Elizabeth and Georgiana took Darcy's small coach for their visits. Often they made their rounds on horseback or in an open curricle, but Georgiana suffered from a head cold, and Elizabeth would take no chances with Miss Darcy's health in the bitter weather. "We have only two more baskets," Elizabeth said. She accepted Murray's hand as she climbed into the coach. He closed the steps, setting them inside. "Thank you, Murray. Tell Mr. Stalling we will see the Baines and the Taylors."

"Yes, Mrs. Darcy."

Mr. Stalling turned the carriage toward the hedgerow leading to the main drive. "We will keep our visits short," Elizabeth told Darcy's sister. "I can tell you are not at your best today."

"My head feels so full. Perhaps I should remain in the carriage. Both the Baines and the Taylors have a houseful of children. It would not be the Christian thing to share my illness." Georgiana sniffled and reached for her handkerchief.

"That might be best." Elizabeth straightened the seam of her dress. "I will make the call; you stay in the carriage and keep your feet on the warming brick. Then I will see you home. I am sure Mrs. Reynolds has a special poultice to make you feel better."

"Thank you, Elizabeth." Georgiana sniffed again.

Elizabeth adjusted the blanket across Georgiana's lap. "Fitzwilliam will be distressed to know you feel poorly."

"He does worry about me." Georgiana Darcy leaned back into the thick squabs of her brother's carriage. Elizabeth remembered the first time she had seen the girl, who had been little more than sixteen at the time. Darcy had brought his sister to the inn in Lambton to meet Elizabeth after finding Elizabeth and her aunt and uncle visiting Pemberley on holiday. It had been the beginning of her life together with Darcy.

Although Elizabeth was four years her senior, Darcy's sister was taller and on a larger scale. She was less handsome than her brother, but there was sense and good humor in her face, and her manners were perfectly unassuming and gentle. Everyone who knew Georgiana Darcy esteemed her for her compassion and her goodness. Elizabeth treasured having Georgiana in the household. Having left a houseful of sisters in Hertfordshire, Elizabeth appreciated having female companionship.

"Your brother has spent his adult life caring for you."

Georgiana closed her eyes, trying to concentrate on feeling the brick's warmth, but a shiver shook her body. "I will be happy to find my own bed."

Elizabeth touched the girl's forehead with the back of her hand. "You are not warm—no fever."

"I simply ache all over, and my head is so tight with pressure," Georgiana rasped out.

The carriage came to a bone-jolting halt. "I will be only a few minutes." Elizabeth opened the door. Murray assisted her to the ground before handing Elizabeth one of the two remaining baskets he carried.

"Murray, I want to see Miss Darcy to the house as soon as possible. Would you mind delivering the basket you carry to the Taylors? Give them our regards and explain the situation. I will call on Mrs. Baine."

"Certainly, Mrs. Darcy." The footman headed toward the Taylors' cottage, less than a quarter mile down the main drive.

Elizabeth glanced quickly at Georgiana to assure herself the girl would be well while alone in the coach. Then she strode toward the small, white washed cottage. Before she reached the door, it swung open, and a burly-looking man greeted her.

"Mrs. Darcy, let me be helpin' ye with that."

"Thank you, Mr. Baine." Elizabeth entered the house and removed her gloves. She glanced around quickly to inspect how well the Baines maintained their home. Darcy did well by his tenants, but he expected the cottagers to uphold the property and not to destroy what he gave them.

"Ye be alone, Mistress?" Mrs. Baine looked to the threshold.

Elizabeth gestured toward the coach. "Miss Darcy feels poorly. We both thought it best to not bring an illness into your house. In fact, I only have a few minutes. I wish to see Mr. Darcy's sister in her own bed's comfort."

"Certainly, Mrs. Darcy." Mr. Baine set the basket on the table.

"There is flour, sugar, some potatoes, ham, and turnips in the basket." Elizabeth slipped her gloves on, preparing to leave.

"We be thankin' ye," Mrs. Baine said and lifted the cloth to peer at the things the Great House had sent to them.

"Of course, there are sweets for the children." Elizabeth touched a tow-headed boy of four. "You may dole them out when you deem appropriate."

Mr. Baine picked up a blonde girl of two. "The little ones be our greatest gift."

The Baines had six children, and Elizabeth chuckled at the irony of the statement. "Then you are indeed blessed, Mr. Baine. Mr. Darcy says the weather will turn dangerous, so be sure everyone is inside. Maybe you should bring in some extra wood for the fire."

"We be thinkin' the same, Mistress." Baine stroked the child's head as it rested on his shoulder. "We be well, ma'am."

"You know if you need anything, just send someone to Pemberley. Mr. Darcy will help if he can."

"We be knowin' it, ma'am." Mrs. Baine joined them as they stood by the door.

Elizabeth glanced toward the carriage. "I really must see Miss Darcy home. Please excuse me; we will visit longer the next time."

"You see to the master's sister," Mrs. Baine said as she reached for the door handle. "We be puttin' Miss Darcy in our prayers."

"My sister will appreciate your thoughtfulness."

Georgiana Darcy pulled the blanket closer. She hoped Elizabeth would not be long. She really just wanted to go to bed and sleep for a few hours—maybe even have Mrs. Jennings heat up some chicken broth.

Reluctantly, she sat forward to check on Elizabeth's return, but saw no one. Georgiana scooted the warming brick closer; it quickly lost its heat in the chilly air. She reached out and slid the curtain aside to look for Elizabeth again. Then she saw him, and a different kind of shiver ran down her spine. He just stood there in the tree line. A blond-haired man, wrapped in a black cloak and wearing a floppy-brimmed hat, leaned against a tree. Georgiana felt her heart skip a beat, and her breathing became labored.

The sound of Elizabeth's approach drew the girl's attention for a fraction of a second, and when her eyes returned to the trees, the man was no longer there.

"Did you see him?" she pleaded as Mr. Stalling helped Elizabeth into the coach.

"See who?" Elizabeth turned expectantly. "Was someone there?" She searched where Georgiana stared, but all they saw was a bare headed Murray walking toward them, slapping his jacket to keep himself warm.

Elizabeth sat next to Georgiana, and slid her arm around the girl's shoulder. "Might we take Miss Darcy home, Mr. Stalling?"

"Yes, Mrs. Darcy." The driver stored the coach's step inside before motioning Murray to climb aboard the back of the coach.

As the carriage circled to return to the house, both women stared out the opposite window, looking for something neither of them hoped to see again. "He is not there," Georgiana whispered.

"No one is there, Georgiana." Elizabeth let the curtain fall in place. "Would you tell me what you saw?"

"A man—all in black—wearing an unusual hat—like those in the books from America." Georgiana's eyes widened. "Do you believe me?"

Elizabeth tightened her hold on the girl. "Your brother thought that what I saw yesterday was a bear, but what you just described was what I saw in my mind's eye. Except I could not make out the man's face."

"Neither could I," Georgiana whispered although they were alone in the moving carriage. "What does it mean, Elizabeth?" The girl grabbed her sister's hand.

Elizabeth did not answer; she simply pulled the blanket over both of them. "We will tell Fitzwilliam. He will know what to do."

CHAPTER 2

~ ~ ~

ADAM LAWRENCE, THE FUTURE earl of Greenwall, was
traveling from London to Cheshire. Against his better judgment,
he had agreed to escort his mistress, Cathleen Donnel, to her home
country. Her uncle had taken ill, and the family had summoned
relatives to his bedside. Cathleen had been his lover less than eight
months, and Adam knew he should not cater to her, but despite
his reputation as a rake, he never treated his women disrespectfully,
and the news had greatly distressed her. She had considered not
going, but Adam had known that she would regret it always, so he
had insisted that she go and that he accompany her. His coachman, Morris Johnson, pressed the horses, as the party anticipated a
winter storm, and Adam cursed himself for placing them in danger.

Green-eyed Cathleen Donnel was an actress of sorts. Actually, she had no talent in that respect, but she possessed a beautiful
singing voice and previously made her living on the stage. And
Cathleen was a most pleasing mistress. She had dallied with several
other short-term patrons prior to Lawrence, but it was he who
paid the rent on her upscale townhouse on Mayfair's fringes. Adam
preferred his women to have some experience but not be well
worn, and Cathleen met those qualifications, as well as meeting his
passion with her own. Besides, he thought that she possessed the
greenest eyes he had ever seen this side of a spring meadow. Cathleen's auburn Irish hair had attracted him at first, and her petite,

buxom figure, pouty mouth, and mesmerizing eyes ensured that he stayed infatuated with her.

Adam glanced at Cathleen as she slept on the opposite seat. Using her cloak as a blanket, she curled up on the coach's bench. For a brief moment, he wondered why he let her have her way. It seemed he always let other people influence him—tell him what to do, actually. His father—his tutors—his professors at the university—his mistresses—his friends—they all made decisions for him. Easier, he supposed. It was easier when others assumed the responsibility for what happened.

Adam never discussed his aversion to responsibility with anyone. At five and twenty, he accepted no real accountability. His father, Robert Lawrence, made all the decisions: where Adam lived, where he attended school, how much money he could spend, and where he bought his clothes and his horses. His father never needed Adam to do more than be his heir. Most of the time, Adam felt quite useless. However, he never let anyone see that side of his personality. To the world, he showed an aristocratic face and an inscrutable nature. He received what he wanted, when he wanted it—so why complain.

Glancing at Cathleen again, Adam saw her stir. She looked exceedingly appealing with her disheveled hair and dress. Cathleen groaned and stretched before sitting up. "Did I sleep long?" she asked huskily, sleep still lingering on her tongue.

"Less than an hour," Adam answered before moving next to her. He quickly gathered Cathleen into his arms. "You look delicious." Adam brushed his lips across hers.

As she should, Cathleen laced her arms about his neck. After all, Lawrence was completely masculine—narrow waist; well-formed chest and back; muscular legs and hips; dark, straight hair—actually worn a bit too long for her taste; and gray—actually, silver—eyes. He was the kind of man that women desired immediately. And he was good to her. Only recently, Adam had bought her a gold-leaf book, one she had seen in the window of an upscale bookstore and wanted immediately. A collection of fairy tales, most from the Brothers Grimm, the book was not a first edition but a limited printing, and Cathleen loved it more than many of the jewels and gowns she earned with her body. She had never owned a book—she read well, but her family lacked the wealth to own books other than the Bible. The uncle she rushed to comfort was a minor Irish nobleman—a baron, but nothing like the relatives that her handsome lover, Lord Stafford, claimed. Her uncle's family worked the land; Cathleen was sure Lord Stafford would bolt if someone even suggested that he might dirty his hands.

"Do you desire *delicious?*" she asked teasingly, sliding her tongue along the line of Adam's lips.

"I am more than hungry," he growled and then nibbled her earlobe to emphasize his point.

Cathleen laughed lightly. "You are always hungry, my Lord."

"Do you object?" Adam pulled back to take in her countenance.

"Absolutely not. I am a blessed woman; you chose me."

Lawrence knew Cathleen uttered the words he paid her to say, but a part of him wanted her to care about him simply because he was Adam Lawrence, not because he would someday be an earl. Dismissing such thoughts, he deepened the kiss. Then he said, "We will try to make it to Cheshire itself this evening, although Mobberley may be an impossibility before dark."

She kissed along the line of his cravat. "Then we have time?"

"Plenty of time," he murmured.

When his butler, Mr. Baldwin, announced the arrival of Lady Catherine de Bourgh, Darcy shot a quick glance at Elizabeth before ordering the man to show his indomitable aunt in. He and Elizabeth were sharing time in his study, as had become their habit. In reality, Darcy did not like to be too far from his wife; they did not always talk or even keep each other company, but he liked to look up and see her in his home. Before he had won Elizabeth's heart, he had envisioned such moments—had seen her everywhere—on the main staircase, at his table, in his garden, and in his bed. Today, Elizabeth worked at her embroidery, something not necessarily her forte. She bit her bottom lip in frustration as her thread knotted again. No matter. Darcy found contentment in the scene.

Now, Elizabeth's eyes widened. Neither of them had seen his mother's only sister since that day the woman had actually taken the trouble to journey from her home seat of Rosings Park in Kent to Hertfordshire for the sole purpose of breaking off Darcy's and Elizabeth's supposed engagement. This was before Darcy had proposed to Elizabeth Bennet a second time. She had vehemently refused him the first, and he had striven to prove himself worthy of her love. However, his aunt had held a starkly different opinion of their possible union, and she had made no bones about her objections.

That day, Lady Catherine had verbally attacked Elizabeth—quite ungraciously—accusing his future wife of industriously circulating scandalous falsehoods. His aunt had lambasted Elizabeth, saying, "Your arts and allurement may, in a moment of infatuation, have made Darcy forget what he owes to himself and to all his family."

When Elizabeth had steadfastly refused to succumb to Her Ladyship during this extraordinary visit, his aunt had rushed to London to enumerate the miseries of a marriage with one whose immediate connections were so unequal to those of her and Darcy's family. What Lady Catherine had not considered was the violence of the love her nephew felt for Elizabeth Bennet. His aunt's words, instead of turning Darcy from the woman he loved, had taught him to hope as he had scarcely allowed himself previously—actually not since before he erroneously thought Elizabeth to be expecting his attentions during that first ill-fated proposal. He had known enough of Elizabeth's disposition to be certain that had she been absolutely and irrevocably decided against him, she would have acknowledged it to Lady Catherine frankly and openly. When he had been approached, Darcy abruptly ended his aunt's interference in his life and immediately boarded his coach, returning to Longbourn to judge whether Elizabeth might finally accept him.

Unfortunately, Darcy's engagement and ultimate marriage to *his Elizabeth* had served to sever ties with his aunt. Lady Catherine preferred to "control" everything within her own "parish." The minutest concerns of her tenants were Her Ladyship's domain; in the same way, she expected to lord her power over her family, as well. When her cottagers were disposed to be quarrelsome, discontented, or too poor, she sailed forth into the village to settle their differences, silence their complaints, and scold them into harmony and plenty. When Darcy had defied her orders to abandon his fascination with Elizabeth Bennet and instead honor what his aunt saw as an engagement to his cousin Anne, Lady Catherine had indignantly declared herself to be finished with him.

Following propriety, Darcy had written to her to announce his engagement and the impending marriage. Lady Catherine had given way to all the genuine frankness of her character in her reply, sending her nephew language so abusive, especially of Elizabeth, that for some time all intercourse between Darcy and his aunt was at an end.

But, at length, by Elizabeth's persuasion, he had been prevailed on to overlook the offense and to seek a reconciliation. Darcy admired Elizabeth's ability to forgive, although he suspected her insistence came from the fact that his wife missed her own family desperately, and like it or not, Lady Catherine and the Matlocks were his only family, besides Georgiana. The woman had guided him when his mother had passed, and Darcy knew her heart to be in the right place. So although she had yet to respond, for the past six months, he had written to her monthly with family news. At least, she had not returned his letters unopened; he had supposed that to be a positive sign. Now she had arrived, unannounced, at Pemberley. Darcy expected trouble.

"Show Her Ladyship in, Mr. Baldwin," Darcy stood to acknowledge the woman he had thought never to see again.

Elizabeth placed her sewing on a side table and rose to receive their guest. He noted how she fidgeted with the seams of her dress and patted her hair to make sure nothing was out of place. When she saw him watching her, Elizabeth colored. Darcy chuckled and winked just as Lady Catherine's footsteps heralded her appearance. Mr. Baldwin opened the door farther and announced, "Lady Catherine de Bourgh," before stepping aside.

She swept into the room, all haughty grandeur, but Darcy noted immediately the gauntness of her face under the thick cosmetics she wore "Aunt," he said, "I am pleased to see you at Pemberley again." He bowed to her and came forward to accept the hand she offered. "Come, let me show you to a chair before the hearth."

Without waiting for Lady Catherine condescension, Elizabeth established herself as the manor's mistress. She dropped a curtsy to the woman before adding, "Welcome, Lady Catherine. Is Miss de Bourgh not joining us today?"

The woman answered the query in a shaking voice without looking directly at Elizabeth. "I sent Anne and Mrs. Jenkinson to their regular rooms. The trip has taken its toll on Anne's constitution; she has always been of a delicate nature."

"I see." Elizabeth ordered tea for three from Mr. Baldwin. Then she said to her husband and his aunt, "If you will excuse me, I will see to Miss de Bourgh's comfort."

"Of course, my Dear," Darcy replied. Lady Catherine remained silent. As Elizabeth turned to leave, Darcy added, "Please rejoin us at your convenience."

When the door clicked behind her, Darcy seated himself beside his less-than-affable aunt. He pasted a smile on his face before speaking. "Lady Catherine, although unexpected, you are welcome in my home." Darcy could not help but note her trembling hands. "I assume, Aunt, that this is not simply a social call."

"Hardly, Darcy," she declared, more strength in her voice this time. "I need your help or else I would never lower myself to return to this estate, especially with that woman here."

Darcy had expected as much, but her words set him on edge. "Your Ladyship, as much as I have always held an affection for you and have esteemed you, I must caution you regarding your word choice. Elizabeth is my wife, and I will tolerate no disrespect where she is concerned. I have never been happier, and before I will let you ill-use her, I will send you from Pemberley permanently." Darcy paused to emphasize the truth of his words. "Now, I am more than willing to serve you with those stipulations."

"If you had fulfilled your obligation to your cousin, I would never be finding a need to seek your relief," she asserted.

"As much as I respect Anne, we would not have suited each other. I needed a woman at Pemberley who could help me bring the estate to right; with all the temptations of fast money the cottagers see in the bigger cities, it takes a different temperament to address the changes coming to this country. Mrs. Darcy is that woman—a woman of resilience and adventure."

"Adventure?" she said and snorted. "If that was what you sought, then Anne would have been a better match."

"With no disrespect," Darcy spoke with a twinge of irony lacing his tone, "the words *Anne* and *adventure* are not ones I would think in harmony."

Lady Catherine snapped, "That shows how little you know of our Anne. Typically, a man sees only the shell."

Darcy refused to argue with her. "Tell me the matter, Your Ladyship, and let me determine how I might be of service."

She impatiently tapped her foot; Darcy knew that to be a sign of extreme agitation in his aunt. "I do not want a word of this to escape. It would be a great disgrace if others knew. I have sent Mr. Collins and his wife for a family visit to Hertfordshire rather than have them know my shame." When Darcy said nothing, she continued, "Deeply moved by *your* desertion," she intoned, "Anne needed extra attention, and despite my better judgment, I allowed your cousin, the colonel, to bring some of his fellow officers for a visit before reporting to Dover."

Again, Darcy remained silent, waiting for the whole of the story. He recognized her dramatics—had dealt with them on more than one occasion over the years. He would not let her bait him. "I knew better," she chastised herself, "but I succumbed to Anne's need for company. A mother allows her only child freedoms when sound reason says otherwise."

"You have always been most charitable," Darcy said, silently wishing that his aunt would just come to the point. "And I cannot imagine our cousin would pollute your drawing room with unsavory characters."

Darcy counted his cousin Colonel Fitzwilliam as one of his closest friends. They served as joint guardians for Darcy's sister, Georgiana, and they knew each other as well as two very private men could. In fact, there had been a time when Darcy worried that he might lose Elizabeth to his cousin. They had taken to each other immediately, often falling into easy conversation of Kent and of Hertfordshire, of traveling and staying at home, of books and of music. After her initial refusal of him, Darcy had spent many miserable nights imagining that she might have readily accepted Edward, but his cousin's position as a second son of an earl demanded that he choose a woman of fortune. Edward held a title, but he could not afford to fall in love with a woman of Elizabeth's small means. For Darcy, this had proved little comfort during those months when he pined for a "lost" Elizabeth.

"One of your cousin's associates is a Lieutenant Harwood, a man of no consequence," Lady Catherine said. "Although Edward Fitzwilliam brings honor to our family, I admit to finding the military an objectionable occupation. It brings persons of obscure birth into undue distinction and raises men to honors, which their fathers and grandfathers never dreamt of. A man is in greater danger in the military of being insulted by the rise of one whose father, his father might have disdained to speak to."

Before Darcy could offer her another caution, Mr. Baldwin interrupted with the tea service. They waited until the man had retired before continuing their conversation.

"And I assume this Lieutenant Harwood paid Anne undue attention," Darcy encouraged.

"He did, but I remained unaware for some time. The man subversively began to correspond with Anne, sending her letters under the guise of writing to her maid, pretending to be the girl's brother. The chit will be seeking other employment as soon as we return to Kent. She will rue the day she helped Anne to defy me!"

Darcy thought he might find the girl another position before that time. He would not blame a servant for doing what his cousin had obviously asked her to do, even if that request denied reason. As Anne was shy and withdrawn, her maid had probably rejoiced at her employer's interest in the man. They all wanted Anne's happiness. "So you brought Anne to Pemberley to remove her from this man's attention?"

"I wish that it were that simple." She sipped her tea. "Under the guise of going to London to see her modiste, Anne, after many weeks of this secret correspondence, made a trip to Liverpool to meet Harwood." Her voice wobbled, and her hand trembled.

Darcy reached for her cup and returned it to the tray. He took her gnarled hand in his. "Tell me, my Dear."

"I found her…my Anne…in a room in a seedy inn…one this Harwood character had arranged for her. Oh, Darcy, what will I do?" she whined. "I certainly cannot have Anne marry such a cad."

Darcy fought back the smile creeping across his face. His cousin Anne had finally defied her mother. Possibly, "this Harwood character" did see his cousin as an easy mark and wanted to secure a quick marriage to claim Anne's substantial dowry. As Rosings Park came unentailed to Lady Catherine after her husband's passing, Anne's husband would take control of a vast fortune soon enough. Then again, possibly, the man had developed a true affection for Darcy's "sickly" cousin. Darcy would need to ascertain which case prevailed. "Do you wish me to speak to Anne?"

"Darcy…would you do this for Anne?" She actually looked pleased.

He smiled. "You and Anne will be my guest for a few days. I anticipate a winter storm is headed our way, and I will not have you on the road in bad weather. Winter turnpikes in Derbyshire can be quite treacherous."

"The storm was just settling into Manchester as we departed. We have outrun it so far." She seemed suddenly very weak for a few moments.

"Come, you will find safety here until it passes." He patted her hand. "As head of the Darcy family, I will not have you on the road in unsafe conditions. You and Anne are under my care for now."

"Thank you, Darcy."

"No thanks are necessary. Mrs. Darcy is preparing for a visit from Mrs. Wickham later today. A few more guests will be most welcome." Darcy took some pleasure in watching his aunt stiffen with the news.

"That girl!" she began. "The one of the infamous elopement? That of the patched-up business at the expense of your wife's father and uncle? Mrs. Darcy brings that girl to Pemberley? Are the shades of Pemberley to be thus polluted?"

Darcy warned her with a one-word reprimand: "Enough."

Lady Catherine stifled her next thoughts.

"Aunt," he said ominously, "as I said earlier, you will control your tongue. I do not accept Mr. Wickham as my brother; however, I will not deny Mrs. Darcy the company of her youngest sister." He wondered what Lady Catherine would think if she knew that it had been he, not Elizabeth's father or uncle, who had arranged Lydia Bennet's marriage to George Wickham. Nothing was to be done that he did not do himself. He had done it purely for Elizabeth. Lydia's elopement had brought shame to her sisters, and Elizabeth's sobs had torn his heart apart. He loved her, although at the time he had not believed that she would accept him. The wish of giving happiness to Elizabeth had added force to the other inducements that led him on. He had thought only of her when he acted. "Mrs. Wickham will be welcomed, as will you and Anne. If you do not believe you can comply with my wishes, I will see you into Lambton—to the inn. I will secure comfortable rooms to tide you over."

"I will tolerate the girl," Lady Catherine hissed.

"And with civility?" Darcy ordered.

"I will be a paragon of the nobility's best."

Darcy accepted her avowal. "I expect nothing less, Aunt." He rose to end the conversation. "Let us settle you in a comfortable room, my Dear." He helped her to her feet. "Later today, I will seek Anne's company and see what I may deduce from our conversation."

A torrential rain met the public stage as it made its way toward Lambton. "I do not like the looks of this," mused Mrs. Williams, widow of Admiral Samuel Williams of the British Navy. Lydia found it amazing that, in reality, Mrs. Williams was only in her early thirties; she appeared older. Evidently, the lady had followed her husband in his service to England, and the sea had taken its toll on the woman's complexion. The admiral had lost his life in the Battle of San Domingo. Now, Mrs. Williams traveled to Macclesfield to take up residence with her late husband's family.

Lydia followed the woman's line of sight. "Shall we make it to Lambton?" Even though she often felt out of sorts with her husband, Lydia would have been very happy to have him traveling with her at present. The road conditions frightened her; she no longer thought it so grand to be her own woman.

The man who had kept her company earlier joined the conversation. That day, they had been the only occupants of the coach for several hours. "We will reach Lambton, but no farther today, even though the light could take us into Cheshire. Such rain ruins even the best-kept roads. Loaded down as we are, we risk becoming stuck in some mud hole or sliding into a ditch."

"How long, Mr. Worth?" Lydia's eyes rested on the horizon beyond the coach's window.

Nigel Worth, a second son of a minor nobleman, was an affable man and loved to talk to anyone who would listen. He had flirted with Lydia periodically, especially when Mrs. Williams slept, although he held no illusions of her finding him appealing. It was just his nature. He actually did know of the girl's husband indirectly. As a solicitor in a neighboring county, he had once represented a man in court trying to recover the gambling debt that George Wickham owed him. Of course, Worth had not disclosed to Lydia the fact of his dealings with the girl's husband. From what Nigel had discerned Mrs. Wickham held no real knowledge of her husband's base nature. The man had left several residents in Middlewich holding his gambling blunt. "Close to an hour, Mrs. Wickham—should not be much longer than that." He looked at his pocket watch before depositing it in a side pocket of his waistcoat.

∾ ∾ ∾

"My Lord." Cathleen's voice disturbed Adam's sleep. He had taken pleasure in her body along the winding roads from Nottingham and then contentedly nodded off, allowing the coach to rock him to sleep.

Adam slowly opened his eyes to find his mistress looking distressed. "What is it?"

"Listen," she instructed.

Fully on alert now, Lawrence sat up, straightening his clothes as he did. "It sounds menacing." He moved the shade from the window to have a look for himself. The rain came down like liquid bullets tapping out an incessant rhythm on his coach. He considered speaking to Mr. Johnson through the trap, but he doubted that his coachman could hear him over the rain's pounding. "You might move closer to the strap," he cautioned, trying to keep his voice even. "We may be in for a bumpy ride."

"Will we have trouble?"

"Mr. Johnson can handle the coach," Adam declared. "We will have no problems. I have complete confidence in the man, but you should understand that such conditions may affect whether we reach Mobberley in time for you to see your uncle before his passing." Adam touched her hand in sympathy. "I am sorry."

"You have done more than most men, my Lord. Even if we are too late to give my family comfort, I will cherish your kindness." Cathleen dropped her eyes; she did not often speak so personally to her benefactor. "You truly are the best of men."

"There are many who would disagree with you, my Dear."

Cathleen looked him in the eye. "That is because they do not know you as I do." And in her opinion, Adam Lawrence was truly everything she said. A kind and generous man, he held a reputation as a rounder, but she saw none of that. Often she wished she could have known him as his social equal—where he might actually love her—where she might help him become the man he wanted to be—a man quite different from the façade he presented to the world. But she knew she was not the woman to bring Adam Lawrence such love—such contentment. Cathleen would give him what she could while they shared their time together.

Reluctantly, she wondered what her family would think when she arrived in Mobberley unchaperoned and in Adam's carriage. His livery would announce their relationship. She would bring shame to her mother and father, as well as her younger sisters, and for that, Cathleen despaired. Perhaps Adam might allow her to return home alone. When they reached Mobberley, she would ask him to leave her and move on to Manchester or even to Warrington. She would take a public conveyance and follow him there. At least, Viscount Stafford cared enough for her not to allow her to travel a great distance alone.

≈ ≈ ≈

"Elizabeth, are you ready to be to Lambton?" Darcy had found his wife in their joint sitting room. "Mrs. Wickham's coach should arrive within the hour."

"I worry for the roads." She sat on a window box, looking out across the formal garden. "The rain has turned icy."

Darcy came to where she sat. Resting his hand on her shoulder, he peered through the fogged-up glass. "All the more reason to take our leave now—to give Mr. Stalling extra time to negotiate the roads. Your sister will have no transportation... if we do not venture forth." He leaned down to kiss the top of her head. "I could go alone," he volunteered.

Elizabeth turned to gaze into the face she found most comforting in the world. "No....no...I will bring Lydia here. I shall not send you alone to bring Wickham's wife to Pemberley. You show me a kindness, my Husband, by tolerating my sister's intrusion upon your life and your home." She stood and caressed his cheek.

"Our home," he corrected. "Pemberley is *our* home, and Mrs. Wickham is your sister—and mine, too. If you must endure my aunt's intrusion, then I can allow Lydia's naïve exuberance to permeate the hallowed walls of Pemberley. As long as I sleep with you in my arms, I am a happy man. Very little else matters in the scheme of things." He bent his head to brush his lips across hers.

"I love you, my Husband," she whispered close to his mouth, "with all my heart."

Darcy smiled mischievously. "I surely hope so, Mrs. Darcy, as we are about to be snowed in with Attila the Hun and Kathryn Howard. If nothing else, the mixture should be entertaining: our own little circus—it will be a juggling act, keeping them apart."

"Fitzwilliam Darcy, you are a wretched man!" she chastised him.

"I know you, Elizabeth Bennet Darcy," he scolded. "You take as much pleasure as I in observing the foibles of our neighbors and family."

Elizabeth chuckled as her arms encircled his neck. "You may be right, my Love. I just wish we had married sooner, so that we could compare our appraisals of those we found most entertaining." She judiciously omitted the fact that for a time, he had been among those she found amusing.

Darcy drank slowly from her lips. Breaking contact, he inquired, "And who might that be?"

Elizabeth pressed herself closer to him and rained kisses across his face as she recited the names. "Caroline Bingley." *Kiss.* "Louisa Hurst." *Kiss.* "Mr. Hurst." *Kiss.* "Mr. Collins." *Kiss.* "Sir William Lucas." *Kiss. Kiss.* By then, Darcy had forgotten both the question and Lydia's impending arrival. All he wanted was her—*his Elizabeth.* "Do we have time?" she whispered as he edged her toward a nearby chaise.

"Not to sleep in each other's arms," he groaned, "but enough for me to show how much I desire you, my darling Elizabeth."

Elizabeth lowered herself to the sofa, taking Darcy down with her. She knew him—knew the true Fitzwilliam Darcy, a man who would move heaven and earth for those he loved, but also a man one did not want to cross. He passionately protected those he loved. And he loved Elizabeth most of all.

Thirty minutes later, Elizabeth rushed through their private quarters, knowing that Darcy waited for her in the main foyer. She slid her arms into the sleeves of her new fur-lined pelisse, one of Darcy's Christmas gifts. As she walked, she tried adjusting the fit without tripping on the hem. She had descended the first two steps when she heard one of the maids call out to her.

"What is it, Megs?" she asked, a bit annoyed. Darcy disliked being kept waiting.

"Pardon, Mrs. Darcy." The maid bobbed a curtsy. "I be wondering, ma'am, if ye knew the whereabouts of the candelabra, the one we keep on the table by Miss Darcy's room."

Without thinking, Elizabeth stepped to the hallway and glanced in the direction of the table, almost expecting to see the candelabra in its usual place. "I am afraid I have no idea, Megs," she murmured. "Did you ask Miss Darcy?"

"Yes, ma'am. Miss Darcy—she likes having it close by. When Miss Georgiana cannot sleep, she goes to the music room and plays until she feels more peaceful like. That be why we leave it there for her. Even when Miss Darcy returns to her room, she leaves the candle stand in the hall so we can change out the wax for the next time. Miss Darcy says she has not used the candleholder for nearly a fortnight. It be there earlier today." The woman looked frightened of being accused of taking the item.

"I am sure there is a logical reason." Elizabeth reached out and lightly touched the woman's arm. "When do you recall seeing it last?"

Meg closed her eyes to remember. "I suppose it be when I first came on—before I changed the bed linens."

Elizabeth heard Darcy's footsteps on the lower level. "Megs, Mr. Darcy waits for me. We must retrieve my sister at the Lambton inn. I will make it part of my afternoon duties to help you locate the holder. Possibly, Mr. Darcy's aunt or his cousin took it to their rooms without realizing Miss Darcy's nocturnal habits. We will laugh when it reappears in some very obvious place."

"Yes, ma'am." She curtsied again. "You be right about that." The maid glanced toward the stairs. "Mr. Darcy seems impatient, ma'am," Megs ventured.

Elizabeth chuckled. "What man is not so?"

"None I know of, Mrs. Darcy, but ye better hurry. I would not want to be the source of Mr. Darcy's fluster."

"Neither would I, Megs." Elizabeth smiled as she slipped her left hand into her muff. Then she hurried down the stairs to meet her husband.

CHAPTER 3

~ ~ ~

THE FIVE MILES FROM PEMBERLEY to the Rose and Crown took much longer than either she or Darcy had anticipated. The earlier pounding rain had turned bitter cold and become icy. Small pellets were accumulating in the ditches and on the dried grassy patches. The temperature had dropped quickly, and a thin layer of ice skimmed the tops of the mud holes.

Darcy kept the information to himself, not wishing to alarm Elizabeth, but he could not remember conditions ever changing so suddenly. The coach's wheels still easily broke the icy crusts over the brown puddles, but if they had to wait long for Mrs. Wickham's coach, the return trip could be a different story. Instead of sitting across from Elizabeth in the rear-facing seat he usually occupied, Darcy chose to sit beside her—to keep her warmer and to protect her if Mr. Stalling lost control of the coach.

Adam Lawrence's temper rose quickly. He and Cathleen had made it to Lambton's inn, but found it full because of the quickly deteriorating road conditions. "And where do you suggest I find a room for the evening?" he demanded in his best aristocratic voice.

"I am most apologetic, Your Lordship." The innkeeper mopped his brow. "I have already doubled people in rooms. I suppose that I could convince some of our more esteemed citizens to offer you a room, my Lord." Cautiously, the man shot a glance at Cathleen. "I might have more difficulty convincing them to also accept *your cousin*."

Adam hissed, "So you would send *my cousin* and me back out into the storm?"

"I would not wish to do so, Your Lordship." However, before the innkeeper could continue his back-door apology, Darcy and Elizabeth entered to look for Lydia Wickham. Leaving Adam with a swallowed curse still on his lips, Mr. Lawill quickly greeted Darcy. Most of those in town depended on Pemberley directly or indirectly for their well-being. The inhabitants of a small market town knew to whom they owed allegiance.

"Mr. Darcy, sir," the man said as he offered a bow, "how may I serve you?" The first time Elizabeth had stayed at this inn, she had discovered Darcy's true value. Now, entering on his arm, she appreciated how people admired and respected him. The locals knew her husband to be a liberal man, one who did much good among the poor, and they rushed to meet his needs.

"Good afternoon, Mr. Lawill. We were to meet Mrs. Darcy's sister on the afternoon coach." Darcy purposely did not refer to Lydia Bennet Wickham by her name. He wished to keep the memory of her husband, George Wickham, at a psychological distance. The man had left a trail of bad debts in the area when he had suddenly left Pemberley with three thousand pounds, a pecuniary advantage in lieu of the preferment of taking his orders. Like so many other times, Darcy had covered the debts rather than have the Pemberley name besmirched by association.

"Mr. Buckley deposited his passengers thirty minutes ago, sir. I am at my wit's end trying to find accommodations for all the travelers the storm has driven our way."

Elizabeth touched Darcy's arm. "I will see to Lydia," she whispered.

Darcy nodded before returning his attention to the innkeeper. "You will prevail, Mr. Lawill." Then Darcy's eyes fell on Viscount Stafford, a man he knew casually through his cousin Charles Fitzwilliam, Edward's older brother and the future Earl of Matlock. "Stafford, fancy meeting you on this side of Leicestershire," he called as he stepped around Lawill to greet the viscount.

"Darcy!" Adam Lawrence offered a bow before extending his hand. "I had forgotten of your being in Derbyshire."

They exchanged a few pleasantries before reaching the situation's crux. "I was to go to Cheshire." Lawrence glanced quickly to where Cathleen stood watching the storm out the window. "*My cousin* rushes to her uncle's beside at her family's request." Adam guided Darcy to the side where others could not hear. "However, the storm has delayed us, and now we find no rooms available. I suppose I will have Mr. Johnson press on."

"That would be unwise," Darcy insisted. "The rain has frozen. I do not imagine even the best coachman could traverse another twenty miles without incident. And who is to say that you would not find a similar development there?"

Lawrence took in Cathleen's profile. "What do you suggest I do, Darcy? I cannot abandon the lady. It would be unfair to leave her to the locals' censure. Mr. Lawill has already expressed his displeasure. Even if I chose to accept the hospitality of one of Lambton's citizens, no one would extend Miss Donnel such a courtesy. If it were for but one evening, she and I could simply spend the night at Mr. Lawill's tables, but you and I both know the conditions of country roads. We will be lucky to be here less than three days."

Darcy thought about what he should do. Propriety demanded that he extend an invitation to Stafford but, like Lambton's citizens, he could not take the viscount's mistress to his own home. "Unfortunately, Stafford, my aunt Lady Catherine de Bourgh and her daughter are at Pemberley, and my sister…" Darcy felt the shame of being inhospitable.

Adam pleaded, "But if Miss Donnel plays the part of my cousin? The lady is an actress. I will stay away from her, Darcy—be the perfect gentleman—and charm your aunt and your sister."

Darcy snapped, "You will avoid my sister, Lord Stafford." He glanced at the woman waiting patiently by the window. "If I extend what society demands, you will create a story through which even my aunt will not see. I will allow this, Stafford, but if Miss Donnel cannot play the role, I will claim that I was deceived by you and turn you out, no matter what the conditions. Miss Donnel will be a lady, and you will act a gentleman's part around my wife, my sister, my family, and my staff."

"My reputation precedes me," Lawrence murmured.

Darcy spoke in hushed tones. "I do not wish to offend you, Stafford. I barely know you, and under normal circumstances, I would gladly open my door to you at any time. As my cousin Matlock's friend, I owe you as much. Yet, I have a sister to whom I serve as guardian, and I will not have her exposed to your arrangement with Miss Donnel. You may assume me full of pride and full of prejudice, but I will protect Georgiana."

Adam Lawrence stared at Darcy. Despite his seething anger, Lawrence could not help but respect Fitzwilliam Darcy for his vision and his sense of purpose. The man knew his place in the world—knew his duty. Adam had always wanted that type of confidence. His own confidence was no more than bravado. "Miss Donnel and I will be decorum's models, sir. You have my word on it."

"Then explain things to the lady while I speak to Mrs. Darcy and her sister." Darcy moved away, leaving the viscount to do what he had promised.

Elizabeth had rushed from Darcy's side, trying to locate Lydia and tone down her sister's "welcome" before she said something offensive to Darcy. From the time she had finally realized the perfect goodness of the man who loved her, Elizabeth had done all she could to shield him from the frequent vulgarity of her family.

"Lyddie." Elizabeth approached her sister from behind. "There you are—."

Before Elizabeth could finish her sentence, Lydia had her in her embrace. "Oh, Lizzy, it has been so long!"

And despite all those little private moments in which Elizabeth had dreaded welcoming the wife of Darcy's worst enemy as a guest in their home, Elizabeth rejoiced. Her family, even her dearest sister, Jane, was in Hertfordshire, and she missed them desperately. Having Lydia before her increased Elizabeth's loneliness, but it also appeased it at the same time.

"Lydia," she said, her eyes welling with tears. They hugged for a long moment. When she released the girl, Elizabeth said, "Let me look at you. Oh, my, you are growing up."

"Of course I am, Lizzy," Lydia declared, dismissing her older sister's sentimentality. "I am a married woman."

Elizabeth caught Lydia's arm. "Let us return to Pemberley. My husband worries for the roads. I fear that you came to us just as Winter offers her worst. Mr. Darcy speaks to Mr. Lawill. Come along."

"But I cannot leave Mr. Worth and Mrs. Williams." Lydia planted her feet and refused to budge. "I told them that Mr. Darcy would not allow them to sleep on the floor. Surely they can come to Pemberley with us."

Elizabeth put more pressure on her sister's arm, trying to maneuver the girl away from the man and woman seated nearby. "Lydia, you cannot simply invite people to Mr. Darcy's home," she hissed under her breath.

A little too loudly, Lydia announced, "Your husband, Lizzy, has always been …most disagreeable. He would leave my friends here. I am your sister, and he is so high and so conceited that he would—"

"Would what, Mrs. Wickham?" Darcy's voice came from behind them.

Elizabeth whirled to see him standing there. Immediately, she tightly grasped Lydia's arm, smiling politely all the while. "Apologize," she quietly warned her sister while pasting a smile on her face. She realized the whole inn watched them.

"Oh, Mr. Darcy," Lydia bubbled as if nothing had happened. "I am so pleased to see you again." She wrenched her arm from Elizabeth's grasp before dropping a quick curtsy.

Elizabeth walked casually to where Darcy stood and slipped her arm through his. "It seems, Fitzwilliam, that Lydia has made friends with her two traveling companions. I was just about to extend an invitation to Pemberley to Mr. Worth and Mrs. Williams, as we certainly could not have them sleeping on Mr. Lawill's common room floor." She smiled up at him, but her eyes told Darcy that she did not like the situation any better than he.

"Certainly, Elizabeth." Darcy dramatically brought the back of her hand to his lips, demonstrating to all eyes their devotion. "Let us meet Mrs. Wickham's new friends."

Lydia liked the idea of having gotten her way with Mr. Darcy. It might, she mused, bode well for her convincing him to use his influence to help Wickham. Perhaps she could save her marriage to George Wickham. "Mr. Darcy and Elizabeth, may I present Mrs. Evelyn Williams, the widow of Admiral Samuel Williams. Mrs. Williams, this is my sister Elizabeth Darcy and her husband, Fitzwilliam Darcy."

Mrs. Williams stood during the introduction. She immediately acknowledged the Darcys with a proper curtsy. Then she thanked them for their charity.

"It is our pleasure, Mrs. Williams," Elizabeth said.

"And this is Mr. Nigel Worth," Lydia pronounced.

"Mr.-Mr. Worth," Darcy stammered, having recognized the man and wondered why he traveled with Wickham's wife. "You are welcome as well, sir."

"Your graciousness speaks well of you, Mr. Darcy." Worth bowed to both the Darcys.

Darcy turned to Elizabeth. "It seems that I, too, have extended an invitation to Pemberley. An associate of my cousin Charles finds himself on his way to Cheshire. Viscount Stafford will inherit Greene Hall in Leicestershire. I have asked him and his cousin Miss Donnel to join us. They had been traveling to the bedside of an uncle, but now, like all these others, they must seek shelter from the storm. Mr. Lawill has no more accommodations."

"Of course, Fitzwilliam." Elizabeth recognized Darcy's half-truths. His tone always told her when her husband asked her to read between the lines. "We shall have a merry household."

"Let us retrieve everyone's luggage, Elizabeth? We must return to our home."

She released his arm. "I will ask Mr. Lawill's man to help with the trunks. Might Mr. Worth ride with Viscount Stafford? It would make things more comfortable."

"I will speak to His Lordship." Darcy squeezed Elizabeth's hand before walking away. His wife—his incomparable Elizabeth—a woman he had once thought beneath him—inferior in her connection—she understood him and protected him. Now, he too comprehended: From the first moment he had laid eyes on her at the Hertfordshire assembly hall, Fitzwilliam Darcy had thought of no one but her. She consumed him, and he loved her with a passion that surprised even him. Elizabeth would understand and would even find the mix of people about to inundate Pemberley as amusing as would he.

Within twenty minutes, the inn's staff had loaded the trunks onto Darcy's large coach, and both carriages had set out for Pemberley. For his own reasons, Darcy purposely had placed all the ladies, except the viscount's mistress, in his coach. He would not subject Mrs. Williams—or even his wife's sister, who had acted quite shamelessly with George Wickham—to Miss Donnel. He would tell Elizabeth of the lady's true nature so that his wife could help him keep Georgiana apart from Cathleen Donnel.

The icy rain continued, but feathery flakes of snow also appeared. Darcy knew that Mr. Stalling was fighting the elements from his perch on the box. The ice pelted the carriage's sides and roof, while the snow thickened, covering the layer of ice and making the road slick. The horses wanted to bolt—to escape the dampness—but Stalling held them in check, making the animals walk rather than giving them their heads. Each time Darcy looked, it seemed that the snow grew in its intensity—blinding his view. It came—part icy rain and part snow—covering the trees and the ground in a crusty frost.

"We will arrive soon," he told them, although he knew that there were more than two miles to the house. At the moment, he wished that the drive from the gatehouse to the front circular drive were shorter.

"It seems that many of our guests travel to Cheshire, Fitzwilliam," Elizabeth said out of nowhere. When she was nervous, silence drove her to distraction; Darcy realized that his wife's fears had increased, so despite propriety, he slid his arm around her, resting it easily against the back of the seat, while the tips of his fingers touched her shoulder in a gentle caress.

"Unfortunately, my Dear, Lady Catherine says the storm followed her from Manchester. I suspect Cheshire is not the place to be at the moment."

"Lady Catherine?" Lydia gasped. "Is Her Ladyship at Pemberley also? Why did you not tell me, Lizzy?"

"Lady Catherine pays us an unexpected visit, but we are pleased to receive her and Miss de Bourgh."

"Oh, my," Mrs. Williams looked around frantically, giving the appearance that she had suddenly changed her mind about accepting the invitation. In the pale light of the afternoon, her eyes darted from side to side, as if looking for an escape. "I do so appreciate Mrs. Wickham's kindness, but I feel that we have thrust undue obligations on you, Mr. Darcy."

"Nonsense, Mrs. Williams," Darcy assured her. "Pemberley is capable of hosting a large number of people, and it is only for a few days, until the roads improve."

His mention of the roads drew everyone's attention to conditions outside the coach. "I worry so for Mr. Stalling," Elizabeth remarked as she stared at the falling snow.

Darcy patted her hand. "That is because you have a kind heart, my Dear. We will insist that Mrs. Jennings fix our Stalling and the viscount's driver some hot soup and then see them both to bed. We would not want either man to catch an ague."

To pass the time, Elizabeth told Lydia and Mrs. Williams about the first time she had seen Pemberley, when she had come to Derbyshire on holiday with her Aunt and Uncle Gardiner. Her relatives had insisted on seeing Pemberley. She explained, "I was apprehensive about the possibility of seeing Mr. Darcy again. As Lydia knows, early in our acquaintance, I misjudged my dear husband. However, at Pemberley, I suddenly considered how as a brother, a landlord, a master, how many people's happiness were in his guardianship; how much of pleasure or pain it was in his power to bestow; how much good or evil must be done by him, and I began to think of his regard with a deeper sentiment of gratitude than it had ever raised before."

Darcy listened in amazement. Elizabeth had never spoken of this previously. She had shared her first thoughts of his home and of how Mrs. Reynolds's praise had opened her mind, but his wife had never confessed how her opinion of him had changed once she had seen for herself all his responsibilities.

"I understand, Mrs. Darcy," Mrs. Williams said. "I would watch the admiral right before a battle and realize how much of the world depended on him—on his decisions. At such times, I would feel an overwhelming love for my husband."

A long silence followed Mrs. Williams's declaration. Her words had been pretty, yet something about her speech bothered Elizabeth. It sounded rehearsed. Often women professed their love for a husband who was tyrannical. *Is the widow trying to preserve the late admiral's reputation?* Elizabeth wondered.

"Well, I am sure that my dear Wickham would be a fine leader," Lydia asserted.

Elizabeth started to point out to her sister Wickham's shortcomings, but a squeeze of Darcy's hand reminded his wife of Mrs. Williams's presence in the coach. Besides, Murray was pulling open the door to let down the steps. "We are pleased that you returned safely, Mr. Darcy."

"Thank you, Murray. I will see to the ladies. Have someone help Viscount Stafford's party. Unload the trunks as quickly as possible. I want everyone inside."

"Yes, Mr. Darcy."

Darcy turned to those disengaging from Stafford's coach. "Everyone into the house. My staff will see to the belongings and the horses." With a flick of his wrist, he directed footmen to support the ladies on the icy steps leading to the main door, while other members of his staff hurried to bring umbrellas, which offered some protection from the elements.

"It certainly is miserable," Adam Lawrence remarked before following the women up the steps.

Darcy glanced back to make sure that everything was as he had instructed. Assured that all was well in hand, he turned his attention to the house and the open door. Then out of the corner of his eye, he saw him, standing partially behind a drawn drapery in the east wing, in a room not currently occupied, one under remodeling. For a split second their eyes met, but then the figure disappeared, almost as if it had never been there. The drape did not move, but the shadowy image withdrew. Darcy shook his head to clear it. Had his eyes, blinded by the rain and the snow, played a trick on him? Of course, even if someone was truly there, it could easily be one of his staff checking on the rooms, making sure things remained secure. Yet none of those explanations gave him any comfort. Instead, a shiver ran up his spine, and Darcy found his eyes searching the window once more.

"Fitzwilliam!" Elizabeth's voice called from the open door. "Murray has control of everything. Come before you find yourself soaked to the bone."

Closing the carriage door, Darcy quickly followed the rest of his party up the steps. He stamped his feet to remove the mud clinging to his boots. Then he handed Mr. Baldwin his greatcoat. "Have someone bring us tea in the green room, Mr. Baldwin," Darcy ordered.

"Both Miss Darcy and the Mistress have placed like orders, sir." The man smiled slightly.

Darcy chuckled. "I suppose I must abdicate some duties to the women in my life," he whispered.

"It seems a wise decision, sir."

"Obviously, we will need additional rooms available. Besides a room for Mrs. Wickham, another four rooms should be readied. Place the women in proximity to one another and the men likewise."

"Yes, Mr. Darcy."

"And have Mrs. Jennings prepare—"

"Mrs. Darcy again, sir," his man interrupted him.

Darcy smiled at the man who had served the family since Darcy was a boy. "I will leave you to do your job, Mr. Baldwin. You know it better than I do." With that, he followed his party to the drawing room—to the warmth of the fireplace and hot tea.

"Oh, Fitzwilliam, I was so worried." Georgiana greeted him as he stepped into the room.

Darcy slid his arm about her waist. "As you see, other than a bit chilled, we are all safe." He glanced toward the hearth where Elizabeth stood. "Did Elizabeth introduce you to everyone?"

"Yes, Brother." Georgiana, who was always a bit shy, clung to his hand. "It was kind of you and Elizabeth to bring the others to Pemberley."

"It is only for a few days." Then he whispered in her ear. "At least with the others here, Lady Catherine will not offer you her usual caustic censure."

Georgiana smiled at that idea. "Let me help Elizabeth with the tea service." She moved away from him. The absence of his aunt and the influence of his new wife had given Georgiana a large dose of confidence this past year, but he feared that the appearance of Lydia Wickham at Pemberley might be a setback. At age fifteen, Georgiana had aligned herself with George Wickham, a man with whom she shared a familiarity. He, in turn, had claimed to love her, but as it played out, her dowry of thirty thousand pounds and possible revenge on Darcy had interested the man more. Darcy had learned of Wickham's planned elopement and arrived in time to send the man packing. The effect of this disappointment on Georgiana persisted. She lacked confidence in social situations, always wondering if people liked her for herself or for her wealth. Having

Lydia as a reminder of her mistake could prove detrimental. Darcy would guard against that happening. He would not deny Elizabeth her sister's company, but he also would not allow Lydia Bennet Wickham's presence to hurt his sister.

At the moment, even with Anne's situation with Lieutenant Harwood, Darcy was thankful for his cousin's presence at Pemberley. Anne always catered to Georgiana, and his sister could keep company with Anne and her companion, Mrs. Jenkinson. That way, Lydia would scarcely notice Georgiana.

Thirty minutes later, Mr. Baldwin appeared at the door. Darcy met him there and then turned to the group. "Mr. Baldwin assures me that your rooms are prepared with comfortable fires burning in each. I am sure most of you would like time to freshen your things after such a harrowing day. Your trunks are in your chambers. If you are in need of anything, please do not hesitate to ask any of my staff. I am afraid we keep country hours. Supper will be served at half past five."

"If you will follow me," Mr. Baldwin instructed the guests.

The guests rose and made their way to the door. As each one passed Darcy, he or she murmured words of gratitude once again — everyone except Lydia, who seemed to think of herself as more than a guest. "You will have someone bring me water for a bath, Mr. Darcy?" She offered her most beguiling smile.

"Certainly, Mrs. Wickham."

With everyone's departure, Georgiana excused herself to practice her music. Finally, it was just he and Elizabeth. Immediately, she moved into his embrace. For several moments, they simply held each other. "I suspect after this week, we will be more than happy to isolate ourselves at Pemberley once again," Darcy said.

Elizabeth rested her head on his chest. "I am sorry for my sister's impudence," she said, near tears.

"None of that, Elizabeth," he warned her. "I have known no greater joy than I have found with you this past year. Have you not realized that I would move mountains to make you happy? I can tolerate the inconvenience of a few extra people for the pleasure of seeing you enjoying your family."

"But Lydia is so uncontrollable," she protested.

He countered, "And Lady Catherine is not?"

She wound her arms about his neck as she confessed, "Well, perhaps we are even." Elizabeth lifted her chin to look at him. Darcy tightened his hold on her, drawing Elizabeth closer to him. "You are my heart," she whispered as her lips parted in anticipation of his kiss.

"No, Mrs. Darcy. I never found the candleholder," Megs reported. "I searched all the nearby rooms to be seein' if it be there, and I askt' Margie and Lilly to be checkin' Her Ladyship's room like ye be sayin', but it be not there either." She appeared more than a bit upset.

Elizabeth puzzled over this mystery. "It certainly makes no sense," she muttered. "I thought surely it would turn up by now."

"I be sorry, Mrs. Darcy." Tears began to fill the woman's eyes.

Elizabeth heard the trembling in the maid's voice. "My goodness, Megs. Do not do that. No one is blaming you. The candelabra will reappear, just as I said this morning."

"I would not want ye to be thinkin' poorly of me, ma'am—like me did not do me job. I like it at Pemberley. So much better than at the Johnsons'." She blurted out the words in a rush of emotions.

"I assure you, Megs," Elizabeth said calmly, "that we have no complaints regarding your work. The holder will reappear. In a house the size of Pemberley, it could be anywhere. We will continue to search for it."

"Yes, ma'am. Thank ye, Mistress." The woman bobbed a curtsy before leaving to do her duties.

Without thinking about what she did, Elizabeth began to search the rooms along the hallway leading to Georgiana's private chambers. Even as a child, Elizabeth had hated an unsolved puzzle, and although she knew it would reappear, she wanted to find the candleholder to solve this particular mystery. However, after thoroughly going through three bedchambers, she realized the futility of such a search. There were just too many places at Pemberley to look. She would alert Mrs. Reynolds and Mr. Baldwin—have everyone on the lookout for the missing item.

"Mr. Baldwin, I was wondering if we had men working in the east wing today?" Darcy, as he always did when he hosted guests at Pemberley, was double-checking all the details for the evening's entertainment.

"Not of which I am aware, sir." The butler lit the wall sconces in the main hallway. "Should I inquire, sir?"

Darcy glanced toward the main staircase. "I thought I saw someone in the window when we returned from Lambton. I may be wrong, but I would like to know for sure."

"I will check with Murray, sir."

"Be discreet, Mr. Baldwin. If one of our men is shirking his duties and hiding out in the unoccupied rooms, I wish to catch him in the act." The more he considered those brief seconds of eye contact the more convinced Darcy was of actually seeing someone in the darkened room. A footman being where he did not belong was the most logical explanation.

"I will see to it personally, Mr. Darcy."

Elizabeth tapped lightly on Lydia's chamber door. "Lydia," she said as she opened it just a crack, "may I help you dress?" Elizabeth wanted a few minutes alone with her sister. She had not seen Lydia since the day her youngest sister and George Wickham had left Longbourn for Newcastle. That had been before Darcy's second proposal—before her double wedding with their oldest sister, Jane, to Charles Bingley. Of course, the Wickhams claimed that his military duties and the great distance prevented their attending the wedding, but Elizabeth knew the real reason to be the unspoken feud between Darcy and Mr. Wickham.

"Come in!" Lydia called from behind the screen where she dressed.

"I thought we might have some time together." Elizabeth came closer to the screen. "It has been more than a year since we had a five-chit chat." It was what they had once called that time at the end of the day at Longbourn when the five Bennet girls gathered to share gossip and hopes and dreams. Beside the long talks with her father and her uncommon need for Jane as her confidante, it was what Elizabeth missed most about her Hertfordshire home.

"Sure, Lizzy." Lydia grunted, obviously struggling into her clothes.

Elizabeth indulgently came around the screen. "Let me lace that for you." She took up the strings of her sister's corsets. "I will ask Mrs. Reynolds to find someone to serve as your maid while you are at Pemberley. Would you like that, Lyddie?"

"Just listen to you." Lydia turned to really see her sister. "Are you not the be-all, now that you have married Mr. Darcy. Back at Longbourn none of us had our own maid. We all shared the Hills and Harriet."

Elizabeth spun Lydia to where she could tie off the last of the strings. "Well, I did marry Mr. Darcy, and if that makes me uppity, then so be it." Elizabeth walked back toward the room's seating area. "So do you wish the help of a maid or not?"

Lydia followed her as they took a place before the hearth. "Why should I not live in luxury while I may," she replied.

Elizabeth pulled her feet up under her to sit comfortably. "Jane's last letter said that you and Mr. Wickham had moved recently. I will need your new directions."

"It is not much." Lydia straightened her dress's seams, trying not to make eye contact with her sister. "Obviously, nothing like what you or Jane has." She glanced about her. "Just four rooms. You know—military quarters are not much by Pemberley's standards."

Elizabeth knew that her sister had changed quarters three times since her marriage. Elizabeth and Jane had agreed to aid their younger sister, knowing Lydia's tendency to spend foolishly. Elizabeth sent such relief as it was in her power to afford by the practice of what might be called economy in her own private expenses. She refused to ask Darcy to provide the Wickhams with any more financial support. It had always been evident to everyone that the couple would know no economy, and that such an income as theirs, under the direction of two persons in their wants and heedless of the future, must be very insufficient to their support. "But you and Mr. Wickham—I mean—you are happy, are you not, Lydia?"

"It is easy to be happy when you live like this." Lydia gestured to the room's finery. "It is a bit harder when…well…it just is, Lizzy."

Elizabeth sat forward. "I want you to be happy, Lydia; you must know that." She, too, gestured to the room's decorations. "*This* is not from where my happiness comes. For me, it comes from Fitzwilliam. I would be happy to be one of Pemberley's cottagers if he was there."

"Then you are lucky." Lydia stood. "I affect Mr. Wickham—I really do, Lizzy. He is so handsome in his blue coat and all." She walked to the fireplace and stood there with her back to the roaring fire.

Elizabeth had realized from the beginning that Wickham's affection for Lydia was not equal to Lydia's for him. Their elopement had been brought on by the strength of her love rather than by his. She often wondered why, without violently caring for Lydia, he had chosen to elope with her at all. Now she understood that his flight had been rendered necessary by distress of circumstances, and Wickham was not the young man to resist an opportunity of having a companion. Lydia had been exceedingly fond of him from the beginning. He had been her *dear Wickham* on every occasion; no one was to be put in competition with him. He did everything best in the world. It was an idealized love.

"I know that you have always found the best in Mr. Wickham." Elizabeth felt very sorry for her sister's situation—for her own beloved Lydia's foolishness.

Lydia turned to stare into the fire. "I wish my husband did me the same honor. He finds me quite silly, and I suppose I am at times."

"You are still very young, Lyddie."

"Am I?" The girl's shoulders began to jerk with silent sobs. "I am old enough to know what my husband does on these trips when he sends me off to visit with Jane and now you." Her tone turned sarcastic. "Can you imagine *my dear Wickham* not keeping company with some other woman when he is at Bath or London?"

"You do not know that for certain, Lydia." Elizabeth said the words to comfort her sister, not because she truly believed them.

Lydia wiped at her face with her sleeve. "No...I do not know for certain what my husband does on his travels." She wore bitterness on her face when she turned to her sister. "The colonel's wife says that it is a man's way—that a woman must accept her lot. But I will not spend my life with a man who does not love me. I fancy myself still capable of attracting a man of consequence—the same as you and Jane."

"Lydia, you cannot be thinking of leaving Mr. Wickham!" Elizabeth's heart sank as she inwardly acknowledged the possible scandal. A divorce would be ten times more controversial than Lydia's elopement, and it would not be something that even Darcy could cover up, even if it were possible for Wickham to execute. Divorce was usually granted only to those of a particular social class and those with deep pockets, neither of which described the Wickhams.

"Why not?" Lydia went to the mirror to style her hair. "He has no qualms about leaving me—whether it be to Bath or London or even simply to his own bed. Well, I will have no more of it, Lizzy—I will not be tossed aside at seventeen. When Mr. Wickham left, I told him that I expected a renewal of his affections when he returned, or I would speak to the colonel about what happens behind our closed doors."

Elizabeth did not want to ask, but she did so anyway. "What happens, Lydia?"

Her sister did not turn to speak directly to Elizabeth, but she spoke to her sister's reflection in the beveled mirror. "Mr. Wickham drinks, Lizzy, and he is not a man who holds his liquor well."

"He hits you!" Elizabeth said, aghast. She had observed George Wickham being rude to Lydia, but it was always when Lydia had made a spectacle of herself, but Elizabeth had never thought it might be more than embarrassment mixed with irritation.

"Not hit exactly—more like shove or fling or pinch or bend. But I will no longer tolerate my husband's ire, and I told him so before I left Nottingham. I told Mr. Wickham to get whatever it was out of his system before he returned to Newcastle."

"Good for you." Elizabeth moved to stand behind her sister. "I am proud of you, Lyddie." She took up the brush to style Lydia's hair.

"Are you truly, Lizzy?"

"Indeed, I am."

CHAPTER 4

~~~

"SO, WORTH, WOULD YOU LIKE to explain to me how you ended up in a carriage with the wife of a man you previously prosecuted for gambling debts?"

Worth leaned back in his chair. "Would you believe it was purely coincidence?"

"Not in the least." Darcy sat forward to press his point. "I prefer the truth. Mrs. Wickham is Mrs. Darcy's youngest sister. If the lady's husband has brought additional shame on this family, I have a right to know."

Worth played with his pocket watch, opening and closing the case. After several moments, he responded, "Mr. Wickham has made some unsavory connections."

Darcy paused and then asked, "What should I know?"

"Nearly a month ago, Mr. Niall O'Malley, a former associate from Cheshire—sent me a letter. He is practicing in Newcastle and had received several complaints by merchants and officers regarding George Wickham. It took him some time before he made the connection to the case we had brought in my home shire against your wife's brother." Remembering Darcy's contempt for Wickham, Worth was careful not to refer to the man as also being Darcy's brother. "My friend asked me to come to Newcastle to identify the man. When I arrived, I also learned that Mr. Wickham's commanding officer entertained the idea that the gentleman in question had ill-used Mrs. Wickham on more than one occasion."

Darcy made no comment. He comforted Elizabeth when she had returned in tears to their shared chambers with news of Lydia's accusation against her husband. Nigel Worth's words only underscored Darcy's opinion of George Wickham. "That still does not explain how you ended up as Mrs. Wickham's *newest friend*."

"In reality, it was a coincidence. According to your wife's sister, Wickham left her in Nottingham to wait for the public coach to Pemberley. I had no idea of Mrs. Wickham's identity until she shared it during one of our conversations."

"And what is your connection to this new case against George Wickham?" Darcy needed all the facts—needed to know how to ensure his family's well-being.

"I would testify to the repetition of Mr. Wickham's offense—to his proclivity for gambling debts—assuming they decided to bring charges."

Darcy had to ask. "Do you have any idea of the extent of these debts?"

"Somewhere in the neighborhood of nine thousand pounds, I believe, sir."

A sickening feeling flooded his stomach. Barely eighteen months earlier, Darcy had settled a large sum on Wickham to marry Lydia Bennet, plus he paid the man's gambling debts in Hertfordshire and Brighton. He could not afford to bail his enemy out again, no matter what the emotional cost to his family. Enraged, he wondered, *How could Wickham go through so much money in such a short time?* If it would not affect the Bennets, and, ultimately, the Darcys, by association, he would lead the party to lock Wickham away.

"You are not thinking of paying Wickham's accounts again, are you, Mr. Darcy? It would be throwing good money after bad." Worth spoke the truth, although Darcy did not wish to hear it.

"I will not take money from my sister's future to save Mr. Wickham. Plus, I will not rescue the man if what you say is true regarding his actions towards his wife."

"I assure you that it is true, Mr. Darcy."

Darcy stood to end the conversation. "I thank you, Mr. Worth, for being so candid. You have given me much on which to think."

"Let me know, Mr. Darcy, if I may be of service." Worth made his obligatory bow to leave. "You and your family need to openly dissociate yourself from any dealings with Mr. Wickham."

"Unfortunately, you may be correct, Mr. Worth." Darcy led the way to the door. "However, how do I convince my wife to set aside her feelings for her sister and to allow the lady to flounder in the situation she has created?"

Despite Lady Catherine's objections, Darcy insisted that Elizabeth sit opposite him at his evening table. He placed Lady Catherine on his right and Viscount Stafford on Elizabeth's right. He kept Cathleen Donnel away from Georgiana, placing her between Lydia and Nigel Worth.

"It does appear that the storm is not going away anytime soon," Worth observed. "We may be in your debt, Mr. Darcy, longer than we originally had intended."

"I am sure that my nephew knows his duty," Lady Catherine declared to the whole table. "As is our family's nature, we take our responsibilities to the neighborhood seriously. My brother, the Earl of Matlock, is the most magnanimous of men."

"I was unaware, Mr. Darcy, of your relationship to the earl," Mrs. Williams raised her head to join the conversation. She seemed a bit disturbed by the news of Darcy's connection, but she said, "My late husband and I had the honor of making the acquaintance of the Earl of Matlock at a celebration dinner hosted by the Naval Board at Whitehall."

Lady Catherine puffed up with pride. "My brother is known for his strong support of our military efforts. In Parliament, he often urges more funding for our troops. His own son is a colonel in the army. Colonel Fitzwilliam shares guardianship of my niece with Darcy."

Darcy would have preferred that these complete strangers would have no knowledge of his private affairs, but he realized, from years of trying to squelch his aunt, that it was an effort in futility.

Georgiana, seated on Elizabeth's left, ventured a comment. "I do so wish that the colonel might call at Pemberley more often. It seems a long time since he was here."

"It has been only a few weeks," Elizabeth remarked. "He was here during the Festive season."

"It seems longer."

Georgiana's participation did not go unnoticed by Darcy, who realized that six months earlier, it would never have happened.

"If Mr. Worth's evaluation is true, Lord Stafford, you may not arrive at your relative's bedside in time. That would be a great tragedy," his sister observed.

Her words caught Adam Lawrence's attention in more than one way. He and Cathleen had not discussed how they would explain their supposed trip to Cheshire to comfort a loved one. "It would indeed be a tragedy, Miss Darcy."

Lady Catherine asked, "Whom did you intend to visit, Lord Stafford?"

Adam stammered, "A–a dis–a distant relative for me, Your Ladyship, but it is my cousin Miss Donnel's uncle. You understand how extended families come together in times of adversity."

"And your uncle, Miss Donnel—he has a title?" Lady Catherine demanded.

"An Irish baron, Lady Catherine." Cathleen kept her eyes lowered; Adam had warned her of Darcy's threat, and she played her part.

Lady Catherine's disdain showed. "Irish?" She wrinkled her nose.

"We all must come from somewhere, Aunt," Darcy said.

"I suppose," she said and *tsked*, taking the time to cut the slice of ham on her plate. "It is kind of His Lordship to escort Miss Donnel to Cheshire, considering that you are not blood cousins."

Adam found Lady Catherine's attitude amusing. If he had not promised Fitzwilliam Darcy to maintain propriety for the rest of the party's sake, Adam would have enjoyed putting the woman in her place by saying something scandalous. "Miss Donnel and I are *close,* nonetheless, Lady Catherine. I am just not close to her maternal uncle."

"I must observe, Viscount Stafford, that you and your cousin make a striking pair."

Adam could not resist. "So you think my cousin an appropriate match, Lady Catherine? I have never taken with the British practice of marrying one's relatives—be they distant or not." Adam purposely avoided looking at Darcy, knowing what his host might think of such a remark. He also avoided what he assumed played across Cathleen's face. He had openly admitted that he held no desire to marry her.

"Nonsense, Your Lordship." Lady Catherine swelled with self-righteousness. "A family must keep the blood lines pure. I had once entertained the idea of my nephew and my Anne making a match. It was the favorite wish of his mother, as well as my choice. However, it was not meant to be."

"Mother, please!" Anne whispered loudly.

Darcy warned, "Aunt, we will *not* revisit this issue."

"Of course, Darcy. I apologize." The woman looked anything but apologetic.

Adam had taken some pleasure in subtly needling Darcy's aunt, but he had no understanding of the animosity lurking behind the woman's conversation. He knew nothing of how or why Darcy had chosen his wife, but it was obviously a sore point for Lady Catherine. Adam had taken an initial liking to Darcy's wife, and he regretted that he might have inspired Lady Catherine to embarrass the woman.

"Well, as for me, I will follow in your nephew's footsteps, ma'am, and choose a woman I can truly love. It is capital to witness such a perfect couple as we see in Mr. and Mrs. Darcy. Very few men would object to such a match." With these words, Adam hoped that he had laid the groundwork for the Darcys' forgiveness of him.

"Mrs. Darcy is a phenomenal woman." Darcy raised his glass to Elizabeth in acknowledgment of the woman he loved.

"Thank you, my Husband." Purposely, Elizabeth had not reacted to Lady Catherine's insult. She had expected something of the sort from Darcy's aunt. She would not sink to the woman's baseness. Elizabeth recalled Darcy's second proposal: *As a child I was taught what was right, but was not taught to correct my temper. I was given good principles, but left to follow them in pride and conceit. Unfortunately, as an only son, I was spoiled by my parents, who though good themselves, allowed, encouraged, almost taught me to be selfish and overbearing; to care for none beyond my own family circle; to think meanly of their sense and worth compared with my own.* Luckily, her husband had changed his ways. Sadly, Lady Catherine would never see beyond the end of her aristocratic nose.

"Perhaps, Georgiana, you might entertain your brother's guests after our meal." Lady Catherine's suggestion was a thinly veiled edict.

Georgiana flushed. "I...I could not, Aunt."

"Nonsense, child. You most certainly will do your duty. Why spend so many hours practicing if no one ever is to hear you play? I am sure you possess more skill than Mrs. Darcy for she was never one to practice. I told her at Rosings several times that she will never play well unless she practices more. Yet even with her limited experience, Mrs. Darcy managed to entertain both the good colonel and your brother for an evening."

Darcy came immediately to his wife's defense. "No one admitted to the privilege of hearing Mrs. Darcy could think anything wanting." Darcy provided a solution of his own to calm his sister. "Perhaps, Elizabeth, you might offer us the pleasure of hearing you sing, with Georgiana's accompaniment, of course."

Elizabeth smiled archly. "I would enjoy that, Fitzwilliam. Oh, please say you will indulge me, Georgiana!"

Georgiana knew this woman—knew that Elizabeth, like her brother, would walk through fire to protect her. "That would be most pleasant, Elizabeth. You have a beautiful voice."

"Possibly my cousin will share a song also; she is quite talented," Adam Lawrence observed, again ignoring Darcy's possible censure.

Darcy asked smoothly, "Might you honor us with a song or two, Miss Donnel?"

Her initial expression was one of mild alarm, but the lady answered, "Thank you, Mr. Darcy, for asking. If it is your wish, I cannot refuse. You have opened your home to my cousin and me. It is the least I could do in return."

Worth took a sip of his wine. "Sing for your supper, Miss Donnel?" he inquired jovially. As a solicitor, Worth considered himself a keen observer of humanity, for he met all kinds. As such, something told him the viscount and this lady held no blood relationship. He thought her "talents" lay elsewhere.

"It is not necessary to repay our hospitality," Elizabeth interrupted, "but I would appreciate not being the only one to perform this evening. Please do join me."

As usual, Lady Catherine wanted the last word. "Music! It is of all subjects my delight. There are few people in England, I suppose, who have more true enjoyment in music than myself, or a better natural taste. If I had ever learned I should have been a great proficient; and so would Anne, if her health had allowed her to apply."

Darcy watched as his cousin sank lower in her seat, trying to symbolically disappear. Obviously, Anne's *health* had improved enough for her to sneak off to meet *her lieutenant*. Darcy had not yet had an opportunity to speak privately with Anne. When he had stopped by her room that day, she claimed a headache. He would need to give her a day or two before he could approach his cousin on her indiscretion. Darcy would not chastise her, though. He had mistakenly done so with Georgiana; now she struggled to gain her social confidence. Despite the fact that Anne held eight years on Georgiana, his cousin lived under Lady Catherine's thumb. As such, Anne de Bourgh possessed little social confidence. Actually, he found her "rebellion," so uncharacteristic, encouraging. Possibly, Anne's *indiscretion* would be a turning point in her life. He simply wanted to guarantee that the man did not perform a farce in his profession of love. If Lieutenant Harwood's affections proved legitimate, Darcy would not stop the man from pursuing Anne. His cousin deserved to know true affection.

"Let us not stand on propriety then. Shall we retire to the music room?" Darcy stood to end the conversation. Elizabeth followed him to her feet. She came to his end of the table to greet him. In reality, he should escort his aunt, but Lady Catherine's ill breeding and high-handedness irritated him. "Come, my Dear." He placed Elizabeth's hand on his arm and led her from the room.

"Will you not come to bed, my Husband?" Elizabeth stood at the door of his study. United, they had weathered their first evening with their eclectic guests. Both she and Miss Donnel had entertained the group, and Georgiana finally agreed to play several solos——with everyone's praise. They had found the evening actually quite pleasant, with the exception of Lady Catherine's continual remarks on the various performances and her many instructions on execution and taste.

"I have a letter to my solicitor," he noted. "I shall join you by the time you finish your ablutions." He smiled at her; he knew Elizabeth did not like to sleep alone. At Longbourn, she and her sister Jane had shared more than confidences. They often shared the same bed, needing each other's company to feel complete. His wife had transferred that "need" to him. Of course, Darcy did not complain. Lying with her in his arms was exquisite. His loneliness—his own "needs"—found completion in her love.

Elizabeth pursed her lips and blew him an air kiss. A smile played across her countenance. "I shall wait up."

He recognized that look—a love promise. "I shall not be long."

Giggling, she dropped him a curtsy and was gone.

Darcy returned to his letter. In it, he asked Mr. Laurie to seek information on Wickham's reported affairs, as well as the extent of the man's latest debts. He also requested any details that Mr. Laurie might glean on Lieutenant Harwood's financial soundness. Darcy did not fool himself into thinking that the letter would go out anytime soon: The snow had continued to fall all evening, covering everything in a thick layer of whiteness. However, he would have it ready for when the postal service started up again.

A tap at the door drew his attention away from his task. He raised his head and found Mr. Baldwin waiting patiently for his acknowledgment. "I beg your pardon, Mr. Darcy. Might I speak with you, sir?"

"Certainly, Mr. Baldwin. Come in, please." He motioned to a chair, but the well-trained domestic refused with a nearly imperceptible shake of his head. However, the man remained on alert, and Darcy quickly recognized his butler's agitation. "What might I do for you, Mr. Baldwin?" He knew that for Baldwin to approach him, the matter must be significant. Darcy had, long ago, relegated management of the household staff to the man.

"As you requested, Mr. Darcy, I checked the rooms in the east wing myself." He paused, searching for the words to explain the situation. "Sir, the room with the Chinese pattern…"

"Yes, Mr. Baldwin."

"The mattress, Mr. Darcy…and the…the bed linens…they are missing, sir."

Darcy's expression showed his irritation. "What do you mean, Baldwin? Missing?"

"Missing, sir! As in not there…not in the room at all…not in any of the rooms, sir!"

"Are you sure, man?" Darcy was on his feet, moving closer to his butler, as if that would bring back the missing items.

"Completely, Mr. Darcy. I looked myself. I searched every room in the east wing, as well as all the empty ones in the west wing. I even searched the servants' quarters. I found nothing, Mr. Darcy— not a pillow or a blanket or even a sheet—nothing, sir."

"How is that possible, Mr. Baldwin? A complete bedding set does not sprout wings and fly away!" Darcy's frustration became more evident.

"I wish I had an explanation, sir. Where could it be? And why bed linens? None of it makes sense, Mr. Darcy."

Darcy paced the room—he disliked not being in control of his surroundings. "Tomorrow morning, I want you to take Murray and Hastings and search every room in this house—even those oc-cupied by my guests. If they object, tell them that I have ordered you to inspect every window and fireplace flue to make sure that they can withstand the elements. Methodically move from room to room—none is to be left without inspection. I want to know the whereabouts of this said bedding. And while you are at it, look for the candelabra usually kept outside Miss Darcy's room. Mrs. Darcy reports its sudden disappearance also."

"Yes, sir. I will see to it personally, sir."

His man waited, expecting Darcy to say more—to express his anger about the butler's incompetence. "Just find it, Mr. Baldwin. Someone plays games in my house, and I will have none of it."

"Yes, Mr. Darcy."

"Extinguish the lights. I am to bed. Be sure that everything is secure."

"Yes, Mr. Darcy."

Too annoyed to even finish the letter, Darcy strode from the room. Only in Elizabeth's arms could his anger be lessened.

They made love twice: The first time eased his dissatisfaction with the unexpected onslaught of intruders on his domain and with the equally unexpected disappearance of his household items. The second time Darcy brought her to completion, taking time to please her, slowly teasing Elizabeth with his ministrations. They lay wrapped in each other's arms, sated. Elizabeth drifted into the early stages of sleep. Darcy watched her even breathing, as he did nightly. From their first time together, he had watched her—guarded her as she slept—amazed by how easily she gave herself to him.

He had spent a year in suspense, trying to win her love, although he had refused to even acknowledge the power she held over him. "By you I was taught humility," he murmured softly as he lightly stroked Elizabeth's cheek.

She turned in his arms, snuggling into his chest. Her hand reached up to cup his jaw line. Dreamily, Elizabeth mumbled, "I love the way you smell—sandalwood and my Fitzwilliam." She breathed him in and returned to her sleep.

Darcy gently kissed her forehead and brushed her hair from her face. He closed his own eyes to dream of his wife and their life together. All his dreams rested in her.

Finally, deep in sleep—satisfied by their lovemaking and by the total trust he placed in Elizabeth, when the first scream came, it penetrated his subconscious, but did not register in his conscious mind. However, the second one pulled him from the depths of his dream and brought Darcy upright. He stumbled to the middle of the room.

"Georgiana." Elizabeth's whisper behind him sent him bolting from the room, a robe loosely wrapped about his form. Darcy slid to a halt at his sister's door, her screams ripping out his heart.

Without knocking, Darcy shoved the door open to find a terrified Georgiana on her knees in the middle of the bed, clutching her gown to her as she shook with fear. She continued to scream, not seeing him—not understanding he was there. Candlelight reflected in the mirror told him that Elizabeth followed behind him, but he did not turn around. Instead, he focused all his energy on helping his sister.

"Georgiana," he whispered as he edged forward. She no longer screamed, but she shivered uncontrollably. "Georgiana, I am here. Nothing will harm you." Slowly, comfortingly, he took her into his embrace, holding her tightly to him. Cooing gently, Darcy whispered in her ear—told the girl how he would never let anything hurt her. Finally, her body relaxed. "Georgiana," he said while watching Elizabeth use her candle to light the others. "Can you tell me what frightened you, my Dear?"

"Oh, Fitzwilliam," she sobbed. Darcy automatically pulled her closer.

"What is it, Darcy?" Lady Catherine demanded from the open doorway. Anne stood silently behind her mother.

Darcy did not look up; his attention remained on Georgiana, so Elizabeth took charge. "It is nothing, Lady Catherine." She began to turn the woman from the room. "Georgiana simply had a girlish nightmare. Sometimes her fears act on her mind." Elizabeth caught Anne's arm to walk her to her guest room; she knew that Lady Catherine would follow. "We are sorry that your sleep was disturbed, Miss de Bourgh."

"As long as Georgiana is unharmed," Anne murmured quietly.

"I shall not rise until noon," Lady Catherine grumbled. "It will take me hours to settle my nerves."

"I will have Mrs. Jennings send up some warm milk, Lady Catherine," Elizabeth offered.

"Make it chamomile tea with a dash of brandy," Darcy's aunt ordered as she entered her room, closing the door in Elizabeth's face.

Elizabeth smiled in amusement. "Might we send something to you also, Miss de Bourgh?"

Anne shot a quick glance at her mother's closed door. "I believe I shall finish my letter," she whispered conspiratorially.

"As you wish." Elizabeth patted the woman's hand before seeing Darcy's cousin safely to her room.

Returning to Georgiana's chambers, she saw Darcy easing his sister backwards onto the pillows. "Would you like me to stay with her?" Elizabeth asked.

He came closer, where he might speak to her ears alone. "Please...at least until I am more appropriately attired." Suddenly, she realized that he wore nothing beneath his robe.

"I prefer you this way," she said mischievously, hoping to ease the real concern she saw in Darcy's face.

"You are a wicked woman, Elizabeth Darcy." He recognized her ruse and kissed her upturned nose. "I will be back in a moment."

She squeezed his hand. "Have someone take chamomile tea with brandy to your aunt," she whispered before moving to comfort Georgiana. Darcy nodded and quickly left the room.

Elizabeth curled up beside Georgiana on the bed. "I am so sorry, Elizabeth," the girl started an apology.

"There is nothing for which to feel sorrow." She gently placed the lose strands of her sister's braid behind Georgiana's ear. "It was a nightmare—nothing more. We all have them at one time or another."

"But I was not asleep!" Georgiana protested. "At least, not all the way." She gripped Elizabeth's hand. "You must believe me!"

Elizabeth cupped the girl's chin in her palm. She raised her head so that she might fully see Georgiana's countenance. "Of course, I will believe you. You are my sister, Georgiana; I am always on your side." Darcy reappeared, wearing breeches and a loose shirt. He lovingly handed Elizabeth a silk robe. "Might you tell your brother and me what happened?"

He moved to sit on the end of the bed, leaving his sister's care to Elizabeth's tender encouragement. Darcy would simply listen. This was what he had always wanted for Georgiana—someone she would trust, and she did trust Elizabeth, just as he did.

Georgiana stared deeply into Elizabeth's eyes, allowing her brother's wife to make things right. "I went down to the music room because I could not sleep. I was so excited after everyone praised my playing; I wanted to work on a new piece to show them I could do something more complicated, actually earn their praise."

"That was admirable of you." Elizabeth eased away from Georgiana, encouraging the girl to draw on her own personal strength. Then she curled up before Darcy, accepting his symbolic protection and telling Georgiana they would see her through anything.

"I returned here after an hour or so, finally relaxed." Georgiana's attention remained on them. "I blew out my candles and curled down into the blankets, trying to ward off the chill. Finally, I started to reach that point where I was drifting off to sleep—you know, that moment when you are between the two worlds: wake and sleep." Elizabeth nodded for her to continue.

"Anyway, I felt a sudden cold, as though someone had opened a door to the outside, and the icy air rushed in. I burrowed deeper trying to find warmth, and then I saw a light floating in the air. It kept coming closer and closer. I could see it in my dresser mirror; it was coming for me. I feared it might burn me—might float right through my body. Then it spoke my name. It said, *Georgiana, lovely Georgiana* in a voice barely above a whisper. I was so frightened…I tried to move away, but it kept coming after me. Finally, I found my voice, and I started to scream. That is all I remember; I closed my eyes and screamed."

"Did the light move away when you screamed?" Darcy wanted to know.

She stared at him—not engaged with anything but her tale. "I do not know, Fitzwilliam. When I opened my eyes again, you were here and holding me."

"Let me have a look around." Darcy picked up the nearest candleholder and began a minute inspection of the room, looking for anything out of place. He checked the windows for cracks or drafts, but he found nothing out of the ordinary. Elizabeth's and Georgiana's eyes followed his progress. When he stepped to the other side of her dressing screen, Georgiana's attention became more intense.

Elizabeth caught the girl's hand. "What is it, Georgiana?"

"There!" The girl pointed to the cheval glass mirror beside her dresser. "That is what I saw!"

Elizabeth turned to where the girl pointed. She could see it also: Darcy held his candle high, and it reflected in the mirror. "Fitzwilliam, stay right there," she ordered. Quickly, Elizabeth rushed about the room extinguishing all the candles she had lit earlier. Then she closed the door so that the dim lights in the hall could not be seen. She returned to sit beside an equally enthralled Georgiana. Together, they stared into the mirror. "Move slowly toward us—around the screen, Fitzwilliam," Elizabeth uttered cautiously, her eyes locked on the light in the mirror.

Darcy started forward. "No, wait!" Georgiana insisted. "You are too tall, Fitzwilliam. Do it again and bring the candle down to your chest."

Reluctantly, Darcy turned to the back wall and retraced his steps. When he swiveled to the front again, he carried the candle lower. "Hold it away from your body more," Elizabeth suggested softly.

"That is it!" Georgiana declared. "That is what I saw." She and Elizabeth watched as a seemingly disengaged light *floated* toward them—the light reflected by the mirror, moving on its own.

"It is quite remarkable," Elizabeth whispered. "Come look, Fitzwilliam; give me the candle." They switched places. Elizabeth, being so petite, could not bring about the effect, but Darcy could easily imagine what Georgiana had seen.

"Someone was in my room," Georgiana gasped. "But I saw no one when I came in from the music room." She thought aloud. "I was all over the room—sat at the dresser—combed out my hair— put my ribbons away—found some stockings for my feet were cold." She mentally watched herself move about the room. "Where was he hiding?" Frantically, the girl's eyes searched the depths of the room.

Elizabeth moved immediately to relight some of the extinguished candles, hoping the light would drive away her sister's fears.

"Maybe Mrs. Reynolds came to check on you," Darcy reasoned.

"Then would she not have said something?" Georgiana began to tremble again. "And would you not have seen her leave—the room is at the end of the hall. One must retrace one's steps to reach either the main stairway or the servants' stairs."

"That settles it." Elizabeth took charge. "You will come back to my room tonight. Tomorrow morning your brother will have additional locks installed on the door, or we will move you to an entirely new room." She began to gather some of Georgiana's belongings.

"But I could not," Georgiana protested.

"You most certainly will." Elizabeth's voice said that she would brook no objections. "You and I can share my bed. Back at Longbourn, my dear Jane and I regularly shared the same bed. Or I will leave you to mine alone and join Fitzwilliam in his." Most aristocratic couples kept separate beds—separate chambers, even—but everyone at Pemberley knew that the Darcys nightly slept in the same bed.

Darcy was less inclined to speak about his and Elizabeth's sleeping arrangements, but he added, "Elizabeth is correct. You are too upset, my Dear, to find a proper night's sleep in this room. You will come back with us." He maneuvered Georgiana toward the door.

"If you are certain, Fitzwilliam." Georgiana leaned into his shoulder as he slipped his arm about her waist to lead his sister away.

For a second time, Elizabeth began to extinguish the candles. When she closed the door to follow her husband and sister, she impulsively looked back. Suddenly, she felt it, too—a cold rush of air from behind the screen, which stood at the side of the room. A deep shiver shot down her spine. Frightened of the unknown, she hurriedly closed the door and raced down the hall to find the comforting arms of her husband.

CHAPTER 5

~ ~ ~

"ARE YOU CERTAIN THE DRAFT did not come from the hearth?" Darcy and Elizabeth rested together in his bed. They had spent an additional hour distracting Georgiana and making her comfortable in Elizabeth's chambers before retiring to Darcy's room.

"I am positive, Fitzwilliam," she insisted. "It came from behind the screen, where Georgiana claims that she saw the light. It was not a dream, Fitzwilliam. Something is not right—something is happening at Pemberley."

They whispered together. The adjoining doors to their dressing rooms remained open, in case Georgiana felt uneasy. "What has happened has a logical explanation," he declared. "I do not believe in ghosts or other apparitions. Whatever is happening here is manmade."

"But you do believe Georgiana."

"I believe that someone will pay for invading my home with his perfidy," Darcy growled.

"We must not involve our guests," his wife cautioned. "Might you secure Lady Catherine's discretion as far as Georgiana is concerned?"

Darcy adjusted her in his embrace. "It will be difficult, but I will insist on my aunt's secrecy."

Elizabeth kissed along his chin line, feathery touches of her lips and tongue dancing along the sensitive part of Darcy's neck. "You were very tender with Georgiana this evening."

"Georgiana is my sister, and I protect those I love." He now loomed above her, poised only inches from her mouth.

She smiled seductively at him without looking away. "Then I am blessed, my Husband, that you love me." Her voice was husky.

Darcy felt a bit lightheaded, as he always did when he realized that Elizabeth belonged to him forever. When they had met in Hertfordshire, her eyes had engaged him from the beginning, and he had found himself falling into their depths. He had fought valiantly—had tried desperately not to fall in love—but he was in the middle before he knew that he had begun.

"Have I told you today how beautiful you are?" he asked, his voice a raspy whisper. Darcy lowered himself against her, pressing his chest against her body. He heard Elizabeth suck in a slow breath. Darcy's mouth found hers, and he quickly deepened the kiss. "I love you, Elizabeth Darcy," he murmured close to her ear before kissing down the length of her neck.

"Fitzwilliam," she pointed out, "Georgiana is in the next room."

He moved against her. "I can be very quiet."

Elizabeth murmured, "I doubt that, my Husband."

"Then I will prove it to you, Mrs. Darcy." He took her lips again, his tongue invading her mouth. Instinctively, Elizabeth moaned and moved closer to him. Darcy stifled the groan in the back of his throat. He let his touch speak for him. Lost to sensation, neither Darcy nor Elizabeth heard the faint click of the lock along the inside wall.

Mr. Baldwin reported his lack of success: "I searched every room, Mr. Darcy."

"And nothing?"

"Nothing, sir—nothing except a very angry Lady Catherine."

Darcy snorted. "My aunt is generally dissatisfied with one thing or another."

The butler smiled faintly.

"We have a problem—missing bed linens, missing candelabra...." Darcy purposely omitted the mystery in Georgiana's room the preceding evening.

"Missing food," Baldwin added.

"What do you mean?"

Baldwin nervously shifted his weight. "A round of hard cheese, sir, and two loaves of dark bread and one of Mrs. Jennings's rhubarb pies."

"You jest?"

"No, sir—the lady swears she made six, and there are but five."

"This becomes more bizarre by the moment. Do you have any inkling—even a glimmer of an idea who might be to blame, Mr. Baldwin?"

The man looked around sheepishly to observe if anyone could overhear. "The staff, sir, some…they think it is one of the Shadow Ghosts…while others say it is the work of Black Shuck."

"Tell me, Mr. Baldwin, you really do not believe such poppy-cock. Black Shuck?"

"The snow, Mr. Darcy, you cannot deny this is an unusual storm—just like the unusual storm back in Suffolk all those years ago. People swear that Black Shuck appeared at the Bungay and Blythburgh churches in 1577, and only this past week, Mr. Stalling says he saw a black shaggy dog near the Darcy family cemetery."

Darcy closed the door to ensure privacy. "Mr. Baldwin, you must stop this nonsense. We are not living in the times of our Anglo-Saxon ancestors. The Vikings left England long ago, and they took the legends of Thor's Shukir and Odin's huge dog of war with them. We live in a time of industrial advancement. I cannot have you and the rest of the staff repeating such stories. I am well aware of Reverend Abraham Fleming's version of what happened in the sixteenth century in Suffolk. I, too, once thought it a great tale of mystery, but I left those stories behind when I left childhood."

"I understand, Mr. Darcy. Such tales are for those of a lower house. I will convey your message to everyone." Baldwin started to bow out of the room.

Darcy put a hand on the man's arm to stay him. "I realize it is important for people to explain the unexplainable. People have a need to be in charge of their lives. I am sure that Blythburgh and Bungay suffered greatly, but the appearance of a stray black dog had nothing to do with lightning striking a church tower. What is happening in this house has no connection to a dog or to ghostly apparitions. No malevolent shadow person is haunting this house. I guarantee it."

"Yes, Mr. Darcy."

"I need your agreement on this, Mr. Baldwin."

"Mrs. Reynolds and I will speak to the staff, sir."

The butler was nearly out the door before Darcy remembered his letter. He called to the man's retreating form, "Mr. Baldwin!"

His man reappeared immediately. "Yes, sir."

"Did you place my letter from yesterday evening on the salver to be posted?"

"I have not seen the letter, sir."

Darcy came around the desk. "I was writing it when you came in yesterday evening."

"I remember your being behind the desk, sir, but you left everything after we spoke. You gave me no letter to post."

Darcy looked around in dismay. "I did not finish the letter," he muttered. "It was on the desk—a letter to Mr. Laurie. Are you sure you did not see it?"

"No, sir."

"It is no longer there." He gestured toward the papers piled neatly in three stacks along the edge of the desk.

Baldwin did not know how to respond. "Was it of a personal nature, sir?"

Darcy thought of his request for information on George Wickham and on Lieutenant Harwood. He could have no one else know about either matter. "It is of a nature I would prefer not to share with everyone." He looked about confused. "Maybe I misplaced it; I will look again."

"Yes, Mr. Darcy."

"That will be all, Mr. Baldwin."

Lydia Bennet Wickham dressed for the day. This Pemberley trip had been a mistake. She had hoped Elizabeth might introduce her to people of fine society. But with the snowstorm the likelihood of meeting anyone other than those sequestered with her was nearly nonexistent, at least for the next week. True, there was Lord Stafford, but he had an affinity for his cousin Miss Donnel, no matter his many protests to the contrary.

That left only Mr. Worth's company as a possibility. Of course, Lydia never considered the company of other women to be "fine society"; she needed a man's attention to feel important. Nigel Worth was pleasant company, and he did pay her compliments, but he was too old for her. However, he held a respectable position in the community. That would be a better situation than what she currently endured.

Lydia did not know where to turn; misery rode on her shoulder. She had made a terrible mistake the day she left Brighton with George Wickham. She had thought to best her sisters to the altar, and had foolishly believed his pretty words. Only afterward had she realized that he had ill-used her—only when Mr. Darcy came to find them did that become crystal clear.

Even then, her pride had kept her from betraying Wickham. And despite a small voice in her head, which said she should follow Mr. Darcy's advice, she had stubbornly clung to the hope that George Wickham might learn to love her as much as she fancied herself to love him.

Yet, instead of their growing closer after their nuptials, they had begun a campaign to destroy each other. Mr. Wickham openly flirted with every attractive woman he met, and when she complained, he told Lydia if she objected that she could return to Longbourn's warmth. In retaliation, she had set about attracting his fellow officers' attentions. Of course, the difference came in the followthrough: She flirted and flattered, but remained true to her marriage vows where Mr. Wickham openly flaunted his conquests—from the lowliest barmaid to his former commanding officer's wife.

A sigh escaped her as she took a closer look in the mirror's reflection. She was still young enough to find another if her husband took her threat seriously. Lydia did not wish to declare to the world that she had failed as a wife, but she knew deep in her soul that she could not spend the rest of her life pretending that Mr. Wickham's indiscretions did not hurt. A separation would bring scandal, but she could face down the gossips if necessary. "I will survive this," she whispered to the image staring back at her.

However, a breeze—a gush of cold air—in the room seemed to ask mockingly, *Can you?*

Lydia jumped to her feet to see what had caused the chilly wind. But try as she might, she could find nothing unusual in her quarters, although she searched behind furniture and inside items.

She did, however, find a box of mementos hidden in the bottom of the wardrobe. When she took out the wooden box, the contents surprised her. The items were a diverse mix of some of her sister's memories and some that obviously belonged to Mr. Darcy. What amazed her was how soon Elizabeth's things and Darcy's things had become *their* things. Sadly, Lydia doubted that she and George Wickham would ever be so joined. Elizabeth knew a perfect love despite Mr. Darcy's stiffness—his overwhelming pride. Lydia began to lift items from the box. She had seen Elizabeth's keepsakes many times: a smooth rock painted blue with white clouds, a gift from their eldest sister, Jane, on Elizabeth's fifth birthday; a monogrammed handkerchief from Grandmother Bennet; a book of prayers inscribed "To My Lizzy," from their father; and a pair of white lace gloves Elizabeth had worn to her first adult party.

Mr. Darcy's spoke of his life: a drawing in crayon signed by Georgiana Darcy; a diamond stick pin with a bent tip, likely belonging to his father or another close relative; a newspaper notice of his mother's passing; and, surprisingly, a miniature—a portrait of her own husband—of Mr. Wickham as a young man. Impulsively, Lydia retrieved it from the bottom of the box. Dusting it off against her dress, she stared at a man she did not know—a boy, really— with innocence and hope clearly evident in his eyes. She had never met this young gentleman, who had the whole world before him. The Wickham she knew was really two men. One was completely charming to everyone he met. His appearance was greatly in his favor; he had all the best part of beauty—a fine countenance, a good figure, and very pleasing address—a happy readiness of conversation—a readiness but at the same time perfectly correct and unassuming. The other George Wickham was a frightening force—one that hid the hostility he felt—masked his voice's harshness—ruled with fear. He was a careful schemer, handsome and charming.

Lydia returned the other items to the box and replaced it in the wardrobe, but she kept the small portrait of her husband to set beside her bed. "I would have liked to have known this young man. We could love each other until death do us part." She patted the frame, treating the miniature as a symbol of their renewed relationship. Feeling much more content, she turned for the door. They would take the afternoon meal soon, and Mr. Darcy preferred his guests to be prompt.

Lydia stepped into the hall, only to find Cathleen Donnel also exiting her assigned room. The sleeping quarters followed a T-shaped hallway. The main guest chambers were situated in the vertical line of the T. The Darcys took the left branch of the horizontal line of the T, and their aristocratic guests took the right. Lydia's room lay where the lines intersected—the perpendicular point—and Miss Donnel's, the farthest away from her room, at the far end of the vertical line of the T. Lydia idly wondered about the arrangement. Should not Miss Donnel be closer to her cousin?

Cathleen did not speak, but Lydia nodded her head in the direction of the approaching woman and stopped to wait for her. They could enter the dining room together.

At that moment, Anne de Bourgh turned the corner, entering the main hall from the right. Lydia paused long enough to offer the woman a curtsy. "Miss de Bourgh!" Lydia gushed. "Is it not uncanny that we meet at Pemberley? I have heard so much of you and of Lady Catherine from my cousin Mr. Collins."

"Mr. Collins is a ninny," Anne grumbled as she approached. If the girl wanted to offer her some civility, mentioning her mother's clergyman did not play well. In Anne's opinion, Mr. Collins was nothing more than a walking mouthpiece. He spoke only of what he thought his patroness Lady Catherine might approve. It was not beneath the man to gossip and to fawn over Lady Catherine to stay in Her Ladyship's good graces.

"Of . . . of course, Mr. . . . Mr. Collins, can he somewhat pretentious," Lydia stammered.

"That would be an understatement," Anne insisted.

Both women moved toward the main staircase. Miss Donnel reached it before they did. As the three women prepared to descend the stairs—catching up their skirts to steady their steps—Mrs. Williams opened her door to follow. Both Anne and Lydia paused—mere seconds to observe Mrs. Williams. But Cathleen did not do so; she began her descent.

The next twenty seconds seemed to both speed by in pure chaos and simultaneously pass as slowly as a snail through a peculiar mix of events. Cathleen boldly stepped forward, only to find herself tumbling through the air, banging against the railing and support wall, before coming to a stop on the landing eight steps below. Her scream of surprise and pain echoed off the walls.

As one, Lydia's and Anne's heads turned to behold a flurry of muslin and lace wrapped around Cathleen Donnel's legs while she fought for control—arms flailing. They watched and squealed, both terrified and mesmerized.

Evelyn Williams saw the woman take the first step—observed the horror on Cathleen Donnel's face, but she could not move quickly enough to make a difference. Pushing against Mrs. Wickham and Miss de Bourgh, Evelyn tried to prevent the accident, but this was impossible. Her scream joined Cathleen's in a cacophony of sound.

Adam Lawrence strolled casually along the hallway. At least, Pemberley offered a refined sophistication. The rooms were lofty and handsome, and their furniture suitable to the fortune of their proprietor—neither gaudy nor uselessly fine—with less of splendor

and real elegance than the furniture found in many homes he visited. He and Cathleen could be stranded in a run-down inn right
now. Lawrence decided that even with the inconvenience of Darcy's
terms for his stay, this was decidedly better.

However, just as he turned the corner to the main hallway,
Adam heard her—heard Cathleen scream. Immediately, he reacted,
shoving his way past a stunned Anne de Bourgh to catapult himself
down the carpeted steps to reach a crumpled and twisted body on
the landing.

"Cathleen," he pleaded as he moved her hair away from her
face. "Speak to me. Come on, Sweetheart." When he cradled her
head in his hands, a groan told him she was conscious.

Darcy replaced the pen in its holder. Unable to find the original, he had rewritten the letter to Mr. Laurie. He had retraced the
events leading to Mr. Baldwin's recent evening visit to his office,
and Darcy knew that on that evening he had not folded the letter
in preparation for posting. He left it lying on his desk. And so for
an hour today, he had moved everything in this room, carefully
looking under and behind furniture. The letter was nowhere to be
found, another spoke in a wheel of mystery.

He was deep in thought, so when the initial scream came, followed closely by a choir of dismay, it took him by surprise. Instinctively, he ran toward the noise, afraid that it signaled a problem
for Elizabeth or Georgiana. Taking the steps two at a time, Darcy
quickly covered the distance, and discovered a very upset viscount
comforting his mistress as she lay writhing in pain on the landing.

"What happened?" Darcy asked as he knelt beside Adam Lawrence.

Lawrence did not look up—his concentration was on the
woman as he began to check for broken bones. "I am not certain—
I heard a scream."

Darcy looked up to see three women staring down at them.
"Might any of you speak to what occurred?" He stood slowly to
survey the area.

"I saw Miss Donnel lose her balance," Evelyn Williams said. "But I could not reach her in time."

Anne stared in disbelief at Miss Donnel. "I do not believe that either Mrs. Wickham or I can add anything, Fitzwilliam."

Mrs. Jenkinson had followed Anne de Bourgh from the room. She had returned to their adjoining chambers to retrieve a shawl for the woman she admired and respected. Mrs. Mildred Jenkinson had served as a companion to Anne de Bourgh since before the girl turned sixteen, nearly twelve years earlier. As much as possible, she shielded Anne from Lady Catherine. Her Ladyship was a difficult employer, but Mildred stayed because she thought that otherwise Anne might crumble in submission to her mother. With Mr. Darcy's marriage to Elizabeth Bennet, Lady Catherine had become harder to predict. In her anger at her nephew, Her Ladyship often lashed out at the closest person—her daughter Anne.

Lady Catherine had for years planned a union between the cousins, despite the daughter's subtle objections and Mr. Darcy's open refusals. In Mrs. Jenkinson's opinion, such a joining would be marital suicide: their dispositions were too much in opposition for a relationship to succeed. Mildred had watched Mr. Darcy's reaction during that ill-fated Easter dinner when Miss Elizabeth Bennet visited the Collinses and dined at Rosings. She had been amused by Mr. Darcy's response to the interactions between his cousin Colonel Fitzwilliam and Miss Bennet. Mr. Darcy, usually so cool and reserved, had left his aunt in midsentence in order to station himself by Miss Bennet's side. Unfortunately, Lady Catherine had observed this, also. Her Ladyship immediately launched a campaign to belittle Miss Bennet at every opportunity.

Yet it had all been for naught. Mr. Darcy had married Miss Bennet, finding the happiness that eluded him for years. Now, if her dear Anne could prove so lucky, Mildred could rest easy. She understood everyone's concern regarding Lieutenant Harwood because Anne knew so little about the man. But Mildred Jenkinson could not harbor ill feelings toward him. Farce or not, the lieutenant's mindfulness of Anne's good qualities brought sparkle into the life of the woman Mrs. Jenkinson so dearly loved. Only Lady Catherine saw the situation as deplorable, and her disapproval had driven Anne to a desperate act: Anne arranged a tryst. Mildred did not approve, but she understood.

Shawl in hand, she had followed Anne at a more leisurely pace. However, when she had heard the scream, she rushed forward, fearing the worst, but found only a man in the Pemberley livery blocking her way. "What is going on?" she cried. She peered around the man's shoulder. He stood perfectly still. "Move!" she ordered as she tried to press past him.

"I would not," he growled.

Mildred looked up into his eyes, which were red with anger. The man frightened her, but she mustered her best duenna voice—the one she had used years earlier for misbehaving children—and ordered, "See to your duties, sir, and remove yourself from my way."

The man leaned menacingly over her, but he said no more. When she raised her chin in defiance, he whispered in a gravelly voice, sounding much older than his appearance indicated, "Beware, old woman!" And then he left, disappearing in the direction of the family quarters.

Mildred stared after him for a few brief seconds, overpowered by his rudeness, but as he withdrew, her sensibility returned, and she rushed to Anne's side.

Darcy glanced down to where Lawrence continued to tend to his mistress. "Can she be moved?" he asked as he knelt again.

"I can find no obvious injuries, but I am no physician," Lawrence said. "Yet, I think we can move Cathleen to her room."

Darcy started to motion for a waiting footman, but Lawrence shook off the offer. The viscount circled to the opposite side of the woman, where he might lift her without hurting Cathleen or himself. However, before he had made a move, his eyes fell on the first step. "What is that?" He indicated with his eyes for Darcy to look to what he saw.

Darcy obeyed the urgency in the viscount's eyes. "I do not know." He bounded up the eight rises and reached for what he and Lawrence now realized had caused the accident. A thin piece of hemp—pulled tight—stretched from the banister's spindle and hooked around a decorative nipple in the wall's baseboard.

"What the hell?" The viscount ran his finger along the line. Angrily, Lawrence jerked on the looped thread and broke it. "Cathleen could have been seriously hurt," he hissed. "Is this some sort of perverted trick?"

Darcy did not like the man's accusation. "We have never experienced anything of this sort at Pemberley, sir—at least, not until we were beset with unscheduled visitors. We opened our doors out of kindness. If you and Miss Donnel wish to withdraw, I will make no an effort to stop you." Darcy stood erect, arms akimbo—his fists opening and closing.

Lawrence, equally as tall, stood also—toe to toe; they took each other's measure. "I shall see to *my cousin's* well-being, and then you and I will speak of this at greater length, Darcy."

"It would be *my pleasure*, sir," Darcy snapped.

Adam returned to where Cathleen now pushed herself to a seated position. "Let me help you, Darling," he murmured softly to her. "Can you tell me where it hurts?"

"My ankle," she muttered. "And my head."

"Let me see you to your room." Adam lifted her to his chest and began to climb the steps again. When he reached the point where Darcy still stood, he snarled, "Might you send someone to my cousin's room, sir?"

Darcy felt sorry for Miss Donnel's injury, and he understood the viscount's anger, but he objected to the man's tone. "Mrs. Reynolds will see to it personally, Lord Stafford."

When Adam reached the hallway, he let Lydia Wickham lead the way to Cathleen's room. "Allow me to get the door and turn down the bed, Lord Stafford."

"Thank you, Mrs. Wickham."

Adam gingerly placed Cathleen on the bed. He wanted to examine his mistress's ankle himself, but a gentleman would not conduct himself as such, even with a cousin. Luckily, Mrs. Reynolds rushed through the door, carrying bandages and several medicine bottles. "I will tend to Miss Donnel, Your Lordship."

"I know this may be unseemly, Mrs. Reynolds, but I will wait on the other side of the screen in case you have need of my assistance."

The housekeeper did not think that would prove likely; yet, she simply nodded her assent. "Where might be the most pain, Miss?" Mrs. Reynolds gently raised Cathleen's chin to look in her eyes— to determine the clarity within them.

"The back of my head." Cathleen reached to feel a raised lump behind her right ear.

Mrs. Reynolds replaced the woman's hand with hers. Gently, she removed two pins from Miss Donnel's hair and probed the affected area. "I see no laceration," Mrs. Reynolds announced. "You should probably remain in bed for a day or two just to be sure— until the swelling goes down." The housekeeper looked up to see Lydia Wickham still lurking by the door. "Mrs. Wickham, might I trouble you to send one of the maids to me?"

Curious about the interactions—Lord Stafford's more-than-familiar relationship with Miss Donnel and his less-than-friendly confrontation with Mr. Darcy moments earlier—she volunteered, "I will find someone and return to help you also."

Mrs. Reynolds had lost all respect for George Wickham many years earlier, and she fought to not transfer those feelings to the man's wife; however, the girl's foolish interference irritated her. "That will not be necessary, Mrs. Wickham," she stressed. "Please join the master in the dining room; my staff and I can handle Miss Donnel's injuries. I am sure that your sister—that Mrs. Darcy— will call on Miss Donnel herself. The mistress is all charity," she pronounced with the assurance of a skilled servant long in her position.

Lydia wanted to speak to Lord Stafford—wanted to assess the situation personally—as this was the most interesting thing in the house right now—but she relented. "I will see to it." She flounced from the room.

Seconds later, a maid entered. "You sent for me, Mrs. Reynolds?"

"Miss Donnel will need cold compresses for her head, Detanne."

"Probably for my ankle, as well," Cathleen muttered from behind them.

Mrs. Reynolds jerked her head around. "Oh, my, Miss, I did not realize." She lifted the sheet. "Which ankle, Miss Donnel?"

"The left."

The housekeeper raised the woman's lower leg and cradled the ankle in her hands. "Might I rotate it?" she asked as she touched the tender joint.

"Yes."

Gingerly, the older woman circumvolved the injured foot, while bracing it from the back. "I observe no breakage, Miss." She turned it again just to be sure. "The ankle is swollen and quite bruised. We should elevate it." Mrs. Reynolds took several pillows and placed them where she might rest Miss Donnel's foot on the cushions. "We will need compressions for the ankle as well, Betanne, and have Mrs. Jennings send up some oil of chamomile."

"Yes, Mrs. Reynolds." The girl curtsied and departed.

Mrs. Reynolds spread a blanket across the young woman's lap. "You may join us, Your Lordship," she called out to the viscount.

Adam reappeared immediately.

"I am assuming, sir, that you overheard what I have told your cousin."

Adam sat beside the bed and took Cathleen's hand in his. "I did, Mrs. Reynolds."

"It seems important to keep your cousin in bed where she might rest. I would also like to give Miss Donnel a dose of laudanum; the medicine will ease her pain."

Adam patted Cathleen's hand. "I suggest we ask Mrs. Reynolds for a tray. Once you have eaten, the laudanum will not have such a dramatic after effect. I will remain with you until you are asleep."

"Thank you, Adam." Cathleen knew he felt affection for her: Adam Lawrence would protect her even though she was no more than his mistress.

"Let me see to a tray, Your Lordship. I will be back in a few minutes." Darcy's servant disappeared.

Adam shifted to sit on the edge of Cathleen's bed. "I am so sorry, Sweetheart." He kissed her forehead. "I wish I could change this for you."

"I will recover," Cathleen assured him. "I will be able to escape the possible censure of Mr. Darcy's relatives if I remain in bed and out of sight."

"I beg your forgiveness for that also." He traced lines up and down her arm with his fingertips.

"For what must you ask forgiveness? You went beyond the boundaries most men would offer in a relationship such as ours. You tried to see me to Cheshire to be with my family. Only Nature's full fury stopped us; I will never forget your kindness." Cathleen caught his hand and brought the back of it to her lips.

Adam leaned down to kiss her cheek. "You are a beautiful woman, my Dear—both inside and out." He returned to his seat in the nearby chair before someone saw them acting like lovers, not cousins. "Can you tell me what you remember of your accident?"

Cathleen's brow frowned in concentration. "I do not believe there is much to tell. Mrs. Wickham and Miss de Bourgh both entered the hallway about the same time as I. We all moved toward the top of the stairs. Mrs. Williams came last. When the widow opened her door, Mrs. Wickham and Miss de Bourgh paused to wait for the lady, but I continued on. When I started to descend the steps, I lost my balance."

"Then any of you could have been the first one down the steps? I mean...Mrs. Wickham did not purposely hold Miss de Bourgh back or vice versa?" Adam attempted to visualize what she described.

"Mrs. Wickham was already in the hall when I left my room." Cathleen tried to see the action in her head.

Adam reasoned aloud, "Really? I wonder for how long."

Cathleen looked puzzled. "I assumed it was for only a second or two. It was time for the afternoon meal."

"But it could have been longer?" Adam put together the pieces of the mystery.

"Miss de Bourgh came after I started for the dining room. I remember her coming from the right hallway, where your room is."

Adam's countenance turned grim. "Someone rigged a thin line of rope across the step. It was difficult to see it in the dim light. I suspect that you were not the intended victim, but purely an innocent bystander. Now, I am trying to determine who might have had the opportunity to do so."

"You suspect Mrs. Wickham?" Cathleen tried to reason it out, but could not fathom the purpose of such a trap.

Adam's voice spoke of anger—of regret—and of determination. "I suspect everyone until I know otherwise."

CHAPTER 6

~ ~ ~

FITZWILLIAM DARCY SILENTLY FUMED as he oversaw the afternoon meal. Mrs. Reynolds had informed him of Lord Stafford's request for a tray for himself and Miss Donnel. Darcy understood the man's concern, but he did not relish the idea of pretending a disinterested calm before the rest of his guests. It was bad enough that in addition to the viscount and his mistress, three others had witnessed what was evidently an attempt to cause someone real harm. Between the recent disappearances, Georgiana's nighttime "visitor," and now this staged trap, Darcy's nerves strained for control.

"I came down thirty minutes earlier," Mr. Worth bemoaned missing the incident. "I took no note of anything unusual at that time."

Mrs. Williams sipped her soup. "I pray Miss Donnel suffers no continuing injury."

"My housekeeper reports that the lady has a badly bruised ankle and a sizable bump on the back of her head, but Miss Donnel should recover quickly," Darcy assured everyone.

Georgiana offered, "I think it admirable that His Lordship sees to his cousin personally. I imagine that Edward would be as attentive for Anne or me."

Darcy noted Elizabeth's questioning stare, but he ignored her silent demand for answers. "Lord Stafford does seem most concerned. The family is suffering with the illness of a loved one, compounded by the inconvenience of being stranded by the storm."

"I still say the man affects his cousin," Lady Catherine remarked to no one in particular.

"It should be none of our concern," Anne said evenly.

The fact that his cousin offered an opinion of any kind caught Darcy off guard. He had no time to intercept his aunt's response. "One could hardly help but take notice," Lady Catherine snarled. "And who are you to correct me? Since when do you censure me—your mother—the woman who suffered to bring you into the world?"

"And what a lovely world it is, Mother!" Anne stood suddenly, throwing her napkin on the table. "If you will excuse me, Fitzwilliam," she mumbled as she rushed from the room.

"Well, I never!" Lady Catherine began.

However, Darcy cut her remarks short. "I am sure, Aunt, that my cousin meant no harm. It could have been Anne or Mrs. Jenkinson or Mrs. Williams or Mrs. Wickham lying in that bed right now or even worse. Anne is sensitive; I beg you not to dwell on her unintended aspersion."

His aunt said grudgingly, "I suppose, Darcy."

Elizabeth caught Darcy's eye. "Maybe Mrs. Jenkinson might see to Miss de Bourgh."

"That is an excellent idea, Elizabeth. Mrs. Jenkinson, please send us a report on Anne's recovery when you deem her settled."

"Certainly, Mr. Darcy. Thank you, sir." The lady gave Elizabeth a quick nod of gratitude and followed Anne to their adjoining quarters.

"Anne," the older woman called as she came through their connected dressing rooms, "are you well?" Anne lay prostrate across her bed, clutching a lace handkerchief in her left hand—her shoulders shaking with muffled sobs. Mildred Jenkinson sat on the edge of the bed, lightly stroking Anne de Bourgh's back. "Oh, Anne, my darling girl. I hate having you so distraught."

Sniffles and sobs escaped as Anne buried her face into the pillow. "I cannot go back there!" she wailed. "I simply cannot return to Rosings." She sat up suddenly to look at the only friend she had ever had. "If I return to Kent, I must accept never having any freedom until my mother leaves this earthly world. I cannot bear it, Mildred."

Mrs. Jenkinson slid her arm around Anne's shoulder. "We will think of something. Maybe Mr. Darcy can convince Lady Catherine to soften her reproaches." Mildred rarely spoke honestly about what she observed in the de Bourgh household, but she knew that Anne would not chastise her for speaking aloud what they both thought. "Or perhaps the Darcys might extend an invitation for you to remain at Pemberley when Her Ladyship returns to Kent."

Anne grasped at this hope. "Oh, Mildred, do you believe that possible? Even though Lieutenant Harwood may not be here, it would be heavenly to simply have the peace that Pemberley provides. I could learn to play the pianoforte at last. I have always wanted to play."

"I know, my Girl." Mildred tightened her embrace.

Anne closed her eyes as if picturing a different future. "And I could take a long walk if I chose or read a novel by Mrs. Radcliffe or paint a picture. There would be no one to say 'She is quite a little creature' or anyone to remark that I might become quite accomplished if I applied myself." Anne sighed.

Mildred hesitated. "I must offer you a caution: Even Mr. Darcy may choose to accept Lady Catherine's dominion over you."

Anne refused to give up on her dreams. She wiped the tears from her face. "Help me to freshen myself. I must speak to my cousin immediately. If Fitzwilliam refuses to help, then I need to know before this storm lessens. I must have all my options present." She rushed to her dressing room and poured fresh water in the bowl. Taking a folded cloth from the stack on the dressing table, Anne dipped it in the water and wrung it out. Dabbing at her eyes, she looked at herself in the mirror. "I hate the way my lids swell when I cry." She pressed the cool cloth to her eyes and held it there. It was as if she washed away her troubles. "You will come with me, Mildred, when I speak to Mr. Darcy."

"I am sure the gentleman would prefer not to discuss familial relationships in my presence." Mildred watched Anne's demeanor.

She had noted the subtle difference in Georgiana Darcy now that she was under Mrs. Darcy's care. She would like to see Anne earn some confidence of her own.

Anne came to kneel before her companion. "Oh, Mildred, you must come with me. I would not be able to approach Fitzwilliam without your support." She took the older woman's hand and brought it to her cheek. "You are my only true friend; you know my deepest secrets."

Mildred Jenkinson stood, bringing Anne to her feet also. "Come, my Girl. You know I can never deny you."

Forty-five minutes later, they sat with Darcy in his study. Mrs. Jenkinson appreciated the kindness that Mr. Darcy showed as he listened carefully to Anne's plea for asylum. He made no commitment, saying that he would need to speak to Mrs. Darcy and to the Fitzwilliam faction of the family before he chose to involve them in what would likely be another tiff with Lady Catherine.

He questioned Anne regarding Lieutenant Harwood, specifically asking whether the man offered marriage and asking about anything else she might know of him. "It cheered me to know the good colonel was the one who introduced you to Harwood. I trust Edward's opinion of a man's character." Darcy spoke the truth—he did trust his cousin's judgment. But he also paid Harwood arf indirect compliment to gain Anne's confidence. Attacking the man had gotten Lady Catherine nowhere.

"You would like the lieutenant, Fitzwilliam. One finds the easiness, openness, and ductility of his temper. He is just what a young man ought to be: sensible, good-humored, lively, and I never saw such happy manners!—so much ease, with such perfect good breeding!"

"Then Harwood is of family?" Darcy still wanted to know more of the man than his cousin's idealized opinions. The fact that Harwood had met Anne privately at an inn bothered Darcy. Theoretically, the man compromised his naïve cousin; he chose to learn more of the man because Anne needed protecting.

"The lieutenant is a second son; his brother Rowland will inherit. Robert has two sisters—one still at home and the other married to another officer in the service."

Darcy steepled his fingers, deep in contemplation. "I see." He paused before he added, "Anne, I am concerned, and I intend to learn more about the lieutenant. I want you to understand that I do so out of affection for you and not out of some mean spiritedness."

Anne glanced at Mrs. Jenkinson, who sat obediently in the corner, pretending not to hear. "Mrs. Jenkinson will speak to my conduct, Fitzwilliam. I would wish that you feel free to ask her anything, and I release her to be completely truthful regarding what she knows of me and of the lieutenant."

Again, Darcy weighed his words carefully. "I do not believe that necessary at this time, but I may consider it as the situation develops."

"Thank you, Cousin, for listening to me." She prepared to stand, but he motioned for her to remain.

"Might you tell me what you know of Miss Donnel's accident?" He sat forward, interested in her account.

"I am unsure of what you speak, Fitzwilliam."

"Simply tell me the chronological order of the events. Did you see anyone else about? Did Miss Donnel seem aware of what awaited her?" Darcy could not shake the feeling that as Miss Donnel made her living as an actress, the *accident* held more questions than answers.

"Mrs. Wickham and Miss Donnel were in the hallway when I left our quarters and joined them. When Mrs. Williams opened her door, Mrs. Darcy's sister and I turned to greet her, but Miss Donnel continued. She came from the opposite direction toward the main staircase."

Impulsively, Darcy's attention now fell upon his cousin's companion, a woman to whom he had rarely spoken over the years unless during a game of casino or quadrille. He knew something of the woman's respectability. Mildred Jenkinson had come to Rosings after losing both her husband and her child in a typhoid epidemic that hit her village in Oxfordshire some fifteen years earlier. A traveling carnival and a group of gypsies had reportedly spread typhoid to three communities in the midlands that summer before the disease was contained. Having traveled extensively with her husband, who served in a diplomatic position, the lady had the disposition and the qualifications to serve as his cousin's companion. Anne turned to the woman for affection, and the woman protected Anne from Lady Catherine's frequent censure as best she could. "Mrs. Jenkinson, you were in the hall when I helped His Lordship. Did you observe anything unusual?"

Brought to the center of attention, at first Mildred stammered. "I-I was a few sec-seconds behind Miss de Bourgh, sir, as I returned to her quarters for a shawl. Lady Catherine is most mindful of cold drafts." It was the woman's way of saying that Her Ladyship could be demanding, and she simply tried to anticipate her employer's idiosyncrasies. "There was a man in Pemberley attire blocking the way, and when I could not reach her, I feared for Anne's safety." Mrs. Jenkinson paused before telling Mr. Darcy the rest. She was still a servant, even though she shared Anne's confidences, and she preferred not to report poor service. Mildred did not wish to see the man lose his position. "I hesitate, Mr. Darcy, to criticize this man's conduct."

"Was a member of my staff unpleasant, madam? If so, I wish to be informed," he insisted.

Mildred rose and came closer to the desk, where she might speak without being overheard from the hall. "The man blocked the way, and when I tried to move around him, he refused to budge. I was most anxious to assure myself of Miss de Bourgh's safety, and I spoke harshly to him, demanding that he move. At that point he told me to beware and called me an old woman."

"Why did you not tell me, Mildred?" Anne reached out to take her companion's hand.

"It was really nothing." She looked away in embarrassment. "The thing was, Mr. Darcy—it was not so much his words, but the pure animosity found in his countenance."

"Would you recognize him again?"

"Of course, sir."

"Then I will ask Mr. Baldwin to gather the male staff. If you will indulge me and identify the man, I would wish to speak to him about his rudeness to a guest." Darcy thought the man's actions suspicious.

"As you wish, Mr. Darcy."

An hour later, Darcy summoned Mildred Jenkinson to the downstairs ballroom. Several rows of men and boys stood awaiting her appearance. "Is this everyone, Mr. Baldwin?"

"It is, Mr. Darcy." He bowed respectfully. "I checked off everyone against my household records. All the men are accounted for, sir, except young Lawson, who rode out with Mr. Steventon to check on the sheep. The boy wishes to apprentice with the steward."

"How long have they been away?" Darcy wanted the lady to examine the entire staff.

"I believe, sir, that they left at first light. I let the boy go because Mr. Steventon seems to like Lawson's company."

Darcy bit down his frustration. "I understand." He would need to see the lad separately when the footman had returned from his outside duties. "Mr. Baldwin, have each man walk toward us and then return to his duties."

"Yes, Mr. Darcy." The man moved off to deliver his instructions.

Placing the woman's hand on his arm for support, Darcy stood beside Mrs. Jenkinson. "As each man passes, observe him carefully. Once you have noted your unknown opponent, you may tell me then. I will make no comment until we have seen them all. In fact, I will wait until you have returned home before I address the man, so as to remove the blame from you."

"Thank you, Mr. Darcy."

Then the procession started. One by one, the men walked past them, and Mildred purposely made eye contact, but after looking at all thirty, she found no one who resembled the man she had seen in the private hallway. "I apologize, Mr. Darcy, but it was none of these men."

"Yet the man you saw wore the Darcy livery?" They were the only ones left in the expansive room.

"It was the same, sir, as what your men wore today. The man I encountered was near your age and several inches shorter. He had a muscular build and what would have been a pleasant-looking face if he had not been so angry. He had dark, wavy hair, and a square jaw. He spoke fiercely and then moved away to the private family rooms."

"He entered my family's quarters?" Incredulity played through his voice.

"I did not see him enter the rooms, but he walked in that direction, and the hall ends with those rooms."

The situation dumbfounded Darcy. "I want to find this unknown man, Mrs. Jenkinson. At the moment, you are the only person who has seen him. Will you help me identify him?"

She recognized Mr. Darcy's protective nature: She had observed it on more than one occasion when he dealt with Miss Darcy and even with her beloved Anne. "Of course, Mr. Darcy——anything, sir."

From behind the gold-trimmed door leading to the linen closet, James Withey watched. Each of the men employed by Fitzwilliam Darcy as part of the household staff paraded by the opening, which was only an inch or two——but large enough for him to see all he needed to see: the old woman from earlier in the day exited the room on Darcy's arm. He did not know her——had not expected to confront her as he had made a timely exit. He had taken a chance with the string——wanted to see if it could possibly help him eliminate his target. However, he would need to be more careful in the future. He could not afford for anyone else to see him.

Yet he thought it quite amusing, really, how Fitzwilliam Darcy had always portrayed himself as the kindly master, the man who treated his staff as family. Today, James had walked among that *fam-*

ily, and no one recognized him. Even more detrimental for the Darcys, no one had questioned his right to be in the house—to move through the private quarters. James had held conversations with many of them in the execution of *his duties.* He had even flirted with a chambermaid named Lucinda—Lucy, as she preferred to be called. He might even enjoy himself by partaking of her charms, but not tonight. Tonight he would simply watch and learn. He fancied that he knew the Darcys, but he had not anticipated the others being guests at Pemberley. The storm had driven in the riff-raff; however, they would not keep him from his task.

Adam Lawrence had not joined the rest of Darcy's houseguests the previous evening. Fleetingly, Darcy had thought to discuss the *unknown* intruder with the viscount, thinking to solicit Lawrence's help in apprehending the culprit who had set up yesterday's accident. Then Lord Stafford ignored Darcy's request that he and Miss Donnel not let the rest of Pemberley's guests know of their relationship by staying in the lady's room all night. Darcy had been forced to instruct Mr. Baldwin to quash any gossip by the household staff and had agreed aloud with Mrs. Williams and Mr. Worth when they praised the viscount's concern for his cousin. Inside, Darcy seethed with anger at His Lordship's impetuous actions.

So when the viscount entered the morning room, Darcy fought his natural instinct to chastise the man for his poor choices.

"How is Miss Donnel's injury?" Elizabeth asked when Lawrence joined the others at the breakfast table.

"My cousin is healing nicely; thank you for your concern, Mrs. Darcy. Please convey my respect to your staff for their tender care of Cathleen's injuries. I suspect that by this time tomorrow, she will be able to join us for some of the day." Lawrence speared one of the kippers that he had piled on his plate.

"That is pleasant to hear." Darcy motioned for a footman to refill Elizabeth's cup of chocolate. Of late, it seemed to be her morning favorite, and he readily indulged her.

Elizabeth's eyebrow shot up when the footman approached. "Fitzwilliam," she said affectionately from across the table, "Lydia and I thought that we might take advantage of the weather. Do you suppose that Mr. Steventon might bring the sleds out of storage? We could use the hill leading to the orchard."

Darcy had no desire to participate in winter sledding; he had estate business with which to deal, in addition to a "phantom" employee to locate, but he could not deny Elizabeth, and he knew his duty as a host. "That is an excellent idea, my Dear. I will make arrangements after we break our fast. I hope that everyone will join us." He directed his last comments to the entire table.

"Oh, that sounds entertaining, Mr. Darcy, but I am unsure that a woman of my age—" Mrs. Jenkinson began.

"Mildred, you must," Anne interrupted.

Mr. Worth took up the cause. On the first evening, he had sat beside Mrs. Jenkinson during the musical entertainment. They had enjoyed a pleasant conversation, which he would not mind resuming. "You will not let these young folks," he gestured to Lydia and Georgiana, "have all the fun, will you? You may traverse the hill with me."

His attention caused Mildred Jenkinson to blush. "Thank you, Mr. Worth." She dropped her eyes in embarrassment.

"You will come, too, will you not, Your Lordship?" Lydia coyly flirted with the viscount.

"I should remain with my cousin," he insisted.

Elizabeth took the lead. "Please indulge us, Your Lordship. We are greatly lacking in males." She indicated the abundance of women at the table. "There are only the three of you, and we could use your expertise on the hill. I will ask Betanne to sit with Miss Donnel if you can see your way clear to join us."

"Thank you, Mrs. Darcy, I will call on Cathleen first and then make my decision."

While the others prepared for the outdoor activities, Elizabeth followed Darcy to his study. "I apologize, Fitzwilliam, for taking you from your work." She stood in the doorway, waiting for him to acknowledge her. "I should have asked you prior to announcing my plans for the day."

Darcy came forward to catch her hand and bring her into the room. "Did you think me angry with you?" He brought her hand to his lips to kiss her knuckles.

"You, my Husband, were angry with *someone* at that table." She winked. "I have not slept in your arms every night for more than a year without taking note of the nuances of your personality." Elizabeth and Darcy knew each other well, often communicating without words.

Darcy smiled mockingly down at her. "Since when are you so perceptive, my Love?"

Elizabeth's hands fisted on her hips. "Do not change the subject, Fitzwilliam."

He kissed her upturned nose. "Yes, Mrs. Darcy."

"Yes, what, Fitzwilliam?"

"Yes, I was angry." A sigh of exasperation escaped his lips.

"And?"

Darcy pulled her into his embrace. "Would you rather not spend time in my arms than talking?" He nuzzled behind her ear.

She moved even closer to him. "This is not fair, Fitzwilliam," she protested while sliding her arms around his neck. "You know how you affect me."

"I know how you affect me, Mrs. Darcy," he murmured into her hair as his hands began to search her body. "I wish to never be without you in my life."

With a shaky exhalation, she whispered, "I love you, my Husband, even when you refuse to answer my questions."

Darcy took her mouth fully, just to satisfy his constant need for her. When he finally raised his head, he rasped, "I suppose I will have to tell you, or you will kiss it out of me."

"If that is what it takes, Mr. Darcy." Elizabeth leaned into him. "I would willingly sacrifice my lips for the truth."

Her taunt made him chuckle. "It would be no sacrifice on my part, my Love." Darcy kissed her again, only more tenderly this time.

Elizabeth's breathing became shallow. "We have our best *conversations* in each other's arms, but I insist on knowing what is going on. Has it something to do with Miss Donnel's accident?"

Darcy's thoughts went to the missing items, and to the Pemberley staffer who had spoken so disrespectfully to Mrs. Jenkinson and likely set up the trap on the stairs. Addressing those issues with Elizabeth created a conflict for him. He felt a need to keep unpleasantness away from her. Finally, he said, "I found it inappropriate for Lord Stafford to spend the evening in Miss Donnel's room."

Elizabeth ran her fingertips through Darcy's hair. "Well, the lady *is* his cousin."

Darcy reluctantly released her and led Elizabeth to a nearby settee. "Miss Donnel is not His Lordship's cousin; she is his mistress. I insisted when Lord Stafford accepted our hospitality that he and Miss Donnel keep their relationship secret. I tried to shield you and Georgiana and the others."

This revelation surprised her. "I see. I am all astonishment, my Husband, that you would tolerate such a situation."

"It was not to my liking, but His Lordship is an acquaintance of Edward's older brother, and I could not send the viscount out on the road with the ice and snow. I would have no man's death on my conscience—or the death of his mistress." Darcy paused, debating whether to share his concerns. "I understand His Lordship's concern for his mistress, while disapproving of his actions. He discovered a piece of hemp strung across the top step—high enough to catch the foot of the person who descended the stairway first. Miss Donnel's fall was likely no accident."

"Oh, Fitzwilliam, please say it is not so." She took his hand in hers. "Do we have any idea who may be at fault?"

"I wanted to speak to Lord Stafford yesterday evening, but he remained with Miss Donnel." Again he paused, and he filtered out what he did not wish to share with his wife. "Mrs. Jenkinson accosted a man dressed in Darcy livery in the hallway to the private quarters. I asked her to view each of our male staff members, but she could not or would not identify the man."

Elizabeth leaned forward to assure more privacy. "Why would the lady not wish to label the man?"

"I do not suspect coercion," Darcy confided. "Mrs. Jenkinson has served Anne faithfully for years, and has been my cousin's closest confidante. I simply believe that Mrs. Jenkinson is, first and foremost, a servant. I fear the lady might not wish to be responsible for another servant meeting my wrath or possibly losing his position."

"So you think that she might purposely not identify the culprit."

Darcy frowned, never liking anything out of the ordinary in his life. "At this point, I am unsure what to believe. If I take Miss Donnel's accident and combine it with all the other unexplained incidents of late, I am at my wit's end."

"Should we not share our concerns with the others?"

"Share what exactly?" Darcy stood to pace the room. "All we have are suspicions—a phantom footman or worker and some missing items. I would not wish to tarnish Pemberley's reputation by spreading rumors of a disgruntled employee."

Elizabeth watched him closely; she knew Darcy thought best when he was on the move. "Then we simply become more observant."

"At the moment, I think that best."

An hour later, the Pemberley party gathered on the south lawn. Darcy assigned two footmen to help. Each of the three male guests took on the duties of escorting the ladies down the hill. Elizabeth rode with Darcy, and so did his cousin Anne. Mr. Worth squired Mrs. Williams and Mrs. Jenkinson. The fact that Lord Stafford took Georgiana by the arm caused Darcy to bristle, but Elizabeth pulled him to one side, assuring him that the man's innocent attention would bolster Georgiana's confidence. The viscount knew Darcy's expectations, Elizabeth explained. And as a gentleman, she continued, His Lordship would not offend Georgiana's sensibilities. Darcy also felt some qualms about his sister sharing the sled with Lydia Wickham. He did not wish to remind Georgiana of George Wickham's betrayal, but again Elizabeth saw the advantage of the situation. "Georgiana must face her mistakes and grow from them," she told him. Reluctantly, he saw the logic in what his wife said, but that did not make it any easier to accept.

Repeatedly, the gentlemen climbed the slopes, tugging the sleds behind them. The footmen helped the ladies settle onto the wooden runners. For Adam Lawrence, the innocence of Georgiana Darcy fascinated him. Some man would eventually earn her love and her devotion and be a very lucky man. He could have done without the clinging Mrs. Wickham. The woman wrapped herself around him when they sped down the hill. He enjoyed physically peeling her fingers from his arm and waist.

Mr. Worth respectfully accompanied the two older women. He found Mrs. Jenkinson charming, for although the woman had earlier declared herself too old to participate in the winter fun, she embraced the experience with an unexpected enthusiasm: She shrieked and giggled like a girl enjoying her first outing. Mrs. Williams, obviously more frightened than Mrs. Jenkinson, closed her eyes tightly and said a prayer as the sled hurtled toward the flat land.

Darcy placed Elizabeth in front of him, spooning her body with his and allowing her to help him steer the sled. He nuzzled her neck while he pulled the ropes to turn the sled as it zoomed to the bottom of the hill. Elizabeth screeched her delight, leaning into him and plastering her back to his chest. "That was *magnificent,* Fitzwilliam!" she squealed as she scrambled to her feet.

He brushed the snow from her. "Indeed, it was." He caught her hand to lead her to the top of the slope again. "Are you ready, Cousin?" he asked as he set the sled for his next descent.

"I have not done anything like this since we were children, Fitzwilliam," she confessed.

"It is time you lived again, Anne."

She hesitated for only a moment and then seated herself behind him on the slick wood. "I am ready, Fitzwilliam, to be that girl again."

"Then hold tight, Cousin. I mean to give you the ride of your life." The footman gave the sled a mighty shove, and they were off, the trees a blur as they sped by them. Darcy listened for Anne's scream, but it never came. Instead, she sang a note of joy—laughter exploding from her. He found that he liked the sound. If Lieutenant Harwood had given Anne the courage to laugh again, the man had earned a measure of Darcy's respect.

When he helped her from the snow bank, along which they had skidded to a stop, Darcy leaned down to tell her, "You should laugh more, Cousin: You are beautiful when you do."

"Thank you, Fitzwilliam. Today, surprisingly, I feel beautiful."

Once, two sleds raced to the bottom. Darcy and Elizabeth won, just barely edging out the viscount and Georgiana. "That was so close," Stafford asserted. "If it had been my servants helping to shove off instead of yours, Darcy, I believe the results might have been different."

Darcy laughed heartily. "Maybe so, Stafford—maybe so."

As the men returned to the hill, Elizabeth and Georgiana waited for Mrs. Williams and Mr. Worth to reach them. "Is this not great fun?" Elizabeth called as Worth helped the widow to dismount the wooden sled.

"Great fun!" he yelled back genially. "It has been too long since I have done anything so impetuous."

Mrs. Williams motioned him on. "I wish to speak to Mrs. Darcy a moment."

Worth turned to the hill and the climb once more.

"Mrs. Darcy," the woman said as she caught Elizabeth's arm. "I have a problem." She glanced around to assure their privacy. "My petticoat, ma'am. The bottom of it has come loose. I caught it on the runner's edge. I cannot go about with a lace ruffle hanging below my skirt. Do you have a suggestion? Should I return to the house?"

Elizabeth glanced down at the offending garment. "Is it just the lace ruffle?"

"I believe so."

"Can you simply pull it free?"

"I do not see why not."

"Then how about the storage shed? No one will notice, and you can slip in there and free the ruffle before it becomes entirely unraveled."

"I would be mortified if that happened."

Elizabeth motioned to Georgiana to precede her on the climb. "Do you need my assistance?"

The woman glanced toward the small outbuilding. "As long as the door is unlocked, I can manage. If you go with me, it will bring more notice. Just tell Mr. Worth that I needed to catch my breath for a moment; he will not worry so much then."

"I will do just that."

Thirty minutes later, they all gathered at the bottom of the slope, shivering, but none of them willing to give up the camaraderie. When Elizabeth scooped up a handful of snow and struck Darcy on the shoulder with it, a melee broke out. Soft snowballs struck them all as a mist of snow filled the air, a splatter of white on a brown and green background. "Enough!" Elizabeth ordered as Darcy picked her up by the waist, threatening to dump her in a snow bank.

Deep baritone laughter and soft soprano giggles indicated everyone's enjoyment. Lydia Wickham suggested a snowman. Again, teams formed, and they rolled small snowballs over and over, the frozen spheres collecting volume and becoming crude circular masses.

Bases fully formed, the men sat about stacking the globes one on top of another, while the women began to search for branches and nuts to use for decoration.

"Mildred, what are you doing?" Anne said as she came sauntering over.

After breaking an icicle from an overhead branch, the older woman began to suck on the frozen stick. "Have you never enjoyed an ice treat, Miss Anne?"

"Of course, she has," Darcy called as he straightened from lifting the mass to the second level. "Only my cousin prefers her icicles flavored."

Georgiana bubbled, "I love flavored ice, too. May we add some flavors, Fitzwilliam?"

Always one to indulge his sister, Darcy sent Lucas to ask Mrs. Jennings to send out some oils of cinnamon and clove and licorice. When the footman returned with the oils, he also brought a small bowl of crushed walnuts and some plum preserves and some loose sugar. Everyone gathered around the tray the man held, each with his own tasty icicle.

"Try this." Darcy placed two drops of licorice on Elizabeth's frosty rod.

She let the licorice roll down the short stick, turning it to leave a trail of intense flavor in the ice before placing the coldness to her tongue. "Mmm!" she said in approval.

"This is delicious." Mildred Jenkinson followed Anne's lead and spread plum preserves on the side of her frosty rod.

"I knew that you would love it," Anne teased her companion.

"Here are a few smaller ones," Mrs. Williams handed out the ones she had gathered.

"This one has sugar already on it."

"Yes, I thought to use the sugar, but I can fix another one."

"Are you certain?"

"Oh, my heavens, yes. One or two of these are more than enough for me," the widow shared. "I prefer my treats warm, in fact."

"Hot tea sounds heavenly right now," Lydia declared.

Adam Lawrence slapped his hands to shake off the snow. "Let us finish this snowman and then get everyone inside."

With a renewed effort, the men lifted and supported the three stacking globes as Elizabeth, Anne, Lydia, and Georgiana smoothed and shaped their creation. However, Mrs. Williams helped Mrs. Jenkinson to indulge in one more frozen treat before Lucas returned the flavorings to the house.

Georgiana found a branch with five pointed twigs to represent the snowman's fingers. "I think I am as cold as you, sir," she said to the snowman as she shoved the branch into the side of the middle ball.

"Why do you not return to the house?" Darcy suggested.

"No, I would like to stay, Fitzwilliam," she whispered. "I want to be a part of the group."

He argued, "But you could ask Mrs. Jennings to prepare hot cider for everyone." Elizabeth squeezed his hand in a tender warning to listen to his sister and not exert his will over her each time.

Georgiana swallowed uncomfortably, her throat working up and down, but she stood her ground. "Please, Fitzwilliam. It is important to me."

Darcy bit back the words, trying to trust Elizabeth—they had on more than one occasion discussed his tendency to be overprotective of his sister. He had served as Georgiana's guardian for the past seven years—after their father's passing. He was as much father as brother. "Very well, my Dear," he whispered softly.

Lydia interrupted, "Well, *I* will ask Mrs. Jennings for the hot cider." She made her way to the house.

"What do you think?" Anne asked the group. They all turned to look at their snowy embodiment of a man.

"He looks formidable." Mr. Worth shook the snow from his coat. A chorus of agreement followed.

"I suggest we partake of hot cider." Darcy ushered everyone toward the house.

Anne caught Mildred around the waist. The woman still sucked on a flavored ice. "Thank you for coming out with me today. I felt young and hopeful. I know that sound ridiculous, but I have spent a lifetime nearly empty of feelings. This was all new to me."

"You, my Girl, must never return to being that person," Mildred said. She spoke unusually candidly. "You are too precious to suffer so. It is not necessary for you to completely defy Her Ladyship, but do not let your mother define you. Be Anne de Bourgh in all her glory."

CHAPTER 7

~~~

SHEDDING THEIR SNOW-COVERED outerwear in a small room off the kitchen, the group made their way to the blue drawing room. Mr. Baldwin had built a roaring fire in the hearth, and the cozy sitting room offered the warmth they all desperately sought.

"Ah, this is perfect," Mrs. Williams commented as she took one of the arranged cups of heated apple cider and headed for a chair near the fireplace.

"Oh yes," Lydia Wickham asserted, spreading her fingers around her cup of hot liquid.

Each took comfort in the steaming brew. "This is excellent cider," Mr. Worth declared.

"You should send a cup up to Miss Donnel, Lord Stafford."

Adam ignored Mrs. Wickham's suggestion, pretending not to hear her as he walked toward the bay windows.

Anne laughed lightly. "The rest of us are devouring the spicy mixture, and Mildred still partakes of her icicle. Are you not cold, Mildred?" Everyone's attention fell on the older woman.

"It is cold," she admitted, "but it is so refreshing." The lady slid the last inch of the stick into her mouth.

Mr. Worth came up behind Mrs. Jenkinson. "I think the lady very practical. She uses the ice to offset the heat of the cider she will soon drink."

Blowing on the cup she held to cool it down, Anne added, "My companion is a very practical woman."

"I bend to your wishes," Mildred Jenkinson said and nodded her head in acknowledgment of their good-natured teasing. She reached for the tray's last remaining cup, as did Elizabeth Darcy, who had just entered the room. She had given Mr. Baldwin orders regarding their guests' cloaks, coats, and gloves. "Ah, Mrs. Darcy, please." Mildred quickly withdrew her hand. "You must have the last cup."

"Nonsense, Mrs. Jenkinson." Elizabeth gestured to the steaming mixture. "The cider is yours. You must take it—I insist."

The older woman hesitated. "But it is your home, ma'am."

Elizabeth knew how to put people at ease. "Please take it, Mrs. Jenkinson. If you do, I will have a legitimate excuse to send Mr. Baldwin for another cup of the hot chocolate that I so enjoy of late."

"If you are certain, Mrs. Darcy."

"Absolutely."

Mrs. Jenkinson appreciatively took the offering and swallowed a mouthful of the spicy drink. "I have never tasted better cider," she commented before taking another large sip.

"I told you the ice would increase your tolerance of the heat," Worth announced.

Mrs. Jenkinson laughed at herself. "I suppose you correct, Mr. Worth." She took a third sip and struck up a conversation with that gentleman about the many places she had visited with her late husband.

The exuberance of the party waned as the warmth of the room seeped into their bones.

"I believe I shall freshen up," Mrs. Williams announced to those who sat nearby.

"That is an excellent idea," Anne agreed. "Mildred, I am to our rooms."

The lady lightly touched Anne's hand. "I will be there in a moment, my Dear. I want to finish telling Mr. Worth about the late Mr. Jenkinson's love of Denmark."

"Take your time." Anne squeezed the woman's hand. "You so

rarely have a chance to share your wonderful stories with someone other than me."

Adam returned his cup to the tray. "I shall check on Cathleen." He bowed and quietly left the room.

Within minutes, everyone had deserted the blue room for his or her own quarters. Everyone, that is, except Mrs. Jenkinson and Mr. Worth. The two seemed to have a real affinity for each other, and they chatted away in front of a full fire on that winter day.

"Mr. Darcy." Murray stopped him in the front foyer before Darcy climbed the stairs for the evening. "Might I speak to you, sir?"

Darcy, weary from the day and from his constant worries, considered putting off the conversation until morning, but he indulged the man. "What may I do for you, Murray?"

The footman motioned Darcy to a private corner. "I-I have," he stammered. "That is to say, sir—"

"Yes?" Darcy glanced toward the main stairs, needing to be with Elizabeth and a night's peace.

The footman swallowed hard. "Well, you see, sir...I thought of something earlier, and Mr. Baldwin says I should tell you."

Darcy's full attention now rested on his servant. "Go on."

"I thought you should know, sir, that I have spoken to young Lawson on three different occasions about not fulfilling his duties."

"What do you mean, Murray?" Lawson was the one footman that Mrs. Jenkinson had not seen that day.

"The boy disappears for long periods of time, sir." Immediately, Darcy wondered if Lawson was the one he had seen in the east wing. "I have addressed him twice. Plus, a fortnight ago I caught him in the music room with Miss Darcy. It was one of the evenings that your sister came down to play after everyone else had retired. We were having trouble with the fireplace in there, so I waited until everyone was asleep to clean it out."

"Caught him in the music room with Miss Darcy?" Darcy's rage rose quickly. "What do you mean?"

"Nothing untoward, sir. They sat together in the room on the music bench. I simply did not think it appropriate, sir."

Darcy would need to consult with Elizabeth. The last time he had confronted his sister regarding her speaking to a man while unchaperoned, he had done Georgiana more harm than good. His wife would know how to approach the subject without giving offense. "Would you tell Lawson I wish to speak to him before he goes off duty in the morning?"

"Yes, Mr. Darcy."

"And, Murray, I do not want the boy to have access to my sister alone late at night again—maybe we should see about transferring him to Mr. Steventon now. I wanted to wait until he turned eighteen, but we should see to it sooner."

"I agree, Mr. Darcy." Murray took the safety of the family personally. "I am sure that nothing happened, sir," he added.

Darcy glanced toward the stairs again. The phrase *Georgiana, lovely Georgiana* rang in his head. Could Lawson be Georgiana's intruder? "Just let me speak to the boy first—I have some questions to which I require answers."

Murray nodded and bowed and departed. Slowly, Darcy trudged up the stairs. He hated the disorder surrounding him at the moment. *Maybe Mr. Baldwin is right,* he thought. *Maybe a curse besets this household.* No other explanation seemed as plausible.

In the middle of the night, a light but persistent tapping brought Darcy to his wife's bedchamber door. He almost expected to see Georgiana huddling in the dimly lit hallway—perhaps her nightmares had returned. Finding his cousin took him by surprise.

"Anne," he whispered, trying to let Elizabeth go back to sleep. "What is the matter?"

Tears ran down his cousin's cheeks. "Please come," she pleaded. "It is Mildred. She is very ill. I cannot...I cannot lose her."

Darcy shoved the door open. "Let me—" he began, but then Elizabeth slipped his shirt into his hand. "Lead the way," he indicated, pulling the shirt over his head as they hurried through the hallway.

He heard Elizabeth behind them. When she turned toward the servants' staircase, he intuitively knew that she sought Mrs. Reynolds for medical help. He followed Anne to Mildred Jenkinson's small room. The woman's gaunt figure thrashed about in pain. Darcy rushed over to steady her, making sure that her violent movements did not cause her to fall from the raised mattress.

"Light more candles, Anne," he ordered as he touched the woman's head, checking for a fever. "She is cool and damp to the touch. Bring a cloth and some water." Darcy took the woman's shoulders and repositioned her in bed.

Mrs. Reynolds, followed by Elizabeth, rushed into the room. Both women were wearing muslin gowns and robes, with their hair in long braids down their backs. He often considered how his housekeeper had taken on the role of Elizabeth's mother some time ago, but this picture solidified the image. Mrs. Reynolds pushed him out of the way so that she could examine the woman. "Tell me what you know of her illness," she demanded. She touched Mrs. Jenkinson's stomach, and the woman recoiled in pain. "She has a tenderness in her lower abdomen."

"Mildred ate so little at supper," Anne barely whispered as she came to the bed's end. She handed Darcy the water bowl and the cloth. "She said she did not feel well; we thought maybe she took an ague, being out in the cold so long today." Elizabeth moved beside Anne, sliding an arm around the woman's waist. "She took a tray in her room, saying she was chilled." Anne caught the post for support, swaying in place. "Mildred never complains, so I knew that she was not well; I kept checking on her. She has been experiencing stomach pains for several hours. I came for you, Fitzwilliam, when she brought up her meal in the chamber pot I held for her."

Darcy moved to where he could see the pot. He knew from his parents' final illnesses that the contents of one's stomach give clues to the illness. The yellowish tint of the congealed liquid in the pot told him that his cousin's companion suffered greatly. Mrs. Jenkinson's body shook with pain. "If I did not know better," Mrs. Reynolds spoke for Darcy's ears alone, "I would suspect cholera. I saw cases of it when I was a mere child, and this woman shows all the signs."

He shook his head in denial, and the woman who had served him for six and twenty years swallowed her words. "Let us try some warm barley water to settle her stomach. Mrs. Darcy, will you ask Mrs. Jennings to send up some barley water and maybe some peppermint or ginger?"

Elizabeth nodded and rushed from the room. Mrs. Jenkinson's eyes flew open in terror. She fought to reach the edge of the bed. Darcy brought the pot to her as Mrs. Reynolds supported the woman's body. Mildred Jenkinson retched repeatedly—her body convulsing. Blood and saliva seeped from the corners of her mouth; however, nothing but dry heaves came from her efforts. "Rest now," Mrs. Reynolds whispered as she gently pushed the woman back against the pillows.

"Anne, come closer...my Girl." The hoarseness of Mildred's voice caused Anne to tear up again, but she went to sit by her only friend. With much difficulty, the woman offered Anne peace. "I will...see my...husband and baby girl soon."

"No!" Anne pleaded, grasping the woman's hand in hers, kissing it gently.

The pain caused Mrs. Jenkinson to contract, but she continued her farewells. "Find your heart ...my Girl...let love...guide you." A paroxysm shook her—and then a shudder released it slowly through her clenched teeth as the woman collapsed in a final peace. Mildred Jenkinson breathed her last breath.

Moments later, Elizabeth rushed into the room to find a terrible tableau. Mrs. Jenkinson lay lifeless on the bed, with a sobbing Anne de Bourgh lying across the woman's body. Mrs. Reynolds stood with her face buried in Darcy's shoulder as he lightly stroked the woman's hair. Elizabeth gasped and froze like the others for a brief moment before she took charge. "Come, Anne," she said and pulled her husband's cousin into her embrace. "Let me take you from here."

His wife's voice brought Darcy out of his trance. He turned Mrs. Reynolds in his arms before catching Elizabeth's eye. His wife mouthed "Georgiana," and he nodded his agreement. He would not entrust Anne to her mother's care this evening. Lady Catherine could not offer the compassion his cousin needed.

"Mrs. Reynolds," he sat the woman away from him, "find Mr. Baldwin. Move Mrs. Jenkinson's body to the other wing. I do not want it where it might remind my cousin of her loss. It is too cold and the ground too frozen to bury the lady right away. Clean this room from top to bottom in case of disease, although I do not suspect any such condition exists here. We will need to move Miss de Bourgh to other quarters and assign someone to be with her at all times."

"Yes, Mr. Darcy." She wiped her eyes on her gown's sleeve.

"I will want to speak to everyone in the morning. Set up the main drawing room. We need to reach the bottom of this—the missing items, Miss Darcy's visitor, Miss Donnel's fall, a phantom footman, and now this."

Mrs. Reynolds frowned in puzzlement. "Do you suspect foul play? Not at Pemberley, sir!"

"Something is rotten in the state of Denmark," he murmured as he pulled the sheet up to cover Mrs. Jenkinson's face. "Please send Mrs. Jennings to my study right away."

"Yes, Mr. Darcy."

Nearly an hour later, Elizabeth found him in his sanctuary. He stood before the fireplace, his head resting on his arm as he leaned against the mantel for support. "I brought your robe, as well as stockings to warm your feet."

Darcy glanced as his bare toes. "I hardly noticed."

Elizabeth came forward to hold the robe for him. Absentmind-edly, Darcy slid his arms into the sleeves. Going on her tiptoes, she straightened the material across his shoulders and turned him around to cinch the cloth belt in front. Darcy allowed his wife to address his needs, but he never saw her: He watched a scene of horror over her shoulder—seeing what no one else saw. "Come," she pulled on his hand and led Darcy to a nearby wing chair. "Let me pour you a brandy." Elizabeth found the decanter and a glass and filled it. Handing it to her husband, she ordered, "Drink this." Then she dropped to her knees before him and began to cover his feet with stockings. "I brought your old dance shoes," she explained. "I did not think I could wrestle on boots."

Darcy sipped the drink, slowly becoming aware of Elizabeth's tender care. "Anne?" he asked as his wife rested her chin on his knee.

"Mrs. Reynolds gave her something to help her sleep. She shares a bed with Georgiana. Your sister showed such mature compassion; I was very proud of her."

"How do we handle this?" Darcy's voice sounded far away.

Elizabeth came up on her knees, where she might give him comfort. "We cannot reach the magistrate. Mr. Baldwin says it is snowing again. You will need to do the investigation yourself. There has to be a logical explanation: A woman who is thoroughly enjoying herself, as Mrs. Jenkinson was today, simply does not suddenly up and die."

Darcy gave a little tug on Elizabeth's hand, and she came willingly into his embrace, curling up on his lap. "Nothing like this has ever happened at Pemberley," he whispered into her hair, resting his head on hers.

"Then we aggressively seek the culprit." Elizabeth's words held a resolve. "The Darcy name will not be blackened in the country."

"I wish I were as sure as you." He tightened his arms around her as she snuggled against his chest. "I watched my father devote his every breath to protect this estate, and I was groomed in his image. I always thought the threat would come from without— the factory's draw on the workers—but the real demon is within these walls."

"We will find who performs this farce if we have to tear down the walls to reach him."

Darcy stroked her back as he contemplated what to do next. "I intend to speak to our guests in the morning. As much as I do not wish to frighten them, I must make them aware of what goes on in my home." Elizabeth heard the defeat in his tone.

"Maybe someone saw something and took no notice of it originally. Your words tomorrow may jog a witness's memory and help us unwind this mystery. Please, Husband, you must believe this will resolve itself."

"Oh, Elizabeth, what would I do without you?" He kissed her forehead before tasting her mouth. Raising his head, he looked deeply into her eyes. "You will not leave me if this turns bad?"

"Never!" she declared. "Listen to me, Fitzwilliam Darcy. I will never be disloyal to you. You are my world. If you ever hear me repeat a disparaging word about you, then you will know I am being made to do so under duress. I would fight your enemies with the ferocity of a she-bear." She cupped his chin in her palm. "I love you to distraction."

Darcy's smile turned up the corners of his mouth. "A she bear? You are too petite, my Love." He kissed her tenderly. "Thank you, Elizabeth. I needed to hear your determination in order to put my desolation aside. Of course, we will find the culprit and bring him to justice."

"Let us to bed. Although neither of us will sleep, I do not intend to spend what is left of the night curled up in this chair." Elizabeth stood and offered him her hand.

Darcy followed her to his feet. "You brought life to this house after it had been silent for so long. I will not allow death to hold us hostage again."

At eight in the morning, Darcy summoned everyone to the main drawing room. He told no one what had happened, only that he needed to see everyone—no exceptions. His aunt objected, but

Darcy brooked no challenge to his authority. He even requested that Anne join them, although he spent time offering her his comfort first.

Thirty minutes later, they all gathered in his favorite room—an earth-toned drawing room off the main foyer. Darcy hated to sully it with his program for the day, but he needed the peace it gave him in order to face his guests. He and Elizabeth took up positions before the windows. He ignored his guests' requests for information, instead directing them to the tea and biscuits he had ordered as a prelude to breakfast.

"Well, Darcy, I hope this is important." Lady Catherine wore a brocade dressing gown, having refused to dress that early. However, he noted that she had styled her hair and rouged her cheeks before making an appearance. For a moment, he allowed himself to imagine Her Ladyship's disdain if any of the others had chosen to appear thusly.

"Please have a seat, Aunt. This shall not take long." He gestured to the maid to pour Lady Catherine some tea.

Finally, Georgiana entered with a distraught-looking Anne de Bourgh clinging to the girl's arm.

Lady Catherine placed her cup down hard. "Darcy, what is this? You promised me that you would keep things private."

"And I shall." He helped Anne to a nearby settee, pausing to caress her cheek and to whisper words of sympathy. "You make assumptions, Your Ladyship." He returned to Elizabeth's side. "We shall begin," he announced in a steady tone he perfected over the years.

Nigel Worth glanced around the room. "We must wait on Mrs. Jenkinson," he offered.

The mention of her companion's name set Anne sobbing again. Georgiana slid her arm around her cousin's shoulders to support her.

"That is part of why I have summoned you here this morning. Mrs. Jenkinson took suddenly ill and passed during the night."

A collective gasp filled the room. Tears slid from Miss Donnel's eyes, but she valiantly asked, "How is that possible, Mr. Darcy?"

"I will attempt to answer that question if you will bear with me for a few minutes."

However, before he could continue, Lady Catherine shot to her feet. "I will take Anne to her room, Darcy. She should not be here."

"Your Ladyship, I ask that you remain. Anne understands the importance of addressing everyone. Mrs. Darcy and my sister have tended my cousin for hours; she is in good hands. Besides, Anne is stronger than any of us have ever given her credit for. My cousin holds great fortitude." He and Lady Catherine had a staring match, but his aunt finally succumbed to his request. Only a grumbled "I never!" escaped before she reached for her cup again.

Darcy motioned for his servants to leave before he continued. With the door securely closed behind them, he began his tale. "Two days before your arrivals, my wife's horse spooked and threw her."

"What does that fact have to do with Mrs. Jenkinson's death?" Worth demanded.

"Please let me tell it all, Mr. Worth; I will keep my comments brief; but you must hear the complete tale." Darcy paused until he received agreement. "I saw nothing before Mrs. Darcy found herself dumped unceremoniously on the ground, but she thought that she had seen a man hiding behind the trees. Although I searched, I found no traces—no footprints or broken tree limbs. Thinking it an animal, we resumed our lives. However, the next day, my sister thought she saw someone lurking about the cottagers' houses."

"Darcy," Lady Catherine began, but she swallowed her objection when he glared at her.

"The next evening, Georgiana had what we thought to be a nightmare—she saw a light moving in her room." Again, he anticipated their questions, but when none came, Darcy continued. "She also thought she heard a voice."

Viscount Stafford leaned forward. "What did it say, Miss Darcy?"

Georgiana blushed with his notice. "Nothing really—simply called me by name."

Darcy stepped forward to draw the group's interest again. "Then my staff began to report unusual happenings. Mr. Stalling saw a shadowy figure in the Pemberley graveyard. Megs reported a missing candelabra. Mr. Baldwin followed with an account of missing bedding from a room in the east wing. I even thought I saw a person at a window in one of those rooms. It was the day we returned from Lambton—the day of the storm. Since that time, we have experienced Miss Donnel's accident. His Lordship and I found a string across the steps leading us to believe that someone had planned the incident."

Again, gasps filled the air. Instinctively, Elizabeth slipped her hand into Darcy's, presenting a united front. She knew how much this madness hurt him, and she needed to remind Darcy of her complete devotion. He rewarded her with a gentle squeeze of recognition. The rest of her husband's story would bring disbelief to the room's occupants. "As Viscount Stafford and I dealt with Miss Donnel's injury, Mrs. Jenkinson had a confrontation with a man she assumed was a staff member. This unknown man offered her a warning. Now, the lady is dead."

Mr. Worth was on his feet and moving toward Darcy. "Surely, Mr. Darcy, you do not believe Mrs. Jenkinson's passing an act of murder!"

"I do."

A terrible silence smothered the room—Anne's whimper being the only exception.

"You jest, Darcy!" Lady Catherine's voice rang clear. Her incredulity spoke volumes.

His words' gravity settled on everyone's shoulders. "It is not a subject in which I might find humor, Aunt."

Darcy listened with some relief when Adam Lawrence recapped for the room what Darcy had just shared. He thought, despite the man's impetuous nature, that he could be one of Darcy's greatest allies in this trouble: He needed another perspective. Then Lawrence inquired, "May I ask if Mrs. Jenkinson identified this phantom employee?"

"When I became aware of the lady's accusations, I made arrangement for Mrs. Jenkinson to observe my male staff. However, she could not identify the man she encountered in the hallway. At first, I thought the lady protected a fellow servant, but I soon came to believe otherwise."

Lawrence gazed at Darcy. "And why did you not tell us before now about your suspicions?"

Darcy swallowed hard. *How can I explain that the reputation of my family's name took precedence over my vigilance in this matter? I will be forever at fault in the lady's death.* "None of the events seemed connected. Often poachers appear on the property, and something is always misplaced in a house of this size. In retrospect, I know that I should have shared my concerns. But I thought that rumors of shadow people were simply my servants trying to explain the unexplainable."

"And why might you now believe Mrs. Jenkinson's death to be murder?" Lawrence's tone remained accusatory.

"Because of the lady's symptoms." Darcy spoke softly, "Anne, might I prevail upon you to describe Mrs. Jenkinson's progression?"

His cousin dabbed at her eyes, but her voice held a strength that Darcy admired. "After speaking to Mr. Worth, Mildred finally returned to our rooms. Shortly afterward, she complained of a mild headache and lightheadedness." Anne glanced around suddenly, realizing that she spoke to the whole room—a completely new experience. For a moment, she panicked, but a squeeze of Georgiana's hand gave her the courage to continue. "The stomach pains came next. We tried some dry toast, and I foolishly teased her for eating so much of the preserves when we were outside. Little did I know how she suffered: Poor Mildred relieved herself of part of her small meal several times. When she tried to speak, my friend's voice was hoarse. Soon the blood and saliva seeped from her mouth." The description of her companion's demise brought on new grief and restarted her sobbing.

Mrs. Williams said aloud what all of them thought. "The lady seemed perfectly well when we attacked the hill yesterday."

Viscount Stafford took up the questioning again. "Might you share with us, Mr. Darcy, what you believe killed the lady?"

"Arsenic." The word reverberated off the walls. Unaware of her husband's assumption, Elizabeth swayed and caught at Darcy's arm, before he pulled her closer.

The viscount was on his feet immediately. "Arsenic? How would the lady consume arsenic?" He came to stand beside Cathleen, taking up a defensive stance.

"When Mrs. Reynolds tended the lady, she made a private observation that Mrs. Jenkinson's symptoms mirrored many of those found in cholera."

Cathleen caught Adam's hand, but his attention remained on Darcy. "I assume, sir, that your housekeeper spoke out of turn."

"Not entirely." Darcy met the viscount's resolve with one of his own. "Mrs. Jenkinson did exhibit symptoms of cholera, but not just of that disease. Her clammy skin, the tenderness in her stomach, and her dry heaves also spoke of poisoning. Luckily, the cups from yesterday's cider remained in the blue room. One of them has the residue of what appears to be arsenic on the rim."

"A person would not need a large dose to kill another, but would not Mrs. Jenkinson taste the arsenic?" Miss Donnel saw the faultiness of their assumptions.

"The lady had so many flavored ices," Mr. Worth remarked, "that she drank the hot cider without needing it to cool."

Adam sat on the arm of Cathleen's chair. "I suppose she could numb her mouth enough to not taste the poison."

"Women of a certain age consume a little arsenic on a regular basis," Lady Catherine observed. "Possibly my daughter's companion was one of those women. I have been known to occasionally rub a bit of arsenic on my face and arms to improve my complexion."

The men looked a bit confused so Elizabeth explained, "Some women are known to mix arsenic with vinegar and chalk. They believe that if they eat this mixture it will make their skin appear paler. Women often exposed to the sun might resort to such drastic measures to achieve a fashionably pale complexion."

Mrs. Williams remarked, "It amazes me that a woman would consider using a wood preservative on her skin or would consume a compound used for bullets or bronzing or paints."

Lydia Wickham finally spoke. "But how could the murderer know that Mrs. Jenkinson would choose that particular cup?"

"Maybe you can answer that question yourself," Lawrence asserted.

Lydia turned on him. "And what is that supposed to mean?"

"I believe that you know more than you share, Mrs. Wickham." Again he showed his protectiveness, keeping Cathleen close to him. "First, you were the one person already in the hallway when my cousin entered it the morning of her accident. Miss de Bourgh came next, and the two of you turned back to greet Mrs. Williams. Only Cathleen continued toward the stairs. Did you plan on hurting Cathleen or was someone else your target?"

Elizabeth came to her sister's defense. "I assure you, Your Lordship, you are in error."

"I pray I am, Mrs. Darcy, but it seems even more of a concern when one takes into account that it was Mrs. Wickham who returned to the house to arrange for the hot cider." Adam staunchly defended his beliefs.

"I have never heard such poppycock!" Lydia protested. "What motive would I have for hurting Miss de Bourgh's companion?"

Lawrence countered, "Possibly, Mrs. Jenkinson was not your target."

"And who would that be?" Lydia turned red with anger and embarrassment.

"My cousin."

"And why, pray tell, would I wish to hurt Miss Donnel?"

"To get to me."

Lydia charged across the room at him. "I have you know, sir, that I am a married woman!"

"You would not be the first married lady to find her way to the bed of a man not her husband."

Darcy moved to whisper to Georgiana, excusing her from the room.

"You think a great deal of yourself, sir!" Lydia shrieked.

"It was you, Mrs. Wickham, who suggested that I send a cup of the cider to my cousin. It was you who clung to me on the hill in a most suggestive way. It was you who followed me to my cousin's room after her accident, and it was you alone in the hallway." His voice rose with each accusation.

Elizabeth stepped forward to insert herself between them. "Do you not think it more likely, Your Lordship, that the man Mrs. Jenkinson saw in the hallway is to blame?"

"Let me remind you, Mrs. Darcy, that Mrs. Jenkinson took the last cup on the tray, a cup she offered to you, and you adamantly refused."

"So I am a suspect now, Your Lordship?" Elizabeth steamed with anger and contempt.

"I would say we all are, Mrs. Darcy." Lawrence declared.

Darcy placed Elizabeth in the curve of his body. "Neither Mrs. Darcy nor Mrs. Wickham were involved."

"How do you know?" Nigel Worth, a man used to dealing with evidence, ventured.

"I questioned my cook, Mrs. Jennings, after Mrs. Jenkinson's death. She reported only the presence of the new footman in the kitchen after Mrs. Wickham left to find Mr. Baldwin to see that he stoked the fires in the blue drawing room." He paused to allow that vital information to become part of the room's collective knowledge, and then he added, "I have no new footman on my staff." Total silence again. "My purpose this morning was not to frighten you, but to make you aware of what is happening. Unfortunately, with the storm, it is impossible to reach a magistrate to investigate the matter, so it falls to us to do our own inquiry. I will ask His Lordship and Mr. Worth to join me in my study. We will discuss this in detail, and we will ask each of you to make a statement. We will need you to bring to our attention any detail that you might have thought insignificant. Such information may lead us to our wrongdoer. Exercise care until we discover the source of this perfidy."

Slowly, reluctantly, the group rose to their feet. No one made eye contact, but each warily watched the others from behind lowered lashes and furtive side glances. Mrs. Williams helped Cathleen, and Lydia arrogantly flounced away.

Elizabeth came to where Anne now stood. "Let me help you, Miss de Bourgh." She slid her arm around the woman's waist. "I have asked Mrs. Reynolds to move your personal belongings to the room next to Georgiana's."

"I will tend to my daughter," Lady Catherine objected and reached for her only child, but Anne flinched at her mother's touch.

"I will go with Mrs. Darcy," Anne spoke softly but with determination. "Thank you, Mother."

Lady Catherine's eyes reflected the pain she felt, but she regained her composure before saying, "As you wish, Anne." Slowly, she let her hand drop to her side.

Having observed her mother's broken composure, Anne remained motionless for a long moment, but she turned to Elizabeth's welcoming friendship. They left the room, arms encircling each other. Darcy watched as a dejected-looking Lady Catherine followed them from the room. It was a moment he had long hoped to see. He did not wish any pain on his aunt, but he had often wanted to see his cousin Anne assert herself.

Soon, only the three men remained. "Gentlemen," he said at last, "if you will join me in my study, I will send for breakfast."

Glumly, first Worth and then Lawrence followed Darcy from the room. Darcy was master of his estate—his staff hustled to do his bidding. But any guest who looked closely at him would see less crispness in Darcy's step and less authority in his gaze. Darcy would see this through, but the smear to his family name physically hurt him more than anyone knew. He did not look back to see the men following him—Darcy knew they were there. *A woman has died—*

been murdered under my roof. The thought pounded in his head. He had to find whoever had carried out mischief in his house. Darcy would not rest until then.

CHAPTER 8

~ ~ ~

"SO WHAT DO WE DO NOW?" By consensus, the three men led a party of footmen and searched the house, looking for any clue to the culprit's identity.

Nigel Worth, who appeared frustrated with the process, seemed inclined to believe Darcy. He knew Fitzwilliam Darcy as a man of honor—the kind of man to make good on a scoundrel's debts to safeguard his family's name. Plus, they questioned every servant. Many of them spoke of encounters with a new footman—a man who did menial jobs about the estate without complaint—a man who offered genial conversation as he completed his duties. These staffers described the same man: dark, wavy hair; approximately six feet in height; muscular build; clean-shaven; chocolate-brown eyes; a square jaw; and a firm jaw line. Lucinda had spoken to the man on three separate occasions. The chambermaid described him as "extremely fair of face." The only differences in their stories were the names he had given them. They knew him as Samuel, as Giles, as Layton, and as Harry.

Viscount Stafford, on the other hand, had insisted that they satisfy their need to know the truth of Darcy's revelations. Being young and a bit impetuous, Adam Lawrence wanted the business resolved immediately.

"I suggest we take a few hours to digest what we know and what we do not know and meet again after luncheon. I need time to rethink my way through this." Darcy, Worth, and Lawrence stood together in a tight circle in the middle of an unused bedchamber in the east wing. Pemberley's master absentmindedly ran his fingers through his hair.

Worth jammed his hand into a side pocket, seeking a snuffbox, which he nervously opened and closed. "I do not like to walk away when answers are not readily available, but it appears we have no choice." Viewing Mrs. Jenkinson's body had affected him more than he cared to admit. He had taken a liking to the woman, although he suspected that she was several years older than he. They had enjoyed conversations over the past few days, and yesterday afternoon, the conversation had taken a more intimate turn. Mildred Jenkinson had told him of her late husband, and also of herself, and Nigel Worth wanted to know more. Something about the woman—probably her graciousness and her intelligence—attracted him. He grieved for something that might have been.

"I am too distracted to sit around for a few hours. Despite the snow, I will take a look outside. Maybe our reprobate does not stay in the house at all—maybe the outside sightings are the clue," the viscount asserted.

Darcy nodded in agreement. "I was thinking something similar. Do you mind some company?"

"I would appreciate it; you know exactly where the other sightings occurred. I will meet you in the main hall in a quarter hour." The viscount left the room immediately, agitation showing on his face and in his gait.

Darcy touched the solicitor on the shoulder. "Mr. Worth, might I prevail upon you to keep an eye on the ladies while we search the landscape? I fear their sensibilities are thinly stretched, and several may need someone with a clear head when they realize the depth of our situation."

"Of course, Mr. Darcy."

"It is too far to reach the field that Mrs. Darcy and I rode across on the morning of that first sighting," Darcy explained as he and the viscount walked the main drive to the nearest hedgerow, their going laced with difficulty because of the snow accumulation. Beyond it laid the cottages that Elizabeth and Georgiana had visited. "But we will see the landscape that Miss Darcy described."

"I do not like this business, Darcy," Lawrence grumbled.

"None of us do, Stafford." Darcy pointed to the copse of trees where Georgiana claimed to have seen the stranger. "With the snow and the ice, we are not likely to find anything, but it will not hurt to look around."

They separated, each of them circling the trees, looking for broken twigs, loose threads, or anything unusual. Darcy inspected the tree against which Georgiana had sworn the man leaned. "Look here," he called to the viscount as he bent to examine a brown smear some two feet high on the tree.

Lawrence knelt beside Darcy. "It is just a glob of mud," Stafford intoned, his irritation evident.

"Not exactly." Darcy removed his gloves and lightly touched the damp dirt. "My sister said the man leaned against this tree—his back along the trunk—his foot resting against the bark." Darcy took a similar stance on the other side of the tree—mimicking the position Georgiana had demonstrated when he questioned her. In doing so, his wet, muddy boot left a similar mark along the tree. "See what I mean," he summed up.

"Our man was here." Stafford touched the dark smudge—this time with more interest. "Whoever he is, the man is several inches shorter than you," he observed. "See—your mark rests higher on the tree."

Darcy knelt to examine both marks again. "The heel of his boot," he pointed out, "has a squareness about it." He compared the shapes. "What kind of footwear might this be?"

The viscount stood and braced his hand against the tree for balance. He raised his foot to look at the bottom of his boot. "Like yours, mine resembles a horse's shoe—half an oval."

"If we decipher this clue, we might solve our mystery." Darcy looked back toward the house. "I would prefer not to tell the others until we have more to go on."

The viscount followed Darcy's gaze. "You remind me of my father," Lawrence observed. "Your passion is this estate. You can bear nothing that might tarnish Pemberley's reputation. The earl is as obsessed with Greene Hall as you are with your home."

Darcy turned slowly, taking in Stafford's smirk. "There was a time, Your Lordship, that your words would have rung true. That was before Mrs. Darcy, literally, danced into my life. It would grieve me to have what my father spent a lifetime creating to go away. Yet, I would abandon it all to keep Mrs. Darcy with me. When you observe my angst, it has nothing to do with this house or the reputation of this estate; instead, it is my need to protect my wife and my sister and those people who have served me well over the years... I must protect them—all of them—from this madness." Darcy's gaze returned to the house. "Have you ever been in love, Stafford?"

The future earl smiled slightly. "No."

"Someday," Darcy mused. "Someday, it will happen to you. I attended a country assembly with my friend Charles Bingley, and my world shifted on its axis. A woman not of my society caught my eye, and I could not withdraw my attention. Much to my chagrin, Elizabeth Bennet consumed my every thought. When I returned to Pemberley, I wondered what she might think of it."

Lawrence crossed his arms over his chest. "I am sure that Mrs. Darcy saw the advantage of marriage to you."

Darcy barked out a laugh. "Oh, yes, Mrs. Darcy expressed herself quite well. When I proposed the first time, Elizabeth told me that I could not have made the offer of my hand in any possible way that would have tempted her to accept it. Adding insult to her injury, she told me that I was the last man in the world whom she could ever be prevailed on to marry."

"The lady refused you?" Lawrence's eyes lit with mockery.

"Definitely. I had thought that Elizabeth Bennet lacked the proper connections and would seek the opportunity to better her situation. She, on the other hand, thought me devoid of feelings. From her, I have learned to value what is really important in life. When we met again by chance, I used every civility in my power to show Elizabeth I was not so mean as to resent the past, and I hoped to obtain her forgiveness and to lessen her ill opinion, by letting her see that her reproofs had been attended to."

"You changed *your* ways to please a *woman? Good God, man, they* are meant to please *us.*"

Darcy gestured toward the house, and they began their return to Pemberley's warmth. "It seems to me, Stafford, that you have gone out of your way to please Miss Donnel. Yet, even if that were not true, with God's grace, someday you will meet a lady who will see you for the man you want to be. Pleasing Mrs. Darcy makes me a better man. I would attempt anything for the woman. Do not speak to me of brick and mortar. Any concern you detect is for the people I affect."

The viscount said nothing for several minutes. "I always knew you to be a rich man, Darcy; I just never knew the extent of your wealth."

Darcy smiled and nodded. Then he continued, "What I mean to say, Stafford, is if Miss Donnel is of importance, then do not allow your pride to keep you from happiness."

"I care deeply for Miss Donnel, but the lady is not my future countess, and it has nothing to do with our current relationship. Cathleen stirs my senses, but I have never known someone whom I could love. However, I assure you that if I meet such a woman— whether she be a fine lady or of genteel birth or a commoner—I will attempt anything to make her mine. Maybe then I might become the kind of man my father thinks I should be."

Darcy accepted the man's words as truth. "For what it is signifies, I need your strength and your intelligence to solve this mystery."

Lawrence chuckled. "That is something, I suppose, although I am sure that the earl would disapprove somehow. My father reeks with disapproval, and I have perfected the art of disappointing him."

Darcy thanked his lucky stars that he and his late father had rarely argued about his position in the world. He even thought that his father would approve of his choice of Elizabeth Bennet as his wife. "You are young, Stafford. The responsibility of a title weighs heavily on you. You will find your way. I see a greatness in you."

The viscount looked sharply at Darcy, trying to read the sincerity of his remark. After a moment, he said, "Listen to us discussing our legacies as if we knew the dates of our own demises. I appreciate your confidence in me, Darcy, especially after I so out-and-out accused your wife's sister."

"Ah, Mrs. Wickham. If you made the acquaintance of my wife's mother, Mrs. Bennet, or her aunt, Mrs. Phillips, you would understand the source of the lady's boldness, as well as her need for attention. However, despite my constant dismay at Mrs. Wickham's self-absorption, I do not believe the lady possesses the kind of evil needed to orchestra Mrs. Jenkinson's death or Miss Donnel's accident." They reached the main entrance; Mr. Baldwin held the door for them. Neither man spoke of their search before the servants. Handing the butler their outerwear, Stafford followed Darcy into his study before they returned to their conversation.

"Is it possible that Mrs. Wickham is an accomplice?" Adam could not shake the feeling that somehow the mystery involved the lady.

"Anything, I suppose, is possible." Darcy knew Lydia to be easily misled and knew her blind loyalty to a man that Darcy despised. Still, he could not imagine her participating in murder. "Yet I remain far from convinced of Mrs. Wickham's involvement."

Darcy gestured to a tray, and Adam poured himself brandy. "I will bow to your assessment, Darcy."

"No," Darcy demanded sharply. "I want to hear every motive— every possibility. I want no stone unturned."

Adam had no response to his host's insistence. What would his father do if this was Greene Hall? Everything Fitzwilliam Darcy had said to him swirled through his mind. He paused for several long moments before saying, "I believe I will check on Cathleen and spend some time in my room." Stafford moved toward the open door. "I will see you at luncheon, if not before." A few moments later, Adam Lawrence climbed the stairs to his quarters. He had told Darcy that he would call on Cathleen first, but Darcy's earlier question about Adam's regard for Cathleen still rang in the viscount's ears. He was indeed protective of Cathleen. Yet, it was not the same feeling that Darcy held for his wife. He did not know Fitzwilliam Darcy's financial worth, but Adam suspected that he was to inherit a fortune comparable to Darcy's. But Darcy had found true happiness, which outweighed the financial gain either of them would attain. Adam wished that he had the focus—the control—his host possessed. Even though Darcy had said he needed Adam's help, the viscount wondered if the truth was not the reverse.

"Murray, I have not spoken to Lawson. Did you not tell him I wished to see him?" Darcy had summoned his footman to his study.

Murray looked about, in real concern. "No one has seen the lad today, sir. I have checked the boy's quarters, the house, and the stables."

"Mr. Steventon?" Darcy did not need to ask the question. Murray would understand.

"The steward reports not seeing Lawson since late yesterday afternoon."

Darcy nearly groaned with frustration. He did not need another mystery. "Let me know the moment Lawson returns to the house, Murray. In this weather, he could not have gone far."

"Yes, Mr. Darcy." The man bowed and exited the room.

"Mr. Worth, I wondered where you were!" Elizabeth had found the solicitor sitting in a darkened library corner.

The man rose slowly to his feet, his mind engaged elsewhere. "I apologize, Mrs. Darcy. Did you have a concern I could address?"

"I thought that you might need some company."

Worth gestured to a nearby chair. "I am afraid that Mrs. Jenkinson's fate has affected me more than I anticipated. The lady was so happy when we last spoke. Now, she is no more. I am beyond distraction."

"Mrs. Jenkinson seemed content to reunite with her husband and child. Her only concern seemed to be Miss de Bourgh." Elizabeth watched the man's expression. "It might be comforting to Miss Anne if you shared your feelings of loss. I barely knew the woman, and even though yours was a short acquaintance, you and the lady seemed to have an affinity for one another."

Mr. Worth spoke softly. "I would have liked to have known Mrs. Jenkinson better."

Elizabeth sat forward to press her point. "Miss de Bourgh spent the past ten years in Mrs. Jenkinson's company. It might help Mr. Darcy's cousin to speak of her friend with someone else who appreciated the lady."

"You are very wise, Mrs. Darcy." Worth seemed to relax a bit. "Does Mr. Darcy realize what a find he has in you, ma'am?"

Elizabeth stood to leave. "I remind Mr. Darcy of that fact daily, Mr. Worth." She smiled. "I believe Miss de Bourgh hides in the music room, sir."

"I will seek her out, Mrs. Darcy. Thank you for being so perceptive."

"Miss de Bourgh." Worth came quietly into the room. He paused upon seeing the hunched figure of Mrs. Jenkinson's friend. He finally forced himself to approach the distraught Anne de Bourgh. "I thought it might help both of us if we could speak of Mrs. Jenkinson. Of course, if you prefer to remain alone, I will understand." He edged forward, coming to where she sat curled up in the chair.

Anne quickly wiped her eyes and looked up in surprise. "Mr. Worth."

He bowed low. "I apologize for disturbing your privacy, Miss de Bourgh."

"You are not disturbing me, sir." Anne thought of sitting up properly in the chair, but she rejected that automatic response. She was in mourning and needed to follow the promptings of her heart, not the stilted rules of etiquette. "I would appreciate your company, sir. Mildred Jenkinson meant the world to me, and I would like for you to know my friend as I did."

Worth pointed to a nearby chair. "May I?"

Anne de Bourgh nodded her agreement.

For two hours, they sat together. Some tears came, but laughter also peppered the conversation. When a servant brought tea and cakes, compliments of Mrs. Darcy, neither seemed surprised.

"Mrs. Darcy thinks of everything," Worth remarked as he took the tea she offered.

"My cousin chose the perfect woman for himself," Anne observed. "I am afraid that I could never handle an estate the size of Pemberley. I am too faint-hearted."

Worth looked disturbed. "Mildred Jenkinson believed in you, Miss de Bourgh. Although I knew that lady only a short time, I came to value her opinions. If Mrs. Jenkinson thought you capable, I would have the same opinion."

Anne blushed "I have had few opportunities to exercise my will over any situation. Speaking to the whole group this morning was the first time I can ever remember addressing more than two people at one time. Is that not the most ridiculous assertion to ever come from a woman's mouth?"

Worth looked on in feigned amusement. This woman knew Lady Catherine's censure always pressing upon her, holding her down. Yet he had brief sightings of the capable woman whom Mildred Jenkinson described so tenderly. "I would like to see you honor Mrs. Jenkinson's memory by no longer hiding the real you. I believe the lady would smile down from heaven if she knew."

Impulsively, Anne touched his hand. "Do you believe I can be that person, Mr. Worth?"

He brought her soft hand to his mouth and kissed the back of it. "I do, Miss de Bourgh, and while we are at Pemberley, I am going to make it my personal mission to help you find that woman."

As his staff cleared the last course, Darcy looked up to see a very agitated-looking butler standing beside him. Darcy nodded, and the man leaned in to whisper his news. Darcy's heart lurched, and he instinctively gripped the chair's arms. His eye caught Elizabeth's, and he told her with a nearly imperceptible shake of his head that they had more trouble.

Elizabeth rose to her feet. "Ladies, might I have the pleasure of your company in the drawing room. Let us leave the men to their port and cigars."

The men saw the women to the drawing room and then retired to Darcy's study. The door had barely closed before Darcy told the others what he knew. "Gentlemen, I need your assistance. The body of one of my younger footmen has been found outside. I would like for you to accompany me to where he lies and then to a room in the east wing. The light grows thin, and we should examine the scene first."

They made haste, choosing to exit the house through the servants' entrance rather than signaling trouble by leaving through the front door. It took only moments to find the body. The boy lay spread-eagled, face down, in the snow—his face buried in at least six inches of damp whiteness.

"Who found him?" Darcy asked Murray as he slowly turned the body over.

"Lucas saw something from the ballroom window. He was cleaning the wall sconces in there. When he investigated, this is what he discovered."

Adam Lawrence knelt beside Darcy. "When was that exactly?"

"Less than a half hour ago, sir. Mr. Baldwin thought it best to handle this as discreetly as possible."

"Thank you, Murray." His footman stepped back to await other orders.

Worth walked back and forth along the edge of the house, examining the bushes and window casements. Meanwhile, Darcy and Lawrence took note of the young Lawson's injuries. "He has some broken bones, but if he fell from the open window above, that would be consistent with his fall," Lawrence mused aloud.

"As would the contusion on his forehead."

They found nothing at the scene to tell them what had happened, so Darcy led the men to the room above. "These are the chambers where I thought I saw someone when we returned from Lambton that first night." He held the door wide for the others.

The window standing fully wide made the room bitterly cold. However, nothing seemed out of place. They moved cautiously, each of them expecting some sort of evil to be lurking within, but the room was spotless, and everything was pristine.

"I see nothing unusual here," Worth remarked as he circled to the left.

"Only the open window," Stafford murmured.

Darcy crossed to where he could look out the opening. From that position, he could see the image of Lawson's body still in the snow. "He evidently went out head first. There are no scratch marks on the sill, which would indicate that he was not fighting to keep from falling."

"So you do not believe that someone threw him from the window?" Lawrence asked as he came to stand beside Darcy.

"I am not saying that, but I can attest to there being no struggle—no boot marks on the wall or the casing—nothing broken. It seems that he went out…willingly."

"This may explain it." Worth leaned over the bed to peer at a note lying open on the coverlet. Darcy and Lawrence joined him immediately. None of them touched the note, but their eyes searched the words for answers.

Mr. Darcy and My Pemberley Family,

I beg your forgiveness. I done evil and now I must pay. It is said that hell is full of good intentions, and although I intended to

bring honor to me family's memory, temptation and false pride led
me astray. I took some of Pemberley's treasures and sold them for
me own benefit. I be jealous of what others had, and I took what
I thought I deserved, but it be wrong to steal. To make matters
worse, I lost the money in cards. It be a sad life, and I can stand it
no longer. He that knows no guilt knows no fear.

"A suicide note?" Lawrence wondered aloud.

Worth moved to the window. "It would appear so."

Darcy pocketed the confession, knowing he would need to add
it to his extensive notes for the magistrate. "This would answer
the question of the missing items and maybe even the intruder in
Georgiana's chambers, but it says nothing of the string rope or the
arsenic."

"It speaks of doing evil," Worth observed before turning back to
where Darcy stood. "Maybe that is what he meant."

"I think I have as many questions as answers." Darcy examined
the window again before closing it. "We should rejoin the women;
they will wonder what has kept us."

"Are we speaking of this to the ladies?" Lawrence asked as he
picked up the candle.

Darcy followed with a light of his own. "Do we have a choice
at this juncture?"

"I suppose not."

Ten minutes later, they put on their bravest faces and made their
way into the drawing room. "Ah, Darcy," his aunt called. "We
thought to play whist."

He walked past Lady Catherine and straight to where Elizabeth
sat on a settee. Taking a place beside her, Darcy captured her hand
in his. "We should speak about something else, Your Ladyship. If
you would all join us." Darcy gestured to the nearby chairs.

Tentatively, they followed his suggestion, each biting back newfound fears.

"Fitzwilliam?" Elizabeth whispered close to his ear, but he did not respond. Instead, he gently squeezed her hand and then let his thumb trace circles on the inside of her wrist.

When everyone had settled, Darcy cleared his throat. "The viscount, Mr. Worth, and I have spent the better part of the past hour examining a situation in the east wing of the house. The body of one of the Pemberley footmen was found lying face down in the snow while we were still at supper."

"Oh, no!" Mrs. Williams gasped.

"Which one?" Elizabeth demanded.

Darcy turned his head to look at her. "Lawson."

Georgiana audibly caught her breath and reached for Lady Catherine's hand for comfort.

His aunt demanded, "What happened, Darcy?"

Her nephew took up the tale again. "I asked Murray to send Lawson to me today. A report had reached me of the young man shirking his duties—going missing for an hour or more at a time. I felt it prudent to first speak to the boy and then to make my decision to either release him from duties or find a more suitable match for his interests. However, the lad had disappeared. At first, I thought it because he knew of my objections and wanted to avoid our talk. I was in error. The boy, evidently, had decided to punish himself for what he considered to be violations of my trust. It appears from a suicide note that Lawson took his own life by jumping from a third-floor window."

Cathleen voiced the dissent. "That makes no sense, Mr. Darcy."

"I agree, Miss Donnel." He paused before beginning again. "But the room shows no signs of a struggle. Lawson's body has a laceration on the forehead and what appears to be several broken bones, but those could have come from the fall."

"Then what killed the young man?" Lydia tried to understand.

Lawrence provided a possible scenario. "The impact, possibly, or maybe the cold. We have no idea how long the young man lay there before someone noticed him."

"What motive did the suicide note mention?" Anne asked.

"Theft of some of my property, supposedly for spending money and gambling—cards."

Elizabeth became the voice of opposition. "But you gave Lawson a home when he had lost everything—when his father died in the fire. He was always so appreciative. Is it possible that he was still grieving his losses and fell into a depression?"

Miss Donnel asked what none of them could explain. "Even if that was true, Mrs. Darcy, why would the boy add arsenic to Mrs. Jenkinson's drink?"

"Maybe Lawson feared her identifying him. He was out with my steward when the lady viewed my staff. He was the only one she did not inspect."

Lydia chimed in, "But I thought your cook said there was a new footman?"

Elizabeth looked for an explanation. "Lawson has been with us less than three months. Perhaps Mrs. Jennings considers him new in comparison with the others in our employ. We could call her in and ask her."

"Perhaps later, Elizabeth." Darcy gently pulled her closer to him.

Anne's quiet voice interrupted the others. "How do we know the lad took his own life? Other than the note, that is?"

"Just the note, Anne. And the apparent lack of a struggle," Darcy responded.

Worth had joined Anne on a small sofa. "The boy confessed to his thievery and begged Mr. Darcy's forgiveness, Miss de Bourgh. He never admitted to Mrs. Jenkinson's attack, but he claimed to have done evil."

"At least, we know who caused us so many hours of anguish," Lady Catherine murmured.

Suddenly, Georgiana jerked her hand away from her aunt's. As Darcy watched, an acknowledgment of truth passed unspoken between his sister and his wife. "Fitzwilliam," Elizabeth hissed, "you should speak to Georgiana."

Darcy's voice softened, but a demand remained in his tone.

"Georgiana, do you have something to tell us?"

The girl squirmed under everyone's complete attention. "It…it could not," she faltered, "could not have been Lawson who wrote the note."

"How do you know, Georgiana?" Darcy probed.

His sister swallowed hard. "After…after Elizabeth spoke to me today…oh, *Elizabeth!*" she wailed. The tears flowed down her cheeks, and she buried her face in her hands.

"May I?" Elizabeth came to his sister's rescue. Georgiana nodded as she sobbed. "One of Mr. Darcy's complaints against Lawson was that Murray had found him alone with Miss Darcy late at night. I should explain that my sister often goes to the music room when she cannot sleep. Although Murray assured us nothing untoward had happened, I questioned Georgiana regarding the incident. The reason Georgiana knows that Lawson could not write the note is because she was tutoring the boy. Lawson wanted to eventually apprentice under our steward, Mr. Steventon. To do so, the boy needed to learn to read and write. For the past month, Georgiana has given Lawson lessons. She did so without her brother's knowledge because Lawson did not want to admit this lack to Mr. Darcy."

"Lawson could not write a confession." Georgiana raised her head to face the others. "He just recently learned to write his name," she quietly shared.

"Lord," Lawrence nearly moaned, "that compounds the mystery. Someone made Lawson's death appear to be a suicide. If Lawson did not commit the crimes, who did?"

CHAPTER 9

≋ ≋ ≋

THEY ABANDONED THEIR PLANS for cards and music—all thoughts of entertainment gone. Two people had died in the house in less than twenty-four hours, and they had no idea who to blame.

"My Lord, can we not leave—tonight even?" Cathleen whispered as they stood together by the bay window. "I do not think I can sleep in this house another night."

He caught her hand and brought it to his lips. He cared not for the pretense any longer, and if anyone saw, so be it. "I do not see how, my Dear. If it were so, I would have removed you from danger immediately, but I cannot imagine our coach, even unloaded, making it safely to Lambton, or to anyplace else. The snow is too deep. The roads are more dangerous than is this house."

"My Lord, I am frightened." She gripped his hand.

"I will stay with you at night. I will not abandon you. Listen for my knock."

She looked lovingly into his eyes. "Thank you, Adam."

"Mr. Worth, what do you make of this madness?" Anne spoke softly for his ears only.

He shot a furtive glance about the room, assessing everyone's demeanor. "It appears someone has a vendetta against your cousin," he ventured.

"Should I be frightened?" She slid her hand closer to his on the sofa cushion.

Worth saw the movement—saw her fingertips inch closer—and his heart lurched in his chest. Earlier today, he had felt an attraction for the lady's companion—but had he really? Had not Mrs. Jenkinson spent equally as much time extolling the goodness of the woman whose fingertips he now wanted to kiss, as she had praising her late husband? Today, when he and Anne had sat together in the music room, he had remembered everything Mrs. Jenkinson said and realized that the dear lady had wanted him to learn more about Miss de Bourgh. "If you will allow it, I shall place myself as your protector." He moved his hand to where their last two fingers gently touched.

"I would be forever in your debt, sir. You have offered me a peace."

"Lizzy, this is ridiculous!" Lydia Wickham hissed as she pulled her sister toward a nearby alcove where they might speak privately. "This is certainly not why I agreed to come to Pemberley." Lydia crossed her arms across her chest—looking as if she chastised her older sister.

Elizabeth's temper flared, but she forced amusement into her tone. "Well, Lyddie, you said you wanted excitement."

"But not like this," Lydia protested, looking more than a bit irritated with her elder sister's attitude. "I sorely wish I had gone to Hertfordshire instead."

Elizabeth swallowed her initial retort; instead, she said, "In the future, Lydia, maybe you should remember this threat." She clasped Lydia's upper arm. "I am sure that Mr. Darcy and I will celebrate the day that I no longer send you and your wayward husband funds upon which to live. Anytime that you wish to remove yourself from that dependency, I will be happy to receive your tidings. However, until then, you will refrain from making any complaints about these past several days' events. My husband is doing everything humanly possible to resolve this mystery. You will support him with your words and your actions or you can expect your Pemberley money to disappear. Do I make myself clear?"

Lydia jerked her arm away. "Ye-Yes," she stammered. "Yes, I understand."

Evelyn Williams watched the rest of the room. She watched as Mrs. Darcy and her sister argued over something obviously important to Pemberley's mistress. She watched as the young Miss Darcy sought comfort from her older brother and the imperious Lady Catherine de Bourgh. She watched the viscount court his cousin with his eyes and his touch, and she watched Mr. Worth edge his hand toward the one that Anne de Bourgh offered.

The sisterly exchange emphasized the immaturity of one sister and the innate superiority of the other. It had not taken Evelyn long to assess the situation. Mrs. Darcy's obvious intelligence had challenged Mr. Darcy's arrogance, and he had fallen heels over head in love with the woman. The younger sister, however, offered nothing to merit her being in the same family. Lydia Wickham was spoiled and self-centered. Elizabeth Darcy made her point, and Evelyn's estimation of the woman grew.

Georgiana Darcy sat close to her brother. She barely spoke to him or to their aunt, but the girl's eyes did her talking for her. Miss Darcy regretted keeping from her brother her part in the boy's educational plans. She would beg Mr. Darcy's forgiveness in private; yet, despite her shame, the girl's comfort came from her older brother, and she clearly esteemed him above all others. Brother and sister tolerated their aunt in a respectful manner, but neither accepted the lady's precepts.

Viscount Stafford openly demonstrated his affection for his cousin, although Evelyn suspected Cathleen Donnel no relative of the man. They shared no features in common, and the viscount held a reputation, according to Mr. Worth, as a rake. The cut of Miss Donnel's dress said *mistress.* Likely, Mr. Darcy was aware of the relationship and demanded the viscount safeguard Miss Darcy's innocence in exchange for room and board. If the viscount had known the depth of danger into which he brought the woman, Evelyn was sure he would have chosen another shelter.

Finally, she watched Miss de Bourgh and Mr. Worth. It irritated the woman to observe their blossoming relationship. Only yesterday, the man had courted the now-deceased Mildred Jenkinson. His affections shifted easily from one woman to another. However, Evelyn blamed Anne de Bourgh, instead of Worth. The woman blatantly flirted with the solicitor. Evelyn thought she knew Miss de Bourgh's type: the woman who pretended to know nothing of men, but who manipulated hearts on a whim. She held no respect for Miss de Bourgh or the lady's wantonness. Women such as Anne de Bourgh led men to commit desperate acts.

"As the evening is lost, I suggest we retire," Darcy announced. No one voiced dissent; it was as if they had waited for someone to make the suggestion.

Slowly, the party climbed the main stairway. By silent assent, each paused outside his or her respective door, and with a slight nod from Lady Catherine, in unison, they entered their rooms. A succession of locks clicked to block out the evil.

Darcy saw Elizabeth to her chambers and then made the excuse of checking on the household before he retired. She let him go without reproof, knowing that his nature required solitude—time for him to analyze all that had happened.

She, too, needed time to work through what plagued their household. Her husband had not been forthcoming with information, and although she realized Darcy had withheld the details to spare her, Elizabeth took offense. From the day she had accepted Mr. Darcy's proposal, she had envisioned theirs to be a different sort of relationship—one of equals. She appreciated his position as the master of Pemberley and understood his responsibilities; but *she* was the mistress of Pemberley, and those responsibilities were equally hers. Up until these incidents—until this storm—Elizabeth had felt that Darcy shared everything, even the most insignificant details. Now, she saw the pompous, selfish, and somewhat overbearing man she had initially despised. Of course, Elizabeth knew her husband was none of those things—it was her Bennet peevishness shining through. She wanted Darcy to trust her enough to tell her the things he had shared with the viscount and Mr. Worth. She was his wife—his life partner. And they were strangers to each other.

So for two hours, she fumed—she sighed—she stifled her temper—and she waited impatiently for Darcy to return to their shared chambers. She even looked into his room twice to see if he had returned to his own bed without bidding her good night. "Enough is enough," she grumbled as she reached for her robe and slippers.

She took a single candle and made her way to Darcy's study. The door stood ajar, so Elizabeth gave it a mighty shove, sending it slamming into the wall. "Fitzwilliam Darcy, I am your wife," she declared.

Darcy had personally checked all the outside doors, and then he visited the attic, which held both the bodies. He had placed them there and opened the windows to keep them from deteriorating so quickly. He did not know what he would do with them if the storm did not lessen soon. He pulled the sheet away and looked at each face, wondering what could have done differently, somehow preventing this tragedy.

"If it is *I* he wants," he spoke to the empty room, "then I wish he would come for me. Leave the innocents out of this."

Finally, he found his way to his study, where he spent an hour going over every detail of the past few days. *One of my guests*—that was his conclusion—*one of my guests practices murder under my roof.* He had just taken out foolscap upon which to write notes when his study door slammed open and a voice announced, "Fitzwilliam Darcy, I am your wife."

An amused smile turned up the corners of his mouth as he saw his wife framed in the doorway. "I am pleased to hear it, Madam."

Elizabeth flushed. Her declaration had not come out as she had planned, but she shifted her shoulders back, trying to appear taller and more imposing. "Then, sir, I expect you to treat me as such!"

Darcy stood and moved toward her. Despite the dudgeon of his thoughts, his body reacted to his wife's presence. The shift of her shoulders brought her breasts to where they pushed against her gown's white muslin, and Darcy could see them clearly. "And how should a man treat his wife? Have I neglected you, Mrs. Darcy?" He stood before her and reached casually for her hand. Darcy sought to address whatever objection he heard in Elizabeth's voice, as well as the balm her touch always offered. "If it is neglect of which you charge me, I will happily amend my ways immediately and devote myself to you." He brought her hand to his lips, kissing the inside of her wrist.

Instinctively, Elizabeth leaned toward him; then she caught herself. She surreptitiously removed her hand from his. "Your wife does not accuse you of neglect in that realm, sir." She tried to sound precise and chastising. "Instead, I am of the persuasion that you consider me your intellectual inferior when it comes to restoring peace to Pemberley."

The smile of amusement Darcy sported only moments ago quickly disappeared. He realized the seriousness of his wife's charges. "Elizabeth, I have always esteemed your mind. How can you say such a thing?"

"Because you have turned to strangers—relative strangers—when it is I in whom you should place your trust," she asserted. "You expect me to stand beside you—to support you—but you tell me nothing. I hear the news of your investigation at the same time as the other women. I will tolerate it no longer, sir." She tried her best to stare him down—to show Darcy she meant business.

He wanted to reach for her, but he forced his arms to remain at his sides. "Elizabeth, you know I only wished to protect you." He lowered his voice, compelling her to listen to his plea.

However, Elizabeth knew his ploy—had observed this trick in his business dealings and when her husband wished to reason with his cottagers. "Do not try to manipulate me, Mr. Darcy," she warned. "I am not a shrinking violet. And I am capable of protecting myself." She brushed past him, walking closer to the hearth, needing its warmth and also needing to be released from Darcy's intense gaze. "You men seem to think you have the superior minds, but your insights are so narrow—you miss the forest because you study the trees," she asserted.

He loved his wife, but they had argued more than once along these lines. Normally, he took Elizabeth's protestations with good humor, but the strain of the past few days caused Darcy to snap at her. "Then pray tell, my good wife, how you have suddenly found yourself to be so astute."

"Suddenly!" she countered. "I see!" She stormed toward the door. "I will bid you *good night,* sir!"

His initial anger waned as he realized the truth of her charge. She was nearly out the door before Darcy could catch her arm and pull her to him. "Elizabeth." He tightened his grip when she started to resist him. "Do not…" he began. "Do not…walk away from me…Not now, when I need you more than ever before." When she stilled, Darcy cupped her chin. "I love you, Elizabeth," he beseeched her cooperation. "I was terribly terse; it was abhorrent of me." He tugged her closer, so he might wrap his arms about her. When Elizabeth acquiesced and rested her head on his chest, Darcy sighed. "I am truly sorry, Sweetling. I need you every minute of every day. You must know that." He stroked her back.

Elizabeth's arms encircled his waist. Reluctantly, she relaxed into his embrace. *What is the purpose of fighting him?* Anyway, it would be impossible for him to change. He had been born overly protective. "I did not mean my words, Fitzwilliam," she murmured.

Darcy knew her temperament—knew his Elizabeth grudgingly offered an apology. "Please tell me what I missed," he whispered close to her ear. "What does the forest look like?"

"It is nothing," Elizabeth said and shrugged her response.

"It *is* something," Darcy insisted. "If what you felt was important enough for you to bring your anger to my study door, then I need to listen to your thoughts."

She suddenly felt very foolish for losing her temper with him. "It is just a silly feminine whim," Elizabeth muttered before dropping her gaze.

"Although you are all woman, my Love, you are not the type of female to have feminine whims." Darcy smiled at her, but Elizabeth's face said she doubted his sincerity. "Please, Elizabeth. I must know your mind. I concede my own bafflement. I have dwelt on what is happening in this house, and I can see no end to it."

"My supposed insights will not solve the mystery, my Husband." She allowed her index finger to trace the outline of his lips. "I simply saw the fault of your suppositions."

"Then come." He took her by the hand and led Elizabeth to a chair near the fire. He sat and brought her to his lap. Pulling her close, he settled his wife in his arms. "Tell me what you saw that I did not."

"It-it is nothing of genius," she stammered. Elizabeth paused, feeling somehow inept in her husband's presence, but when Darcy remained silent, she continued. "Take young Lawson. Even without Georgiana's story, I knew that he had not committed suicide."

"And how is that?" An eyebrow shot up as he weighed what she had said.

Elizabeth shifted her position so that she might command her husband's full attention. "Let us look at the facts," she stated. "First, in order for Lawson to plunge from the window, he would have needed to step up to the opening, catch the shutters, and step back. Then Lawson would have had to take another step forward, undo the latch, and open the window. Then he would have had to walk a few paces back, turn, run toward the window, and fling himself to the ground. Do you not see the ludicrous position in which you found Lawson? A man set on suicide would not plunge from a window if he literally had to step up three times to throw himself from the opening. A man's nerve would not allow him to step forward, step back, step forward, step back, and then step forward again in order to jump." Excitement now filled her words. "Besides, even if Lawson would have had the nerve to jump from the third floor, he would not have been found lying face down and spread out like an eagle in flight. A man, no matter how desperate—even desperate enough to take his own life—would fight for that same life as he fell through the air. He would not simply spread his arms and legs as if he were a bird and welcome the impact that might kill him. He would have split-second questions about whether he did the right thing. He would try to stop the outcome he had chosen. Such a man would not be so positioned. He would need to be unconscious and pushed from the window in order to be found in the position in which you described Lawson."

"Really? Anything else?" Darcy questioned, awestruck.

"Actually, there is one more important fact that you overlooked."

"And what is that?"

"Well, Mr. Darcy," she said with sarcasm, "you forgot that Lawson was a devout Catholic. The boy would have considered the act of suicide more damning to his soul than the theft of a few household items. He could have offered retribution for the dishonor of the thefts," she declared with certainty. "However, no absolution could be offered for the taking of his own life."

Darcy sat perfectly still, Elizabeth's assumptions weighing heavy on him. "You saw the scene with clearer eyes than I," he muttered.

Elizabeth hid her triumph. "Men and women see life and death differently. Women always see the emotion associated with each act. It is, perhaps, our fate rather than our merit. We cannot help ourselves. We live at home, quiet, confined, and our feelings prey upon us. Those emotions give us a different perspective."

"What else?" he asked impulsively.

"Mrs. Jenkinson's death," she said.

He caught Elizabeth's hands in his; he rubbed his over hers, trying to warm her slender fingers. "What of the lady's demise?" Darcy asked quietly, steeling himself for embarrassment.

She lifted his hand to her mouth and kissed the palm. "I love you, Fitzwilliam." She held his hand to her cheek in quiet devotion. "Maybe we should simply find some sleep. You are exhausted, my Husband."

"I would hear your opinions first, if you please, Mrs. Darcy."

Elizabeth let out a sigh of exasperation. "If you insist, Mr. Darcy."
She regretted the implanted tone as the words escaped her lips; she
recognized the tenuous grounds upon which she stood. She would be
a fool to prove her husband inept—a fool to destroy her marital happiness just to prove a point. "Although I believe," she began slowly, "that
the stranger you seek was in Mrs. Jennings's kitchen the afternoon of
the poisoning, I cannot imagine the phantom footman placed arsenic
in one cup of cider and let Fate guide it to Mrs. Jenkinson's lips."

"But the man threatened the lady." Darcy played the devil's
advocate.

"Exactly." Elizabeth waited for him to draw the same conclusions as she, but when her husband did not follow her thoughts, she
offered up a few hints. "It is not logical, Fitzwilliam." She waited
again. "This is the same man who stole a complete set of bedding
under your servants' noses." Still silence. "Whoever this man may
be, he would leave nothing to chance. If he wanted to specifically
kill Miss de Bourgh's companion, he would devise a practically
foolproof plan to do so. He evidently has access to this house's
many chambers. Poisoning would not be his mode for murder. He
is too ingenious to let Fate guide his hand."

A deeper silence filled the room. "Then you think there is more
to the lady's death than a reported threat from our mysterious staff
member?"

"I cannot say what all the fuss might be. I have made no assumptions. But the facts do not equal such a neatly packaged death.
If you recall, Mrs. Jenkinson offered me the poisoned cup before
she drank it herself. If Fate had taken a twist, it would be I in that
cold attic right now."

A shiver ran down Darcy's back. "Do not even speak such
words," he cautioned. "I could not live without you, Elizabeth."

"Of course, you could. You would remain the master of Pemberley."

Darcy brought her to him, needing to feel her closeness.
"Breathing is not necessarily living, Elizabeth. I never truly lived
until you defiantly breezed into my world."

"Nor I you," she whispered close to his ear. "I should never have fought you."

"On that point, I would agree. We wasted valuable time that we should have spent loving each other."

Elizabeth teased him. "I am ashamed that women are so simple to offer war where they should kneel for peace, or seek for rule, supremacy, and sway, when they are bound to serve, love, and obey."

"Ah, *The Taming of the Shrew*." He lifted an eyebrow. "Shakespeare is correct. Neither a man nor a woman should claim dominion over the other. I should listen not only to my heart but also my head." He stood suddenly, lifting Elizabeth in his arms. "Will you permit me to carry you to our bed, Vixen?"

"I thought you would never ask, Mr. Darcy." She laced her arms around his neck. Resting her cheek against his chest, Elizabeth sighed contentedly.

Nearly at the top of the stairs' first flight, Darcy paused long enough to nuzzle behind her ear. "I need to limit all those cups of chocolate you have devoured of late," he murmured teasingly as his tongue circled Elizabeth's ear.

"What is wrong, my Husband? Married life making you soft?" Elizabeth taunted.

He renewed his efforts and turned toward their private quarters. "I might offer you the same criticism, my Love. Your sweet tooth has grown demanding of late." His words struck a chord, and Elizabeth squirmed to release his hold, but Darcy tightened his embrace. He leaned against the inside wall's painted brocade to steady himself. "Elizabeth, it was a poor attempt at humor." He whispered so as not to wake his guests.

"Put me down, Fitzwilliam," she insisted in hushed tones.

"Do not…do not pull away from me," he pleaded.

"Put me down, Fitzwilliam." Elizabeth repeated.

Slowly, he lowered her to the floor. "Elizabeth?"

But his wife turned and walked purposely away from him, closing and locking her chamber door behind her.

The moment of passion had died—killed by an unwise remark. He rushed to his own door, sending his valet away with just a nod of his head. Darcy did not pause; instead, he traversed the distance between his and Elizabeth's shared dressing rooms and entered her quarters without knocking. "Eliza—" The sight of her froze Darcy in mid stride. She was stretched out across her four-poster, wearing nothing but a smile and her waist-length auburn hair draped about her shoulders. "I-I thought you angry with me," he stammered. His eyes drank their fill.

"Men are so obtuse!" she declared. "I came to my room because what I have to say to you could not be said in a hallway with Pemberley footmen every twenty feet."

Darcy edged closer. "And what would that be, Mrs. Darcy?"

"*I* do not have a sweet tooth, my Husband." She rose to her knees, and Elizabeth lightly rested her fingers on her stomach. "But your *child* certainly does."

Darcy's smile disappeared, and a serious frown wrinkled his brow. Elizabeth watched—pure discontent testing her resolve. Darcy's eyes rested on her fingers; he saw nothing but the way her hand cupped a very slight bulge below her waist. "Fitzwilliam?" she rasped, "did you hear me?"

A nod of his head was all Darcy managed. His eyes remained on Elizabeth's body—the rise of her stomach and the swell of her breasts. He slept beside her each night and had not noticed! "How is it possible?" he murmured.

Elizabeth chuckled. "Surely you do not need for me to explain the mechanics of the act, my Husband."

Darcy snorted. "I meant…I should have realized."

Elizabeth giggled. "This is surreal, Fitzwilliam. I assumed that you would be more demonstrative."

Her words broke the spell. Darcy stepped to the bed and smothered her with kisses. "Elizabeth, how long?" He held her gaze with his.

"Six months."

His hand palmed the swell of her stomach. "Our child." He planted a tender kiss where his hand caressed her. "When may I tell the others?"

"Under the circumstances, with death in the house, it seems incongruous to mention life," she cautioned.

"Yet even with death all around, life goes on. That is the beauty of it—of God's greatest gift to man. Our child, Elizabeth. I am nine and twenty and am a wealthy man at last. Pemberley could fall down around my head, and I would still know happiness, for I will have you and our child."

"Am I to be the only one to undress tonight?" she taunted.

Darcy's smile grew by the second. "I believe I might acquiesce." He loosened his cravat and tossed it on the floor. "Have I ever told you how beautiful you are?"

Elizabeth corrected, "Mrs. Bingley is the beautiful one in my family."

"I beg to differ, Mrs. Darcy. From the moment I saw you, I could not withdraw my eyes from the classic beauty of your face. You possessed me." He kissed Elizabeth's temples, her lips, her cheeks, and the corners of her mouth. "You are the breath—the wind—the sun—my everything." He claimed her mouth and let love consume him. Darcy thought of nothing but his wife and the life she brought to his home. "Holding you in my arms is more exquisite than holding the sky and the stars," he whispered as he loosened the cords holding back the bed's drapery.

James watched from the raised dais behind the fireplace. The sight of Fitzwilliam Darcy making love to his wife—the delectable former Elizabeth Bennet—sickened him. He had once thought it possible that he, too, might know such happiness—a living—a chance to make his name mean something—a wife who would look at him the way Elizabeth Darcy did her husband. As much as James had tried, none of those hopes had come to fruition. With his every *loss,* Fitzwilliam Darcy *gained.* Now, the man was to have his heir—

an heir for the great estate of Pemberley. The Darcy legacy would continue, written in the annals of British history, while his legacy floundered like a fish on dry land. What did he have to show for all his efforts: a rented room, a trade he despised, and a simpering woman clinging to his every move. And all of it was Fitzwilliam Darcy's fault. Every failure came from Darcy. He had not come to Derbyshire to exact a revenge on Darcy, but James would take pleasure in extinguishing Darcy's dreams. When he left Pemberley, he would take Elizabeth Darcy and the man's heir with him. He would leave Darcy nothing—the man had just said that only his wife and unborn babe brought him happiness. Did he not deserve happiness also? Why should Darcy be the golden child?

Secretly, he watched as Darcy undressed and finally released the drape of his wife's four-poster, cocooning them in their love nest. "Enjoy it while you can, Darcy," he whispered to the darkness. "Soon it will be I." He slid the slit closed, locking away the image of contentment he had observed for the past thirty minutes. Picking up the candelabra, he made his way to his makeshift bed. He would need to accelerate the pace of his plan. The worst of the storm had come and gone. Within the next several days, the players would disperse, and he would lose his opportunity to blame Darcy for a series of murders—his chance to destroy Darcy's reputation and his life, an added benefit of his original plan. While he saw to her—saw that she knew misery of the bitterest kind—he would enjoy the Darcy diversion. The reason for his trip into Derbyshire would know the depth of his ire and know how she had brought shame to all who had once revered her name.

CHAPTER 10

∼ ∼ ∼

"MR. WORTH, YOU RESEMBLE the cat licking the cream," Anne de Bourgh teased from across the breakfast table.

The gentlemen slathered blackberry preserves on sliced dark bread. "I had a restful night," he noted.

"Pleasant dreams, then?" Anne's eyes sparkled with girlish mischief.

"Indeed, Miss de Bourgh." Worth assessed the woman's countenance. "I dreamed of infinite possibilities."

Anne's smile grew. "As did I, Mr. Worth."

"I was hoping, Miss de Bourgh, that I might interest you in seeing your cousin's conservatory. Mrs. Darcy assures me that she has cultivated several new species of roses. I am most eager to see them."

Anne shot a quick glance at the other end of the table, where Darcy spoke to his sister. "I would be delighted to accompany you, Mr. Worth." She lowered her voice as if speaking in secret.

Worth noticed her reticence. "Have I placed you in an awkward position, Miss de Bourgh? I would not for the world have you spoken poorly of," he whispered for her ears only.

"No, sir, I have only...only of late taken my life in my own hands, and I, at times, am still unsure of what I should and should not accept." Anne dropped her gaze, staring at the coddled eggs on her plate.

"I assure you, Miss de Bourgh, I have only the highest regard for you."

Anne moved the bits of egg around with a fork. "I will meet you in the hallway leading to the conservatory in three-quarters of an hour."

Worth wanted to say something reassuring, but the lady's mother entered the morning room. He still did not know how best to respond to Lady Catherine—what he would prefer to say to the woman reeked of disrespect, and he refused to allow his dislike for the way the woman treated her daughter to interfere with his interactions with Anne de Bourgh. His courtship of her. Suddenly, Worth realized that it was a courtship. *Out of death comes life,* he thought.

"You are up early, Anne," Lady Catherine remarked.

"I am, Mother." Anne filled her mouth to avoid conversation.

"You must guard your health, Child. You have never been strong; a full night's sleep can only benefit your constitution," Her Ladyship cautioned.

Anne muttered, "I am no longer a child, Mother."

Lady Catherine stared disapprovingly at her daughter. "You are *my* child, no matter your age," the woman declared to the entire table. "And as your mother, I have a responsibility to guide you."

Anne wanted to offer a retort, but a slight shake of Darcy's head warned her to think again. She touched her napkin to her mouth. "If you will excuse me," she announced to the room. "I have some tasks in my chamber to which to attend."

Mr. Worth rose to acknowledge Anne's speedy exit. He had watched the interaction between mother and daughter closely. Anne de Bourgh evidently sought release from the control her mother exerted over her, much to Her Ladyship's displeasure. He wondered how he might fit into the equation. He had developed a fondness for Miss de Bourgh, but he did not wish to be an instrument for the lady's rebellion. As he considered the possibility, he quickly ascertained the disparity in their social status—something he had not considered over the past few days. Being thrown together, society took a back seat to the storm. Now, he saw the futility of such a suit. As the younger son of a minor lord, he had nothing to offer her in rank. He would meet Miss Anne as he requested, but he would make it clear to the lady that he did not have—could not have—designs on her.

"And where is Mrs. Darcy?" Lady Catherine asked sarcastically. "Does she keep city hours in the country?"

"No, Your Ladyship, I do not." Elizabeth swept into the room, pausing only long enough to squeeze Darcy's outstretched hand before taking in the morning table's offering. "I have been in the east wing seeing to the renovations of the last three guest rooms we will be remodeling this winter." After filling her plate with ham and buttered toast, Elizabeth returned to the table, taking the seat on Darcy's left.

"Mr. Baldwin, Mrs. Darcy needs her favorite chocolate." Darcy winked at Elizabeth.

"Yes, Mr. Darcy." The butler motioned to one of the footmen to fill Elizabeth's cup.

Tsk. "Mrs. Darcy should be more observant of her appearance; she should look to her waistline," Lady Catherine observed.

"Actually, Aunt, I find my wife's curves most befitting her position as the mistress of Pemberley. No true citizen of Derby would take orders from a waif of a girl." He gave Elizabeth an enigmatic smile.

"Thank you, my Husband." Elizabeth bit back the laughter bubbling up. They shared a secret regarding their future, and it was lusciously satisfying to know Darcy's devotion to her.

"Well, I still believe a woman who has been *raised* to Mrs. Darcy's standing should be more cognizant of the image she creates." Lady Catherine attacked the eggs and ham on her plate.

Elizabeth feigned humility. "I will take your advice to heart, Lady Catherine." She quickly turned her attention to Mr. Worth. "Do you plan to see the conservatory today, sir?"

"I shall, Mrs. Darcy, with your permission, of course." Worth placed his cutlery beside his plate in preparation for his departure.

Elizabeth smiled at how she had maneuvered Worth and Anne together. "I am most eager for your opinion of my horticultural adventures."

The man chuckled. "Your *manipulations*, Mrs. Darcy, will be carefully noted." He left before he betrayed to the others what he suspected of his hostess.

When the man departed, Lady Catherine observed, "I am not sure that I approve of Mr. Worth's attentions to Anne."

"Why not?" Georgiana spoke before she thought. Elizabeth had asked Darcy's sister's help in convincing Anne of Mr. Worth's sincerity, and the girl thought the whole situation quite romantic.

Lady Catherine glared at Georgiana as if the girl had sprouted horns. "The man is obviously not of the proper social class."

Darcy placed his cup down hard enough to draw his aunt's attention. "Your Ladyship," he spoke in hushed tones, "I have dealt with Mr. Worth previously, and I judge him to be an honorable man. He holds a respected position, and although as a younger son, he has no title, the man would offer the woman he chose something more important—his esteem. If Anne were the object of his affections, I would have no fear that he would run through her fortune. In this age, could a woman ask for more?"

"Mr. Worth?" Anne came up behind him. He stood admiring a set of armor proudly displayed in the access hall.

He turned to smile at her, and Anne felt a certain calm steal over her. She had wondered what he thought of her after her verbal exchange with her mother earlier. "Ah, there you are, at last." He reached for her hand, placing it on his arm. "I feared you might have changed your mind."

"Would that have been a disappointment, sir? You might still enjoy the Darcys' conservatory." She allowed him to lead her along the passageway.

"I cannot imagine the beauty of the place being nearly as inviting without your presence, Miss de Bourgh." He leaned close, speaking softly only to her ears. Less than an hour earlier, he had vowed to make it known to the lady that he would seek his suit elsewhere, but as soon as he had heard her voice behind him, Worth's reason left him.

Anne blushed thoroughly. "I suppose I should have asked one of the maids to accompany us," she noted while looking back over her shoulder, almost expecting one to materialize.

"You have nothing to fear from me, Miss de Bourgh," he assured her. "We have already spent several hours alone together, in a perfectly proper way."

Anne shook her head. "No, Mr. Worth, I can charge you with nothing. You were the perfect gentleman."

He held the door for her. "Then join me, Miss de Bourgh. We will continue to let nature take its course."

Anne took a deep breath to steady her nerves. "To nature," she said softly.

For thirty minutes, they strolled among the plant rows, admiring the predictable, as well as the more unusual offerings. Worth watched as Anne's delicate fingers caressed an orchid's leaves. "Your touch is so tender," he remarked. "It is like the kiss of a butterfly."

Anne paused, hand extended. "I have never been allowed such freedoms," she whispered.

"The freedom to know a flower?" He seemed confused. "Surely you deceive me, Miss de Bourgh."

"I wish I did, Mr. Worth." Anne turned to face him. "My mother convinced me and everyone else that I was of a delicate nature. She would consider this time we spend together as an endangerment to my health—the warm moisture in the air—the exotic plants. Other than to occasionally smell the fragrance of the flowers cut and displayed in vases about Rosings Park, I have never truly experienced the beauty of nature."

"Surely you have elaborate gardens at your home, Miss de Bourgh."

She turned away slightly, ashamed of her assertions. "For years, I have been forbidden to take a brisk walk, spend time in the garden, practice music—to experience life. Is that not strange, Mr. Worth? I am nearly eight and twenty and know less of life than my seventeen-year-old cousin. Until recently, I have never even been anywhere without my mother's presence or without her permission."

Nigel Worth's heart went out to the woman. He directed her to a nearby bench, where they sat in silence for a few moments. "Might I ask, Miss de Bourgh, what prompted you to defy Her Ladyship?"

Anne sat with her eyes down, studying her hands as they rested in her lap. "In truth, the thing that changed everything was Mr. Darcy's marriage. You see, from my earliest memories, I have been told that I was to marry my cousin. My mother claimed that it was his mother's hope, as well as hers. And although I have never felt anything beyond admiration for Mr. Darcy, I accepted my mother's assertions about my future. Her Ladyship protected and cajoled and demanded and loved in her own way, and I am a product of all her ministrations and admonitions. And it never occurred to my mother that Mr. Darcy showed no desire to marry me—barely even spoke to me when he called at Rosings. I experienced no Season—had no taste of Society—possessed not even a friend until Mildred Jenkinson came to stay with me. I have had no flirtation— no broken heart—no great love."

Anne brought her eyes to meet his steady gaze. "Then Fitzwilliam fell in love with Elizabeth Bennet. If you could have seen how he pined for her when she visited her friend Charlotte Collins at Hunsford! Mildred and I spoke of it often over the weeks that Miss Bennet stayed there in the Collinses' household. Fitzwilliam was besotted with the woman, and I knew then that, no matter what my mother did, my cousin would never propose marriage to me. I was an old maid before I had ever experienced my first relationship. Miraculously, Mr. Darcy married his love, and my mother bewailed the *merits* of having a daughter with no redeeming qualities." Mr.

Worth started to correct her, but Anne's glance stopped him cold. "Do not protest my words, Mr. Worth. I know what I possess: I am an heiress of considerable wealth. So I decided that I might use that to my advantage.

"Another cousin, Colonel Edward Fitzwilliam, called recently at Rosings, and with him came an associate, Lieutenant Robert Harwood. The lieutenant gave me the type of attention for which I was starving—the kind I had never known. To make a long story short, he asked me to go with him to Liverpool when his orders changed. Of course, I refused. How could I chance a flirtation of the heart? I had no reason, I thought, to trust the gentleman's sincerity. Yet, within days of the lieutenant's departure, I realized that he could be my only chance to marry; so despite Mildred's adamant warnings, I covertly devised a plan to follow the lieutenant."

Anne straightened her spine. "It is not something of which I am proud, but my mother found me in a Liverpool inn with the gentleman. She took me out of the establishment before the lieutenant returned. I am a ruined woman, Mr. Worth—not ruined in the strictest sense of the word, but ruined just the same. Because I enjoy your company, I had to tell you the truth. It would be unfair of me to do otherwise."

Immediately, Nigel Worth caught her hand, bringing her fingers to his lips. "My dear Miss de Bourgh, if you think anything you just said affects my growing fondness for you, you are mistaken. I would deem it an honor to be allowed to show you the world's simple pleasures. As far as your so-called ruination, I count it as only one of life's lessons. Our time together may also prove to be another of those lessons, but I would prefer to see where this initial interest leads. I am successful in my profession, and although I could not offer you the kind of luxury you have in Kent, I could provide a modest home in Cheshire. You could be the mistress of your own house if that is what you choose. I am to run for the House of Commons in the next election. I have my supporters and my detractors, of course, but I hold a reputation as an honest man, and most people deal with me as such. Would you consider such a life, Miss de Bourgh? Could you see yourself as the wife of a country gentleman—a solicitor by trade?" Anxiety filled his voice.

Anne instinctively caressed his cheek. "How has a man of your integrity escaped marriage for so long?"

He squeezed her hand and returned it to his arm. "Unlike you, I knew love as a young man. However, the object of my affection, despite the understanding between our fathers, chose another. I could not force the lady to share herself with me if she affected another, and so I withdrew my suit. She married the other fellow and has four children about her all the time."

A twinge of jealousy rocked Anne's being. "Then you see her regularly?"

"The occasional country assembly or that sort of thing," he admitted.

Anne's cheeks flushed. "You must have loved the lady violently if you have never married."

"I cannot say that I loved Marion. I think I loved the idea of her, but she needed to know happiness so I released her to Jacob Crumb. To settle my life, I concentrated on my profession, and time went by. In the past few years, however, I have been more open to the possibility of finding a life partner."

"Tell me of your home, your family, and your friends. I wish to know everything about you." Anne spontaneously rested her head on Worth's shoulder. He slid his arm about her and pulled her closer to him. They sat in the conservatory's center, where no one could see them. He relaxed into the recitation, telling her amusing anecdotes about his cousin's fetish for Gothic novels, his mother's favorite bread pudding, and his best friend's recent courtship of the local baronet's daughter. For nearly two hours, they laughed and commiserated and shared and became intimate friends. They compared their tastes in food and in music and in art. Many things they held in common; others, they did not, but their differences were minuscule in the scope of what they accomplished that day.

"I suppose we must return to the main house," he said as he eased Anne away from him.

She bit her lower lip. "We have been here so long; it is probably for the best if we return separately. I would not wish to meet my mother unexpectedly."

"I imagine Her Ladyship would not approve of our keeping company, even if we were chaperoned."

"My mother disapproves of so many things," Anne observed matter-of-factly.

Worth stood to make his leave. "Lady Catherine will see our relationship as one of disparity. My family is landed gentry, but nothing of your quality. My older brother inherited with my father's passing, and I attended the university with the purpose of studying law and building my life around that profession. Yet, you must realize Miss de Bourgh, that when I look at you, I see an interesting woman. I see Anne de Bourgh, an adventurous spirit, not Lady Catherine de Bourgh's only child and heir." He extended his hand to her.

Anne gladly accepted his outstretched hand. "I never thought otherwise, Mr. Worth."

He moved through the darkened passageways, the single candle offering little light. He had traversed these tunnels dozens of times the past few days. Today, he searched for weapons. His friend Gregor MacIves had managed to remove the silver sword displayed with the suit of armor. A bit heavy for normal usage, it could still be used to exact justice. James wished that he had more guns than the two he had brought with him. The chances of locating others in the house appeared slight. He knew from past experience that Darcy kept several under lock and key in his study, but gaining access to that particular room had become difficult since the first death.

Like James, MacIves had foolishly allowed several of Darcy's staff members to see him and even speak to him in the early hours of the operation. At the time, both he and Gregor had thought it quite amusing to move among Darcy's trained staff without being

apprehended. Now, James wished they had kept more to themselves. Because of their carelessness, he could no longer move freely
through Pemberley's hallways, making it more difficult to find food
and additional candles. Plus, the darkened tunnels were cold and
uninviting, and he sorely wanted to be free of them for a few hours.

Carefully, he climbed the stairs leading to the second level. Besides Darcy's study and several sitting rooms, this level sported additional guest quarters and the main ballroom. There were four secret
doorways on this floor. Easing into an empty guest room through
an opening behind the wardrobe, he moved quietly to the door.
He released the lock and opened it a few inches so that he might
observe the goings-on. Servants cleaned wall sconces and picture
frames, but no one seemed to be searching for him, a fact that he
could not understand, but one he gladly accepted.

If the roads had not turned impassable, he might have stolen
some of the rooms' smaller items and taken them to the next village
to sell for a quick profit. But now there was no urgency to fill sacks
with silver candlesticks or cutlery. Besides, the missing items would
increase Darcy's efforts to capture him, and right now, James wanted
Darcy to assume that he no longer "haunted" the main house.

Leaving the servants behind, he returned to the blackened passageways. Giving his eyes a moment to adjust to the darkness, he took
up the candle again and climbed to the next level. Fewer openings
were available on this floor. One was in Georgiana Darcy's room, and
the other in the room originally given to Miss de Bourgh's companion. That room now stood empty, a happy circumstance for him.
There were other openings—ones he used to observe the Darcys,
the viscount, and his objective—mere slits through which he could
watch the comings and goings of the room's occupants without being
detected. The slits were hidden among the items decorating the walls.
One was a three-inch section of painted woodwork next to a light
fixture; another was hidden by the edge of a picture frame. The best
one, in Elizabeth Darcy's room, was the bottom support for a beveled mirror hung over the mantel. James enjoyed watching Elizabeth
Darcy. He marveled at the intimacy the lady shared with her husband.

From the doorway of what had been Mrs. Jenkinson's room, James watched as Anne de Bourgh slipped into the room next to Georgiana Darcy's. Evidently, Darcy's cousin had changed rooms after the first death. That suited him well, giving him some freedom he would not have had otherwise. Miss Darcy followed closely behind her cousin. The girl had matured dramatically over the past two years. Her sweet innocence had become an ethereal sort of beauty. Her pale skin and the soft blonde curls framing her face reminded him of a Greek goddess; he imagined her draped in white satin and posing, statue like. In his imagination, she posed for him before he undressed her and sated himself.

Finally, Elizabeth Darcy entered the hallway, followed closely by her younger sister. "Let us see if the blue muslin will fit you. I think a tuck or two will be just what you need to make the dress work for you. It will go better with your coloring than mine." The women slipped inside Lydia Wickham's room without noticing his peering out at them.

Without further ado, he closed the door gently and slid through the open passageway into the darkness. He would make his way to the secret door in the cold cellar. There he would take a round of cheese and some cold ham. The mid-afternoon meal beckoned. If luck stayed with him, he might also find a carafe of port or wine, maybe even an apple or some other fresh fruit.

Tonight, he might risk sleeping in one of the east wing's empty rooms. Even the extra blankets and counterpanes that he hid in his secret antechamber could not ward off the passage's cold. He wanted Darcy to develop a false sense of security—to think that his "phantom" had departed. He would take care neither to disturb the bedding nor take so much food that it would be easily missed. He would give the impression that the danger had passed. With a satisfaction he had not anticipated, James made his way to the below-stairs level. Soon, he thought—tomorrow or the next day—he must leave. Yet, today would be the day he made it all happen.

CHAPTER 11

A CONSISTENT LIGHT TAPPING came on his wife's chamber door in the middle of the night. A bad omen. Darcy fought his way to consciousness and rolled to the side of the bed. Elizabeth pulled the sheet to her chest as he slipped on his breeches and robe.

"What is it, Fitzwilliam?" she whispered from behind the bed drape.

"I do not know." Darcy made his way to the door and cracked it a few inches to look into the worried face of his butler. "What is so important, Mr. Baldwin, that you wake me at this hour?"

"Forgive me, Mr. Darcy," the man said as he adjusted the candle he carried. "I had the men checking the house, just as you ordered. Jatson reports that the door to one of the rooms in the east wing is locked from the inside. It was not locked when he made his rounds at ten o'clock. I have placed him on guard outside the room, and I have the master key here." He held up a ring of keys.

Darcy opened the door wider. "Let me find some shoes and retrieve my gun." He turned around. Elizabeth stood beside the bed, her gown and robe on. "Stay here," he ordered before she could speak. "Lock the door and do not open it to anyone except me."

"Be careful, Fitzwilliam," she cautioned.

He squeezed her hand before exiting the room. Darcy paused long enough to hear her turn the key lock and then followed his men through the shadowy hallways of his home. His heart raced—the possibility of catching the mysterious intruder made him breathless.

A stranger had invaded Pemberley, and try as he might, Darcy had been unable to capture the man. He possessed a description of the intruder, and Darcy had set his men as guards throughout the house, hoping to detain the interloper without any more deaths. Now, it appeared that his enemy boldly took up residence in one of Darcy's guest rooms. Apprehending the man would give Darcy great pleasure.

Mr. Baldwin, Darcy, and Murray paused at the end of the hallway, preparing their assault.

"Mr. Baldwin will set the key and quickly turn the lock. Then you and I will charge the room, Murray." Darcy cocked the small handgun he carried. "Be careful—all of you." He motioned Jatson to join them. "I want no more deaths in this house."

"I be not leavin' the hall, Mr. Darcy. No one be 'scapin' the room," Jatson assured him.

"Good man." Darcy and the others began to edge toward the designated room. They stepped slowly and cautiously, avoiding the creaking floorboards. Darcy motioned Mr. Baldwin to the other side of the door frame.

Slowly and meticulously, the butler silently slid the master key into the keyhole and steadied his hand. With a nod of his head, Darcy indicated to his man to turn the key and to step back. Mr. Baldwin followed the silent order. He turned the key, the lock loudly echoing in the empty hallway. Immediately, all hell broke loose. Darcy and Murray hit the door together, but it did not give. Instead, a straight-backed chair, lodged under the handle, and a nearby desk blocked the way. They doubled their efforts, hitting the door with shoulders and shoving with all their might. *So much for the element of surprise!*

James entered the east wing guest room after the Darcy household had retired for the night. He made his rounds, checking the rooms to which he had access. He saw, for example, the viscount, attired in a casual manner, leave the room assigned to him. The man checked over his shoulder repeatedly as he made his way down the right hall. James assumed that His Lordship slept elsewhere. He could see the other bedrooms—or at least, the hallway leading to them. But the man did not enter those areas designated for the family. Instead, the viscount turned to his left, moving stealthily through the shadows. Only two rooms in the main hallway were occupied: one by the widow and one by the viscount's extremely attractive cousin. James's intuition told him that the man's cousin was move than a *relative*—likely, the future earl's mistress. The fact that Darcy would tolerate such an alliance under Pemberley's roof surprised him. The master of Pemberley had softened, which would help him defeat Darcy.

Leaving Darcy's guests to their own amusements, he made his way to the house's empty wing. For a change, he would spend the night in a real bed. He would sleep in his clothes, something he did quite often of late. To secure the room, he wedged a chair under the door handle, setting the straight-back chair at a forty-five degree angle. He turned the key softly to lock the door. Finally, he slid a desk to block the door frame. All those precautions would give him time to escape if Darcy and his men discovered him.

He left the secret passage's latch unhooked and the door slightly ajar, making it easier to shove it open, as well as setting the sword at ready. Then, as a diversion, he released the window's locking mechanism. Finally, he crawled into the bed, tossing the counter-pane over him and cradling a pillow. He needed a night's sleep. For a week, he had slept a few hours here and a few more there. The lack of sleep affected his ability to deal with Darcy's household effectively.

He rested for three solid hours. Once James thought he heard someone in the hallway, but the noise moved away, and he drifted back to sleep; so when the key turned in the lock, he did not expect it, but it instantly alerted him. Jumping from the bed, he threw the linens aside. He had planned his escape carefully, and as he hurried toward the secret passageway, he paused only long enough to pull the shutters and the window open.

Krr-thump! His head snapped around at the sound of bodies hitting the barricaded door.

"Push!" He heard Darcy order his servant. He would have liked to stay and see Darcy's face when he realized who the intruder was—but it was too soon. He still had scores to even and vengeance to exact, so he wedged his fingers into the opening and slid the fake door open far enough to fit his body through. Catching the lever on the other side, he swung the door into place and secured the latch just as Darcy and his man hit the door a second time—splintering the legs of the wedged chair and shoving the desk away from the opening.

Darcy and Murray hit the door a second time. Darcy heard the wood split and in the small opening he saw a flash of color move away from the bed and toward the far wall. As he and Murray put their backs into moving the furniture piled before the door, a rush of cold air swept through the opening. A loud click punctuated their efforts.

When the desk finally gave way, and he and Murray managed to squeeze through the narrow opening, Darcy's anger took hold. Even before he made his stumbling entrance into the room, he knew they would find nothing. Turning around once and then once more, he took in the entire room. Other than the chair, desk, messy bed, and an open window, nothing was out of place. "Damn!" he hissed. "What the bloody hell is going on in this house?" Out of pure frustration, he forcibly flipped the desk on its side. If not for the heavy furniture, they could have cornered the intruder.

"I do not see anything outside, Mr. Darcy." Mr. Baldwin leaned out the window, looking for traces of the man's escape. "I see no footprints in the snow."

"I do not think the intruder went out the window." Darcy's eyes searched the walls. He motioned Murray through to the adjoining passage, although intuitively Darcy knew the footman would find nothing.

Moments later, Murray returned empty-handed. "I went all the way through the other room, Mr. Darcy. All the way to the outside hall. The only thing I encountered was Jatson, where we left him. He swears no one came his way. The man had to go out the window. Maybe he went up instead of down?"

"Our phantom scaled the icy walls and entered an open window of the tomb we have created on the upper floor? Absent supernatural powers, that is not possible, Murray."

The footman shrugged. "Where else could he be, sir?"

"I wish I knew, Murray." Darcy released the gun's cocking mechanism. He would not need the weapon tonight. Earlier this evening, he and the viscount had discussed the possibility of the specter's departure. Things had seemed to resume a normalcy as the day progressed. Georgiana had returned to the piano. Elizabeth and Lydia had taken on the alteration of one of his wife's summer gowns for her sister. Mr. Worth and Anne had reportedly sat in the conservatory for hours. Mrs. Williams and his aunt, along with Miss Donnel, had played loo, while he and the viscount had taken up a closely matched game of chess. Throughout, his men had remained on watch, but nothing out of the ordinary had happened, and he had relaxed, thinking the worst over.

Now, he chased a ghost—a shadow. No wonder his people entertained the possibility of a haunting—of a shadow man taking up residency at Pemberley. If he was not a man of logic, Darcy thought he might believe in such legends himself. He simply hoped that warmer weather would make an appearance soon, releasing Pemberley from Winter's icy death grip.

"Close it." He gestured toward the window. "Nothing to see here." He walked about the room, letting his fingers trace the wallpaper, looking for something—he knew not what. "He just disappears—into thin air." His fingers continued their journey.

The sound of a *thud* brought his attention to the hall. "What the hell!" he grumbled as they turned toward the door.

He heard the stirrings from the other side of the darkened passage. James would have liked to see the expression on Darcy's face when he found an empty room, but for now he needed a distraction. He knew Darcy well, and he did not think the man would consider the window a viable exit. Darcy, he realized, would search until he found the secret door.

Therefore, he made his way to this wing's other opening—one where the fire place hearth separated and swung inward. He left the secret entrance standing wide open and made his way across the shadowy bedroom. He eased the door open and blinked at the hallway's muted lights. The one footman stood staring off in the direction of the open doorway. Quietly, he swung the door wide. Taking the sword that MacIves had stolen from the suit of armor, he edged forward until he stood less than two feet away from Darcy's man. He raised the sword above his head and brought it down hard.

Jatson St. Denis stood at his post, watching the hallway. He wished to be a part of the assault on the room, but Mr. Darcy had told him to secure the hallway. He noted the struggle of the young master and Murray, but made no move to help them. Mr. Darcy had given him specific orders to guard the hall, making sure that no one exited the rooms in the vicinity of the one Mr. Darcy had entered. That was what he would do.

Within moments, Murray had opened the door of the adjoining chamber. Despite expecting it, Jatson had still flinched when Murray jerked the door from its frame and spoke to him. "Did you see anything?" the other footman demanded.

"No…no one. I be in this hall since I found the locked door. No one else come this way."

Murray disappeared back the way he had come, but Jatson did not desert his post. He stood his ground even when he heard Mr. Darcy obviously take his frustration out on the bedchamber's furniture.

Patiently, he waited for the next order from Pemberley's master. His job paid better than any similar position in the area, and Jatson, whose wife had recently delivered a son, would do nothing to jeopardize his child's future. They were saving for a small cottage. Deep in thought, daydreaming of his wife and child, at first he was unaware of danger until he observed the long, reflected shadows from the wall sconce. Someone stood behind him.

Jatson wanted to move, but he had heard tales of the Shadow Man all his life, and a small part of him——the part that controlled his feet—believed the legends. His body stiffened as the shadow came closer. Then the phantom raised his hands above his head, and Jatson saw the image of a sword ready to exact justice, and he could no longer remain rooted to the spot.

Swiftly as the sword made its descent, he twirled around, knocking the weapon to the side. The intruder was closer than he had anticipated, and Jatson found himself stumbling backward against the wall. The sword found a home—his arm burned with the weight of the cut.

He raised the blade above his head and brought it down hard. But Darcy's footman turned at the last second, as if the man knew his peril. The watchman staggered from the momentum, and the sword took a jagged chunk from the man's arm.

Knowing he had only seconds to escape, James used the hilt of the weapon to deliver a blow across the side of the man's head, knocking the footman to the floor. Dropping the sword, he fled through the bedchamber door, closing it quickly behind him and rushing to the open hearth. He swung the secret entry closed and grabbed the candle he had left on the inside step. Purposefully, he made his way to the lowest level. While Darcy tended the wounded footman, James would raid the cold cellar again in anticipation of a long day. Hopefully, he could find a loaf of Mrs. Jennings's bread or a few boiled eggs. He would be enclosed in the secret passage until he was ready to make a stand against Darcy—maybe not tomorrow, but soon.

The sound of the *thud* brought Darcy's attention to the hall. "What the hell!" he grumbled as he turned toward the door. "Jatson!" he called, seeing the footman lying prostrate upon the carpet runner. Darcy rushed forward, kneeling by his man. "Jatson," he said again as he lifted his servant's head. His hand came back covered in blood. "Murray, tear one of the sheets from the bed. Jatson needs a bandage."

Murray rushed to the room they just vacated and returned with a sheet trailing behind him. He tore at the material, pulling off long strips.

Darcy reached for the strips and began to wrap them around the footman's head. "Mr. Baldwin, we will need help moving him to one of the other rooms. And send for Mrs. Reynolds."

"Yes, Mr. Darcy." The butler rushed to do his bidding.

"Murray, come here. Hold the bandage—press here to stop the blood flow." Darcy released the folded cloth to his trusted servant. Then he grabbed the torn sheet, stripping off another long piece. He wrapped the man's arm. "This one looks bad, but it does not seem too deep." He tied the piece to secure it in place.

Mr. Baldwin and two others returned at a run. "Let us place him in one of the main hallway rooms," Darcy ordered as the men positioned themselves where they might lift Jatson's unconscious body. "I will tell Mrs. Darcy of our trials and then come to his room."

"Yes, Mr. Darcy."

He leaned against the inside wall, trying to stay out of their way. Watching them go, Darcy gave a silent prayer of thanks that no one had lost his life in tonight's altercation. Instinctively, he picked up the sword. It was his sword; he recognized it immediately. Motioning for another of his men to see to the clean up, Darcy made his way to his wife's chambers. What would he tell her? Would Elizabeth see things he did not, or had her previous admonishments opened his eyes to the evil that had invaded his home?

He tapped lightly on her door. "Elizabeth," he whispered.

She threw the door open and pulled him into the room, embracing him. "Thank God you are well!" Her tears streamed down her cheeks. "I was terrified." She encircled his waist with her arms and snuggled into his warmth.

Darcy kissed the top of her head. "I have only a few minutes. Jatson was hurt, and I must see to his care. Hopefully, he saw the man and can tell us more."

"Then our mysterious visitor was there?" She tilted her head back so she might see Darcy's face.

"He barricaded himself in one of the east wing guest chambers. Evidently, he slept in the room. Murray and I had to push back the desk and a chair before we could enter the room. By the time we did, our phantom had disappeared. I saw a flash of color—actually of his coat when we first made our foray, but that was all. The window stood wide open, but we both know he had not jumped out the window." Elizabeth nodded her head in agreement. "Within a few minutes, we heard a noise in the hall. Jatson was unconscious; he had a head wound and a slice across his arm. The intruder used the sword from the armor."

"The one in the hallway leading to the conservatory?"

"I believe so. I left the sword in the hall; I did not want to frighten you unnecessarily. There is blood on the blade."

Elizabeth released her hold on him. "I want to go with you. Mrs. Reynolds may need my assistance. Help me with my dress." She untied the belt of her robe. "I will wear my old muslin over my chemise." She reached for the dark gray dress. "You will lace me up?"

Darcy took off his own robe and slipped a shirt on. He donned his stockings and boots while Elizabeth put on the day dress. Then he moved behind her to tighten the laces. "You should abandon your corset. It cannot be good for the child." His voice sounded distant; his mind was elsewhere.

"I will as soon as this situation resolves itself. Then we can tell everyone our news." She turned toward the door. "Let us do what is necessary, and then we will find comfort in each other's arms."

The adrenaline gone from his body, Darcy nearly dragged himself along behind her, but his energy revived when he saw Jatson awake and sitting up in bed. Elizabeth led the way into the room, rushing to Mrs. Reynolds's side. "How may I help?"

The housekeeper looked up and smiled. "I knew you would come, Mistress." She handed Elizabeth the bowl of soapy water. "Clean the arm wound so I might bind it."

"Certainly." Elizabeth sat on the bed's edge. She gently touched the servant's arm. "Mr. Darcy and I are remorseful that you were injured, Mr. St. Denis." Elizabeth dabbed at the wound, cleaning away the blood and the loose skin. "And we are very thankful for your dedication to the estate."

"It be nothing, Mrs. Darcy." The man felt the honor of Pemberley's mistress tending to him personally. "I be sorry I did not catch the blighter meself."

"Your safety is more important." Elizabeth soothed the area with the balm Mrs. Reynolds had handed her. "Is it not, my Husband?"

Darcy stood in the open doorway, framed by the hall lights. He watched with pride as his wife assumed the responsibility of tending to his man. He had known all along that Elizabeth Bennet would love his estate and would tend to Pemberley as he did, but to observe her kindness and charity firsthand made him love her even more—made him thankful that he had won her heart—made him count the blessings of having Elizabeth as his child's mother. "Absolutely," he said as he entered the room. "And you are not to worry. We will see that you and Mrs. St. Denis are well taken care of while you heal."

"Thank ye, Master. My Dorothea will sleep better, knowin' our young'un will not suffer while I not be workin'."

Darcy came to the bed's other side. "Do you suppose you might tell us what happened?" He noted how Elizabeth and Mrs. Reynolds continued to work in tandem while tending Jatson's wounds. They did not speak, but a nod of the head or a gentle touch did it all.

"Well," Jatson began, his head turned away from the women's ministrations. "Ye be knowin' how Murray be comin' to ask if I sees anyone."

"Yes…yes, we know all that."

"I be standin' where's ye left me, Mr. Darcy. And I be thinkin' how this be a good job, and how my missus be happy to have the extra pay now that we havin' our Jobe."

Elizabeth looked up from her bandaging duties. Mrs. Reynolds had slipped from the room to get some laudanum from her medicine pantry. "That is right! I had totally forgotten about your new son, Mr. St. Denis. I hope the boy is doing well."

"He be growin' stronger every day, Mistress."

"I am pleased to hear it." Elizabeth tightened the bandage to hold it in place.

Darcy cleared his throat, bringing the man's attention back to his story. Jatson blushed and continued. "Anyways, I be noticin' an eerie feeling, and then I sees it—a shadow person standin' behind me."

Darcy frowned. "How could you see someone behind you?" He purposely ignored the reference to a shadow man. He would give no credence to the superstition.

"I be seein' the man's silhouette on the floor next to mine. Then he raises a sword above his head. I couldn't move at first, but the sword skeered me, so I's turned. I's knocked the sword aways 'fore he be cuttin' off'n me head with it, but it cuts me arm instead."

Darcy asked anxiously, "Did you see the man's face?"

"I sees it, Mr. Darcy, right'n before he's hittin' me head."

Darcy leaned closer, praying there was some logical clue. "Can you describe the man? Did you recognize him?"

"He be lookin' like what ye already be knowin'. I's don't suspect I kin tell ye anything new." Darcy looked away in frustration. Jatson noted his employer's disappointment. "But I's kin tell ye I's seen him before, Mr. Darcy."

Darcy's head snapped around in anticipation. "Where? Where have you seen the man before?"

Jatson dropped his eyes. "I kin't be sayin' for sure, but I sees him recently, sir. Maybe I's kin study on it a bit."

"I would appreciate anything you can remember, Mr. St. Denis." Darcy began to move away from the bed. "I see Mrs. Reynolds has prepared some medicine to help you rest. Mrs. Darcy and I will leave you to mend." He reached for Elizabeth's hand. "Mrs. Reynolds, you will let me know if Mr. St. Denis needs anything else."

"Yes, Mr. Darcy." She spooned the laudanum into Jatson's mouth. "In the morning, I will send Lucas to let Dorothea know why Jatson does not return home. I do not want her to bring the babe out in the cold when we are capable of taking care of her husband here."

"That is most thoughtful, Mrs. Reynolds," Elizabeth said as she returned to Darcy's side. "We will see you in the morning."

"Yes, Mrs. Darcy."

Silently, they returned to their shared chambers and remained silent as they prepared for bed a second time. Darcy stoked the fire and straightened the bed linens as Elizabeth released the loose braid of her hair. Finally, they crawled in bed, burrowing under the blankets, seeking warmth. Only when Darcy released the drapery from its tie-back did they venture to voice their thoughts. "We were so close, Elizabeth." She rested her head on his shoulder while Darcy aimlessly stroked her arm. "I do not know what else to do. I feel that I cannot ensure Pemberley's safety," he confessed in a whisper.

Elizabeth knew Darcy's admittance came with great difficulty. "We are just overlooking something obvious," she assured him. "Have we any enemies—anyone displeased with the way we have dealt with them of late?"

"There is always someone." Darcy rolled on his side, so he might look upon her face. "Yet, even though a merchant might complain, the anger is not enough to commit murder." He caught her hand and brought it to his chest, pressing it to his heart. "Our intruder has likely taken one life—Lawson's—and he tried to end Jatson's this evening. I have known men to take revenge for a supposed wrongdoing, but I have never known such evil. It is beyond my way of thinking. Who sets out to murder another?"

"A madman."

The impact of her words struck them both dumb for several moments. "How do we fight a madman?"

"More aggressively than we have done so to date. We need to make it harder for him to find food…to find a place to sleep. We must flush our phantom out. Right now, we are reacting to his appearances—to his attacks. We need to be the pursuers, rather than the pursued."

Darcy did not respond right away, taking time to reflect on what she had proposed. "What else might we do?"

"We need for Mrs. Jennings to take stock of the supplies in the pantries. We need to block off entrances to the root cellar and cold cellar. I refuse to fill the stomach that wreaks havoc in my household." Her chin rose in defiance.

Darcy took note of her declaration that this was her household. It was what he had always wanted—a woman with the same devotion to Pemberley as he. Elizabeth had made the place her own, and even though she had ordered only subtle changes in the décor, she filled Pemberley's walls with her personality. Since the day he had first walked her up the front steps and into the main foyer, the place carried her mark. She possessed him as much as she did his home. "I will see to it first thing in the morning," Darcy agreed. "Have you other suggestions?"

"We need a pattern of where our intruder has been seen. The east wing is obvious, but which rooms?" Elizabeth knitted her brow. "He was in Georgiana's room. That disturbs me…She may be in danger."

Darcy stiffened with the thought of his sister's possible peril. "You believe Georgiana did not have a nightmare?"

"At first, I took much of what she said as nerves, but I felt the cold air rushing through her room, Fitzwilliam. Yes, I believe the light she saw was our *ghost*."

"She needs someone else sleeping in her room. I will assign two maids to sleep on pallets until we find this man, and Georgiana is not to pay midnight visits to the music room. You and I must insist on it."

"Of course." Elizabeth bit her bottom lip, indicating she had other ideas. Finally, she found her voice. "I know you well enough, my Husband, to know that you have made the connection. We had no problems at Pemberley until we opened our doors to strangers."

Darcy looked relieved. He had drawn similar conclusions the preceding evening. "I have considered," he began slowly, "that one of our guests could be our practitioner—he is one of them. Yet, our so-called *madman* is just that—a man. I cannot give merit to the belief that either Lord Stafford or Mr. Worth creates such chaos. I do not know His Lordship well, but the worst that is said is he is an immature young man, overly fond of his own pleasures. But I also know he treats his servants well, and he contributes regularly to several charities. He does not have the nature of a murderer."

"And Mr. Worth?" Elizabeth prompted.

"I met Worth several years ago when I settled Mr. Wickham's numerous debts in Cheshire." Darcy paused, choosing his words carefully.

"What is it, Fitzwilliam? You must tell me what you know."

Darcy lovingly caressed her cheek and brushed the hair from Elizabeth's face before he spoke. "Mr. Worth was returning from Newcastle, where a colleague had summoned him. It was purely by happenstance that he traveled in the same coach as Mrs. Wickham. Your sister's husband has accumulated additional debt. Much more debt than I can assume without borrowing from Georgiana's dowry or jeopardizing our child's inheritance. I will do neither to save the man. Plus, Worth also reports that Mr. Wickham's adultery and his physical abuse of Mrs. Wickham are now common knowledge among those stationed at Newcastle. We cannot disassociate ourselves from your family, but we must find a way to minimize their impact on us—for Georgiana's sake."

Elizabeth swallowed hard, fighting back the tears flooding her eyes. Her shame when she had shared with Darcy the news of Lydia's elopement returned. Her husband had acted honorably, saving her and the rest of her sisters from public humiliation. Her husband had done it all without taking credit and without her knowledge— because it required an explanation that would rob her Uncle Gardiner of his borrowed feathers and give the praise where it was due and because Darcy loved her more than even she had realized at the time. Her aunt and uncle had given way to Darcy because they had given him credit for another interest in the affair—her heart, which he owned completely. "Oh, Fitzwilliam," she moaned, "My family and I cannot repay you for how you saved our reputation."

"I told you before. Your family owes me nothing. Much as I respect them, I thought only of you at the time. And you owe me nothing. I think only of you still. I love you with all that I am. I will love you with every ounce of my being until my last breath. And I will love you beyond that."

"I do not deserve you."

"Let us not dwell on these issues, Elizabeth," he declared as he rolled her to her back and covered her body with his. "To-morrow..." he murmured close to her lips. "Tomorrow we will deal with our problems. Tonight...tonight, I wish only to show the woman I love how very perfect I find her." He claimed her mouth, deepening the kiss and losing himself in her passion.

Lydia Wickham spent another restless night at Pemberley. Her sister's pure happiness made her own marriage seem that much worse. Elizabeth had chosen the most disagreeable of men, but her sister had proved them all wrong. Mr. Darcy devoted himself to Elizabeth's happiness: Lizzy had a beautiful home and true love.

As for Lydia, she had chosen the more amiable George Wickham—a man who possessed a handsome face and a way of pleasing all onlookers. Her husband was the type of man toward almost every female eye turned, and Lydia had originally prided herself upon being the woman he had chosen. Initially, everyone in Meryton had believed her husband's disgraceful lies regarding his relationship with Mr. Darcy. Even Elizabeth had accepted Wickham's tales of malicious revenge and justice. It was only after Lydia's ill-fated elopement with him that the world had known her Wickham for his true colors.

Yet even then, she had foolishly believed him—accepted his words of love as legitimate and rejected the efforts of her father and of her aunt and uncle and of Mr. Darcy to salvage her reputation—and declared herself perfectly happy to remain with *her dear Wickham* until he could bring himself to marry her. Unfortunately, it had been only under duress that Wickham agreed to make her his bride—not a solid basis for a marriage.

They lived in rented rooms, surviving upon Jane's and Elizabeth's goodness. She did not know what else to do. She had never learned economy in her mother's home—frivolity, yes; economy, no. She possessed no household arts. If she were in either of her sisters' positions, she would have servants who knew how to maintain a household, and even though she realized it not fair to Jane or Elizabeth, Lydia thought it quite unreasonable that she should suffer alone. Only recently, her mother had written to announce that Mary had attracted the attentions of one of Uncle Philips's clerks, and their mother expected the man to declare himself soon. Lydia felt the injustice of knowing that even plain, moralizing Mary might find contentment when she did not.

Evelyn Williams opened the cloth purse she hid each night under her pillow. It contained all she had of value in the world. Fifteen gold pieces caught the glint of the fire—solid gold—worth a small fortune. She lifted one of the circular discs and rolled it about in her fingers. Slowly, Evelyn brought it to her lips and kissed it for good luck.

Next, she took his ring into her palm. Somehow, it felt warm, as if it still held the heat of his hand in its metal. Again, she brought the item to her mouth, but this time it was his face she saw—the face of the man she loved. Their marriage certificate lay folded and small on the white bed sheet. Reverently, she unfolded it, smoothing out the edges, letting her fingertips trace the raised letters. Reading the solemn words silently, Evelyn placed her hand upon the page and drifted off to sleep.

"Adam?" Cathleen whispered as she turned in the man's arms. They had made love and fallen asleep, arms and legs entangled. "I need to say something to you."

"What is it, Darling?" Fully sated, Adam Lawrence would have preferred only to rest in her embrace.

"When this is over, I want to travel to Cheshire alone. My family would not understand my traveling in your company."

Adam forced his eyes open, hearing a touch of finality in her tone. "Then you mean to leave me?" He stared deeply into her sea green eyes.

"I will never know a more generous man, and I will regret it all my life, but it is for the best. The fragile thread of life is too easily broken. The evil we have experienced at Pemberley convinces me I need to return to the girl I once was and to the life I once knew." She tenderly caressed Adam's face.

He did not move. He had known this moment would come soon enough, although he had expected to be the one to end their relationship. Adam appreciated Cathleen for her alluring combination of innocence and sexuality. He found the woman most appealing, and he did not wish to replace her; yet, Adam would not beg her to stay. "I would prefer to remain with you until we are safely away from Pemberley. I will see to your journey and make an appropriate settlement upon you."

"I remain in your debt, my Lord." She slid her arms around his neck. Leaving him would be the hardest thing she ever did. She had been in love with him from their earliest days together; however, she had no choice but to leave him. Adam Lawrence must never know the depths of her love.

Nigel Worth turned over in bed. The mattress was a little softer than he liked, but tonight, he had no complaints about his accommodations—about the forced confinement of the storm—about missing his Cheshire appointments.

Tonight, he thought only of Miss Anne de Bourgh's merits. Lovely and personable—thick-lashed eyes that saw the world as an innocent globe—a sharp mind, open to new ideas and new adventures. He felt like a young man with her, although he also wanted to protect and to father her at the same time. She created a calmness deep in his soul, and also an exhilarating stimulation. Worth did not fool himself. He knew that others would see him as a fortune hunter, but he honestly had known very little of the woman's financial situation when he had first found himself attracted to her. Now, he contemplated the possibility of wooing the lady and making her his own. Those thoughts rocked him to sleep—the mattress he had greatly despised on the previous evenings was less of an issue tonight.

CHAPTER 12

~ ~ ~

PETER WATCHED LYDIA WICKHAM as she dressed for the day. The maid, known as Lucinda, laced up Lydia's corset, but not to the woman's specifications. James objected to his watching, but Peter took note of how much James had enjoyed Mr. and Mrs. Darcy's coupling and, therefore, had ignored his friend's warning. "I said tighter," the girl demanded.

Behind her, Lucinda turned red in the face as she strained to meet the order. "Yes, Mrs. Wickham."

"I would hate to tell my sister of your incompetence," Lydia threatened.

The maid pulled again as Lydia sucked in her breath. "No, Mrs. Wickham."

Corset finally in place, Lucinda stepped away to retrieve the long-sleeved dark violet dress, which Lydia indicated she would wear for the day. Another round of lacing followed. At last, Lydia's appearance seemed to please her. "You have probably left me black and blue," she chastised the maid as she preened before the long mirror, "but I do cut a nice figure, do you not think?" Lydia twirled in place, admiring herself from all angles.

"I be apologizin', Mrs. Wickham. I never be dressin' anyone before."

Lydia took a quick look at the servant—a moment of regret making her take a kinder approach. "Well, we all must learn, I suppose."

"Yes, Mrs. Wickham." The maid turned to pick up the articles Lydia had left strewn across the bed and chair. "Might I be of service some other way, ma'am?"

Lydia headed toward the door. She gestured to the clothes to which the woman now attended. "Just iron some of those and see to my laundry."

"Yes, Mrs. Wickham."

Peter continued to watch all this from the security of his hiding place. Lydia Wickham's condescending attitude did not sit well with him. His father insisted that quality people treated others well. The woman he watched today had never learned humility—never learned to value anyone else's needs but her own. She had never learned to love herself. Consequently, she could not truly recognize the value of another. Maybe that was why he despised everything for which Lydia Wickham stood and why he continued to watch her— why her shallowness mesmerized him. *She should be taught a lesson,* he concluded. It was up to him to teach her—the way his father had taught him—with a good switch and a cane if necessary. "Later," he whispered to the darkness. "Later today, she will know my wrath."

"I will see to it, Mr. Darcy. Immediately, sir." Darcy was meeting with both Mr. Baldwin and Mrs. Jennings. He had followed Elizabeth's suggestions from last evening. His butler would scan the rooms once more and record any sightings of the Pemberley phantom. They already knew which staff members had seen or had spoken to their mysterious intruder. Now, the Pemberley butler would document the when, where, and time of day each encounter occurred. Darcy also instructed his man to remove from the rooms anything that might be used as a weapon. "We will not provide our mystery man with devices to bring about our own demise."

Darcy instructed Mrs. Jennings to take a count of what supplies and foodstuffs were available. He specifically stressed the necessity of securing those areas of the house where foods not needing a fire to make them edible might be found. "Hard-boiled eggs are different from fresh eggs," he explained to her.

Earlier, he had spoken to Mrs. Reynolds regarding bed linens, toilette items, towels, candles, and lanterns. He wanted everything that the intruder might need to survive within Pemberley's walls locked up. "Open up the east wing's rooms—doors remain open. No fires in the fireplaces. Inventory each room's furnishings down to the mantelpiece's smallest figurines." Having spent a combined three quarters of a century in service to the estate, the two staff members were ready to respond to the threat to Pemberley's reputation and to fulfill their own responsibilities to keep it secure.

Satisfied that they would complete their tasks as he instructed, and having started his day with a visit to Jatson St. Denis, Darcy now turned his attention to what to tell the viscount and Mr. Worth. Since speaking candidly to Elizabeth, he wondered about the wisdom of being so open with his guests. He knew intuitively that he needed to acknowledge the troubles besetting Pemberley—to allow his guests to protect themselves with a large dose of caution. Yet, he could not shake the feeling that somehow one of them had participated in this duplicity. Only earlier that morning, Darcy had learned that Lord Stafford had not slept in his own bedroom the previous night, and despite Darcy's knowledge of the viscount's relationship with Miss Donnel, a small part of him wondered if Adam Lawrence could be involved somehow. His lack of command over the events exploding in his household weighed heavily on him. He could not take care of all of them. It was a fact that Darcy did not take lightly, but he had decided during the long night that his first responsibility was to Elizabeth and the child she carried, along with Georgiana. They would be his priority in this peril. He would tend to the others, but only after his ladies and his child were safe.

Since Elizabeth's revelation, Darcy's mind had drifted often to how he would secure his child's future. Milder weather could not come too quickly for him. Besides being the end of the nightmare plaguing the estate, Darcy eagerly anticipated meeting with his solicitor and making a proper settlement on his child. Although he wished for a son—an heir for Pemberley—he had actually dreamed the past two nights of an auburn-haired little girl curling up on his lap and falling asleep. A daughter would bring him a different type of contentment. Darcy missed how Georgiana had once clung to him—how she would climb on his outstretched legs and beg her big brother for a horsey ride. His imagination told him that Elizabeth's child would bring such happiness again. With her mother's wit, the child would challenge him to be more than a family figurehead. He would be a father—a man who taught his children responsibility while giving them love.

A knock at his study door brought him out of his musing. "Enter!" he called.

Anne edged the door open. "You wished to speak to me, Fitzwilliam?"

Darcy came automatically to his feet. Circling the desk to meet her, he led his cousin to a nearby chair. "Yes, my Dear." After seating her comfortably, Darcy returned to his place behind the mahogany desk. "I have several items about which I wish to speak with you if you are of a mind."

Anne smiled politely, but she worried. Would Darcy reproach her for her actions the past few days? Brought up on constant censure, she expected it from everyone. She said cautiously, "Of course. I have enjoyed our newfound closeness."

"So have I," he admitted, and she released the breath she had held. "It is ironic that we have shared a lifetime and only of late can say that we share a friendship."

"Unfortunately, it took your defiance in claiming Mrs. Darcy as your own to open communication between us." Anne chortled, and Darcy noted how laughter made her appear years younger. "It is probably indelicate to say this," she continued, "but the sword of Damocles hung over us for too many years—our prescribed union kept us from developing a caring relationship. I pray for this new knowledge of each other to continue when I am forced to leave Pemberley's security."

Darcy chose his words carefully. "And do you feel secure at Pemberley? Despite everything that has happened?"

"Notwithstanding the tragic loss of a woman I admired more than anyone else in my life, I have found moments of pure joy at Pemberley." Anne shifted in her chair. "I love my mother, Cousin, and like you, I understand her bitterness. She was the eldest child of the Fitzwilliam family and a bit spoiled by all those at Matlock. Even though your father and mother taught you what was right and gave you good principles, they certainly left you to follow them in pride and conceit. I say that not to criticize you, Darcy. It is but a fact." Darcy simply nodded his head in acknowledgment of her words. "If your mother, Lady Anne, my namesake, offered you such guidance, you must realize that she and my mother were instructed by our grandparents on the nobleness of their line." Again, Darcy gave no verbal confirmation of what his cousin said, but he made no move to correct her. He had heard his aunt declare on more than one occasion the idea of the "perfection" of his and Anne's lineage—the same noble lines—respectable, honorable, and ancient families. "However, as my cousin, you—more than most people—recognize the censure with which I have lived for years. Since birth, I have been my mother's disappointment. She needed a son to truly please my father. Although Rosings Park is not entailed upon the male line, a son would have meant that she had not failed him as a wife."

"Sir Lewis adored you," Darcy observed.

"He was my world, and I never felt unloved, but my father left us too soon, forcing my mother into the role of both master and mistress. She could let no one take note of a woman's weakness, including her own daughter. When my father left us, I also lost my mother."

"Some day you should explain your *defiance* in just those terms," Darcy suggested. "I have seen the pain in Lady Catherine's eyes when she experiences the inadequacy of her own futile attempts at motherhood. For years, I have been of the persuasion that my aunt taught you docility because she wished never to risk losing Rosings. If we had married, you would have become the mistress of Pemberley and have no need for another great estate. Yet, if you married another, your husband would take control of the property, and Lady Catherine would assume the position of dowager: Rosings would be yours. Actually, I prefer your explanation for Her Ladyship's harshness rather than the thought of her manipulating you for her own benefit. It eliminates a point of honor."

Anne sat silent for several moments. "It is a conundrum. All I know for sure is that I must discover my own identity and become my own person. I am seven and twenty and have never known the thrill of another's attention."

"That brings me to another topic of discussion. I wished to know of your continued recovery from Mrs. Jenkinson's death and of what appears to be a blossoming relationship with Mr. Worth."

Anne blushed profusely. "Is it not shameless that I am here because I followed Lieutenant Harwood to Liverpool; yet, I am finding comfort in building a friendship with Mr. Worth?"

"What I know of Nigel Worth tells me the man is honorable."

Anne looked surprised. "You knew Mr. Worth previously? I was under the impression that you met him when he came to Pemberley with those seeking refuge from the storm."

"I dealt with Mr. Worth several years ago in a legal matter regarding one of our former Pemberley employees." Darcy stretched the truth, even with Anne, but he realized she would think he *interfered* in his cottagers' lives—as if that were the normal way for a landed gentleman to behave. He could not admit to her that he had paid Wickham's debts without also revealing the man's betrayal and attempted seduction of Georgiana.

Anne asked impulsively, "Do you believe Mr. Worth's attentions honest?"

"I assume you question whether the man's interest is based on your fortune?"

"I am painfully aware that Rosings Park is my best asset," Anne openly confessed.

Darcy's expression softened. "You cheat yourself, my Dear, if you make the assumption that is the only reason any man might find you attractive. Yet, with Mrs. Darcy's insights, I have learned that women often have a poor opinion of their own true appeal and must learn, in their own way, to love themselves and accept themselves." He paused to allow Anne to digest his words thoroughly. "As for Mr. Worth, I believe he would not choose to show attention to someone he might not truly find attractive. A man will flirt with a woman he knows he cannot have, just to say he tried; but when his heart becomes engaged, his demeanor changes to one of protection and caring. I have noted such a change in Mr. Worth since discovering your beauty. Worth has a successful practice and a comfortable home in Cheshire. Although he would welcome your wealth, it would not persuade him to make you an offer. As a point of reference, we must assume that the man would know how to see to your interests and to make them grow profitably."

"Whereas Lieutenant Harwood would not?" Anne asked weakly.

"I do not know the lieutenant's motives, Anne. I can speak only of what I know of Mr. Worth." Again, Darcy paused for emphasis. "What I wish to ask, my Dear, is whether I am to pursue my quest for information about Lieutenant Harwood? I had planned to assure myself and you of the man's intentions and of his truth once the storm subsided."

It was Anne's turn to pause; she needed time to word her response. "If you would not mind postponing your inquiry, Fitzwilliam, I would like the opportunity to see where Mr. Worth's addresses lie. My intuition tells me my future may find itself in that direction. I never felt Lieutenant Harwood's commitment to me the way I do with Mr. Worth."

"Very good," Darcy said with relief. "I wish you happiness, Cousin, and it appears that Mr. Worth wishes you the same." He stood, bringing an end to their conversation. "If you care to remain at Pemberley when Her Ladyship returns to Kent, Mrs. Darcy and I would be honored to play your hosts. It would make it more feasible for Mr. Worth to continue your courtship. Pemberley is not so far that he could not arrange a day trip. It might be a way to determine the depth of the man's interest. If he is willing to withstand the discomfort of a long carriage ride or one on horseback to spend a few hours in your company, then we can count him a legitimate suitor." Darcy chuckled, thinking of how he would have traveled from Derby to Hertfordshire in a heartbeat if Elizabeth had given him reason to do so. "It would demonstrate most clearly his intentions."

"I suppose it would. Thank you, Fitzwilliam, for understanding."

"Think nothing of it. If I cannot fulfill the position of husband, at least, I can portend the role of brother."

"That is most comforting." They caught hands as he led her to the door. Anne turned to him before making her exit. "Mrs. Darcy is a very fortunate woman. She married into the highest realm of the land, and I do not speak of Pemberley's wealth." Going up on tiptoe, she kissed Darcy's cheek.

"Go and find your happiness, Cousin," he murmured.

"I will, sir," she replied. Then she swept from the room.

Anne found Georgiana and Evelyn Williams in the rose-colored drawing room. Both worked at their embroidery, a task Anne found tedious. "What say you," she asked as she joined them, "to performing a play? I thought it might be a way of passing the hours. We could create costumes or just use our everyday clothing. Nothing spectacular—just us, enjoying one another's company."

"I have never tried to act," Georgiana began. "I am not sure I could deliver a line without choking on the words."

"Even if you forgot your lines, no one would care." Anne reached for Georgiana's hand, needing her family to agree to her first attempt at defining herself. "Do you think I have ever enjoyed such freedoms? We would experience it together. Besides, we have a predominance of women in the house. We can take the part of men and lose ourselves in the roles."

Georgiana asked, "Do you believe the others might agree?"

"How do we know unless we ask? This is the first time I have ever suggested something that my mother has not prompted." Anne was intoxicated with the possibilities before her.

"What of you, Mrs. Williams?" Georgiana asked as she turned to the older woman. "Might you care to join us if we can persuade the others?"

Mrs. Williams vehemently declared, "My late mother believed the theater leads to the worst vices."

Anne flinched with the woman's censure, but she forced herself not to succumb to her own feelings. "I would not call what we attempt *theater*, Mrs. Williams, but if you choose not to participate, we understand. Come, Georgiana, let us find the others." Anne gently pulled the girl to her feet. "I am sure that Mrs. Wickham will be happy to perform with us."

"I hope Elizabeth will also agree to take part." Arm in arm, they walked toward the open door.

Finding several of the guests still lingering in the morning room, Anne, a bit embarrassed but willing to try something new, cleared her throat to catch their attention. "Georgiana and I thought we might perform a play among ourselves to pass the time—nothing elaborate, just us trying to put the storm and the gloom of the past few days behind us."

Cathleen's eyes lit with eagerness. "That sounds like something I might enjoy. I missed the outside day because of my accident. I would like to get to know the others better. Have you chosen a piece to perform?"

Laughing at herself for not having thought that far ahead, Anne glanced quickly at Georgiana for suggestions. The thought of performing had occurred to her only after she had left Darcy's study. He had told her to find her happiness, and Anne had always wanted to perform plays. It seemed a natural consequence of their heartfelt conversation. "I do not believe that either my cousin or I hold a preference for a particular play."

"Might I make a suggestion?" Cathleen continued. Anne and Georgiana nodded their agreement. "A tragedy under the circumstances seems inappropriate. A comedy, probably something from Shakespeare, seems feasible. How about *Much Ado About Nothing*?"

Georgiana confided, "Elizabeth loves that play!"

Anne thoroughly enjoyed Georgiana's growing excitement. "Then *Much Ado About Nothing* should be our choice. Thank you, Miss Donnel, for your suggestion and for accepting our idea as your own."

Mr. Worth looked up from an old copy of the *Times*. "I am not much of a performer, but you may count on me, Miss de Bourgh." He caught Anne's eye and winked.

"Thank you, Mr. Worth."

"And you, Your Lordship?" Georgiana prompted.

"Why not?" Adam Lawrence placed his napkin beside his plate. "It is not as if we have had much else to entertain us."

"May we all meet in the ballroom in an hour?" Anne quickly organized the group before they could change their minds. "I suppose we must find a copy of the play. I am sure Mr. Darcy owns at least one copy of the work."

"I believe I saw copies of Shakespeare's works in the gentleman's library," Worth announced as he rose to his feet. "Let me help you find a copy, Miss de Bourgh." He came around the table's end to where Anne stood.

His presence sent a shiver down Anne's spine, but she managed to send Georgiana to secure Elizabeth's and Lydia's consent. "We will see you in an hour," she declared as she took Worth's proffered arm.

"Where could Mr. Darcy keep his copies of Shakespeare?" Anne asked as she scanned the shelves for the books. Having confessed to Darcy her interest in the man who accompanied her into the library suddenly made Anne nervous.

Worth stepped behind her. He had dreamed of Anne de Bourgh the previous night. Speaking softly, close to her ear, he said, "I believe you will find Mr. Darcy treats his library as he treats his life: The man cannot tolerate disorganization. The books are shelved alphabetically by the author's last name. We simply need to find the letter *S*."

Anne turned to face him, expecting Worth to step back, but he held his ground, and she found herself only inches from the man. "Shall we," she murmured nervously, "look for that letter?"

Worth touched her cheek lightly with his fingertip. "You have beautiful eyes, Miss de Bourgh. They haunted my dreams last evening."

Anne blushed immediately. "Mr. Worth, although your words give me pleasure, I cannot encourage you to speak so forwardly." She tried to look away, but Worth's intensity held her gaze.

"Miss de Bourgh, I am in my late thirties. If I am to finally choose a woman who holds my interest, I do not intend that my wooing game be an extended one. It is inappropriate to declare my desires so soon after your loss, but when the arrangements for dear Mrs. Jenkinson are complete, I will press my suit."

Anne flushed once more, but she gathered her nerve to catch Worth's hand with hers and turned to kiss his palm. "I would be pleased to accept your regard. Mildred would love the possibilities; I believe it to be one of her last wishes."

Worth brought Anne's hand to his lips and kissed her fingertips. "I am your servant, Miss de Bourgh."

Anne smiled brightly. "We have a play to find, Mr. Worth."

"That we do, Miss Anne." His laughter filled the room. He turned toward the shelf holding the many volumes of Shakespeare. "I believe what we seek can be found over here," he said loudly for the benefit of any servants lurking in the hallway.

"You are correct, Mr. Worth," she announce just as loudly. Anne watched as he stretched and retrieved the tome. The man possessed an interesting face and a solidly built body, and Anne knew him to be a man of compassion—a man who could care for her and her alone.

"And what do you wish me to do?" Elizabeth had cornered Darcy in one of the servant entrances to the below-stairs area.

"I expect you to enjoy your exploits in the performing arts." He leaned close, so that only she might hear. "And, more importantly, use your intuition. Please watch and listen and be my eyes and my ears. I need to know more about our guests, and I am depending on you to supply me with that information." Darcy nestled her in the curve of his body, touching Elizabeth's back—his right hand splayed over her hips.

She smiled up at him mischievously. "Your hand tells me you wish something else, my Husband.

Darcy's left hand caressed the side of her face, while his right nudged her forward. "All you must do, Elizabeth, is smile at me or walk into a room or speak my name, and I am lost to you and you alone. I am even more besotted with you now that you carry our child." His warm breath teased her ear. "In you, I know both affection and passion."

Elizabeth laughed softly, reaching up to brush away the lock of hair falling over his forehead. "As for me, I have no notion of loving people in halves. My attachments are always excessively strong. I believe my feelings are stronger than anybody's," she said. "I am sure they are too strong for my own peace of mind."

"Well, I suppose my obsession is perfectly appropriate then." Darcy brushed her lips with his. "You have placed me under your spell." The fragrance of lavender, which always clung to her skin, swept over him.

They had come from different worlds, but knew the same desires—possessed the same perspectives. Their need for each other ran deep—a profound connection. Elizabeth ached for him—could not deny her need for his approval, even when she had foolishly thought that Darcy disapproved of her. Then one day, he had opened himself to her—let her see his vulnerability—see his fears and his hopes—see the part of him that Darcy secreted away from the world. From that moment forward, she had begun to comprehend that he was exactly the man, who in disposition and talents, would most suit her. "I will join the others now," she rasped, hearing the approach of one of the servants at the end of the passageway. Darcy reluctantly released her. "Until later, Mr.

Darcy." Elizabeth dropped a curtsy and disappeared through the side door.

Darcy watched her go, his eyes tracing her form. "It is a truth universally acknowledged, that a single man in possession of a good fortune, must be in want of a wife," he whispered to the empty hallway. He chuckled. *When I was single, I feared that notion; only now do I understand its wisdom—for the man of wealth and the man of modest means.*

James observed the group gathered in the ballroom. He rested against the backside of an Athenian column supporting the main wall. Hidden by a balcony-like façade, he observed closely the dynamics of the group as they planned a theatrical performance. He knew most of the players, but no one had told him of Nigel Worth's presence at Pemberley. He would have a little talk with Peter about not keeping him informed. He did not like surprises, and Peter Whittington knew him better than anyone else—knew his likes and dislikes intimately. Although James had not seen Worth in nearly five years, he remembered his distaste for Worth's arrogance and his envy of Worth's knowledge of the law. James had once considered the study of the law, but his talents had taken him elsewhere—to the underbelly of society.

Now, he wondered if he might not include Worth in his plan for revenge. "Two birds and one stone," he muttered. Worth seemed quite taken with Miss Anne de Bourgh. *Darcy's cousin*, he thought, as he closed and locked the opening through which he had peered. The lady might serve as a means to exact revenge on both Darcy and Worth. He would use the information about Worth and Anne's flirtation to his own advantage. As he was well aware, the de Bourghs were very wealthy, and he always needed money. "Something good this way comes," he added as he made his way to his makeshift bed. "Pemberley is a house of infinite possibilities."

"Then we are agreed." Anne led the group's discussion. "We will select poignant scenes to recreate the main plot of the play. Some of us will enact more than one part, especially as we have only two males, and they must be Benedick and Claudio."

Elizabeth caught Georgiana around the waist. "Well, I, for one, am looking forward to playing a man's role, and I am sure my sister, Miss Darcy, feels the same." She squeezed the girl to her teasingly. "After all, Shakespeare had men playing the female roles."

"I think it quite generous of you to offer to perform many of the minor parts, Mrs. Darcy," Miss Donnel remarked. "It will take some creative staging to tell the story with so few performers."

"It will be great sport," Anne asserted, before organizing the papers strewn on the floor. "We will stage the masque, the plot against Benedick and Beatrice by the Prince, Borachio's seduction of Margaret, the first wedding scene, Beatrice's demand that Benedick kill Claudio, Dogberry's questioning of Don John's men, the second wedding, and the lovers' declaration. Is that the extent of our scenes?" Anne quickly surveyed their faces for approval. When no one offered objections, she settled back into her role as the group's leader. Only eight and forty hours earlier, she could not have filled the role of director; or, at least, she would have believed it impossible. *Be daring, Anne,* she urged herself. *It is the way forward.* "Then let us read through the scenes and meet back here in, let us say, two hours to begin our rehearsals."

As the others stood, Elizabeth heard Lydia complain, "I do not see why I must play Margaret. I would make a more plausible Hero."

Georgiana intervened. Until that moment, Darcy's sister had avoided Mr. Wickham's new wife. It was as though Anne's new approach inspired Georgiana. "It would be more fitting for Miss Donnel and Lord Stafford to commit to the roles. They are close and can say hurtful lines without offering an offense. Would you not think so, Mrs. Wickham?"

Lydia begrudgingly agreed, but she remained less than happy about the choice.

"Mr. Worth consented to be your Borachio," Elizabeth said encouragingly. "That is an agreeable situation, and you do have one of the more *provocative* scenes." Elizabeth smiled teasingly. "Hero is too bland a character for your talents, Lyddie. Be part of my and Miss Darcy's group of minor characters." She brought the two younger girls together in a tight circle. "I propose we do something of our own to spice up our roles as men." Elizabeth glanced around to be sure no one else could hear them. "I say we dress in men's clothing."

Georgiana gasped. "We cannot, Elizabeth!"

"We can, Georgiana. It will be great fun. I will have Mr. Darcy help us find some men's breeches and some shirts." Amusement danced in her eyes.

"Oh, Lord." Georgiana turned pale. "Fitzwilliam will never tolerate it."

"Lizzy has a way with Mr. Darcy," Lydia asserted. "I never thought to see the day when Mr. Darcy would even consider dancing with Elizabeth, let alone marrying her. If anyone can persuade him to permit such a scheme, it is my sister."

Georgiana paused, recalling those early days after Elizabeth's arrival at Pemberley. At first she often listened with an astonishment bordering on alarm at her new sister's lively, sportive manner of talking to her brother. He, who had always inspired in Georgiana a respect, which almost overcame her affection, she saw the object of open pleasantry. Her mind received knowledge, which had never before fallen in her way. By Elizabeth's instructions, Georgiana began to comprehend that a woman may take liberties with her husband, which a brother will not always allow in a sister more than ten years younger than himself. Georgiana giggled nervously. "I have always wondered about the freedom men's clothing affords."

"Then I will see to it." Elizabeth smiled. "Let us find some tea in the rose drawing room, and then we will map out our scenes. I wish to be Dogberry; his mutilation of the King's English fascinates me." She led them toward the main door, her arms wrapped around their waists.

Suddenly, Georgiana froze in place. "Oh, Elizabeth, you must say that word!" she exclaimed, both terrified and amused.

Elizabeth paused, trying to imagine Georgiana's horror, repeating the play's lines in her head. Then she snorted. "I will, will I not, Georgiana? I must say the word *ass* repeatedly. Ooh, I do so love this play." She gave Georgiana a quick hug. "Come, girls, I will need much practice to say my lines without blushing."

CHAPTER 13

~ ~ ~

"WE HAVE ONLY ONE more scene through which to read," Worth told Anne, as they hid themselves away, by common assent, on the same bench they had occupied previously in the conservatory. It offered them privacy. If anyone questioned their withdrawal, they would place the blame on the need to practice their scenes. They played lead parts, Beatrice and Benedick.

"Scene four of act five," Anne noted, "after the second wedding scene." She flipped through the pages to find the place. Sitting close together, they read from the same book. "Are you ready, Mr. Worth?"

"Absolutely, Miss de Bourgh."

Anne pointed to the passage. "You may begin, sir."

Worth cleared his throat before declaring, "Soft and fair, Friar. Which is Beatrice?"

Anne moved a bit closer. "I answer to that name. What is your will?"

"Do you love me?" Worth gazed at Anne's profile.

She huskily whispered her lines. "Why, no, no more than reason."

Worth returned his attention to the play. "Why, then your uncle and the Prince and Claudio have been deceived. They swore you did," he read.

Anne asked flirtatiously, "Do not you love me?"

"Troth, no, no more than reason."

"Why then my cousin, Margaret, and Ursula are much deceived, for they did swear you did."

Worth caught Anne's hand in his, letting his finger trace a circle in her palm. "They swore that you were almost sick for me."

Anne copied his teasing tone. "They swore that you were well-nigh dead for me."

"'Tis no such matter. Then you do not love me?" He raised an eyebrow and his partner burst into laughter.

Composing herself, Anne read, "No, truly, but in friendly recompense."

Worth looked down at the script. "Then Leonato, Claudio, and Hero produce the poem Benedick has written to Beatrice and Beatrice's letter to Benedick." He held up his invisible prop, a letter, and studied it. Then he read the lines, "A miracle! Here is our own hands against our hearts. Come, I will have thee, but by this light I take thee for pity."

Anne said faintly, "I would not deny you, but by this good day. I yield upon great persuasion, and partly to save your life, for I was told you were in a consumption."

"Peace! I will stop your mouth." Worth lifted his hand to caress her face. "We should rehearse the kiss if you are willing, Miss de Bourgh."

"If you wish, Mr. Worth," the lady responded breathily.

"I wish very much, Miss de Bourgh." The man lowered his mouth to hers, kissing her gently. Their lips touched briefly—no embrace—no overt sexuality—simply an early courtship kiss—a declaration of a commitment between them. "I look forward to the actual performance so I might repeat the pleasure of tasting your lips, my Anne."

"Am I yours, Mr. Worth?" she murmured.

"If I have anything to say on the matter."

Anne slid her arms around his neck. "I believe I am in need of more practice, sir."

"As am I." Worth chuckled as he pulled Anne closer.

Hours of separate and group rehearsals brought additional laughter, along with some frustration. They considered postponing their performance an additional day to allow more time for perfection, but Lord Stafford insisted that they were as ready as they might ever be; and after some desultory debate, the gentleman's reason prevailed. After dinner, they would offer up their version of Shakespeare's comedy for the delight of one another, as well as Darcy, Lady Catherine, and Mrs. Williams.

Elizabeth had talked Darcy into her idea of wearing men's clothing, but she had forgotten that Lady Catherine would be in the audience. *Now, I will just prove my inappropriateness,* she chastised herself. *Even worse, I have involved my sister and Georgiana. What was I thinking?* However, as her entrance approached, Elizabeth took a deep breath and stepped, or rather galloped, to center stage. She played the part of the ineffectual constable Dogberry, with his ever-present sidekick, Verges, who was portrayed by a terrified Georgiana.

Elizabeth heard Lady Catherine's snort of disapproval, but Darcy's simple "Excellent!" gave her the courage to portray the foolish Dogberry with pure abandonment. She spoke with all the pomposity of the man who considered himself learned when the world recognized him as an incompetent fool. "Why, you speak like an ancient and most quiet watchman, for I cannot see how sleeping should offend. Only have a care that your bills be not stolen. Well, you are to call at all the alehouses and bid those that are drunk get them to bed. But if they will not, why then, let them alone till they are sober. If they make you not then the better answer, you will say they are not the men you took them for."

Darcy laughed heartily. In his opinion, Elizabeth was a natural, but then she always amused him, even when they were in opposition. He had loved her handling of the infamous Caroline Bingley's obvious barbs back in their Netherfield Park days. It was one of the qualities which had attracted him to her in the first place. Her presence lightened his heart and brought him joy. Knowing Georgiana had upcoming lines in the play, Darcy returned his attention to his sister's look of pure delight. Six months ago, a sultan's fortune could not have induced his sister to perform in a play and place herself in a position for censure or for praise.

Tonight, infected by Elizabeth's enthusiasm, Georgiana hobbled along as his wife's partner. "If you hear a child cry in the night, you must call to the nurse and bid her still it," she declared. Darcy's smile exploded. *She will recover,* he thought. *Her heart will heal, thanks to Elizabeth.* "Bravo," he said loudly enough for Georgiana to hear. Quietly, he added, "Bravo, my dear sister."

"Darcy," Lady Catherine hissed under her breath, but he immediately hushed her.

"None of your usual censure, Aunt," he warned. "Let them know the day's distraction."

"But . . ." she began; however, a glacial stare from Darcy silenced her immediately.

Peter ventured a quick survey of the ballroom thespians. The ladies—Mrs. Darcy, Miss Darcy, and Mrs. Wickham—flaunted a freedom not rightly theirs and abused the precepts of propriety with their performances. He despised women who crossed the boundaries of society's unwritten laws. Women, and society as a whole, often found him disagreeable because he fancied himself a discerning critic—not blind to the follies and nonsense of others. He knew that affectation of candor is common enough; one meets with it everywhere. Of the three women, Mrs. Wickham bothered him the most. Her behavior had not been calculated to please in general; and with more quickness of observation and less pliancy of temper than the others, he was very little disposed to approve of the woman.

He found Lydia Wickham not deficient in good humor when she was pleased, nor in the power of being agreeable when she chose it; and although rather handsome, she was in the habit of spending more than she ought, a grievous error in a lady as far as Peter was concerned.

"No," he whispered, "not Mrs. Darcy or the girl." The mistress of the estate, although occasionally bordering on impertinence, had an affectionate nature, which added to her virtue. He had heard that Miss Darcy was exceedingly proud, but the observation of a very few minutes convinced him that the girl was only exceedingly shy. In fact, Peter rather liked Georgiana. Despite his disapproval of Mrs. Darcy's and of Miss Darcy's choice of attire for the play, only Mrs. Wickham gave true offense. "Outrageous," he muttered. Like his father, he held the opinion that the loss of virtue in a female was irretrievable; that one false step involved her in endless ruin; that her reputation was no less brittle than it was beautiful; and that she could not be too guarded in her behavior toward the undeserving of the other sex.

Peter was well aware of the history of George Wickham and his wife. Though he did not suppose Mrs. Wickham to have deliberately engaged in an elopement without the intention of marriage, neither her virtue nor her understanding had kept Lydia Bennet from committing the ultimate transgression—possessing nothing but love, flirtation, and officers in her head, she had succumbed and entrapped at the same time. Peter had never understood Wickham's choice. What attractions had Lydia Bennet beyond youth, health, and good humor? What could make him for her sake forego every chance of benefiting himself by marrying well?

"No, it must be Mrs. Wickham," he repeated. "She is the most deserving."

Darcy became engrossed in the Pemberley rendition of Shakespeare's comedy. His sister playfully came alive, and despite the troubles plaguing his household, he accepted the possibilities of Georgiana's future—of her finding a match appropriate to her station, but also a loving relationship. He would not give his consent, no matter the man's title or his wealth, to any suitor who did not engage Georgiana's heart.

As the final scenes developed—leading to the masked wedding, where love prevails—Elizabeth slid into the empty chair on his left. Darcy caught her hand in his and brought the back of it to his lips. "Thank you," he mouthed. She understood his meaning without his expressing the words.

"I love this scene," she whispered.

Darcy smiled, "I recall." During their courtship, Elizabeth had often asked when he had recognized his growing affection for her. On one such evening, Darcy had turned the tables and pleaded with her for words of devotion, and they had repeated Beatrice's and Benedick's lines from the second scene of the play's final act to each other. That evening, he had truly realized Elizabeth returned his love. Through the play, she spoke the words he most needed to hear. Now, he listened as Worth and Anne offered their interpretation of the characters.

Nigel Worth, as Benedick, took Anne's hand as he spoke the words of affection, and Darcy found he caressed Elizabeth's in anticipation. "And, I pray thee now tell me, for which of my bad parts didst thou first fall in love with me?"

Anne smiled wryly. "For them all together, which maintained so politic a state of evil that they will not admit any good part to intermingle with them. But for which of my good parts did you suffer love for me?"

Worth touched Anne's cheek. "Suffer love! A good epithet. I do suffer love indeed for I love thee against my will."

"In spite of your heart, I think. Alas, poor heart, if you spite it for my sake, I will spite it for yours, for I will never love that which my friend hates."

"Thou and I are too wise to woo peaceably." Darcy glanced at Elizabeth as Worth continued his recitation. Her lips moved in a silent mirror of the play's action. It was true; they certainly had not "wooed peaceably"—more a resemblance of a fencing match, but now Elizabeth answered his every prayer—she brought Georgiana along; she admirably fulfilled the role of Pemberley's mistress, and she carried his child. All the blessings of his life rested in her.

"I must go," she murmured as she leaned closer. "I have one more scene."

"Hurry back," Darcy answered, reluctant to allow her to depart. He heard Lady Catherine's deep "hurmph" of contempt, but

Darcy said something positive he was sure she would not cross. "Anne shows a true talent, Aunt." He smiled to seal her agreement.

Her Ladyship spoke softly. "I would expect nothing less. She and Georgiana outshine the others."

Darcy thought that an impossibility. He knew Miss Donnel to have at one time in the not too distant past earned her living on the stage. Stafford's mistress may have left the performing arts behind, but she expressed the confidence to face an audience without blushing, something not found in his sister or in Anne. Yet, he graciously accepted the compliment meant for Georgiana and just as graciously ignored the cut aimed at his wife. With his aunt, Darcy had learned to pick his battles. "I am sure Anne and Georgiana would greatly appreciate your praise, my Dear."

"However, I do not like the way that man mauls my daughter," she hissed under her breath.

"It is part of the play," he responded quietly, as they waited for the group to switch the scene. "And I believe Mr. Worth would treat Anne with respect under all circumstances."

"Well, one would certainly hope so!"

The group's return brought their attention to the stage. He observed that throughout the performance Mrs. Williams remained aloof. The lady did not laugh—did not politely applaud. She simply stared at the raised dais, a sour expression frozen on her face. He knew from his sister's report that Mrs. Williams disapproved of the theater, and Darcy wondered why the woman bothered attending under the circumstances. He supposed she could find no way to politely refuse, and now the lady suffered in silence.

The viscount and Miss Donnel claimed love as Claudio and Hero, and then it became Beatrice's and Benedick's turn. Elizabeth, Georgiana, and Mrs. Wickham joined the audience, taking up positions behind Darcy, Lady Catherine, and Mrs. Williams. Lord Stafford produced the paper supposedly inscribed with Benedick's love poem and handed it to Anne. In like form, Miss Donnel produced Beatrice's love letter and presented it to Mr. Worth.

Worth and Anne pretended to read the incriminating words in opposition to their denials of affection. Worth declared the papers to be proof of their true feelings, even as Beatrice declared that she would love him only to save his life. And as they had rehearsed it earlier, Worth delivered the line, "Peace! I will stop your mouth." Then he took Anne in his arms and kissed her thoroughly.

Elizabeth and Georgiana giggled and clasped hands in excitement. Darcy barked out a surprised laugh, but Lady Catherine gasped out her daughter's name, instantly bringing the scene to its close.

"Anne!" Lady Catherine was on her feet. "You are becoming overwrought," she declared in an autocratic tone. "You will retire immediately to your room."

Anne flushed with embarrassment, but she refused her mother's order. She spoke calmly and with respect, but her resolve remained firm. "Mother, this is only a play, but even if it were not, I am seven and twenty—too old to be sent to my room, as if I were a misbehaving child."

Elizabeth rushed forward to offer Anne her support. "You are mistaken, Lady Catherine. Miss de Bourgh treated the scene with professionalism."

Her Ladyship spit out, "What can one expect from a woman with no connections, who prances around in men's attire and who corrupts the minds of her sisters in life and in marriage!"

With an effort, Elizabeth spoke calmly. "I found Miss de Bourgh's and Mr. Worth's performances tastefully executed, Your Ladyship."

"Mother, please!" Anne cried.

"Obstinate, headstrong girl! I am ashamed of you! Is this your gratitude?" Lady Catherine prepared for another assault as Darcy caught her arm and hurried her from the room.

"Darcy!" she protested, but he said nothing, only continued to escort his maternal aunt along the corridor from Pemberley's ballroom to a nearby sitting room. Once the door had closed, however, he turned on her. "How dare you speak so disrespectfully to my wife and my cousin in my house and in front of my guests!" He seethed with anger still unspoken. "This family has tolerated your scathing disdain for years out of respect for your position as my dear mother's sister. However, any latitude you have been allowed ended with your attack on my wife before my marriage. I swore then that all intercourse between us was at an end. I accepted your coming unannounced to Pemberley for my cousin's sake and because that woman you abuse at every opportunity—my wife—has prevailed on me for some time to overlook the offense and to seek reconciliation. Mrs. Darcy has the most generous of natures and why she would agree to tolerate your continued censure is beyond my limits of understanding. It only speaks of Mrs. Darcy's devotion to her family!"

Lady Catherine considered making an objection, but a warning glare from Darcy made her change her mind.

"You have a wonderful daughter, and your caustic words are driving her from your life. Do you wish to spend the rest of your days alone? Never knowing Anne's happiness? Never to meet your own grandchildren? Do you wish to know my heirs or those of Georgiana?" He stalked away from her, needing distance from the woman. "Anne believes that she lost both parents when Sir Lewis passed—that you hardened yourself in order to run Rosings without a husband." Darcy returned, looming over the woman. "I saw your motives for keeping my cousin under lock and key as more self-serving. I assumed you bullied Anne so you might maintain control of her fortune. You and I both know she inherits it all at age thirty or before, if she marries. Did you fear, Aunt, that the view from the dower house would not be as grand as the one from the main house? Is that why Anne never experienced a Season? Has never known a suitor?"

Lady Catherine's shoulders sank with each of his accusations. "It was never my intent for Anne to suffer," she murmured.

"Yet, she did, Aunt. The blame for Anne's lack of social skills and her overabundance of naïveté lies clearly at your feet. It is my hope that Mr. Worth pursues a relationship with my cousin. If so, I pray you will have the good sense to swallow your pride and welcome a country gentleman into the family. The man will care for Anne and guide her and give her the open affection she has never known. Please remember my words, Your Ladyship; Anne is of age, and she is determined to find her own place in the world. You may either be part of her transition or be left behind to brood over your loss. It will be your choice, as it is hers."

Darcy started away from her, unable to be in the same room with Lady Catherine any longer. "I expect you to offer Mrs. Darcy a genuine apology or order your maid to begin packing your bags for an early morning departure. As always, I welcome your insights into running an estate, but I will sanction no disrespect in your interactions with Elizabeth. I shall not question your intelligence, Aunt, by asking if you understand me. I am my father's son, and he never accepted your disdain under his roof." Darcy strode from the room, needing to find his family and make things right. Elizabeth, Georgiana, and now Anne needed him to provide them a safe and comfortable home—a place where they knew love and acceptance. He would not fail any of them.

"Mr. Baldwin."

"Yes, Mr. Darcy."

"Please send Her Ladyship's maid to escort my aunt to her room." The butler bowed. "Immediately, Mr. Darcy."

Peter knew where all the important members of the household were, so he made his way stealthily through the darkened passageway from the rooms formerly occupied by Miss de Bourgh and her companion to the suite given to Lydia Wickham for her Pemberley stay. He had taken a perverse pleasure in watching Mrs. Wickham. His father would reprimand him thoroughly for ogling a lady—maybe even take a cane to him—but he justified watching a woman in some of her most intimate moments because of his need to know about the opposite sex. His father certainly would not enlighten him, even if Peter asked him for information. He would consider it sinful to even have such thoughts. Besides, Peter did not consider Lydia Wickham a lady in the strictest sense of the word. He paused twice—waiting for the estate footmen to attend to their duties—before entering Mrs. Wickham's chamber.

He moved cautiously across the room, lighting two candles along the way. Entering the main bedchamber from the sitting room, Peter slowly surveyed the area, taking in the disarray occupying every corner and draped across every piece of furniture. Clothes—gowns, corsets, chemises, and stockings, every piece of apparel possible for a woman to own—were strewn about the room. Apparently, Mrs. Wickham spent some time in a state of indecision as to what to wear. The way the lady treated her belongings spoke volumes of the woman. Her spoiled behavior—the total disregard for the work she made for others—irritated him. Peter had been brought up to know that all things held a place, and a true person of character never allowed himself to live in squalor. "Everything in its place," his father had said many times. Yet, despite Mrs. Wickham's unworthiness to be called a lady, Peter could not help being excited by the idea of touching her personal items. He had never been close to a woman—not like his cohorts—and actually touching a woman's intimate clothing brought a flush to his skin and made his breathing quicken.

As he gently touched one of the lady's corsets, he tried to drive from his mind the image of her breasts being raised by the garment. *This touched her,* he thought quite traitorously. Needing to push the thought from his mind, he forced himself to think of the precepts his father had instilled in him—a gentleman's responsibilities. *One must treat those who serve with respect if one expects respect in return.* That was the one quality that elevated Mrs. Wickham's sister to a lady's status.

Peter picked up a rose-hued gown from the floor, examining the quality. "A woman who treats her best wear as if it was rags deserves to be dressed in rags," he whispered to the room. Impulsively, he caught the seams of the gown in both hands, pulling the threads until they gave—a rent opening the material. "Nice," he murmured as he draped the dress across a chair's back. "This will be great fun…quite capital to see the lady's things in shreds. She will learn respect in the same way my father taught me respect."

Reaching for another gown—one lying crumpled on the bed's end—he took a blade from his boot and sliced the bodice to the waist. "Mrs. Wickham, is this a new style you sport?" he laughed sinisterly as he held up the ruined garment. "What is this?" He grabbed a pair of silk stockings. "One little…two little…three little cuts." He sliced up one of the expensive leggings, tossing the pieces into the air over his shoulder before moving on to the next item. Without thinking, he slid the second of the pair into his side pocket.

Next, he slit the laces of a deep burgundy day dress. Some pieces he ignored; others he purposely ruined. Slowly circling the bed, Peter left his mark on much of what Lydia Wickham had left behind.

Then he saw it—a miniature of the lady's husband—a man he knew well and of whom he violently disapproved. "Well, well… what have we here? Mr. Wickham, I presume." He palmed the frame and brought it closer to examine it. The face, although familiar, did not resemble the man he knew—the portrait showed a man with a future. "No future for you, George Wickham," he grumbled, "especially not married to such a woman. Can you not see what Mrs. Wickham made me do?" He gestured largely to the chaos surrounding him.

"What be ye doing here?" a soft voice asked close behind him.

Peter stayed in the shadows, but turned slowly, expecting the worst, only to find one of the Pemberley maids. "Doing?" he brought himself up to his full height. "What *would* a gentleman be doing in a lady's bedchamber?" His voice squeaked with anticipation.

"Be ye tryin' to 'sinuate that Mrs. Wickham be taken up with a servant—and a boy at that?" She gestured to the Pemberley livery he wore.

Peter glanced down at his attire before inclining his head with cold civility. "I suppose not." He attempted to saunter away, casually setting the miniature on the bed's end.

However, as he moved into the light's circle, Lucinda recognized him, and then she saw the room's condition. "Wait!" she barked out, trying to stop his retreat. "It be you." She rushed toward the bed. "What have ye done?" The maid grabbed up one of the ruined garments. "My God!" she gasped. "Mrs. Wickham will have me job! How will'n I be explainin' this mess?"

He did not stop to enlighten her on why he was in Mrs. Wickham's chamber. Instead, Peter moved through the connecting room door, trying to rid himself of the woman. *What would a man do?* He kept asking himself as he quickened his pace. James would certainly know what to do. James would turn and seduce the woman. But he, Peter, had no such worldly experience.

"Ye be goin' nowhere. I not be takin' the blame for what ye be doin'." She rushed forward to catch his arm and turn him away from the sitting room and an escape. "The Master be wantin' to talk to you."

Peter looked disgustedly at where her fingers rested on his sleeve. "I would advise you to remove your hand immediately," he warned menacingly. "No one touches me—not you—not your master. No one but my father has that privilege."

"Ye not be foolin' me. I be Lucinda...remember?" she challenged him.

His brow furrowed in a question. "I know not of what you speak, Madam," he said in a clipped voice.

"Ye know me. We talked before...before the Master be lookin' for someone who be makin' trouble." As the words she spoke took root in her consciousness, Lucinda became fully aware of her mistake in confronting this man. She moved away while his face turned gray and hers blanched. "I be sorry," she whispered as she backed into the sitting room door.

Peter swiveled slowly to face her. "Not nearly as sorry, my Dear, as you will be."

"No be hurtin' Lucinda," she begged as he closed the distance between them.

"'Hurting Lucinda,'" he mocked as he caught the maid's wrist. "Why would a gentleman hurt anyone beneath him?"

"Beneath who?" she rasped as she tried to ram the door closed, attempting to break his grip and shut him out of the bedroom. "Ye be no gentleman!" she shouted.

Peter anticipated her movement and braced the door with his shoulder. Her attempt to thwart him inflamed his temper—made him the man his father was when Peter disobeyed. "Who are you to judge your betters?" He wrenched her arm behind her, pulling the maid against his muscular chest, tightening his hold on her as she struggled to free herself.

"I sees no betters," Lucinda declared, although her countenance spoke her fears; she jerked her head to the left, searching for an escape.

Peter's arm came across her neck; while he increased the upward pressure on her arm, she kicked helplessly at his legs. She fought him, jabbing him in the ribs with her elbow and throwing her head back hard against his chest. Lucinda fought for air, but the young man crushed her neck in a viselike hold. He tightened his hold, minute degree by minute degree. "Why?" he murmured in regret. "Why did you not let me leave? Why did you make me do this? Why did you pick this day to die?"

In one last effort, Lucinda doubled up her fist and tried to plant him a facer over her shoulder—an act of futility. She flailed—she writhed—she churned—finally, she collapsed against him. "Yes, my Dear, your better," he snarled. Peter supported the maid's limp body against him. Suddenly, he panicked. "Now, what am I to do with you?" He jerked her to a standing position. "I must take you to James. James will know what to do."

He lifted the maid into his arms and made his way to the inside door. He crossed into the empty chamber, which adjoined that of Mrs. Wickham's to the darkened suite. It felt odd to carry a woman—any woman—thus, but especially a woman of the working class. His father's edicts demanded that a gentleman not see his servants as vessels for his own pleasure nor should such a man inflict pain on those who served. That thought stayed him—caused him to go weak in the knees. His father would definitely not be pleased. Peter would need to find a way to hide this one away—away from his father's ever-watchful eye. "Lord, the old man will take a cane to me for sure." *James,* he thought again. *James will solve this.* He would take her to James—to his friend. *Is James my friend?* he wondered suddenly. He was, Peter supposed, as much as any adult was who took a liking to a boy. Either way, James would know what to do—it would cost Peter, but he would turn the care of the woman over to James Withey.

The issue settled in his mind, Peter's feet moved again. He slowly pushed the empty chamber's exterior door open and surveyed the hallway, looking for Darcy's men—listening for the other maids. Sensing no one else moved through this section of the house, he slid along the wall, needing to reach a room with an opening before someone spotted him.

The woman's weight slowed his progress, and Peter had to stop twice to catch her to him again. "Mr. Darcy feeds you well, my Dear." He chuckled lightly as he reached the door of Georgiana Darcy's private chambers. Shifting Lucinda to a semi-standing position long enough to toss her over his shoulder like a bag of flour, he turned the latch and entered the girl's bedchamber. He liked this room—it spoke of the girl he sometimes watched—lilac and sunshine yellow—it reminded him of her—of the sweetness he suspected she possessed. Miss Darcy—the epitome of English innocence—the kind of English womanhood to which a gentleman of the realm aspired and which he revered. He never watched her the way he watched Mrs. Wickham. Despite Miss Darcy's little episode of make-believe he had witnessed in the ballroom earlier, Peter considered the girl a beautiful English flower—a delicate yellow rose. Yellow roses—he would find yellow roses in the Darcy conservatory and bring her a rosebud—one for her pillow. Peter glanced quickly at the girl's bed; he should not be here—not in Miss Darcy's bedroom. He had been furious the night he discovered that James had invaded the girl's room, actually watched her sleep, wanting to compromise the woman inside the girl.

He could not imagine why he tolerated James Withey. Of course, the man could be useful—useful with problems such as the one he carried over his shoulder, but truly the man was vile. James's crude tastes—his rakehell manners—his depravity—left a foul taste in Peter's mouth. His acquaintance with James was another of Peter's sins to which his father would certainly object.

Hurrying through the room toward the passage's entrance, he disappeared behind the screen. A commotion in the hallway gave him pause. When he heard Lady Catherine chastise her maid for doing her duty, Peter increased his pace, reaching for the lever and stepping back to allow the wall to swing toward him. The cold air gushed into the room, but he plunged into the icy darkness, knowing which way to turn to escape the danger of recognition. With another swoosh of air, the wall returned to its usual position—a wallpaper-trimmed panel sporting a light sconce and several bric-a-brac shelves holding miniature silver thimbles and ceramic pianofortes and horses—all Miss Darcy's childhood remembrances—her virtue disguising his transgressions. Placing Lucinda's body against one of the inside walls, he walked away toward his bedding. "Where did I leave that book I was reading? I am always losing things."

Darcy returned to the ballroom to find his family and to lessen the effects of his aunt's open censure. Mr. Worth stood speaking privately to Anne, who wept.

His partner noticed Darcy's entrance, and her head snapped up in recognition. "My mother?" Anne's bitterness masked her obvious tears.

"Her Ladyship decided to retire for the evening. She sends her regrets." He tried to smile. His wife, he observed, looked like an embattled angel, her outrage barely hidden. There was a deceptive calmness about her, which worried him.

"Indeed," Anne murmured, and Worth moved closer to her.

Darcy glanced about the room; they all waited for him to set the mood—to restore the levity of the performance. "I say we take this party to the rose sitting room. Let us celebrate your triumph tonight. We will send for tea and wine and brandy, along with some of Mrs. Jennings's famous chocolate tarts." He addressed a plea of cooperation to Elizabeth with his eyes.

Automatically, his wife fell into her role as the household's mistress. "I, for one, have developed quite an appetite. Who knew the theater was such a demanding occupation?" she announced to their guests as she caught Georgiana and Lydia around their waists. "I believe I have a new respect for those who trip the boards."

"The theater is a most demanding career." Lord Stafford placed Miss Donnel's arm on his own and followed Elizabeth Darcy's group from the hall. "Come along, Worth," he called.

Darcy moved to where he might speak to Anne privately. "I am sorry, my Dear, that I allowed Lady Catherine such latitude. I find it hard to break the habit of permitting Her Ladyship to vent. But I shall not fail you again. I have given my aunt an ultimatum—to either recognize the error of her ways or to leave Pemberley immediately. In either case, you will remain with us. I will not sanction your mother's domination of you any longer. You are under my protection from this moment forward. I shall speak to our uncle, the earl, as soon as possible and secure his agreement."

Anne's fingers reached out to touch his face. "How might I ever repay you, Cousin?"

"Be happy." He took Anne's fingers and brought them to his lips. "Find the type of happiness I discovered as Elizabeth's husband—know the gratification of something deeper and more meaningful than all the wealth of the land."

"Mrs. Jenkinson said that you already loved Elizabeth that Easter when you came to Rosings and Mrs. Darcy visited the Collinses." Anne turned to take Darcy's proffered arm.

"Madly," he whispered close to her ear. "Have Mrs. Darcy tell you how she refused my first proposal during that country sojourn."

"She did not!" Anne gasped. "Elizabeth refused you?" She laughed. "The evening that Mrs. Collins begged my mother's forgiveness for Miss Bennet's absence—claiming the lady suffered from a headache—that is why you made an untimely departure yourself—Mother felt quite put upon by your desertion!"

"Like Mrs. Jenkinson, Her Ladyship recognized what I tried gallantly to hide. I expected Elizabeth to be aware of my consideration, and I called on the cottage that evening to plead my case. Unfortunately, I did not anticipate Elizabeth's stubbornness or her knowledge of my involvement in separating Mr. Bingley from Jane Bennet."

Anne caught at his arm, forcing Darcy to pause. "Tell me, you did not!"

"In all my pomposity, I committed the ultimate of sins," he confessed.

"And Mrs. Darcy turned you away?" Anne queried.

"She said I behaved in a most ungentlemanly manner," he chuckled. "Quite astute—my wife. She declared most emphatically that I was the last man in the world upon whom she could ever be prevailed to marry. Gave me my comeuppance."

Anne giggled, amused by the image of a distraught Darcy. "I would say the lady taught you humility, Cousin."

"Humility and love," he admitted "But do not breathe a word of this to anyone else," he warned.

"I understand, Cousin. You have an image to maintain."

"I only tell you now, my Dear, as a lesson in what life may hand you. Do not let a seeming defeat be the end of what you know is important—what you need to survive. The worst you will suffer is a bruised ego."

CHAPTER 14

~ ~ ~

"YOU WERE MAGNIFICENT," Darcy murmured close to Elizabeth's ear.

Worry still playing across her face, she glanced up at him. "Thank you, my Husband."

"You are not to blame." He placed Elizabeth's hand on his arm. "I was never prouder of you," he continued. "Georgiana's eyes said it all, Elizabeth. She is alive again, willing to face censure, while taking the high road in each of her dealings. That is because of you." She started to object, but he shook his head. "Yes, because of you, Elizabeth, Georgiana has a safe port. After the incident with Mr. Wickham, my sister clung to me with all her might for a time—like a small child afraid of the monsters under her bed. But with you, Georgiana has learned a resolve—a willingness to try new things."

"Even when I insist on dressing her in male attire? You say such despite my poor behavior?" Elizabeth's eyes remained downcast in embarrassment.

Darcy maneuvered her out of the earshot of the others. "Elizabeth Darcy, you are spontaneous and sometimes impulsive, but you are never without a heart. Anything you do is done with enthusiasm and with great generosity. Those are the characteristics you taught my sister—and your own—today. I can offer you no disapproval." He leaned close again. "Besides, I found the sight of your buttocks, accentuated by the breeches you wore, quite fetching."

"Mr. Darcy!" She blushed, but obviously pleased by his words. "You are a scoundrel."

"Only where you are concerned, my Love." He breathed the words into her hair, his lips barely moving as he exhaled his want.

Before Elizabeth could answer, Mr. Baldwin interrupted. "Mr. Darcy," the butler spoke softly, "there is a gentleman who requests your attendance, sir."

"At this hour?" Darcy wondered how anyone might travel the roads under the current conditions.

Mr. Baldwin edged a bit closer. "Shall I send the gentleman away, sir?"

"Do we know the man's identity?" Darcy's gaze took in the whole room, noting the gaiety of the participants after an invigorating performance. Even Lady Catherine's verbal attack had not dampened their spirits. It pleased him to see the trials of the previous days set aside for camaraderie.

The butler slipped a calling card into Darcy's palm. "I thought it best not to draw attention to the man's presence under the circumstances, sir, by serving the card on a salver." Baldwin's eyes rested on Worth and Anne as they laughed comfortably with Lydia Wickham.

As unobtrusively as possible, Darcy read the card. "Mother Mary," he groaned. He turned to block the others' views while he passed the card to Elizabeth.

"Darcy!" she gasped.

He caught her hand in his before turning his attention to his servant. "Place the gentleman in my study, Mr. Baldwin."

"Yes, Mr. Darcy."

With the man's exit, Elizabeth hissed, "What should we do?"

"See if you cannot convince everyone to retire for the night. I will see what our visitor wants."

"Do you expect to keep the gentleman from seeing anyone this evening?" She touched his arm in concern.

Darcy nodded his agreement. "I would ascertain the man's motives. If possible, I will postpone his reunion until tomorrow, giving you and me time to discuss what we should choose to do next."

He left her then, excusing himself to the others by saying that he would see to the house's closure for the night. "It was a most delightful evening. I wish to thank the talented actors and the appreciative audience." He bowed to the room and made his way to his study. What must he do now? Just when he had thought the chaos of the past few days had turned to the positive, a man who could upset the apple cart had arrived on the doorstep. Taking a deep breath, he placed his hand upon the latch and opened the door to his next catastrophe.

James Withey found the woman's body lying carelessly against the secret door to Georgiana Darcy's room. "Another mess for my special touch," he grumbled as he lifted the Pemberley maid to his shoulder. "His Lordship's young vengeance is my dirty work." He clasped the deadweight to him and picked up the lantern he had taken from the stable.

Then he made the descent to the tunnel leading to the open field south of the main house, along the turnpike road. The fertile Peak District land surrounding the Darcy holdings left the steps damp from seeping groundwater. He guarded his footfalls, the moisture and mold making each bricked landing and each set of wooden steps dangerously slippery, but he knew these tunnels like the back of his hand. As a child, he often hid here when he should have been attending to his studies. It was Pemberley's maze that had taught him that he was a creature of the night. In these passageways, he played pirate and highwayman. He had seduced his first conquest in one of the lowest levels, a girl too afraid of spiders and the possibility of snakes to go more than a hundred feet into the tunnel.

Now, he traversed the area to rid Peter Whittington of his latest mistake. The man—a boy, really—pretended to have impeccable manners, but in James's estimation, all the man-child truly possessed was a nasty temper and a skewed sense of morality. "Needs a good tumble in the sack," he said aloud as he pushed aside the boarded-up opening, hidden quite effectively by a natural waterfall, now frozen solid, of course. He moved along the rock face and into the open.

A nearby copse of trees was his destination—the woman's weight and the deep snow combined to slow his progress. He posed

Lucinda against a tree. Both he and MacIves had flirted with the girl when they had openly moved about Darcy's house. James even thought about taking his pleasure with her. "His God Almighty Lordship should have lost himself in the heat of your sweetness, my pretty, instead of crushing your lovely neck." He reached into his pocket, brought out the silk stocking left from Peter's foray into Mrs. Wickham's room, and tied it tightly around the woman's neck. "Rest well, sweet Lucy," he said as he kissed each of her eyelids. Slowly, he rose and returned to the passage. "A few more days," he murmured, noticing the melting snow and the accumulating slush in the crevices and ditches. "A few more days and this will be over."

"How might I serve you, sir?" Darcy swung the door to his study wide and strode confidently into the room.

The man scrambled to his feet and offered a bow. "Mr. Darcy, I am pleased to have your acquaintance at last." He offered his hand in greeting.

Darcy took it briefly and then gestured for the man to return to his chair. "It is rather late for a social call, sir, and I am surprised to receive anyone under the current weather conditions. I was unaware that travel was possible."

"You know of me, Mr. Darcy?" the visitor asked cautiously.

"You have presented your card, sir, so I am aware of your name. If you ask if I am familiar with your relationship with other members of my family, I assure you, Lieutenant, there is little that transpires in the Fitzwilliam family of which I am uninformed." Darcy sat back in his chair and tried to appear relaxed and in control.

The lieutenant took pleasure in observing Mr. Darcy. The man held a reputation as a shrewd negotiator. Harwood had spent the better part of a week learning everything possible of Darcy before he had appeared on the man's doorstep. "Then I am to assume, Mr. Darcy, that my intended has taken refuge at Pemberley?"

Darcy's stomach tightened. "Your intended, Lieutenant? Am I to offer my good wishes?"

"Is Anne here?" Harwood ignored Darcy's attempt at changing the subject. "I traced Her Ladyship's carriage to the area before I recalled your connection to the de Bourghs. I prayed Anne sought safety from the storm in your home."

"May I ask, Lieutenant, how you managed to travel in such extreme conditions?"

Harwood allowed the diversion this time; he had anticipated having to answer such inquiries when he decided to make a Pemberley appearance. "Actually, Mr. Darcy, your part of Derbyshire took the brunt of the storm. Only the last ten to fifteen miles were treacherous. Cheshire is wet and a bit slippery, but it can be traveled by horseback, although carriage travel is still quite limited."

The fact that this man had compromised his cousin upset Darcy. Originally, he had hoped to welcome the man to Pemberley, but the lieutenant's flagrant disregard for Anne's reputation made Darcy wary. Plus, Harwood called at Pemberley late at night when Darcy would have no choice but to extend an invitation to remain with them. Darcy did not like such manipulative behavior. "I see."

Darcy made no other comment. He had found that a pause at an unexpected time would throw an opponent off balance. Tonight, the strategy worked perfectly. Harwood waited through a few strained moments before he stammered, "I-I will ask a-again, sir, if Miss de Bourgh is at Pemberley?"

"If you are truly my cousin's fiancé, then you must be aware, Lieutenant, that Her Ladyship and I have come to a parting of the ways."

"Anne shared no such confidences, but your cousin, the colonel, left the issue quite open to interpretation."

Damn! Darcy had hoped to trip up the man by introducing the subject of the family feud. Although he had just met the lieutenant, the man's sincerity did not ring true, and Darcy had learned over the years to listen to his instincts.

The officer forced a smile and asked nervously, "Am I to assume, sir, that your cousin has not taken shelter with you? If so, I must press on, and I do not wish to dally with guessing games. I will seek your cousin's estate in Matlock instead."

Darcy smiled enigmatically. "I am not a man who shares confidences with complete strangers. Suppose you tell me why you seek the de Bourgh party, and I shall respond accordingly."

Harwood's own smile faded with Darcy's reticence. "I am unsure, Mr. Darcy, of the depth of your knowledge of my relationship with Miss de Bourgh, but I will summarize it by saying that Anne and I developed an affection for one another during my short stay at Rosings Park. When I recently left for Liverpool, I implored your cousin to accept my proposal, but instead, Miss de Bourgh accepted Lady Catherine's estimation of me and refused my hand. Dejected, I returned to my post and my duties, but as luck would have it, Miss de Bourgh experienced a change of heart and followed me to the seaport. There, I secured lodgings for her and made inquiries regarding having the banns called. Unfortunately, while I made arrangements for the ceremony to make Miss de Bourgh my wife, your aunt arrived and removed Anne."

"Then, if my cousin chose to leave with Her Ladyship, may I ask why you think Anne might now seek your company? It would appear that the lady spoke volumes when she agreed to accompany her mother to Kent."

Harwood took note that Mr. Darcy still did not confirm what he knew. He had done reconnaissance before presenting himself this evening. A carriage bearing the Rosings livery rested in one of Pemberley's stables. "We are both aware, Mr. Darcy, of Miss de Bourgh's timidity when it comes to her mother's approval. Any decision Anne might make under Lady Catherine's watch is likely to be in Her Ladyship's best interests rather than in her daughter's."

Darcy heard the unspoken words. "I am under the assumption that my cousin is of age, and her decisions are all her own. I am not sure, Lieutenant, that you give Anne enough credit. Or perhaps you overestimate my aunt's influence!" Darcy knew where this conversation would lead—had known it before he entered the room. Now, he maneuvered the man into revealing his true nature.

Harwood blustered, "I assure you I offer no offense, Mr. Darcy. I realize that the de Bourghs are your family. My comments are based on personal observations only, and they may be in error, of course."

"Of course." Darcy twirled a pen aimlessly, giving the impression of boredom. After another pregnant pause, he turned on the man. "I return to my previous question, Lieutenant Harwood. If my cousin left of her own free will, why do you deem it necessary to chase her across an ice-covered Peak District?"

Harwood squirmed in his seat. "I have sought Miss de Bourgh in an honorable manner, Mr. Darcy, because many in Liverpool know of her presence at the Salty Sailor. An unmarried female in such an establishment is under close scrutiny, and despite our discretion, word of your cousin's abrupt departure has dramatically increased the rumors. I seek Miss de Bourgh so I might renew my proposal and save the lady's reputation."

"Let me see if I understand you, Harwood. You played on my cousin's vulnerability at Rosings, making her believe that you found her your perfect match. Foolishly, Anne followed you to Liverpool; at which point, you took advantage of her naïveté by finding her quarters in an unsavory establishment, where you openly called upon her, making sure others were aware of your clandestine relationship. Now, you feign a concern for extricating Anne from a situation of your own design. Something along those lines, Lieutenant?"

Harwood sprang to his feet. "I have never—"

"Of course, you have, Harwood." Darcy's mouth turned up at the corners. "Now, have a seat and let us be honest with each other." Darcy gestured to the chair Harwood had just vacated.

Fuming, Harwood sat. He would play out the hand he had been dealt. "Then Anne is at Pemberley?" he repeated.

"My cousin dwells under my protection, Lieutenant Harwood." Darcy did no more than raise one eyebrow, betraying no emotions.

"Then I am to present myself to you, Mr. Darcy, instead of Her Ladyship."

"We return to your second proposal. Am I correct, Lieutenant? As my aunt has no knowledge of the first, I am unsure which you mean."

Harwood sat up straight, attempting to convey honesty and dependability. "I am willing to marry Miss de Bourgh and give her the protection of my name, if that is what you mean, Mr. Darcy."

"And willing to accept Anne's very substantial dowry in return?" Darcy poured himself a brandy. Uncharacteristically, he did not offer one to Harwood—a direct cut.

"A man expects his wife to bring something to the marriage," Harwood asserted.

Darcy thought of Elizabeth and her settlement of a thousand pounds. "What if all the lady has to offer is her ardor?"

"That is ridiculous, Mr. Darcy. I am well aware of Miss de Bourgh's financial situation."

Darcy had expected nothing less from the man who sat before him. He felt sorry for his cousin—sorry that Anne had once had so little self-confidence that she had become involved with such a cad—also sorry that he had not protected her. He did not know how just yet, but he would disentangle his cousin from this sham of a marriage proposal. "And if my cousin chooses to weather the rumors and refuses your kind offer?"

"Why would Miss de Bourgh consider such insanity? Once a woman loses her good name, she is not likely to find an honorable man."

Darcy smiled before asking, "And you are an honorable man, Lieutenant?"

"I am, Mr. Darcy."

Darcy rose slowly to his feet. "It is late, Harwood. I will offer you a bed for the evening, and you may present yourself to my cousin in the morning." He moved to the bell cord. "I assume that will be acceptable, sir."

"That is most generous of you, Mr. Darcy, under the circumstances."

Mr. Baldwin arrived immediately. "You rang, Mr. Darcy."

"Yes, Mr. Baldwin. The lieutenant will join us for the evening. A room on this level seems appropriate."

Baldwin knew Darcy always placed his most disagreeable guests on the second level of the house. "I will see to it personally, Mr. Darcy."

"And send Lucas to me." He nodded slightly. "We must see to the lieutenant's mount."

With a smug look of triumph, Harwood followed the butler from the room. Darcy returned to his desk. Within moments, Lucas was at his door. "You sent for me, sir?"

Darcy motioned the man forward. "For this evening, I need you to attend to Lieutenant Harwood's horse. I wish the gentleman to believe that he is secure in what he hopes to achieve at Pemberley."

The footman did not understand, but he agreed with what his employer told him.

"More important, Lucas, I need you to take a message to my cousin at Matlock. I am reluctant to send you out in this weather, but this is urgent. I will finish writing instructions to Colonel Fitzwilliam for you to deliver. The lieutenant informs me that this part of Derbyshire suffered the hardest with the storm. He claims Cheshire is already recovering, but as you are heading in the opposite direction, I am afraid the going may be quite rough. I need my cousin's insights, but not at the risk of your life. Take no undue chances. I will provide you funds with which to take shelter, if necessary."

"Matlock is usually a three-hour ride, sir. Even with the weather, I should succeed in no more than double that time. I will not fail you, Mr. Darcy."

"I am most grateful, Lucas. Be ready to ride at first light."

"As you wish, Mr. Darcy."

Elizabeth followed her sister up the main staircase, exhausted by the day and by the chaos of late. She wanted to announce to Georgiana and to Lydia and to Jane and her parents, and even to Lady Catherine, that she carried Darcy's child. She wanted to tell Mrs. Reynolds and Mrs. Jennings and Darcy's cottagers—tell the world that she bore the heir to Pemberley and to accept their good wishes and to go back to the way it had been before the ice storm—before the phantom of Pemberley had become a reality.

She wondered what Lieutenant Harwood would do to the happiness she had observed on Miss de Bourgh's face this evening. Elizabeth almost wished that Darcy's aunt would refuse the apology he had demanded and that Lady Catherine would take her leave in the morning. It would be easier to handle Harwood and Anne without the benefit of Her Ladyship's temper.

"I will see you in the morning, Lyddie." Elizabeth found the day's earlier excitement had quickly dissipated. She wondered if her sudden tiredness had anything to do with the baby. Darcy was correct; she needed to think of her child first. No more corsets and no more overexerting herself—and no more hiding her happiness.

Elizabeth had just reached for the bedchamber door handle when the sound of her sister's scream sent an icy dagger through Elizabeth's heart. Instantly, she was on the run. Seconds later, she burst through Lydia's door. Screaming at the top of her lungs, her sister stood in the room's center. Elizabeth caught Lydia around the waist and pulled her away from an unknown danger, dragging Lydia toward the dressing room.

The impact of her sister nearly knocking her to the floor stopped Lydia's screams but not her anger. She fought Elizabeth to return to the bedchamber—to right the wrong. Catching Elizabeth's arm, Lydia whipped her older sister from her, driving Elizabeth face first into an interior wall and sending her stumbling backward. That was when her foot caught in the fringed edge of a Persian-inspired carpet. Elizabeth crashed to the floor with a breath-stealing thud.

Craving his wife's company, Darcy left his study behind, dreading telling Elizabeth about the perfidy Harwood had brought into their home. If he ever rid himself of his current guests, he would, he swore, bar Pemberley's doors to any but his immediate family. In the future, he would pay others to offer charity to anyone coming uninvited to Pemberley.

His foot touched the first step leading to the private quarters just as the initial scream rang out clearly from the chamber suites. Immediately, he bolted up the stairs, followed closely by Murray and Lucas. Taking the steps two and three at a time, he heard the second round of screams begin as he gained the main hallway. Thankfully, the screams were not Elizabeth's or Georgiana's. *Who is screaming? Why?* Turning to the left, Darcy saw the open door and lunged toward the sound of a tussle. He burst through the passage to see Elizabeth's arms flailing in the air as she crashed to the floor. Before he could reach her, she went limp.

"Damn!" he cursed as he shoved Lydia Wickham out of the way, trying to reach his wife. "If you have hurt her," he began a threat, but a gasp of air took him to his knees beside Elizabeth. "Lizzy," he cooed as he cradled her in his arms. "Elizabeth, please." Her eyes opened slowly, but when she smiled at him, Darcy clutched her to him. "Thank God," he whispered as he kissed her forehead and brushed the hair from her face. "Let me take you to your room."

"Lydia," she choked out.

Darcy shot a quick glance at Murray, who motioned that he had found nothing amiss in the room. "I will have you settled, and then I will see what troubles Mrs. Wickham." He lifted her from the floor and turned toward the open door. "Murray," he ordered, "ask Mrs. Reynolds to come to Mrs. Darcy's rooms."

"Yes, Mr. Darcy."

Elizabeth buried her face in his chest. "Fitzwilliam, this is not necessary."

Darcy paused in the doorway, shifting her in his arms to maneuver her through the opening. He saw them all—summoned by Mrs. Wickham's screams—all his guests and family, but he made the declaration just the same. "Elizabeth, it *is* necessary. You carry our child, and I will take no more chances with your life."

"Elizabeth!" Georgiana exhaled her name as she touched her sister's arm.

"Come sit with me, Georgiana," Elizabeth declared as Darcy carried her to her room. The others trailed along behind him as if he were Hamelin's piper and they the village children.

Striding into her familiar chamber, Darcy lowered Elizabeth gently to the bed. "Rest, my Love, while I see to the latest crisis."

"Do not be long," she whispered as she caressed his cheek.

"Stay with her, Georgiana, until I return. Your sister is not to rise from that bed, no matter how much she protests." Darcy would brook no argument. Elizabeth's eyebrow rose in amusement.

"Yes, Fitzwilliam." Georgiana caught Elizabeth's hand and squeezed it tenderly.

He shot his wife a warning glare for good measure and then plunged into the crowd gathered outside Elizabeth's room.

"Mrs. Darcy is with child?" Anne touched his arm as she walked quickly to keep up with his long strides.

Darcy stopped suddenly outside Lydia Wickham's room. "She is." He glanced down at his cousin. "And I will have my wife protected at all costs."

"Might we see her?" Anne whispered.

Darcy took in the others clustered around. Thankfully, his aunt had chosen not to join them, or perhaps the noise had not disturbed her rest. He suspected the first. "Tomorrow...please allow Mrs. Darcy her rest this evening, and then I am sure my wife will happily receive your good wishes." Motioning Worth and the viscount to follow him, Darcy reentered Lydia's still-open doorway.

"Elizabeth?" Georgiana whispered conspiratorially as Darcy drew the others away from his wife's door. "Is it true? Are you with child?"

Elizabeth giggled. "Yes, Georgiana. Is it not magnificent news?" Her smile could no longer be contained.

"How long have you known? When will the babe arrive? Do you wish for a son or a daughter? Will I be allowed to hold the child?"

Elizabeth laughed aloud. "Slow down, Georgiana. We have plenty of time—the babe will not come tonight…in early summer. Our child will grace this house in early June."

Mrs. Reynolds rushed into the room after a single knock on the door. "What seems to be the trouble, Mistress?" She displaced Georgiana on the bed's edge and placed her hand on Elizabeth's forehead to check for a fever.

"It is really nothing, Mrs. Reynolds," Elizabeth assured the woman, whose face appeared unusually pale and grim. "I simply stumbled over a rug and took a tumble." The woman turned immediately to checking Elizabeth's arms and legs for bruises and lacerations.

"Elizabeth, it is more than that," Georgiana protested. "Fitzwilliam was not simply concerned about a twisted ankle."

Elizabeth rolled her eyes in supplication. Only a quarter hour earlier, she had wished that she could tell everyone. *The prayer the devil answers!* With a sigh of exasperation, Elizabeth stopped Mrs. Reynolds's ministrations short. "Mr. Darcy has summoned you because I fell and had my breath knocked from my lungs."

"And?" Georgiana prompted.

"*And* I am with child.…I will deliver an heir for Pemberley in a few months."

Tears misted the housekeeper's eyes. She had tended the Darcys for more than six and twenty years, and she had prayed for this moment more than once. "Oh, Mistress," she said and caught at the bedpost. "You brought Mr. Darcy solace when no others would satisfy. Now, you bring all of Pemberley a future." Impulsively, she moved to embrace Elizabeth. "You will remain in bed," she ordered. "I will see to everything in your name." She took Elizabeth's hand and kissed the back of it. "Bless you, Mrs. Darcy."

Elizabeth knew she could not bear to stay in bed for even one full day, let alone six months. "I agree that I should remain abed for several hours to assure everyone of my health, but I will not become a lady of leisure. I have a household to run." When Mrs. Reynolds began to object, Elizabeth silenced her with a tilt of her head. "However, I will promise to adjust my duties and allow you to shoulder some of them. Yet, how may I serve Pemberley and my husband if I am nothing more than an invalid?"

Mrs. Reynolds listened carefully; she had admired Elizabeth Bennet Darcy from the first time she had laid eyes on her when Elizabeth was a Pemberley visitor. When she had realized the young master's interest in the woman, she had intuited that Mr. Darcy might truly know happiness with Elizabeth. She had been proven correct: Elizabeth Darcy was exactly what the estate and the master needed to survive. "You are wise, Mistress," she agreed. "At least, allow me to attend you for this night."

"To that, I will readily acquiesce."

Mrs. Reynolds sat about helping Elizabeth undress. Georgiana hustled about the room, finding dressing gowns and robes. "Why not simply send for Hannah," Elizabeth suggested, thinking her maid could do the job in half the time.

Mrs. Reynolds grumbled, "That girl will have a few of my words, I might tell you. Surely she knew and has said nothing of your condition. All the silly gossip, and she brings no word of such importance."

"You will do no such thing, Mrs. Reynolds. I swore Hannah to my secret, and you will not reward her loyalty as such." Elizabeth tried to sound stern.

Mrs. Reynolds flushed. "Oh, Mrs. Darcy, you surely know I would not judge Hannah poorly for doing her duty."

Georgiana helped Elizabeth out of the man's shirt she still wore. As she did so, she said, "And you would not rob us of the pleasure of being of use to you."

"No, I suppose I would not," Elizabeth said grudgingly, unaccustomed as she was to people fussing over her. Mrs. Reynolds unlaced Elizabeth's corset. "Mr. Darcy believes that I should abandon the corset, thinking it not good for the child," she offered.

"Many fine women do not agree, but country babes know no such restrictions," the housekeeper observed. "I would see no harm if you chose to do so in your own home, especially with your husband's blessing."

Elizabeth smiled at Mrs. Reynolds's attempt at diplomacy. "I want nothing to happen to this child." She winked at Georgiana. "The clothes we sported this evening might serve me well. A woman could hide a great deal under a man's shirt."

Georgiana barked out an embarrassed laugh. "I do not believe Fitzwilliam would give his blessing to such, Elizabeth."

"It is a shame. I find men's clothing quite liberating," Elizabeth teasingly asserted.

"Elizabeth, Fitzwilliam warned me long ago that you love to say outrageous things simply to provoke a response." Georgiana loosened her sister's braid and prepared to brush her hair.

"And so I do, my Sister." Elizabeth gently touched Georgiana's hand. "When the storm has released its hold on Derby, let us shop together for new spring clothes. I will need additional day dresses to carry me through my confinement, and you have an excellent eye for color and pattern."

Georgiana slid her arms around Elizabeth's shoulders. "I am as blessed as Fitzwilliam is that you have entered our lives, Elizabeth. I have never known such acceptance."

"You are a precious jewel, Georgiana. When I left my sisters in Hertfordshire, I never expected to find a like devotion in my new home. We should celebrate that our dear Fitzwilliam recognized a need in both of us and brought us together." Elizabeth kissed the girl's cheek before she rested against the pillows Mrs. Reynolds had placed behind her head. "You will stay with me until Fitzwilliam returns?"

"Certainly, Elizabeth." Georgiana took a position in a nearby chair.

"May I, Mistress?" Mrs. Reynolds gestured to Elizabeth's body.

Elizabeth nodded her agreement, allowing Mrs. Reynolds to carefully examine the slight bulge. "I neither see nor feel anything unusual. I will ask the midwife to call on you soon, Mrs. Darcy."

Caught by the significance of the housekeeper's words and the sudden realization of what her delivery of a healthy child would mean to the hundreds of people who depended upon Pemberley for their existence, Elizabeth was uncharacteristically silent. "Thank you, Mrs. Reynolds," she murmured.

"I will send up some chamomile tea to help you rest, Mistress." With that, the woman left the room, but Elizabeth noted that tears dampened the lady's cheeks.

"You will like being an aunt, Georgiana?" Elizabeth ventured, suddenly humbled by the earnestness of those who surrounded her.

Georgiana flushed. "Next to knowing my own child, I can think of nothing that would please me more, Elizabeth."

Motioning Worth and Lord Stafford to follow him, Darcy reentered Lydia Wickham's still-open doorway. Standing where Darcy had left her, the young woman sobbed uncontrollably while leaning on a chair for support.

Despite his anger minutes earlier, Darcy thought of Elizabeth and how she would want him to treat her sister. "Come, Mrs. Wickham," he said softly as he wrapped his arm around her shoulders. Darcy motioned to the chair, and she plopped down, her energy gone. He knelt before her. "Now, please tell me what happened." Worth and the viscount waited patiently in the background.

Lydia choked and coughed and her shoulders shook from the force of stopping the flow of her tears. *Drama,* Darcy thought as he gazed at her. *There is always drama surrounding Elizabeth's sister.* He slipped his handkerchief into her hand and encouraged her again to provide an explanation.

"Lizzy?" Lydia moaned as she wiped her eyes.

"Mrs. Darcy will recover," he ventured.

The tears remained, but the sobs ceased. "Lizzy is to have a child?"

"She is." Darcy took Lydia's hand in his and tried to calm her. "Mrs. Darcy is concerned for her sister. When I return to her, I would like to allay her fears. Tell me what frightened you."

Lydia's lip began to tremble, but she took a deep breath and began. "Lizzy and I returned to our rooms. We said our good nights, and I came in here. I rang for Lucinda, and then I went to my chamber." She gestured toward the adjoining bedroom. "Everything!" she wailed. Worth and Stafford slipped into the room to investigate. Sobbing, she said, "Everything is ruined!"

Moments later, Worth appeared in the adjoining doorway and held up a shredded gown in each hand. Darcy nodded his understanding and turned to Lydia again. "The gowns, you mean?"

"The gowns——the stockings——everything." A gasp of frustration escaped.

Darcy fought his contempt. His wife had taken a terrible fall because of a torn gown. "And this caused you to scream as if the world had come to an end?"

Indignation entered her tone. "I screamed, Mr. Darcy, because I felt a sudden gush of cold air from behind me and heard a loud clank of some kind that made me think that your intruder invaded my room. I screamed because I feared for my life."

"And my wife?" Darcy prompted.

Lydia looked away for a moment, trying to visualize what had happened. "I am unsure. Someone grabbed me, and I fought to discover the depth of the crime practiced upon me. The next thing I knew, Lizzy was on the floor, and you were angrily charging into my room."

Drama. "I am still angry, Mrs. Wickham; at least, where my wife is concerned," he cautioned.

"I see nothing in the lady's bedchamber to lead us to whomever did this." The viscount returned to the room. "Someone ransacked Mrs. Wickham's belongings. The room is in disarray, and many of your sister's personal items have been destroyed. I found this on the floor." He handed Darcy the miniature.

Darcy barely looked at the portrait. He knew it well—had seen it displayed daily in his father's study—his own study now. He had placed it in a memory box along with several of Elizabeth's mementos shortly after they had married. "I apologize, Mr. Darcy," Lydia began. "I found it at the bottom of the wardrobe in my room. I did not think you would mind if I borrowed it while I was at Pemberley."

Darcy spoke through clenched teeth, "You are welcome to your husband's likeness, Mrs. Wickham." Bitterly, he wondered if he would ever be free of Wickham's shadow.

Worth joined them in the narrow dressing room. "Are we sure your intruder did this? It seems a petty act of revenge, especially for a man who devises sophisticated murders."

"Then who else?" The strain on Darcy's nerves showed in his tone.

"Lucinda," Lydia asserted. "I threatened to speak to Elizabeth about her poor service."

Darcy's head snapped up in response. "Did you not say you rang for Lucinda when you entered the room?"

"I did, Mr. Darcy."

Lord Stafford voiced what they all thought, "And the maid has failed to report?"

"Might you address this issue to Mr. Baldwin and Mrs. Reynolds for me, Your Lordship?"

"Certainly, Darcy." The viscount quickly disappeared through the passageway.

"I will send another of my staff to attend you, Mrs. Wickham," Darcy said stiffly and rose to go.

Lydia caught at his hand. "Tell Lizzy I am sorry. Please, Mr. Darcy—tell her I meant her no harm."

"You may tell my wife yourself, Mrs. Wickham—in the morning." With that, he and Worth departed the lady's chamber. Outside the now-closed door, he pulled the solicitor aside. "Mr. Worth," he whispered, "I have news of interest to you."

"I am all ears, Mr. Darcy."

"I had a visitor a while ago—a gentleman whom I have placed on the second level, away from my other guests." Worth raised an eyebrow. "My cousin's intended, Lieutenant Harwood, has come to save Anne's reputation by offering the protection of his name."

"Bloody hell!" Worth cursed. "Her intended? What is the meaning of this?"

"Mr. Worth, I have no desire to see my cousin with the lieutenant, but it may take me a few days to dislodge his claim on Anne without a loss of significant fortune. I need you to offer Miss de Bourgh comfort and not to betray my hand. If you hear me support the lieutenant's suit, it will be a ploy." Darcy glanced quickly about to assure their privacy. "I will require your cooperation, Mr. Worth, if I am to rid this family of Harwood and his scheme. I confide in you because I know you to be a man of reason in your daily life. You must practice that reason in this situation, even if your emotions tell you otherwise."

"And I am not to confide this to Miss de Bourgh? Am I correct, Mr. Darcy?"

"Despite Anne's venture into the performing arts earlier this evening, my cousin has not the talent to dissemble—to perform such a farce."

Worth's crooked smile turned up the corners of his mouth. "And I do, sir?"

"Precisely, Worth. You practice law."

CHAPTER 15

~ ~ ~

DARCY CHECKED ON Elizabeth before he joined the viscount and the Pemberley staff members. Finding his wife enjoying a cup of tea, he kissed her and then rushed downstairs to address yet another mystery unfolding under his roof.

"I have instructed the butler and housekeeper to ask about the missing maid and report any details they discover," Adam Lawrence informed Darcy when Pemberley's master suddenly appeared in the main foyer.

"Thank you, Your Lordship." Darcy gestured toward the main drawing room, the one Darcy used when he first welcomed his guests to Pemberley. "Let us see if there is any brandy left in the decanter."

"I thought this madness had taken a vacation." Stafford fell in beside Darcy.

Darcy shook his head in disbelief. "I had hoped. I cannot imagine how I will explain all this to the local magistrate. I have taken to making notes daily so I do not omit anything."

They took up chairs before the dying embers of the hearth. Neither of them bothered with stoking the fire—they would not stay long. "Do you think the maid committed the destruction we witnessed in Mrs. Wickham's room?"

"I no longer know what I should believe." Darcy raked his fingers through his hair. "I pray it is simply a matter of a *rogue* servant taking out her lack of patience with a difficult mistress. As appalling

238

as it would be to have such a person in my employ, the alternative is not something I wish to consider." Darcy paused before adding, "I should tell you, we have a new guest on the second level. He is one Lieutenant Harwood, a compatriot of Colonel Fitzwilliam's and an avowed suitor of my cousin Anne."

Lord Stafford weighed his words carefully. "Your tone says you do not approve of the lieutenant. Is there something else of which I should be made aware?"

Darcy would not mention Anne's possible ruination. "The lieutenant reports this part of Derbyshire suffered the most in the storm. He claims that he rode here from Cheshire. Carriage travel, he says, is not yet fully available. I imagine that it should only be a matter of a few days."

Stafford's quick analysis brought an ironic retort. "Are you telling me that if Cathleen and I had continued on our journey that we might have outrun the storm?"

Darcy chose his words carefully. "*If* the lieutenant is to be believed, then the answer is in the affirmative."

Stafford sat forward in interest. "*If?* What are not saying, Darcy? The lieutenant is not to be trusted?"

"I have no knowledge of the man's true character, Stafford, but I have learned not to accept anything at face value. When you hear the lieutenant speak, listen carefully."

Stafford did not respond; they understood each other. "You will seek my aid if you need it, Darcy." The viscount stood to take his leave.

"Should I apply to your chamber or that of your cousin?"

"If you ask the question, I must assume you already know the answer." The viscount strolled casually toward the open door. "My *cousin* has chosen to no longer accept my protection when this is over." Stafford's voice did not betray his own ambivalence about the situation.

Darcy paused momentarily before adding, "I am sorry to hear it; as *cousins* go, the young lady offers a touch of true class."

"I believe she does."

By the time Darcy climbed the stairs, Elizabeth slept. He joined his men as they searched the house for the errant maid. He really did not expect to find Lucinda Dodd; she had disappeared, just as the Pemberley phantom did every time they had an opportunity to capture him. Frustration filled him as he undressed for the evening. He wanted this over—Darcy wanted to go back to his life before the siege on his household.

He struggled out of his jacket before addressing his waistcoat and cravat. He could not even remember the last time he had depended on his valet to help him disrobe at night. "Yes, you do, you fool. It was your wedding night," he murmured. "The night this goddess gave herself to you." He knew he should let Elizabeth sleep alone—exhaustion plagued her—but he did not believe he could ever again sleep without her next to him. Without Elizabeth in his arms, he felt bereft of life—she had imprinted herself on his soul.

Darcy stripped away his breeches and small clothes and crawled under the blankets with her. His weight caused her to roll toward him, and Darcy scooped Elizabeth into his arms. "Fitzwilliam?" she mumbled.

"You were expecting someone else?" he teased as he stroked the hair from her face and kissed her temple.

Elizabeth smiled mischievously, keeping her eyes closed. "My lover."

Darcy nibbled on her earlobe. "Does your lover make you gasp with anticipation?" He kissed his way down her neck, creating the sensation he had just described. Then his lips brushed hers. "Does your lover make you quiver with his touch?" He brushed Elizabeth's breasts before trailing a line of fire across her hips. He feathered kisses along her chin line. "Does your lover bring you such ecstasy that it is a tempest impossible to control?"

"No, sir," she said as she snuggled into his chest, inhaling his scent—the smell of a powerful male. "Only my husband brings forth such pleasure. He is love incarnate."

He closed his eyes for a moment, and then a curious kind of peace crossed his face. "Then I am thankful that I am your husband, ma'am."

"As am I, Mr. Darcy."

He kissed Elizabeth's upturned nose. "Rest, my Love. Your husband is here to take care of you." He wrapped her in his arms, pulling the blankets over them.

The morning room buzzed with life and noise, the excitement of the previous evening carrying them into the new day. "Well, I am thankful Mrs. Darcy was not harmed by the incident," Cathleen remarked. "A woman with child is in a precarious situation."

"With an estate this size," Mrs. Williams observed, "it is imperative that the lady deliver a healthy heir. Mrs. Darcy must feel the pressure of giving Mr. Darcy a son to assume the estate."

Anne joined the conversation. "I am sure my cousin has never conveyed such an edict to his wife."

Mrs. Williams ignored Anne's defense. "Mrs. Darcy must prove she is worthy of the respectability Mr. Darcy bestowed on her when she became his wife."

"Mrs. Darcy is a gentleman's daughter," Anne asserted.

Evelyn Williams spit out her words: "That may be, Miss de Bourgh, but it is painfully evident that your cousin's connections outpaced his wife's." She turned a deaf ear to Anne's protest; and then she delivered a final cut. "It would seem to me, Miss de Bourgh, that you would count Mrs. Darcy's situation as one of your blessings. If Her Ladyship had her way, you would be Mrs. Darcy and be expected to assume the position of mistress of Pemberley and be the mother of the Darcy line. It would be a daunting task for a woman of such a *delicate nature*. Maybe Mr. Darcy had it right, after all. A woman to serve Pemberley and him equally would have to understand those of a lower class."

Anne charged, "Why do you speak so poorly of your hostess?"

Mrs. Williams smiled wryly. "That is where you are in error, Miss de Bourgh. I admire Mrs. Darcy. She is a survivor—the kind of woman who can adapt to any situation. Mrs. Darcy could follow the drum or host a grand ball for royalty. I understand her husband's foresight in choosing the woman. Other choices would have weakened his position and his bloodline."

"Then your censure is for me?" Anne's cheeks colored.

Instead of giving her an answer, Mrs. Williams turned her back on Anne, ignoring the woman she had come to dislike.

Her actions brought a deeper flush of color to Anne's cheeks. Uncertain how to handle such a strained personal relationship, she retreated, taking her plate to another of the settings, away from the offending woman.

Darcy called on Lieutenant Harwood, wishing to accompany the officer to the breakfast room—not allowing the man to *surprise* Anne. "Ah, Lieutenant, I see you are ready."

"I tend to be an early riser, Mr. Darcy."

"Then let us be about it." Darcy led the way through the dimly lit hallways. As no one else resided in this part of Pemberley, no need existed to light lanterns on the tables. Hearing the noise of the morning room in the distance, Darcy reluctantly contemplated the scene he had constructed to inflict upon those in attendance. He had forbidden Elizabeth from coming downstairs this morning; she had reluctantly agreed, although she had provided her opinion on how he should handle the encounter. Luckily, Georgiana was in the music room. Since his reprimand regarding her late night *sojourns,* his sister had decided early morning seclusion was comparable to nocturnal solitude.

Leading the way, Darcy immediately noted that Mrs. Williams sat apart from the others. The woman had become quite withdrawn over the past few days—a fact which did not sit well with him. Mr. Worth chose items from the morning table, while Anne sat with Miss Donnel and Lord Stafford. Anne looked quite troubled, and for a moment, Darcy wondered if Worth had betrayed his trust. Then Anne's eyes fell on Harwood, and she paled in horror. "Robert!" she exclaimed as she rose shakily to her feet.

The lieutenant bowed chivalrously in her direction. "Miss de Bourgh, I am pleased to have found you safe."

Darcy jumped into the fray. "Ladies and Gentlemen, might I present Lieutenant Robert Harwood, an associate of my cousin Colonel Fitzwilliam. Lieutenant, this is Viscount Stafford, his cousin Miss Donnel, Mr. Worth, and…" Darcy turned to introduce Mrs. Williams, but the woman had slipped from the room. "It seems our other guest has taken her leave unexpectedly. You shall meet Mrs. Williams, as well as my wife and sister, a bit later." Anne remained standing, although she swayed in place. "And, of course, you hold an acquaintance with my cousin."

Anne demanded an explanation. "Why are you here?" Her eyes had not left Harwood's face.

The man smiled—the grin of a cat that has caught the mouse. "I believe, Miss de Bourgh, we should discuss in private the reason for my sudden appearance at Pemberley."

Again, Darcy took control of the conversation. "Anne, why do you not go and ask Lady Catherine to join us. We shall all meet in my study in, let us say, thirty minutes."

Anne nodded weakly and skirted from the room.

"Please, Lieutenant, help yourself. Come join the viscount and me. I am sure Lord Stafford would be interested in the road conditions. He and Miss Donnel had set out to reach a seriously ill relative before being waylaid by the storm."

"Thank you, Mr. Darcy." Harwood moved off to fill a breakfast plate. Darcy motioned a footman to bring both coffee and tea, and then he took a seat beside Miss Donnel, leaving the one beside the viscount available for Harwood. Worth quietly seated himself on the other side of Miss Donnel.

When Harwood finally joined them, Adam Lawrence began. "Mr. Darcy seems to believe you are aware of an improvement in weather conditions. Might you enlighten us, sir? As our host has indicated, my cousin and I hoped to reach Cheshire before the demise of our relative, and Worth, here, has a law practice to which to return."

Harwood stuffed his mouth with bacon and toast—a stalling tactic recognized by three of his table partners. "I came from Liverpool by horseback. The roads are passable but difficult. A carriage might still find it impossible. Derby—at least, this part—appears to have taken the brunt of the storm. It became more difficult the closer I came to Lambton."

"And Pemberley was your destination?" Mr. Worth ground out in a poor attempt at civility.

Harwood should have looked embarrassed, but he boldly announced to the group, "I followed Miss de Bourgh when I realized she had left with her mother and her companion." For a man who wished to save a lady's reputation by an offer of marriage, Darcy noted how easily Harwood himself spread the gossip of Anne's indiscretion. "As I entered Derby and noted the conditions, I remembered, quite unexpectedly, Miss de Bourgh's association with Mr. Darcy. I took the chance the ladies came to him for protection."

"I thought you were a close associate of the colonel?" Stafford asked in a seemingly innocent manner, although Darcy knew it was anything but innocent.

Harwood stammered, "I-I call the colonel my friend. Why do you ask, sir?"

"Oh, no reason." Stafford returned to the kippers piled high on his plate. "These are delicious, Darcy." He gestured with his fork. "I must find out from whom your cook purchases these. I would have them regularly."

Harwood sat forward, trying to recapture the viscount's attention. "No, sir. Really, I must insist. Do you question the legitimacy of my relationship with Colonel Fitzwilliam?"

Stafford now sported the cat-like smile. "It just seemed odd that you would *unexpectedly remember* that the de Bourghs are related to Darcy. First, the lady in question called you by your Christian name, indicating an intimate relationship exists between you. Secondly, the Fitzwilliam family is very proud of their connections. I

had known the Earl of Matlock less than a day before his associa-
tion with both Darcy and the de Bourghs was made known to me.
Finally, the colonel serves with Darcy as Miss Darcy's guardian,
something of which I would imagine a *friend* would be well aware.
It seems more likely to me that you *expected* Miss de Bourgh to seek
Mr. Darcy's protection and his advice, and, therefore you came to
Pemberley expecting to find her here."

"I assure, Your Lordship, that you are in error," Harwood asserted.

Stafford laughed softly, self-mockingly setting the ploy. "I may
be, sir. It would not be the first time, now would it?"

"Nor the last," Worth added good-naturedly.

The viscount nodded in agreement. "Nor the last." He turned
to Cathleen. "How do you feel about a tour of the Darcys' conservatory, my Dear? Worth, here, tells me our hostess has teased several
interesting rose varieties from the ground."

"That would be excellent, my Lord." Cathleen placed her napkin on the table. "I wish to look in on Mrs. Darcy first; then, I will
join you, Adam. Please excuse me, gentlemen."

"I shall wait patiently in Mr. Darcy's well-stocked library." Stafford, too, begged their permission to leave and disappeared from
the room.

"I have a great need to check on my wife, if you have no objections, Lieutenant. Mrs. Darcy took a tumble yesterday evening,
and I am a doting husband, it seems." Darcy shot a quick glance at
Worth, reminding him not to say anything untoward to Harwood.

The lieutenant nodded and returned to his breakfast.

Worth followed Darcy to his feet. "There is something about
which I wish to speak to His Lordship. I hate to leave you to your
own devices, Harwood, but I am sure you will understand." Worth
picked up his pace so he might overtake Darcy in the main foyer.
"Darcy," he hissed as he came close.

"Yes, Mr. Worth," Darcy turned expectantly to the man.

"I want to be part of the negotiations between Harwood and
Anne."

Darcy ignored the familiar use of his cousin's name. "How would that expedite the matter?" Darcy drew Worth away from the servants' ears.

"I am a man of the law, for God's sake. I understand what is legal, and what is not in such situations." Worth's voice spoke of his need to keep Anne from danger, and Darcy appreciated the man's sincerity. He had known the same anxiety when Lydia Bennet eloped with George Wickham and placed her whole family's reputation in peril. "I have developed an affection for Miss de Bourgh, and if I can use my skills to safeguard her, I will. I am not the swashbuckling male that the lieutenant is. But let me prove to Miss de Bourgh that I am the superior choice."

"You will not betray your affection for Anne before the lieutenant?" Darcy cautioned. "My aunt will be hard enough to contain without your passion creating other issues."

Worth smiled slightly. "I will be in the room only as Miss de Bourgh's man of business."

"I like your deviousness, Mr. Worth." Darcy clapped the man on the shoulder. "My study in twenty minutes."

Worth leaned closer to ensure privacy. "Tell Miss de Bourgh that at no time is she to admit more than a friendly interest in the lieutenant. She is to repeatedly deny that she ever had an interest in the man romantically."

"I understand, Worth."

"I spent several hours after we parted yesterday evening trying to determine the best way to handle this. Tell Her Ladyship and Anne to follow my lead."

Twenty minutes later, Darcy escorted an agitated Lady Catherine along the main staircase. She had taken to her room after their encounter the previous evening, agreeing to this meeting only at his insistence. He instructed his aunt on holding her tongue while in the lieutenant's presence. "I have guaranteed Mr. Worth of your cooperation, Aunt," he spoke quietly to her alone. "It could mean the difference between paying the man a substantial sum or sending him packing. Do you comprehend my meaning, Your Ladyship?"

"I thoroughly grasp the gravity of the situation, Darcy. I am a woman very well acquainted with the business of a man's world."

"Lady Catherine, I do not question your intelligence, but like the rest of the Fitzwilliams, you possess a fervor, which sometimes boils over into misspoken feelings." He patted the back of her hand as it rested on his arm.

"I will do my best to perform admirably in your presence, Nephew," she bit out the words.

This time he squeezed her hand gently, suddenly aware of how fragile it appeared—the gnarled knuckles and the no-longer-firm skin. In fact, her hand trembled slightly. "That is all one may ask, Aunt."

He and Lady Catherine entered his study, followed by Anne. The lieutenant waited impatiently by the hearth. Darcy had purposely delayed their entrance—just a few extra minutes to allow Harwood to become uncomfortable with his surroundings. Darcy's father had designed the study as an advantage in his business dealings. Dark mahogany panels, rich forest green. The walls sported hunting trophies, weapons, lead crystal—no sign of femininity anywhere. The room could overpower someone—break him with its strength and masculinity. Darcy often used that fact to his advantage.

Upon seeing them, the lieutenant smiled amiably and offered them all a bow before saying, "Your Ladyship, it is pleasant to see you again."

"Do not feign cordiality with me, Lieutenant!" Lady Catherine barked.

"Sit here, Aunt." Darcy led her to a chair close to the fire. "Shall I send for some tea?"

Lady Catherine waved away his concern. "I shall be fine, Darcy."

He seated Anne beside her mother. Since he had sent her from the morning room, Anne's docility had returned—a fact he had expected. His cousin's newfound freedom was a delicate thing. "Come, join us, Harwood." Darcy clustered the chairs in a relatively tight circle.

"For whom is the extra chair?" Harwood remarked, seating himself in the wing chair beside Darcy's. "Shall I have the opportunity of meeting your wife, after all?"

"Unfortunately, I do not expect Mrs. Darcy to join us until supper. The chair is for my cousin's legal counsel." His words brought a simple nod of recognition for what he planned from his aunt and a renewal of hope from Anne.

"I was unaware that the de Bourghs' man of business traveled with them." Harwood shifted uncomfortably in his chair and looked around, as though he was expecting a judge to materialize and pass sentence.

Darcy chuckled lightly, having seen the effect of the mention of the word "legal" had on the lieutenant. Suddenly, this conversation took on *interesting* overtones. "You misunderstand, Harwood. Mr. Worth met my family at Pemberley to settle some financial transactions."

"Mr. Worth?" Harwood looked surprised. "The gentleman I met this morning?"

Worth strolled in the room casually, playing the part of the disinterested man of law. "I apologize for my tardiness, Darcy. The viscount and I took up a heated discussion on duty and politics: I pray I have not delayed your conversation."

Lady Catherine played her part by saying, "We have just taken our seats, Worth. Please come join us."

Harwood glanced around nervously. "I did not expect a full audience for my proposal."

"People of our connections, Lieutenant, do not even order a sack of seed without legal counsel," Lady Catherine said and sniffed.

Darcy interrupted, "Harwood, why should we stand on ceremony? Please explain to my aunt and my cousin what you told me yesterday evening." He sat back into the chair's cushions, giving the impression of being relaxed.

However, Harwood shifted uneasily in his chair, a point Darcy and Lady Catherine enjoyed. "As you are aware, Your Ladyship, while I visited at Rosings Park, I developed a deep affection for Miss de Bourgh." Lady Catherine started to object, but a warning flick of Darcy's wrist stifled her protest. Constantly clearing his throat, Harwood continued, unaware of the private interchange. "And maybe I flatter myself, but I believe Miss de Bourgh returned my interest. I asked your daughter to make me the happiest of men before I left for my new post, but Miss de Bourgh could not muster the strength she would have needed to inform you of her decision, so I departed for Liverpool alone. However, several days after my arrival on the western coast, I received word of Miss de Bourgh's presence in the city.

"I immediately made moves to protect your daughter by finding her adequate housing. It was not of the best quality, perhaps, now that I consider the situation, but I had hoped to guard against it becoming common knowledge that Miss de Bourgh traveled unchaperoned. Unfortunately, as I made plans to solidify our union, you arrived and whisked your daughter away. Your position made Miss de Bourgh's name recognizable. As such, many in Liverpool now are aware of her ruination. I have followed you to Pemberley to offer your daughter the protection of my name."

Lady Catherine bristled. "You accuse me of ruining my own child?"

"May I, Lady Catherine?" Worth inserted quickly.

"Certainly, Mr. Worth. Please earn your pay." Her caustic tone spoke of her disdain for Harwood.

Worth leaned forward to press his point. "May I summarize, Lieutenant?" Without waiting for a response, he continued. "You are under the impression that Miss de Bourgh, first, is afraid of her own mother and would refuse a man whom she affected rather than address such a wish to Her Ladyship. Secondly, you assume that Miss de Bourgh came to Liverpool specifically to join in holy matrimony with you."

"Of course, Miss de Bourgh came to Liverpool because of my earlier request," Harwood blustered.

"Which Miss de Bourgh had already refused, if I heard you correctly?" Worth's voice overrode Harwood's.

A flash of anger showed on the lieutenant's face. "Yes, she refused. Anne knew her mother would object to our union."

"Let us for the moment give some credence to the possibility that you misunderstood the lady's intentions," Worth retorted. "Might it be in the realm of reason that Miss de Bourgh had another reason to travel to Liverpool besides the inducements of your charms?"

Suddenly, Anne chimed in softly. "May I ask, sir, if I so feared my mother's disapproval, how I might then oppose her? First, I was afraid, and then I was not. Afraid…not afraid. I am seven and twenty, sir—not a child to be punished for misbehavior."

"Exactly, Miss de Bourgh," Worth asserted.

"No matter the circumstances," Darcy parlayed his farce, "should we not consider Harwood's offer? After all, if Anne's reputation is in tatters…"

Worth took the reins once more, just as Harwood began to preen. "So Miss de Bourgh refused your overtures. Then you assumed her appearance in Liverpool meant that she sought you out as her affianced?"

"She came to me in Liverpool!" Harwood protested.

Worth smiled confidently. "I am sure she did. Miss de Bourgh was in a strange city, so she turned to a person she considered a *friend*—an acquaintance who might do the gentlemanly thing and see to her needs without creating a compromising situation."

"And that is what I did. Did I not, Anne?"

Lady Catherine's voice sliced through the conversation. "Lieutenant Harwood, I must insist that you show my daughter proper respect by not using her Christian name as if you were an intimate."

"But we *are* intimates, Lady Catherine," the man asserted. "Less than an hour ago, Miss de Bourgh called me *Robert* before all those in attendance in the morning room." He gripped the chair arm tightly, indicating his irritation.

"My cousin did as the lieutenant described," Darcy confirmed. "Perhaps Harwood has a case, Aunt."

Lady Catherine asked hotly, "Why do you choose to support this scoundrel, Darcy?"

He had only discussed his intentions of portraying the devil's advocate with Worth, but in order to weaken Harwood's defenses, Darcy recognized the need to give the lieutenant a false sense of security. "I certainly do not agree with the lieutenant's *methods,* but it appears he is offering my cousin an *honorable* alternative."

Lady Catherine harrumphed in disgust.

Worth interrupted, "May I ask, Miss de Bourgh, if you have ever verbally agreed to the lieutenant's suit—either at Rosings or in Liverpool?"

Darcy had warned Anne regarding her legal response, and although her cousin's apparent support of Harwood confused her, Anne still followed Darcy's advice. "No, sir."

"I object!" Harwood exclaimed, nearly coming out of his chair with anger.

Worth laughed. "This is not a trial, Lieutenant."

"It certainly has the feel of one!" Harwood blustered.

"I am sure no one wished to place you on the defensive, Lieutenant," Darcy soothed him. "Having always known such opulence, it is difficult for us to see our lives as others might."

Worth leaned back, following Darcy's carefully worded suggestion of not appearing so aggressive. "I agree, Mr. Darcy," he said cannily. "We are jumping the gun. I simply wished to establish early on that, although Miss de Bourgh held an acquaintance with the lieutenant, she neither considered herself engaged nor did she encourage the gentleman to make arrangements for a wedding. Obviously, such an agreement was out of the question. A special license was impossible for Lieutenant Harwood, as he is not part of the aristocracy. Therefore, he would have to take the traditional route of first establishing residency before the banns may be called. Most parishes require a minimum of a fortnight and often as long as thirty days to indicate a resident. He, by his own words, spent only a few days in Liverpool before your cousin's arrival. Add to the residential time the three weeks to call the banns. Surely, the lieutenant is not accusing Miss de Bourgh of being the type of woman who would spend five to seven weeks with a man she had previously refused. And if the lady so feared her mother as to seek a clandestine meeting, Miss de Bourgh could not possibly believe she might avoid a confrontation with Her Ladyship for such an extended period of time." Worth knew firsthand that Anne had no knowledge of these facts at the time, but she certainly would not say so now.

"Then if Miss de Bourgh did not come to Liverpool to seek my companionship, why, may I ask, did she travel in the winter and alone?"

"As her business was of a personal nature, I refuse you knowledge of my daughter's purpose," Lady Catherine declared. "However, to suggest that Anne came to see you demonstrates a certain conceit. I knew of and sanctioned her departure for the western coast. She traveled with my blessing, as well as my instructions. Unfortunately, my daughter made a poor decision when her maid became ill, and she left the miserable girl behind. Anne has explained to me that she did not wish to disappoint me by not fulfilling the first task I had ever assigned to her. As my daughter will soon come into her inheritance, I wished her to begin learning of the many holdings belonging to her father."

Harwood charged, "Then why did you create such a scene when you discovered Miss de Bourgh at the Salty Sailor?"

Lady Catherine wrinkled her nose with the memory of the inn where she found Anne—a seedy establishment close to the waterfront. "I was admittedly distraught not to find Anne where she was to stay. Little did I know that Mr. Worth was out of town on business, and she could not reach him for the proper arrangements. Needless to say, I was beside myself with terror for my child's safety. I behaved improperly, I admit, but I was beyond reason by the time I extricated her from your choice of lodging for a lady." Her glare made the lieutenant flinch, and Darcy realized why he admired his aunt. She had that Fitzwilliam tenacity, which his mother had exhibited, along with his uncle and both of his male cousins. Lady

Catherine's fierceness when someone attacked her own softened Darcy's opinion of her sometimes-rude behavior.

"I was in Newcastle in consultation for an upcoming trial. Her Ladyship had assumed I would be able to meet Miss de Bourgh in Liverpool, as my main practice centers are in Cheshire and Manchester," Worth offered. "As I understand it, when Miss de Bourgh realized her cousin Colonel Fitzwilliam was not also in Liverpool, she sought the only person she knew in the city: you, Lieutenant."

"Then it is this family's position that Miss de Bourgh traveled to Liverpool for reasons unrelated to our relationship?"

Lady Catherine actually smiled. "It is, Lieutenant Harwood."

Harwood saw one of his claims on Anne dwindle away, but *defeat* was not in his vocabulary. "However, the facts remain that your daughter, Madam, did travel alone and did come under my care while in Liverpool. As such, Miss de Bourgh has been compromised. I will, therefore, present myself to you as an honorable suitor for Miss de Bourgh's hand. Although she may see me in an unflattering light at the moment, I am certain I will eventually win her affection. I hope, Miss de Bourgh, that you accept my humble plea."

Lady Catherine could not resist tweaking the gentleman, "And you will, in return, accept Anne's inheritance."

Harwood leveled a steady gaze on the woman. "I assure you that is not my main motivation, but any man would welcome such a dowry from his wife."

"Well, you shall not have it. I will disown Anne if she makes such an alliance!"

"Now, Aunt," Darcy cautioned. "Let us not make idle threats which could hurt my cousin." Darcy wanted to keep Harwood at Pemberley until he heard from Colonel Fitzwilliam. He could not have his aunt send the man away too quickly. "I suggest we invite the lieutenant to join us for a day or two. It will give Anne time to seriously consider Harwood's suit." He held a hand up to quell any protests ready to be voiced by his family or Worth. "And it will give us to determine how to address the lieutenant's honest request."

"But Darcy!" Lady Catherine insisted.

"You must trust me, Aunt. I promised Anne my protection, and I will brook no resistance."

Harwood's shoulders straightened, and he gazed at the assembled group triumphantly. "Thank you, Mr. Darcy, for your confidence in my character."

Before anyone else could object, Darcy rose, effectively ending the conversation. "We shall meet here tomorrow, an hour following the morning meal. Harwood, I am assuming your room suits you."

"It does, Mr. Darcy." Harwood also came to his feet. "I believe I shall return to my chamber. Miss de Bourgh, I pray you will honor me with a few moments of your time later this afternoon." Anne did not say a word—did not move—and Harwood accepted her silence as agreement. "Good morning." The lieutenant strode confidently from the room.

Silence filled the study. When Darcy was sure Harwood had actually returned to his room, he crossed to the door and closed it. Immediately, three voices exploded, each drowning out the other, and each more irate. "Darcy, what means this?" Lady Catherine demanded.

"As I said previously, you will need to trust me. I have a plan, and although it may seem like madness, it is far from it." His calmness soothed some of their initial concerns. "I cannot explain at the moment, but it was imperative to detain the lieutenant."

"Well, whatever you plan had better work," Worth warned.

Before any other discussion could occur, a rapid knock at the study door interrupted them. "Come!" Darcy called to the closed portal.

A distraught-looking butler opened the door. Seeing the dazed and astonished scowl clearly displayed on Mr. Baldwin's face, Darcy crossed to him immediately. "What is it, man?"

"It is Lucinda Dodd, sir," Baldwin rasped out. "Everett in the gatehouse sent word that he found Lucinda's body along the incoming rise."

"I prayed never to hear those words." Darcy's lips thinned in a frown. "Send someone to instruct Lord Stafford to meet me in the foyer. Tell him we are taking a walk outside and to dress accordingly."

"Yes, Mr. Darcy."

Darcy turned to Worth. "I would ask you to join His Lordship and me if you would, Worth. We have another mystery on our hands."

Twenty minutes later, Darcy, Lord Stafford, and Worth joined Darcy's men along the edge of Pemberley Woods. "You found her, Everett?"

"Yes, sir. I sees vultures circling from the gatehouse so I walks in this direction to see what those carrions found. I's expected a deer or even a sheep, but I's never thought to discover no Miss Dodd."

"And you have touched nothing?" Darcy demanded, his hands tightening into fists at his sides.

The gatekeeper's candid response added to Darcy's frustration. "I be sittin' the girl up wheres she slumped over, but that be it, sir, besides checkin' to sees if Miss Dodd be breathin'. She ain't, sir." With a nod of his head, Darcy dismissed his servants to their duties, except the two who would take the body back to the main house. He knelt beside the body, trying to determine the woman's condition.

"A woman's silk stocking about her neck," the viscount noted.

Worth touched the offending item. "It must be the mate of the one we found cut to pieces in Mrs. Wickham's room."

"The girl's been strangled. See the marks on her neck." Stafford untied the leg wear and then pointed to the bruising along Lucinda's throat. "Mrs. Wickham?" he suggested.

"My wife's sister admits to arguing with Lucinda, and although one woman could easily strangle another, it does not explain how the body came to be found so far from the house. In addition, I am convinced that Mrs. Wickham, although self-centered, is no murderer." He glanced toward Pemberley. It was nearly a mile from the turnpike road to Pemberley's front door. Lucinda's body rested halfway between the road and the house. It made no sense.

Worth tried to reason out the possibilities. "Do you suppose that your maid tried to escape the house—ran away in terror—and collapsed at this point?"

Again, Darcy looked at the way they had come. Distinct prints—footprints of his men, hoof prints of Harwood's horse, and footprints of his, Stafford's, and Worth's—lay along the curving drive, but no trace of a lady's shoe showed along the entrance pathway or even across the smooth, pristine surface of the gently rolling woodland defining the park. "I observe no female footprints." He took a close look at her footwear. "Lucinda wears the typical half boots."

Worth and Stafford also took a close look at the footwear and estimated her shoe size. Viscount Stafford stood slowly and surveyed the surrounding area. "It appears that your gatekeeper came from the left," he said, pointing to the obvious boot prints leading to and from the body.

Worth followed his train of thought. "And those are ours and those of your servants," he offered as they assayed the evidence. "I see no others."

"Nor do I," Darcy remarked, "but I do see a trail of sort—from the waterfall toward the trees. Notice how this area is scored—no longer smooth—like someone tried to erase his tracks."

"Exactly." Adam Lawrence braced himself against the wind. "Let us spread out and follow along the edges of these marks—see where they lead."

Moving meticulously along the three-foot-wide pathway, they each took a step, sinking deeply in the snow, and then paused, trying to discern anything unusual. Step. Pause. Step. Pause. Step.

"It was probably a tree branch or a broken limb from a bush." Worth pointed to several branches currently stabbing the roughened surface. "Broken from the icy weight and the snow."

"Makes sense," Darcy noted as he took another step.

"It seems our trail leads toward that copse of trees." Stafford gestured as they approached dense woodlands.

No one spoke as they crossed the open area and entered the tree line. Even there they found the dense snow's scratched surface. Then suddenly, it stopped—no more markings. "It is just some hedges and a boulder." Worth looked back to see if they had made a wrong turn.

"There has to be something," Darcy grumbled. "Keep your eyes open and watch where you step."

Again, they moved carefully—looking for another trail—another clue. After several long, agonizing moments, Stafford called out, "Here!"

As quickly as the deep snow and strong wind would allow, Darcy and Worth joined the viscount. "What is it?" Worth asked as he knelt beside Stafford.

"Here," he said and pointed to the upper branches of a bramble bush. "Threads. Probably from the maid's dress."

"And here." Darcy said. He was kneeling close by, holding the lower branches of a Spanish oak. "See, Stafford, it is the same shape as we found on the tree by the cottages."

Stafford's mouth twisted in an all-knowing smile. "The square heel. When we find the man with the square-shaped heel, we will find your murderer, Darcy."

CHAPTER 16

~ ~ ~

A SUBDUED ATMOSPHERE enveloped the evening meal. Another death. The murders had taken their toll on the group. Despite how often they tried to put it all behind them—to resume their lives—death reared its ugly head and dragged them all back into the abyss. The serving staff performed their duties—an upper house English servant never neglected his responsibility—but without enthusiasm.

Elizabeth joined Darcy, realizing he needed her support. Tonight, he placed her at his right hand, rather than at the other end of the table. He could reach under the cloth to touch her hand or squeeze her knee—to reassure them both of their affection and their unity. The party dwindled to a handful. His aunt, along with Anne, had chosen to take the evening meal in their chambers. Georgiana kept her cousin company. In addition, distraught over the news of the maid's demise, Lydia Wickham had sent word that she would dine alone.

When Lieutenant Harwood entered the dining room, the rest of the guests had begun their meals. "I apologize for my tardiness, Mr. Darcy." Against propriety, the man offered no explanation for his lateness.

"Please join us, Lieutenant." Darcy gestured to a chair beside Adam Lawrence. When the man had settled, Darcy made the introduction. "Mrs. Darcy, may I present Lieutenant Harwood."

Harwood nodded an acknowledgement. "It is pleasant to have your acquaintance at last, Mrs. Darcy. Colonel Fitzwilliam speaks so highly of you."

"My cousin, the good colonel, is one of my wife's greatest admirers," Darcy remarked to the rest of the table.

"Our Edward is most generous in his regard." Elizabeth blushed while slipping her left hand into Darcy's right.

Darcy drew the lieutenant's attention to the lady on the viscount's right. "I might also take the liberty, Harwood, of making you familiar with Mrs. Williams." The woman slowly raised her chin to meet the lieutenant's steady gaze. "I am afraid Mrs. Williams escaped the morning room before you joined us, and you had no opportunity to make the lady's acquaintance."

Elizabeth's hand tightened around Darcy's fingers, alerting him to the fleeting look of surprise crossing Harwood's face. "I am honored, Mrs. Williams," he mumbled in apparent awkwardness.

"As am I, Lieutenant. My late husband served this great country's navy, and I am forever pleased to know any man who takes up the call to arms."

Harwood looked about. "Am I to assume Miss de Bourgh has chosen not to join us?"

"My cousin and my sister, Miss Darcy, have promised to become members of our party a bit later—for some light entertainment. My sister has agreed to grace us with several musical selections. I hope you will honor us with a song, Miss Donnel. You have a most pleasant voice."

Although she flushed, Cathleen accepted readily.

"You have a musical talent, Miss Donnel? I envy anyone who can breathe life into a song. 'Butcher' was the word my tutor always used to refer to my musical expertise." Harwood smiled charmingly at Cathleen.

"I pray I do not disappoint you, Lieutenant."

"A lady never disappoints." He turned to Stafford next. "I neglected to ask, Your Lordship, of your family. Are you simply to tend to a long-suffering relative or to a situation more dire?"

Adam spoke with dignity, trying not to betray his amusement at the lieutenant's ability to say the *right* thing to each person. "Actually, it is my cousin's relative on her maternal side. I am related only through marriage—she through blood."

"It is my Uncle Kennice," Cathleen added. "He is quite ill, and we have little hope for him, I fear."

"Might I ask where in Cheshire your uncle resides, Miss Donnel?" Harwood's false interest went undetected by her, but Stafford, Darcy, and Worth all listened with great interest.

Cathleen enjoyed speaking of her family, even though they discussed a heartfelt sadness. Her recent decision to abandon Adam Lawrence's company and return to the bosom of her relations brought her contentment, and she gladly shared the requested information. "Between Warrington and Macclesfield, south of Manchester."

"Outside Mobberley?" Worth asked. "The Kennices outside Mobberley—I know them."

Stafford smiled. "I should have suspected you would have knowledge of my extended family, Worth. Is there a family in this part of the country of which you have no acquaintance?"

"My firm holds a reputation for honesty, especially in land dealings. Many seek us out."

"I expected nothing less, Mr. Worth." Stafford winked at the solicitor, letting him know he meant no offense.

Harwood recaptured the conversation. "And your Uncle Kennice, Miss Donnel, is of connections?"

"A baron, Lieutenant Harwood." Cathleen blushed profusely. "But he is of Irish extraction—not as well situated as His Lordship or Mr. Darcy."

Worth took up her defense. "Yet Kennice owns an excellent tract of land, quite profitable."

"We will take your word regarding business," Darcy summarized.

"Of course, Mr. Darcy. The details are dry. We men of law understand that others do not see property deeds and liens as dinner conversation."

When the party retired to the music room, they found Georgiana and Anne already in preparation for the performance, so Darcy dismissed the required introductions until later.

"Miss de Bourgh, please come join me," Elizabeth bade as she approached the pianoforte, making sure to steer Anne away from the lieutenant.

Anne gave her a nod of gratitude. "Thank you, Mrs. Darcy." They took up residence on a small settee facing the instrument.

"Shall I turn the pages for you, Georgiana?" Darcy leaned over to whisper to his sister.

She replied softly, "Thank you, Fitzwilliam, for thinking of it. You know what a ninny I can be when I have an audience."

"What I know," he murmured as he arranged the music, "is that when you sit to the pianoforte, my Dear, you are brilliant. Do not forget that, Georgie. We are in awe of your talent."

His sister shook her head, but his words of approval caused her shoulders to straighten and her chin to rise. For the evening, Georgiana had chosen a varied selection, including "Then Farewell, My Tridonotuse-Built Wherry" and Dibdin's "The Soldier's Adieu," as well as the song cycle "Colin and Lucy." Georgiana began tentatively, but soon lost herself in the music—the notes swelling and crescendoing in the well-designed room. Mesmerized by her immersion in the performance, Darcy watched Georgiana's face. He had never seen her look more beautiful. Someday he would have to part with Georgiana—give her to another man, who would protect and keep her. Darcy would consider only a man who would cherish this part of his sister—the creative spirit, which needed nurturing in order for Georgiana to live fully.

"Bravo!" Mr. Worth cheered when Georgiana had completed the first number.

Miss Donnel agreed, saying, "Excellent, Miss Darcy!" Cathleen would sing next, and Georgiana would finish out the entertainment. As Cathleen prepared, the others spoke cordially or sipped on libations.

"Shall you speak to the lieutenant?" Elizabeth asked quietly.

Anne shrugged, looking resigned to the prospect. "Do I have a choice? Fitzwilliam believes I should at least listen to the man, although I do not wish to acknowledge my part in bringing Lieutenant Harwood here. What a gormless, dull-witted action! How could I have fallen for his beautiful face and not noticed his lackluster soul?"

Elizabeth glanced to where her husband sat beside Georgiana. "Sometimes perfection hides behind a mask of ambiguity."

"I wish I had met Mr. Worth long before the lieutenant. If so, I might not have been so easily fooled." Anne's eyes naturally drifted to where Worth sat, interacting with Georgiana.

Elizabeth followed Anne's gaze. "Then you cannot imagine Lieutenant Harwood's declaration to be an honest one?"

Anne lowered her voice, hoping for privacy. "I believe the lieutenant *honestly* desires my dowry, but as to his earnest affection, I am of a different persuasion."

"Then why allow the man the freedom of voicing his hopes?"

"Because the lieutenant knows intimately of my ruin." Tears misted Anne's eyes, and she swallowed hard, trying to disguise her emotions. "Mr. Darcy and Mr. Worth believe my ill-advised actions will cost my mother a pretty sum—my dowry in exchange for a vow of silence. Her Ladyship may never forgive me. I could strike the man dead for his perfidy!" Her heartfelt words signaled the first of her tears.

Elizabeth slipped a handkerchief into Anne's fisted grasp on the cushion's edge. "Trust Fitzwilliam, Miss de Bourgh. He has sworn to protect you, and he is a man of his word. You are safe under my husband's care."

"I am indebted to my cousin's interest," Anne whispered softly.

Harwood noted Anne's distress, which signaled that his mild threats had made inroads into her resolve. Another day or two of pressure would break her composure, and the lady would be more forthcoming.

However, even if his plan failed, he would transfer his affection to Miss Donnel. She was not as wealthy as the de Bourghs, but she could develop into a viable option. Her cousin was a viscount—the future Earl of Greenwall—and her uncle was an Irish baron. Even Worth had commented on the lady's family possessing an excellent income. Plus, he suspected that Miss Donnel might be more willing to share her favors than Anne had been. She dressed more provocatively—in the finest silks and the most fashionable trends. *She will do nicely,* Harwood assured himself.

On his left, the lieutenant became aware of Evelyn Williams, who was sitting beside Mr. Worth. The woman maintained a steady, intent stare. With a very slight shake of his head, he warned her to look away. As he returned his attention to Anne, he quickly noted her preparation to leave. Before he lost his opportunity, Harwood left his seat and approached the settee. "Miss de Bourgh," he said, bowing low. "might I entice you to stroll about the room with me?"

"I am rather fatigued this evening, Lieutenant; I shall withdraw. The day brought me much on which to dwell." Anne stood, curtsied, and slipped from the room.

Harwood watched her go, knowing the lady's distress played into his hands. A smirk formed at the corners of his mouth. He turned away to applaud Miss Darcy's final performance of the evening.

"Hopefully, you play cards, Harwood," Stafford said as he stepped up beside him and gestured toward the door. "Darcy assures me he has set up tables in the green drawing room."

"I am not sure I can afford your game, Your Lordship." He did not wish to lose more money—not until he had the de Bourgh wealth safely in his pocket.

The viscount laughed good-naturedly. "I do not particularly care if we play for matchsticks, Harwood. I just cannot sit to another hand of whist. I need a man's game. So what say you? Care to join me?"

"In that case, I do not mind sharpening my skills." Harwood nodded for the viscount to lead the way.

"Lieutenant," Darcy called to forestall their retreat, "before you retire to the tables, might I introduce you to my sister, Miss Darcy?" He kept Georgiana on his arm as he brought her forward.

"It would be my honor to have the acquaintance." Although his voice lacked the cultured intonation of the upper class, Harwood's stance gave nothing to humility. He bowed over Georgiana's hand.

"Thank you, Lieutenant." Georgiana curtsied. "I understand from my brother that you are a close associate of my cousin Colonel Fitzwilliam."

"We have served together for the past several months."

"With my brother's permission, I would welcome hearing of the colonel. It has been some time since we have seen him. Possibly you might spare me and my sister, Elizabeth, a few minutes tomorrow."

"Naturally." Harwood gave a low laugh—an intimate, husky sound, which sent a shiver of warning through Georgiana. Instinctively, she tightened her grip on Darcy's arm, and unsurprisingly, he covered her hand with his free one.

"We will excuse you this evening, Harwood," Darcy said. "You should not keep the viscount waiting. *Patience* is not in Stafford's vocabulary." After the lieutenant had bowed and left the room, Darcy looked into Georgiana's azure blue eyes. "What is it, Sweetling?" he coaxed.

Georgiana bit her bottom lip—a sign of her anxiety. "I wish I could say, Fitzwilliam." She glanced about the room, assuring herself that they stood alone. "Although I have never met the lieutenant before this evening, he is somehow familiar, and it is not a comfortable familiarity."

Darcy whispered close to her ear, "Listen to your intuition, Georgiana. Do not ignore such warnings. They will serve you well."

"Do you suspect Lieutenant Harwood of duplicity?"

Darcy grumbled, "You are not to be alone with the man until—unless—I am sure of his honesty."

His request stunned Georgiana, but she nodded her agreement. He had given her no such warning about Mr. Worth or Viscount Stafford. "Whatever you say, Fitzwilliam."

"Might I have a word with you, Lieutenant?" Nigel Worth waite in the main corridor.

Harwood fought the urge to roll his eyes. "Of course, Mr. Worth. How might I be of service?"

Worth directed the lieutenant through an open doorway to one of the many drawing rooms. Only a roaring fire provided the light, but Worth needed no light to say what he needed to say. "I will come straight to the point, Lieutenant. Leave Miss de Bourgh alone."

Harwood's eyebrow rose in curiosity. "And what would a country lawyer do if I chose to ignore his advice, Mr. Worth?"

Worth continued doggedly. "The lady has returned from her business trip wiser, thanks to your manipulations. Leave her to her life."

Harwood glowered. "Is that the way it is, Worth? Do you affect the lady for your own? Are you really even the de Bourghs' man of business?"

Worth wanted to call the man out, but instead he stayed with the story he had concocted as Anne's defense. "How much will it cost to be rid of you, Harwood?" he snarled.

"More than you have, Worth." Harwood strolled toward the door. "I will deal with you tomorrow, sir."

"You bastard!"

A few innocent-sounding inquiries told Harwood the layout of the rooms on the third level. Keeping to the shadows and timing his movements carefully, he entered the unlocked room in the early hours of the new day. Closing the door with a *snick,* he turned silently to the candlelight. "I see you were expecting me," he smirked.

"Should I not have been?" The candle on its stand rose to light the way.

He pushed away from the door and strolled toward the bed. "What the hell are you doing here?" He fingered the remains of a half-eaten biscuit, resting on a plate on the table's edge. "I certainly did not expect to find you at Pemberley."

"The snowstorm brought Derby to a standstill; I had no other choice but to take sanctuary under Mr. Darcy's roof."

Harwood worked his way about the room, touching the decorative items, which gave the chamber its atmosphere. "I was distressed to discover you among Darcy's guests, but now that I dwell on it, it may prove to be for the best. I can use your expertise to my advantage."

"*Our* advantage."

He smiled condescendingly. "*Our* advantage." Harwood seated himself in a nearby chair, relaxing into the cushions. "What can you share regarding the de Bourghs?"

"I care nothing for the family. The mother's pretentiousness is irritating, but expected. It is the woman—the one you have made your prey—of whom I speak. As mercurial as Hamlet and as false in her dealings as Shylock himself, the lady ebbs and flows. How can you even assume you have the situation in hand? Has she or has she not refused you?"

"Miss de Bourgh will refuse. We knew that coming into the affair. Obviously, I have no intention of marrying the woman."

A bark of laughter interrupted his summation. "I would say marriage is out of the question under the circumstances."

"Yet, the de Bourghs know nothing of which you speak." He rose and crossed to the door. "Stay close. I may need you to cover for me."

As he eased the door open to slip into the darkened hall, a warning followed him. "This is the last time, Robert. I will not tolerate another manipulation. We will stop our wanderings."

Harwood did not look back—only paused long enough to acknowledge the words with a slight nod.

He closed the door silently behind him and sought secrecy behind a cluster of potted palms at the head of the staircase. Holding his breath, Harwood waited for the lone footman to pass before he made his return to his chambers. He seriously considered taking the short trek to Miss Donnel's room and ascertaining whether the lady might entertain him, but he knew it presumptuous to appear uninvited in her chamber. *Soon,* he told himself as he reentered his room. *She is ripe for the plucking. Despite the warning, I am not finished here.*

The morning brought the hopes of a complete thaw. A steady stream of water dripped from the trees and every overhang as the temperatures rose, and the snow began to melt. From his study's window, Darcy watched the main drive, expecting Lucas's return sometime that day. He prayed the servant had found his cousin at Matlock. Darcy needed a voice of reason in the madness surrounding his household.

"You sent for me, Mr. Darcy?" The butler bowed courteously.

Darcy turned to address his man. "Yes, Mr. Baldwin. I need a man sent to Sir Phillip Spurlock's. Tell Sir Phillip that we need him at Pemberley posthaste in his capacity as the local magistrate. We must deal with the three deaths, and I wish Sir Phillip to speak to my guests before they depart the estate."

"Must we, Mr. Darcy?" The rumors that would follow such news in the community obviously worried Baldwin.

Darcy understood; he, too, dreaded the possibility of others knowing of the events of the past week at Pemberley. "This is not simply a Pemberley matter, Mr. Baldwin. Too many know of what has happened here. Only Sir Phillip can erase the shadow of doubt clouding our horizon."

"Certainly, Mr. Darcy." The butler bowed respectfully. "I will see to it immediately. By the way, sir, I have allowed Jatson to return to limited duties. Although I assured him that you would not expect him to rejoin the staff so soon, Mr. St. Denis feared losing his position. I have met him halfway by giving him abbreviated responsibilities."

"I trust your judgment in the matter, Mr. Baldwin." Darcy returned to the window. "Let me know immediately of Lucas's return."

"As you wish, Mr. Darcy." The butler bowed out of the room.

Within a minute of Baldwin's exit, a light tap on the door brought Darcy away from his vigil. "Mr. Darcy, might we speak for a moment?" Harwood filled the door frame.

"Certainly, Lieutenant. Please come join me." Darcy gestured to his favorite chairs. "How can I serve you this morning? I pray that you have not had second thoughts on your accommodations."

"Absolutely not, Mr. Darcy. My chamber is more than adequate, especially for a man used to cramped military quarters." He settled himself before continuing. "I am afraid, sir, that the accommodations had nothing to do with my sleepless state. My regard for Miss de Bourgh causes my conscience to turn in upon itself."

A dark smile graced Darcy's lips. "You have had no interaction with my cousin since we met yesterday?"

Harwood did his best to keep his expression unreadable. "I attempted to approach Miss de Bourgh yesterday evening, but your cousin was too unsettled for a conversation about the future. I thought it best to follow your suggestion that we speak later this morning."

"If that be the case, Harwood, I do not understand the nature of this discussion." A cold fist struck his heart. Darcy knew this was the moment the real Lieutenant Robert Harwood would reveal himself, and he prayed that his own instincts had not betrayed him.

Harwood eyed Darcy sternly. "For many hours, I have mulled over what is best for Miss de Bourgh." The interloper guarded his words carefully. "I sought out your cousin because I wished to do the honorable thing—to give Miss de Bourgh the protection only a husband can offer a woman. Yet, it appears that the lady does not welcome my plight." Harwood paused, but when Darcy made no comment, he continued. "I care for Miss de Bourgh, and I do not wish to witness her ruination."

"That is most admirable, Harwood."

The officer offered a weary sigh. "I have considered Miss de Bourgh's hasty retreat, and I have tried to anticipate who might know of your cousin's Liverpool stay. If Miss de Bourgh refuses my proposal, I would still like to offer myself up as the lady's *friend*. It would seem there are certain people whose silence must be purchased to keep Miss de Bourgh's reputation pure. I would be willing to act as an agent in securing the discretion of those involved."

Coolly composed, Darcy regarded the man. "That is most benevolent of you, Lieutenant."

"Of course, I hope it does not come to that. I prefer to claim the lady's hand as my own, but if I fail, please consider me as your cousin's champion—to conduct this business tastefully."

"And have you considered what such prudence might cost my aunt?"

Harwood fought the urge to celebrate his victory. Facing Darcy with a stony glare, he replied, "I would imagine several thousand pounds—the inn's proprietor, maids, stable hands, hackney drivers, and many more will need to be brought under the umbrella to shield your cousin properly."

Darcy's fists formed at his sides. "And you wish me to approach my aunt in your name?"

"I thought it best to bring my concerns to your attention. You were the voice of reason in the room yesterday. Having offered your cousin the protection of her family, I assumed you would understand the urgency of making arrangements—before the rumors can no longer be squelched."

Darcy rose to his feet to end the conversation. "I appreciate your candor, Lieutenant. I will keep your advice in mind as I negotiate with my aunt—until we meet a bit later." He offered the lieutenant an abbreviated bow. "Breakfast is available in the morning room."

"Thank you, Mr. Darcy. I shall partake of your kindness and then return to my room until we confer with your family. I thought it might be prudent to make a list of whom we may need to approach to secure their silence."

Darcy knew Harwood preferred the payment to the marriage, but for good measure, he added, "We can only pray that my cousin will accept a marriage of convenience rather than the infinite possibilities of her ruination."

"Of course, Mr. Darcy. We both hope as such."

Sir Phillip Spurlock arrived before the family sat to their morning meal. Darcy met him in the main foyer and ushered him into his study before anyone else could speak with the man. He sent one of the maids to find Elizabeth and Georgiana. He wanted them both aware of Sir Phillip's investigation.

"Your man was most insistent, Darcy." Sir Phillip warmed his hands near the fire. "What is all this about?"

Darcy steadied himself. "There are three bodies in the attic drying room." He watched the horror spread across the baronet's face. Sir Phillip and Darcy's father had attended Eton together—he was a man whom Darcy admired and respected. "All have died of mysterious causes. I have several unexpected houseguests because of the storm, and I assumed you would wish to question them before they departed."

"Three?" Sir Phillip took a nearby chair.

"My cousin's traveling companion and two of my staff. Another, Jatson St. Denis, suffered minor injuries in a confrontation with an unknown assailant."

"I am afraid I do not understand, Darcy. Has someone entered the house illegally or is our culprit someone we know?"

Darcy ran his fingers through his hair. "I wish to God I knew. The phantom of Pemberley has haunted this house for nigh on ten days and nights."

"The phantom of Pemberley?" Sir Phillip stared at him.

"What my staff has dubbed my intruder! At first, they believed him to be one of the shadow people." He pulled the cord to order breakfast. "I have sent for Mrs. Darcy and my sister. I thought we might make our insights known to you prior to your questioning the guests. I have made extensive notes of each day's events since we took notice of a stranger on the grounds and then of the cryptic clues accompanying each of the incidents. I suppose you told your household that you might not return until tomorrow?"

"Will it take that long?"

Darcy moved to answer the door. "As we have eight guests and several staff members to address, I am sure you will be about your duties through most of the day." He opened the door to find Elizabeth and Georgiana awaiting him. "Ah, my Dears." He caught

Elizabeth's hand and led her to where the baronet stood. "Sir Phillip has come in an official capacity; we need to tell him everything we know of our phantom."

"Of course, my Husband." She curtsied to the official and then summoned a waiting footman to bring in the ordered food and drink.

Georgiana shivered. "I pray, Sir Phillip, that you can bring closure to this distressing matter."

"I will do my best, my Dear." He squeezed her hand. "I would have Pemberley as clear as the day your great-great-grandfather built it."

"I do have one piece of news that will bring you joy, Sir Phillip." Darcy passed a cup of tea to the man as Elizabeth continued to pour for the rest of them.

A hesitant smile touched the baronet's lips. "Please share, my Boy. Under the circumstances, I am in need of felicitations."

"My household is to know a new member this summer."

The gentleman beamed at Elizabeth, his eyes glistening with genuine happiness. "Mrs. Darcy, you have brought life back to this estate. I do wish Lady Anne and the former Mr. Darcy were here to know of this day. My old friend would be strutting around like the proudest peacock. I cannot wait to tell Lady Spurlock. She will be beside herself with joy. When the roads clear, you will know how much the Darcys are respected by this neighborhood."

"Thank you, Sir Phillip. Mr. Darcy and I are blessed to know such joy."

"A whole houseful!" Sir Phillip declared. "A houseful of Darcys would please me."

Elizabeth blushed. "We will take our blessings one at a time, Sir Phillip."

"Let us begin." Darcy redirected the conversation. The knowledge that the community would welcome the news of his heir pleased him. Pemberley would survive—even the chaos of the past week would not destroy it. Sir Phillip's words rang in his ears. *Mrs.*

Darcy, you have brought life back to this estate. For the first time in several days, he knew contentment. "Elizabeth, why do you not start with the day you saw the stranger when we were out riding?"

The hearty breakfast satisfied one of Harwood's hungers. Plus, he found Miss Donnel alone in the morning room, and he spent nearly half an hour spouting his best "seductive" speeches. The lady appeared to welcome him. Perhaps he would ease another *hunger* tonight.

Of course, the lady's cousin seemed less inclined to "welcome" him to the family. When he found them conversing privately in the breakfast room, Lord Stafford appeared quite angry. The viscount first offered Harwood a direct cut before sending his cousin scurrying to her room. He had thought he knew something of the future earl's nature after spending several hours the previous evening chatting over cards, but His Lordship's subsequent private warning spoke volumes. *You cannot trust the aristocracy,* Harwood reminded himself. *The viscount will gladly take your hard-earned macaroni, but deny you the pleasure of his cousin's company.* Without thinking, he swung the door to his room wide. Seeing a man in Regular regimentals shaving at the vanity table stunned him. He strode forward. "What the bloody hell are you doing here?"

He made the decision to look for a change of clothes and to seek some other comforts. Since James's altercation in the east wing and Peter's frenzied moment in the family quarters, Gregor MacIves had found it quite impossible to leave the passageways. The Darcys had effectively cut off his supplies. Today, he hoped to find some extra clothes or toiletries stored on the second level. "I be a bit rank." He hit the lever for one of the empty rooms. This was the only part of the house not currently in use or not presently being renovated.

As the raised dais sporting a small writing desk rotated inward, he stepped into the airy room. He could get used to such luxury, but the likelihood of ever knowing the warmth of a place of his own faded a bit more with each passing day. Only one thing held him back—kept him from realizing his true potential. He had come to Pemberley to right a wrong. Looking out the nearest window, he took stock of the changing weather conditions. "It be tonight," he said as he let the drape fall back into place.

He found a bowl and a ewer of water. He stripped off his jacket and searched the wardrobe for clothes stored in the cabinet. "Well, look here." He pulled the shirt from the wooden hanger. "Thank ye, Darcy." He removed the rough linen he had worn for the past week and threw it in the empty bag resting on the bedside end table. He poured water in the bowl, lathered up a cloth, and proceeded to wash his body as best he could. He would prefer a bath, but, at least, he could rid himself of the dust and the cobwebs clinging to his face and arms.

As silently as possible, he raised the smallest window, and then carefully carried the dirty water to it and dumped the water onto the frosty lawn. Then he refilled the bowl and applied the soap to his face. He returned to the dressing room and found a straight razor on the table. "Thank ye a'gin, Darcy."

Taking the blade with him, he looked for a mirror. He found one and began to remove the bristly whiskers decorating his face. "I won'er when be the last time Darcy shaved his own face?" He made smooth, sweeping strokes along his cheeks and then wiped the blade dry on a towel.

He had just run the razor up the right side of his neck to his chin line when the room's door swung open. In the mirror, he saw a man wearing what appeared to be an officer's uniform. The man strode forward. "What the bloody hell are you doing here?" he demanded.

For a split second, Gregor froze, thinking that being discovered meant he would not have to return to the cold passageways after all, and then survival instincts took hold. He spun, razor in hand, and caught the officer with a forearm across the neck. With his free hand, he slashed the blade along the exposed flesh, leaving a jagged cut from the man's left ear to his Adam's apple.

The lieutenant fought Gregor until his opponent made a second cut, and the blood poured forth over their hands, which were knotted together in a struggle. Then his opponent went limp, the front of his well-pressed uniform turning red with his own blood. Gregor stepped back and let the lieutenant slide to the floor. Without thinking twice, he rinsed his hands in the water. He grabbed a second towel, the bag from the end table, and the clean garments and sidestepped around the writhing body. After locking the room door, he headed toward the secret panel. Reaching the hidden lever, he glanced back once to see the military officer pull up to his knees before suddenly going very still. He knew it was a matter of time. Within a few minutes, the lieutenant would know his Maker. A loud click signaled that Gregor's escape waited.

For well over an hour, the Darcys shared what they knew of the mysterious deaths. "It is almost as if there is more than one perpetrator," Sir Phillip remarked. "My study of the law and my twenty years serving as a magistrate tell me that, usually, a murderer follows the same pattern in committing his crimes. These are very distinct wrongs. It makes very little sense."

"I had hoped," Darcy began, "that your years in this capacity would give you insights we others lacked."

"I believe it is time I spoke to your guests." Sir Phillip stood and moved to behind Darcy's desk. "I plan to occupy your work area for a few hours, my Boy."

"Certainly, Sir Phillip. Anything you need." Darcy stood also. "With whom did you wish to speak first, sir?"

Sir Phillip settled in Darcy's chair. "I think the viscount if you do not mind, Darcy. I am familiar with Mr. Worth—testified in more than one of his cases, but I am not aware of the viscount."

"The man is right intelligent, although a bit of a rebel; I believe you will find His Lordship most helpful, however." Darcy pulled the bell cord to call his servant. "In a short while, I have a meeting with my aunt, her daughter, and Lieutenant Harwood, so I will b engaged with a family matter for an hour or so. But Mrs. Darcy will be happy to serve you, Sir Phillip."

"One thing I need both you and Mrs. Darcy to do is to become better listeners. Do not simply take what people say at face value. Someone in this household knows the truth of these mysteries, and I mean to find out who that is. We will succeed, my Boy. Never you fear." Sir Phillip took out foolscap and began to sharpen a pen. Very businesslike, the baronet explained what he expected them to do. "Both the midday meal and the morning tea will also allow us some time to assess your guests. I realize that you previously searched for missing bed linens and candleholders, but we need to complete a different type of search. We must look through drawers and the wardrobe—examine papers—look in the ladies' cosmetics. Someone has arsenic. Someone knows something you have missed because of your sense of propriety."

"I understand, Sir Phillip." Darcy looked about uncomfortably. "My men and I are at your disposal."

Elizabeth and Georgiana gathered the cups and placed them on the tray. "I shall inform the kitchen of the extra setting, Fitzwilliam. Do you suppose Her Ladyship will take tea with us?"

"Possibly we should apprise Lady Catherine of Sir Phillip's presence," Darcy whispered.

"I will see to it. Come, Georgiana." She caught the girl's arm. "I will speak to Lady Catherine. Might you check on Miss de Bourgh?"

The girl nodded, but she was lost in her own musings. Taking a closer look, Elizabeth realized the agitation Darcy's sister portrayed. "What is it, Georgiana?"

The girl stopped suddenly and looked alarmed. She stammered, "I–I just re-remembered where I have seen Lieutenant Harwood before. It is something I have been unable to release since meeting the lieutenant yesterday evening. He was the man by the cottages that first day, the one leaning against the tree."

Darcy was by her side, supporting her weight against his body as she swayed in place. "Are you sure, Georgiana?"

"Absolutely, Fitzwilliam. The lieutenant has been close by since before the snowstorm. He lied about riding in from Liverpool in the past two days."

CHAPTER 17

≈ ≈ ≈

DARCY TURNED GEORGIANA to him. "Do not repeat what you just said aloud where anyone else might hear. You must not share this information with the others. It is imperative that it remain among only we three and the baronet." The girl looked frightened, but she nodded her understanding. "No one, Georgiana," her brother insisted. "Especially not our cousin."

Elizabeth touched his hand lightly, letting him know how his intensity affected Georgiana. "Our sister will do your bidding, my Husband," she whispered softly. "Georgiana understands the sensitivity of your dealings with the lieutenant."

Darcy blinked twice to restore his composure. "I beg your forgiveness, Georgiana. I do not question your loyalty."

"I will be careful, Fitzwilliam."

"I know, my Dear." He gently cupped Georgiana's cheek. "I have always trusted you."

"Come, Georgiana," Elizabeth encouraged the girl. "We must set the stage for your brother's negotiations with your family."

Darcy caught Elizabeth's hand as his sister started away. "You two are to stay away from Harwood," he warned.

Elizabeth acknowledged his caution with a slight shake of her head. "I shall protect Georgiana."

"I want you safe also," he murmured. "You are my life."

Elizabeth swallowed hard. He often said the most startling things at the most unexpected times. Her eyes shimmered, and her lower lip trembled. His earnestness completely captured her. She nodded and offered him a full smile before exiting the room.

Lady Catherine reluctantly accepted Elizabeth's invitation to join the household for tea. She still had offered her nephew's wife no apology, but she kept a civil tongue in her head and prayed it would be enough to pacify Darcy. The thought of deigning to admit her wrongdoing did not sit well with Her Ladyship.

"Sir Phillip," she said in acknowledgment of the man, who stood upon her entrance. "I am pleased to see you again after all these years."

The baronet clicked his heels together before bowing in her direction. "Catherine Fitzwilliam de Bourgh, you are as beautiful as ever." He kissed Lady Catherine's fingertips.

"And you, Sir Phillip, are a perpetual liar." She swatted at his arm with her gloved hand. "Come, sit beside me so we might speak of our days at Matlock."

"As you wish, Your Ladyship."

Soon the room filled with congenial company; Sir Phillip spoke often to Lady Catherine, but Darcy carefully noted how much more often, and with some degree of stealth, the man's eyes drifted to the others enjoying the midmorning's refreshments. Sir Phillip looked at each of them —listening to their words—trying to deduce what each was thinking. Darcy followed the baronet's eyes with his own, trying desperately to observe in his guests what the magistrate saw—looking for something he had not seen previously.

Darcy's gaze fell upon Mrs. Williams. She looked down at her lap, appearing deeply exhausted. When had she become so tired looking? Dark circles rimmed her eyes—charcoal smudges telling tales of no sleep—or of a guilty conscience, perhaps, or of twisted lies. Evelyn Williams did not stir—did not speak—simply stared unrelentingly at her teacup.

"Is something the matter with the refreshments, Mrs. Williams?" Elizabeth had noted his interest in the woman and spoke the words he could not.

Instantly alert, the woman stammered, "Noth-nothing is wrong. Everything is exquisite, as usual, Mrs. Darcy. You set a most admirable table." Mrs. Williams took the cup in hand and returned to her tea, obviously shaken to have brought notice to herself.

"I wonder where Lieutenant Harwood has taken himself off to?" Cathleen Donnel commented as she motioned for more tea from the footman.

"Building up his appetite," the viscount grumbled.

Mr. Worth whispered conspiratorially, "Harwood will show when he thinks our solitude least bearable."

Stafford looked very displeased. "The man does have a knack for a grand entrance—reminds me of a distant cousin on my father's side—likes to come late to every engagement so he might be the center of attention—a deceptive conceit."

Lady Catherine displayed a determined smile. Her words, however, belied her attempt at politeness. "If I were never to see the man again, it would be too soon."

"It appears the lieutenant has a few critics," Sir Phillip remarked to no one in particular. His notice reminded Darcy to listen to what people said between the words, and that even silence spoke volumes. Of course, he expected Nigel Worth would disapprove of Harwood—the man's interest in Anne would make it so, but to hear Stafford voice his dislike surprised Darcy. His eyes first met Elizabeth's and then Spurlock's. They both returned his gaze with interest; they, too, had heard the tone of the viscount's words.

Not unexpectedly, Anne had absented herself from the group. Darcy had anticipated her reluctance to see Harwood before their intended meeting. At Elizabeth's earlier suggestion, he had sent Georgiana to Anne's room to keep their cousin company. "One never knows whether Harwood might speak to Anne privately," he told his wife. "He may try to intimidate Anne or even play on her sympathies." Now, he wondered if his prediction had proved true: Perhaps Harwood had chosen to confront Anne—even going so far as to appear at his cousin's bedroom door. Darcy's first instinct was to rush from the room and to put an end to the man's plan, but Elizabeth, who had graciously abdicated her position of importance at the room's center to his aunt and who now, quite naturally, sat on his right, whispered, "Georgiana will send word if the lieutenant calls unannounced on Miss de Bourgh."

Darcy shot her a surprised look, but Elizabeth remained impassive, feigning no knowledge of what had just passed between them. "How is it that after barely a year of our marriage you are capable of reading my thoughts so expertly?" He leaned toward her—a private moment between husband and wife. If others saw, they would think he gave her instructions regarding a household matter.

Quite naturally, she turned her head and murmured, "We have an undeniable connection—a oneness that spans the universe."

"I love you," he whispered into her hair.

Elizabeth flushed but made no other comment.

"Mrs. Wickham," Lord Stafford spoke sympathetically to the woman across from him, "how long will you remain with your sister? Shall yours be a lengthy visit?"

Lydia had been exceedingly quiet. In fact, few had seen her since her hysterics had sent her elder sister flying across the room. Although she answered civilly, her response lacked her usual exuberance. "If my sister will tolerate my intrusion, I had hoped for another fortnight, at least. My husband will not return from Bath before then. I so despise being in Newcastle without him—going among the officers unescorted is simply not done."

"Going unescorted in society is always frowned upon, Mrs. Wickham," he casually noted.

Lydia nodded passively. "So it is, Your Lordship."

Elizabeth joined their conversation. "Of course, you must stay with us, Lyddie." She knew her younger sister's sense of guilt greatly outweighed the "crime." "You have seen nothing of Pemberley or of the neighborhood, except for the sledding hill. The weather will change shortly, and we will have much to occupy us, I assure you. I do know how you thrive on social interactions."

"Thank you, Lizzy," she murmured. "I would enjoy spending

time with you and with Miss Darcy. I truly miss my sisters and walking to Meryton daily and teasing Mary and Mama and Papa."

Elizabeth smiled indulgently at her youngest sister. Lydia Wickham, although married for more than a year, was but seventeen and was still a young girl. "As do I, Lydia. We shall raid the village shops of their finest, and I will see a smile upon your face again."

The girl gave her sister the shyest of smiles. "I will honestly try, Lizzy."

After the refreshments, Darcy dutifully led his aunt into one of the smaller drawing rooms, away from the main hallway. He sent a footman for Anne and asked Mr. Worth to join them shortly. "I wish to speak to you privately, Your Ladyship," he said as he set the door ajar. Lady Catherine said nothing, but she graciously accepted the support of his arm. Darcy became more aware of her feebleness, but it did not change his resolve to speak honestly to his mother's only sister. Once she was comfortably seated, he continued. "I am gratified by your agreement to remain at Pemberley, Aunt, but it is my understanding that you have made no move to apologize to Mrs. Darcy. I thought I made myself perfectly clear on that point." He seated himself across from her, settling back into the cushions and giving the impression of being completely in control.

"I have had no opportunity." His aunt shifted a bit uncomfortably, adjusting a shawl about her shoulders to fill the awkward moments.

"Did not Mrs. Darcy call upon you earlier to assure your presence at tea?"

He watched her in silence, forcing her to respond. "Yes," she said grudgingly.

When she added nothing more, Darcy frowned. "Was that not an opportunity to address your regrets to my wife? No one would have had reason to hear but Elizabeth."

"I could not find the words." For a brief moment, her countenance softened; then a shuddering gasp for air brought her haughty stare.

Darcy shuttered his true feelings. "Then I suggest not only do you find the words, but you also find the opportunity to utter them in sincerity to Mrs. Darcy, or else I will personally have your belongings packed and will order your carriage."

"You would do such a thing!" she declared.

"Do not cross me, Aunt, for you will lose. If I must choose between you and my wife, Elizabeth will win every time."

"You would turn your back on all I have done for you—turn your back on your family?" Lady Catherine charged.

Darcy sighed in disbelief. "In a heartbeat." Somewhat irritably, he continued, "Besides, my family is here—at Pemberley—Georgiana and Elizabeth and the child she carries."

"Mrs. Darcy is to deliver?" Incredulity peppered the words. With her usual harrumph of disdain, Lady Catherine added, " She will probably present you with a daughter."

"If Mrs. Darcy gives me ten daughters, I would find no disappointment. The estate would simply go to one of Georgiana's children. In fact, I would work twice as hard for my daughter, for she would need a valuable settlement to secure her future, and as much as I would enjoy teaching my son the intricacies of owning this estate, an entailed property is not the end of the world."

His aunt looked at him in surprise. "You mean of what you speak? You affect this girl that much?"

"I do, Lady Catherine. My marriage to Elizabeth was the pivotal moment of my life. Of all I have accomplished, it is the summit." Darcy smiled with satisfaction; he saw that his aunt finally understood.

She tasted frustration first and then shame. At last, Lady Catherine spoke. "I will do as you ask, Darcy. I will offer Mrs. Darcy an apology."

"Thank you, Your Ladyship." Before he could say more, Anne entered the room, followed only seconds later by Nigel Worth. Once they had seated themselves together, Darcy remarked, "We have only moments before Harwood's appearance; I thought we might reiterate what we all know. I suspect Harwood will withdraw his demand for Anne's hand in marriage, for such was never his intention."

"The lieutenant wants money," Worth snarled.

Darcy eyeballed him closely. "How are you so positive of Harwood's motives, Worth?"

"Only yesterday evening, the lieutenant threatened to exact a *fee* for his silence."

"You spoke to Harwood? When?"

"After the evening's performance," Worth admitted. "He and I exchanged words when I warned him away from Miss de Bourgh."

Anne turned suddenly. "You did that? Warned Robert away from me?"

Anne's use of the lieutenant's familiar name bothered Worth, but he made himself ignore it. If she chose him now, what did it matter if she had once considered someone else? "How could I not do otherwise? The man upset you, and I will not look the other way in such matters."

"You take too much on yourself, Mr. Worth," Lady Catherine asserted.

Anne snapped, "Quiet, Mother. If Nigel chooses to defend my honor, I am most gratified."

Actually taking away the earlier sting, the use of his Christian name on Anne de Bourgh's lips thrilled Worth. "I would have said more except for our agreement to make it appear that you traveled to Liverpool to meet me."

"I wish I had been so astute," Anne whispered and dropped her eyes in embarrassment.

Darcy recovered the conversation. "Do we know for how much Harwood will ask?"

"The lieutenant's exact words to me were, 'More than you have.'"

"And how much is that exactly, Mr. Worth?" Lady Catherine asked.

Worth sucked in a deep breath. "Do you ask, Your Ladyship, of my financial soundness?"

"I believe my aunt wishes to know the extent of your—er—worth, Worth."

Nigel rolled his eyes good-naturedly. "As if I have never heard that one before, Darcy." Then returning his attention to Lady Catherine, he became serious once more. "My grandfather left me a small bequest, which I have invested wisely—thanks to my knowledge of law and business. At last accounting…somewhere in the neighborhood of thirty-two thousand pounds. My practice brings in five hundred to six hundred per year."

"Thirty-two thousand!" Anne exclaimed. "Then you do not need my fortune. Why did you not tell me?"

"It is not who I am. I determined some time ago to not spend more than I could afford. A single man has few expenses, and as for announcing my *worth*, I preferred a woman to choose *me*, not my purse strings." He looked deeply into Anne's eyes, holding her gaze. "We will speak more of this once we have properly dealt with Lieutenant Harwood. I shall have you know it all."

"Thank you, Lord Stafford, for agreeing to speak to me." Sir Phillip took up his pen to make some notes.

Stafford leaned back in his chair, casually letting his hand dangle over the arm. "I respect Mr. Darcy and would willingly face anything for him."

"Good… … good." As was his way, the baronet made eye contact with Adam Lawrence. "Mr. Darcy has told me of the various deaths, as well as the attack on his footman. He informs me that you thought his wife's sister to be involved somehow. Might you enlighten me as to what brought you to that conclusion?"

Adam looked away, the intensity of the magistrate's stare bothering him. He hesitated. "How do I say this?" he muttered.

"It is between us," Sir Phillip assured him.

Adam flushed. "As a future earl, I am…am accustomed to having women of various stations approach me. Some are innocents, and I avoid them. Most whom I indulge are married women who seek some excitement from a very dull relationship. Although the lady never expressed in words an invitation to her bed, the invitation remained, just the same. I have heard it many times, Sir Phillip. I did not mistake the intent of Mrs. Wickham's attentions."

"I am well aware of the lady's husband, Lord Stafford. He is trouble, and I do not doubt that his wife might need someone to champion her cause." Sir Phillip laid the pen to the side. "And your cousin, Your Lordship?"

Adam smiled knowingly. "My mistress, Sir Phillip."

"As I assumed, young man." The magistrate's grim features softened slightly. "You care for Miss Donnel?"

"Probably more than I should," Stafford admitted. "But I could never marry her…my father would keel over dead if I dared to marry below what Society demands that I take as a wife."

Sir Phillip frowned. "I care not for the new ways. In my day, a man married the woman whom his father told him to marry, and then he tried to make the best of what Fate had given him—make a tolerable life. Yet, I see men like our host marry for love, and I envy the contentedness written across their faces. Perhaps someday you shall know such happiness, too, Lord Stafford."

"Possibly."

Sir Phillip took up the pen again, indicating they were on the official record once more. "And do you still believe Mrs. Wickham to be party to the murders at Pemberley?"

"I no longer believe the lady to be directly involved, but try as I will, I cannot completely exonerate Mrs. Wickham." The magistrate gestured for Lawrence to continue. "It was Mrs. Wickham's silk stocking wrapped around the maid's neck. And it was her room left in shambles—and her hysterics, which placed Mrs. Darcy in danger. The list could go on and on. I simply cannot shake the uncanny feeling that the lady is more involved than any of us know."

"I shall keep your warning in mind, Your Lordship. I never disregard a hunch—however irrational it may seem on the surface." Sir Phillip made a quick notation. "Now, tell me anything else you believe I should know. Tell me what you saw when you accompanied Mr. Darcy on his investigations."

"How much longer must we wait for Lieutenant Harwood?" Lady Catherine grumbled. "I am not in the habit of waiting for my lessers."

"None of us are, Aunt." Darcy moved to the bell cord. "Let us send to the man's room and determine what delays him."

Anne reached impulsively for her mother's hand. "Mother, I regret bringing such shame upon your household." Anne swallowed hard, but she did not look away. "I hope you can forgive me someday."

Surprisingly, Lady Catherine took her daughter's outstretched hand and cradled it in her two gnarled palms. "You have been an exemplary child throughout the years. We shall deal decisively with this worm of a man."

Darcy nodded to Worth, indicating that his aunt had taken a major step by not chastising her daughter.

"Thank you, Mother," Anne whispered.

"I suppose you will tell me," Lady Catherine said with her usual sarcasm, "that I shall have to tolerate your choosing your own mate—much as your cousin Darcy has done."

Anne glanced quickly at Mr. Worth. "You shall, Mother, but I have learned to think more clearly and less impulsively."

"Then your experience in Liverpool will have been a serviceable lesson."

A light tap at the door curtailed the conversation. "Come," Darcy called from his seat.

Murray bowed to the room. "May I serve you, Mr. Darcy?"

"Yes, Murray. Please seek Lieutenant Harwood in his room and tell the gentleman that we await him."

"Right away, Mr. Darcy." The footman backed out of the room. Yet, before Murray could turn and make his full exit, Mr. Baldwin appeared.

"Excuse the interruption, Mr. Darcy. Booker reports that Lucas has returned, and your cousin the colonel rides with him. They should be dismounting in the drive at this moment."

"Excellent, Mr. Baldwin." Darcy stood immediately. "Let me greet Edward properly, and I shall bring him to see you, Aunt. Do not begin your discussion with the lieutenant until we return. I sent for the colonel because of Harwood's arrival."

"Will Edward help us?" Anne pleaded.

"It is my wish, Cousin." Darcy quickly followed his butler from the room.

Within moments, Darcy strode forward to greet one of the two men he counted as his closest acquaintances. Edward Fitzwilliam, one and thirty, was not handsome, but in person and address most truly the gentleman—he moved with the ease of a well-bred man. When Darcy entered the foyer, he found the colonel disposing of his greatcoat and gloves.

"Edward, you have come!" Darcy called as he embraced the man. "You are a welcome surprise."

Edward Fitzwilliam returned the embrace. "Your letter gave me no other choice."

"Edward," Elizabeth said as she materialized beside Darcy, "we are ever so glad to see you."

Impulsively, the colonel picked her up and spun the petite Mrs. Darcy about. "My goodness, Cousin. Marriage treats you very well." He set her down gently. "You are absolutely glowing."

"Unhand my wife," Darcy half threatened.

"Mrs. Darcy always liked me best," the colonel teased.

Darcy grumbled, "Do not remind me, Cousin, or I may have to run you through." Darcy caught Elizabeth's hand and possessively pulled her to him. "The lady married *me*," he warned with a raised eyebrow.

Edward retorted, "*You* are not a second son."

"Gentlemen," Elizabeth cautioned, "we are all where we were intended to be. Colonel, quit teasing my husband. He lacks a sense of humor in the matter."

"That is why I enjoy bringing it to his attention." The colonel winked at Elizabeth before good-naturedly slapping Darcy on the back. "Where is my ward?" Edward demanded.

"*Our* ward," Darcy corrected.

"Here," Georgiana said from halfway up the first flight of steps. She had rushed from her room as soon as word had come of Edward's arrival.

The colonel's eyes lifted to find her, and his heart lurched in his chest. "You cannot be my Georgiana." He lovingly examined the girl as she slowly descended the last few steps. "You are a beautiful lady, where I was expecting a gangly young girl."

"My sister does not recognize her value," Elizabeth whispered loudly enough for everyone to hear, taking note of the anxiousness in Georgiana's eyes.

"Well, she shall learn it from me," the colonel asserted. He walked toward her, opening his arms to accept Georgiana into his embrace. "You are exquisite, my Dear," he spoke softly to her upturned face before kissing the tip of Georgiana's nose. "I shall have to sharpen my sword to run off all the men when they see you, Sweetling." He turned his younger cousin back to her brother. "Shall we be entertaining the idea of a London Season for my girl this year?" The colonel beamed with pride, but Elizabeth saw the look of disappointment on Georgiana's face. She would need to speak to Darcy's sister privately.

Darcy snaked his arm about Elizabeth's waist. "We may have to wait another year. Mrs. Darcy's confinement shall prevent our spending much time in London this Season."

It took but a heartbeat for Darcy's news to reach Edward's consciousness. "Well, you devil!" He grinned at Darcy. "When had you planned on sharing the news with the rest of the family?"

"As the lady just informed us all in the past few days, the time has not proven available," Darcy declared.

"I cannot wait to share the news with the earl and the countess. They will be ecstatic."

"Edward Fitzwilliam!" Adam Lawrence's baritone voice resonated from the top of the stairs. "Am I ever pleased to see you!" He came quickly down the last flight of steps.

The colonel released Georgiana so he might greet the viscount. "Stafford." Edward extended his hand. "Darcy's letter said you were among his guests. My brother sends his regards."

"Mr. Darcy sent for you?" Stafford questioned as he took the colonel's hand in friendship.

The colonel smiled. "He did, Your Lordship."

"I hate to cut this short," Darcy said to the two men, "but Her Ladyship and our cousin await us in the back drawing room. If you will excuse us, Stafford, we three can catch up after the colonel makes his greetings to our aunt and has time to freshen his clothing."

"Certainly, Darcy. Sir Phillip has finished with me. Shall I send either my cousin or Mrs. Wickham in to speak to the baronet?"

Darcy maneuvered the colonel toward the back hallway. "If Miss Donnel would not mind speaking to Spurlock, I would be most grateful."

"I will see to it, Darcy."

Darcy nodded his thanks before turning to follow his cousin.

"Darcy!" Stafford's voice froze him in place. "Look!" The viscount pointed to the tiled floor, now wet from the tracked-in snow and ice left by the colonel and the footman.

Darcy's eyes followed the viscount's to several clearly marked boot tracks. "That settles it. I want Sir Phillip to speak to Harwood now."

"What is it, Darcy?" The colonel rejoined the other two men in the corridor.

"Your boot tracks, Edward," Darcy murmured, his mind already adding the facts to the mystery. "They are the same shape as the ones we found close to the cottages, where Georgiana saw her shadow man, and the same as those near where we found my maid's body. Our murderer is wearing the same type of boots as you."

The colonel finished Darcy's thought. "A military issue."

"Mr. Darcy." Murray had suddenly appeared on the stairs. "You should come with me, sir."

"What is it, Murray?"

"The lieutenant, sir. His room is locked from the inside, and the gentleman does not answer. I knocked several times and have called out his name, but there is no response."

Darcy grumbled, "Ask Sir Phillip to join us, Murray."

"Yes, sir." The footman reversed direction and headed toward his master's study.

Darcy forced his feet to move. "Bring your keys, Mr. Baldwin. Elizabeth, you and Georgiana are to stay here."

"Yes, Fitzwilliam."

He led the way to the second-floor quarters, Colonel Fitzwilliam and Viscount Stafford close on his heels. In his heart, Darcy knew each step led him to another mystery—another loss of life. *When will this end?* he wondered. *How can I stop this madness?*

Mr. Baldwin fumbled with his keys as Darcy pounded loudly on the door, trying to rouse a possibly sleeping Harwood. "Open it!" he ordered the butler as the others gathered close by. Baldwin slid the key into the lock and turned it to disengage the mechanism. He released the handle and stepped back to give the others access. Darcy burst through the opening, saying a silent prayer that his suspicions would be found wrong, but a bloody heap brought him up short. Sir Phillip, the colonel, and Stafford stacked up behind him. Harwood lay crumpled and broken in the floor's center, and the amount of blood, which was staining the carpet, told them they were too late.

With purpose, Sir Phillip moved from behind Darcy to the body. He caught the lieutenant's shoulders and rolled the man to his back. The officer had pulled up on his knees, apparently trying to seek help or to escape, but he had made it no further. Now, arms spread open, the body stared, wide-eyed, at nothing. Sir Phillip gently touched the lids, closing them. "His–his throat has been slit," the baronet stammered. "Look for a weapon."

Darcy, Stafford, and the colonel fanned out automatically in several directions. "The water," the colonel gestured toward the table, "is full of blood." He traced a circle in the bowl. "Was the lieutenant shaving? The bloody towel is on the floor, but I see no blade."

Sir Phillip still knelt beside the body. "The lieutenant's face sports a fine stubble. I doubt if he shaved today."

"Then who used the razor and soap?" Stafford mused. "And who left the window open?" He leaned out to see the likelihood of someone using it as an entrance or an exit. "It appears our attacker threw water out the window. There is an icy circle on the snow's surface."

"We no longer have to worry about Harwood pressing his suit with our cousin," Edward remarked.

Sir Phillip stood slowly. "I will wish to examine the room again before we move the body. I shall need to make an official report."

"I will secure the room," Mr. Baldwin muttered from somewhere behind them.

"Mr. Darcy, I need to speak to anyone with whom the lieutenant exchanged cross words over the past couple of days," Sir Phillip authoritatively declared.

Darcy nodded his understanding. "That would be much of the household, Sir Phillip. I am afraid the lieutenant had a way of irritating many with whom he came in contact."

"You should well start with me," Stafford admitted. "I warned the man from my cousin only this morning."

Sir Phillip looked grim. "Then rejoin me in Mr. Darcy's study, sir. I will take your statement first. Have your man lock everything up as it is, Darcy."

"Yes, Sir Phillip." He motioned to Mr. Baldwin to follow the baronet's orders. "Edward, you and I should attend to Her Ladyship and Anne. This will come as quite a shock to them. I will send Mr. Worth to you, Sir Phillip. I am aware of an argument between the men yesterday evening, and then I, too, will explain my exchange with Harwood regarding my cousin."

"This grows by leaps and bounds," Edward remarked as he turned toward the open door. "When you have finished your investigation, Sir Phillip, I will need to inform the lieutenant's commanding officer."

The magistrate turned dejectedly away. "Indeed, Colonel. However, we must deal with one fact at a time."

CHAPTER 18

≈ ≈ ≈

"NOW, STAFFORD, WHAT IS this madness regarding Lieutenant Harwood?" Sir Phillip resettled behind Darcy's desk, poised to take the viscount's official statement.

Adam Lawrence returned to the wing chair he had so recently vacated. "As usual, I do not know how to explain the situation." He paused uncomfortably. "Mr. Darcy privately made me aware of the perfidy the lieutenant practiced regarding Miss de Bourgh. Darcy asked that I help him keep an eye on the man. Since his appearance at Pemberley, besides his approach to Her Ladyship's daughter, Harwood had taken a *liking* to my cousin. Keep in mind, Sir Phillip, that other than Mr. and Mrs. Darcy, the rest of the household assumes that Miss Donnel is my cousin—my relative and the daughter of a nobleman. Harwood appeared to have identified Cathleen as his next pigeon. I found them in the middle of a tête-à-tête during breakfast this morning. When Miss Donnel departed the room, I warned the lieutenant from Cathleen. The man feigned innocence, but I know a rake when I meet one. He was already counting his money."

"And what did you do, Lord Stafford, after this confrontation?"

Adam chuckled sarcastically. "Are you asking, Sir Phillip, if I followed the officer to his room and slit his throat?"

"Precisely," the magistrate declared.

"Not likely, sir. As much as I disdain Harwood's type, I am not of the temperament to grotesquely murder a man over a flirtation.

I am a gentleman—if I chose to seek retribution, I would challenge the lieutenant and have him name his seconds. Instead of a bloody razor, I managed to quash Harwood's plans by having a serious conversation with my cousin. I followed Cathleen to her room and warned her of the scoundrel's manipulations."

"And the lady will attest to this?" The baronet placed the pen in its holder.

"She would, Sir Phillip."

"Edward!" Anne called as she rose to greet her cousin. She offered him a genuine welcome—the first he could remember receiving from her. As a young girl, Anne had never participated in their childhood roughhousing—Her Ladyship had always declared her daughter too sickly. Now, she glowed with a newfound independence, and he happily accepted her finally becoming a woman with a future.

"You look well, Cousin," he affirmed as he lifted Anne's chin and gazed into her eyes. "I cannot tell you how your countenance pleases me."

"Thank you, Edward."

The colonel released Anne and made his obeisance to his aunt. "Your Ladyship." He bowed over her hand. "My father and mother send their kindest regards."

"You appear well, Fitzwilliam," Lady Catherine murmured. "Is my brother—your father—in health? How is the earl's gout?"

"Somewhat better, Your Ladyship."

"And the countess?"

The colonel smiled knowingly. Lady Catherine and his mother had had more than one disagreement over the years. "My mother works tirelessly in the name of her charities. She and the earl spent Christmas with my maternal aunt and uncle in Lincolnshire. The Attingboroughs welcomed a new addition to the family a fortnight before the holiday."

Darcy motioned for Edward to have a seat and brought their conversation to a close. "Although Edward is always a welcome diversion at Pemberley, I specifically sent for him because he knew Lieutenant Harwood before the man's arrival at Rosings Park," Darcy announced.

"Where is the scoundrel?" Worth asked impatiently. "Did you not send your man for the lieutenant some time ago? If Harwood thinks this purposeful stall will help his negotiations—"

Darcy's clearing of his throat cut the man short. "I have an announcement of sorts. Murray returned with news of the lieutenant's absence. Stafford, Edward, Sir Phillip, and I entered Harwood's room when he did not respond to our entreaties. We regret to tell you that Lieutenant Harwood has met an untimely death."

Anne gasped and swayed and collapsed into Nigel Worth's arms. Her sobs followed. "Poor Robert."

"How?" Worth demanded as he tried to comfort the woman.

Edward glanced quickly at Darcy. "I do not believe we are at liberty to discuss it at this time. Sir Phillip will wish to speak to each of us as part of his investigation."

"I have nothing to say on the matter," Lady Catherine observed. "Although I wish no man an early death, I welcome the absence of the lieutenant's malice."

Edward moved to the settee shared by Worth and Anne. "I will see to my cousin, sir," he whispered. "Sir Phillip wishes to speak to you."

Anne's head snapped up in disbelief. "Why must Sir Phillip question Nigel? Mr. Worth has done nothing wrong!"

Worth eased her out of his embrace. "It is nothing of consequence," he assured her. "The magistrate simply performs his duty. I expected nothing less." Worth stood and straightened his waistcoat. "I assume, Mr. Darcy, that the baronet occupies your study."

"He does." Darcy stood and reached for his aunt's hand. "It seems most prudent that we discuss Harwood's threats from a different perspective. I suggest we allow Edward time to freshen his clothes." Lady Catherine placed her hand in his. "We shall all retire to the blue drawing room. I will send for refreshments and ask the others to join us. It will expedite Sir Phillip's examination if we discuss everything we know as a group."

His aunt stiffened with disdain. "You would openly consider your cousin's failings before strangers?"

"You know my usual reticence, Aunt, but the ordinary does not currently operate at Pemberley. Four people have lost their lives under this roof in the past week. Somehow everything is connected, and we must clear the air if we are to stop the insanity. I cannot imagine that Anne would wish to hide the truth if it meant a murderer would go free."

"Of course not, Fitzwilliam," Anne said from somewhere behind him.

"It is time for some honesty, Your Ladyship."

"And your relationship with Miss de Bourgh?" Sir Phillip questioned Mr. Worth after having dismissed Lord Stafford.

Worth, used to such interrogations, understood the necessity of Spurlock's probe, but he did not appreciate the invasion of his privacy. "I would not say Miss de Bourgh and I have a relationship. We have known each other for only a few days. However, Mr. Darcy and I agreed that I might provide the lady with a reliable explanation for her attendance in Liverpool."

"And why might you place yourself in a questionable position, Worth, if you and Her Ladyship's daughter have no prior knowledge of each other?"

"I am a gentleman who will not stand idly by and allow a bounder to take advantage of an innocent. Miss de Bourgh made a grievous error by placing her trust in Harwood, but the lady should not face ruination for it. If I err, Sir Phillip, it is on the side of purity."

The baronet smiled, hearing the unspoken words. "And what might you know of Mrs. Jenkinson?"

"The lady served Miss de Bourgh well, offering maternal care and love. I met her as one of Mr. Darcy's guests, and we immediately took a liking to each other. I had fleeting thoughts of pursuing a connection, but the lady simply enjoyed my company. She had a vision of what she wanted for Miss de Bourgh's future, and the lieutenant was not part of that conception. I flatter myself in thinking that Mrs. Jenkinson maneuvered her charge in my direction—the lady took an interest in me because she wanted a stable bond for Miss de Bourgh."

"I thought you said you held no relationship with Anne de Bourgh, other than to serve as her man of business in this matter?"

"I do and I do not." Worth considered all the complications involved in his affections for the lady before he answered. "I hold no acknowledged intimacy with Miss de Bourgh, but that does not mean I have no desire to develop one. When we leave Pemberley, it is my intention to request permission to call on the lady."

"And as such, you warned Lieutenant Harwood away from Miss de Bourgh?"

"What you really wish to know is whether I killed the lieutenant."

The baronet simply nodded: He and Worth had experienced the courtroom together on more than one occasion. Sir Phillip knew Worth's reputation.

"As much as I abhorred the man's public swagger, a crime such as you described earlier, Sir Phillip, is a crime of passion and an act of opportunity. You know me, Spurlock. I am a man of reason—spent a decade in the English public courtrooms. I might go a round of fisticuffs with the lieutenant, but cutting a man's throat and letting him bleed to death is simply not my style."

Spurlock agreed, although he made no mention of the fact to Worth. Something about this investigation bothered him—something he needed to clarify. "Might we join the others, Worth? Mr. Darcy sent word that he has gathered everyone in the blue drawing room. I would welcome your insights into this case."

The household gathered at Darcy's request. He told them nothing until Spurlock joined them, and then he said very little about the reason for their attendance. Sir Phillip would simply listen and observe, at least, initially. "I have asked Sir Phillip Spurlock as the local magistrate to join us," Darcy announced at last. "Some of you met Sir Phillip earlier. As the weather has taken a positive turn, and we will soon be able to properly see to the deceased, we thought it best to address some facts before our parting—to find a resolution." By silent agreement, no one mentioned Harwood directly. Several in the room still held no knowledge of the lieutenant's death.

The baronet stepped forward. "Mr. Darcy, his wife, and his sister have spent an inordinate amount of time defining this past week's events, but I have some questions I wish to address to individuals in this room. As I explained to Mr. Darcy, allowing each of you to hear what the others say may lead to new clues—new facts to solve this dilemma."

No one responded directly, but a nervous buzz spread to every corner of the room. Before the baronet began his interrogation, Darcy took the opportunity to finish the introductions. "Pardon my interruption, Sir Phillip, but I should complete our welcomes."

"Of course, Mr. Darcy."

"For those of you unfamiliar with the gentleman on my left, it is with great pleasure that I present my cousin Colonel Fitzwilliam. Edward, I believe you familiar with everyone except Miss Donnel, His Lordship's cousin." Darcy paused while Edward bowed over the lady's hand. "Mrs. Williams." Pause. "And Mrs. Darcy's youngest sister." So as to explain why his cousin might not already know Elizabeth's sister, he quickly added, "I believe Mrs. Wickham was in Newcastle when Elizabeth and I wed. You would have had no opportunity for a prior acquaintance."

"It is a pleasure, Mrs. Wickham." Edward brought Lydia's hand to his lips for the obligatory air kiss.

"Thank you, Colonel," Lydia cooed.

When Edward turned his head, Darcy noted his cousin's raised eyebrow. He did not know if it was because the colonel realized Lord Stafford possessed no "cousin" among those staying at Pemberley, or whether Edward saw the buffoonery of acknowledging George Wickham's wife. After all, Edward shared the guardianship of Darcy's sister and was well aware of Wickham's attempted elopement with and seduction of the girl. Darcy imagined Edward's sensibilities to be shocked by the irony of both women being Pemberley's guests.

When the colonel settled himself beside Georgiana on one of the settees, the baronet recovered the group's attention. "I understand from the Darcys how you each came to be at Pemberley," he began, "and the events of those first few days. What concerns me first is the fateful afternoon when Mrs. Jenkinson lost her life. I have examined the body and the cup from which the lady drank, and I agree with Mr. Darcy's assumption of arsenic being the method." Sir Phillip took a nearby seat and removed some folded paper and the stub of a pencil from his inside pocket, so that he might make himself some notes. "I understand, Mrs. Wickham," he said, quickly turning to Lydia, "that you were the one to make arrangements for the hot cider and tea after the sledding adventure."

Lydia flushed with the notice. "I came into the house and asked Mrs. Jennings to provide us refreshments," she admitted.

"Did you touch the service, ma'am?" the magistrate continued.

Lydia started to respond, but then she paused with a frown. "If you mean, did I pour the drinks, the answer is no, Sir Phillip." She saw the viscount's head snap up in surprise. "It is true, Your Lordship," she avowed. "I have thought long and hard on your accusations regarding my opportunities for poisoning the lady's drink, but I was not the first person in this room that day."

Adam Lawrence demanded, "Then who was, pray tell? It was you, Mrs. Wickham, who ordered the drinks' preparation from Darcy's staff, and you were partaking of the hot liquid when the rest of us entered the room."

Lydia bristled with the renewal of his accusatory tone, but she did not retreat from his charges. "Mrs. Williams was sitting by the hearth when I arrived in the room," Lydia asserted.

"That is impossible," Worth remarked. "Mrs. Williams entered with the rest of us."

"Yes, and entered the storeroom off the kitchen with the rest of us so that we could rid ourselves of our snow-soaked outerwear," Stafford clarified.

Anne sat forward, feeling a twinge of discomfort with her thoughts. "Yet, Mrs. Williams was the first in and the first out that afternoon. Mrs. Darcy left at the same time, but she stopped to give orders to her staff to tend to our wet clothes. Miss Darcy, Mildred, and I sought a withdrawing room before we came in here that day."

"You are correct, Miss de Bourgh," Elizabeth confirmed. "Mrs. Williams and I did walk this way together, but I tarried to speak to Mr. Baldwin."

"Then I am now accused," Mrs. Williams charged, "of a deed most foul?"

"Blame is not this inquiry's purpose, I assure you, ma'am; I simply wish to know the facts. For all I know, the late Mrs. Jenkinson may have willingly partaken of the arsenic as part of a beauty regime."

The woman protested, "Well, I never!"

The baronet pressed the point. "Never what, madam? Never entered this room before the others? Never planned to hurt Mrs. Jenkinson? Never held knowledge of the potency of the powder? Never liked the lady?"

"How could anyone not like Mildred?" Anne disputed.

"The lady was of the first cut," Worth added his evaluation.

"Never expected to face such censure," Mrs. Williams snapped, not liking the implications.

Darcy glanced uneasily from Mrs. Williams to Sir Phillip. "Would you mind answering the baronet's question, ma'am?"

The lady glowered at Darcy. "I thought I just did."

"No, madam, you have not." A shocked silence filled the room.

Mrs. Williams's face looked thunderous. "I was the first one in the room," she hissed.

"And when I accused Mrs. Wickham before of having the opportunity of performing a 'deed most foul,' as you so kindly put it, why did you not correct my misinformation?" Adam Lawrence charged. "Why did you not assume the truth then?"

"How was I to know whether Mrs. Wickham wanted to hurt Mrs. Jenkinson? She was the first to the house and the first to be around the refreshments that afternoon. Possibly the young lady might choose to place the culpability in my lap. Who might the Darcys believe? Their own sister or a complete stranger? I kept quiet to protect myself. Who could fault me for that?"

"And what do you know of arsenic?" Stafford continued.

The widow looked trapped. "No more than any other well-trained lady."

Anne shivered, her mood somber as a tomb. "And Mildred—what did you think of my companion?" She brushed away the tears forming at the corner of her eyes.

Mrs. Williams choked back her anger. "I barely knew Mrs. Jenkinson; I had no opinion one way or the other."

She thought she might end the conversation there, but Lydia asked, a hint of betrayal playing through her voice, "Was it you, Mrs. Williams, who arranged the cups in the pattern on the serving tray?"

"Again, I am unaware of what you speak!" The woman's expression grew mutinous.

Georgiana ventured a comment, encouraged by the close proximity of her cousin. "In rows—three, then two, then three, and one alone. The one alone was the one over which my sister and Mrs. Jenkinson dickered."

Mrs. Williams rose to her feet. "I do not need to stay and listen to this!"

Sir Phillip's calm voice stayed her. "I am afraid you do, madam. Please return to your chair."

Her face grew cold. "As you wish." The lady resentfully sat once more.

"Now tell us, Mrs. Williams, if you arranged the cups on the service tray."

She gritted her teeth, tightening her jaw. "I did, sir."

"For what purpose?"

"For no purpose, sir, except that I am the widow of a man who spent his life in the military—a man who preferred things orderly—in rows and perfectly spaced—an old habit."

Lord Stafford appeared unconvinced. "Why did you not say so without the baronet's prompting?"

"I am a very private woman, Your Lordship. I recognized how my perversion might appear to the rest of you."

"Then the last cup—the one from which Mrs. Jenkinson drank—was purely a matter of Fate?" Sir Phillip inquired.

Mrs. Williams raised her chin in defiance. "Even I could have chosen that cup. It could have been any of us in this room, including me."

A long silence followed as each of them considered what the lady had said. Finally, Mr. Worth broke the quiet. "I ask again: Did you disapprove of Mrs. Jenkinson?"

The widow looked uncomfortable—every eye in the room surveyed her demeanor. "I thought the lady could have shown more restraint," she declared with some emphasis on the last word.

"Would you explain what you mean by 'restraint,' ma'am?" Sir Phillip asked quickly.

Mrs. Williams sat up straighter, throwing her shoulders back—stiff and proper—unbending in her righteousness. "Mrs. Jenkinson held a position where her actions should be of an exemplary nature, but she set a poor example."

"Mildred Jenkinson was a woman of the first ilk," Anne defensively charged. "When I was at my lowest, she tended to my needs in lieu of her own. Her last thoughts were of my well-being."

"I agree, Miss de Bourgh," Worth expressed wholeheartedly.

Mrs. Williams nearly snarled, "Of course, you would say so, sir. You shared intimacies with Mrs. Jenkinson."

"The lady and I spoke of her late husband—a man renowned for his *diplomacy*."

The starchily virtuous woman straightened an imaginary seam on her dress. "A man's greatness does not define his wife. Mr. Jenkinson's reputation does not expunge that of Mrs. Jenkinson's."

Darcy's cold voice penetrated the tension filling the room. He blamed himself for not asking the obvious questions and for allowing this creature to enter his household. "Beware, Mrs. Williams. The same might be said of you and the admiral."

At first, the lady appeared to want to offer a protest, but then a smile turned up the corners of her mouth. "For once, Mr. Darcy, we are in accord."

"Might we leave Mrs. Jenkinson's case for a few minutes?" Sir Phillip interrupted. "Do any of you have insights into the deaths of either Mr. Darcy's footman or the maid?" When a silence ensued, he clarified, "Even if you believe your thoughts without merit, please do not withhold them. Often, a minor detail is the one which turns the screw."

Lady Catherine cleared her throat. "Darcy, far be it of me to speak poorly of my niece, but I thought it odd that the footman's death followed the disclosure of someone having invaded Georgiana's room."

"I am aware of Miss Darcy's nightmare," Sir Phillip noted, "but do you believe, Your Ladyship, that there was more to the story?"

Lady Catherine shifted to face him. "My niece cried out in fear; my daughter and I rushed to her side, but my nephew and his wife assured us it was no more than a nightmare. Then later my niece disclosed to this group in a similar meeting what she believed she heard a voice repeat in her room."

"Then you consider the possibility the voice belonged to Lawson, the footman," the baronet said, looking very ill at ease. He realized the implications would infuriate Darcy.

As expected, Darcy intervened, refusing to allow his sister to be portrayed in a poor light. He looked positively murderous, and several of the others automatically shrank back in response. "Miss Darcy has admitted what she heard, and she has addressed how she met secretly with the young man, teaching him to read. I do not believe there is a connection between the two, despite my aunt's suspicions." He thought he could easily strangle his mother's sister at the moment and enjoy every second of it. The woman purposely tried to deflect the attention from Anne, a culprit in this mess, and send the attention toward Georgiana. Well, she would pay for this betrayal. His good opinion once lost was lost for good.

"Why not?" Worth ventured, ignoring Darcy's look of contempt. "I mean, none of us are beyond scrutiny."

"Might I, Fitzwilliam?" Georgiana ventured, her lower lip trembling. The colonel lightly touched her arm, and the girl sucked in a deep breath. "It could not have been Lawson because the night the intruder entered my room, Lawson was in Dove Dale for his sister's wedding. Do you not remember, Elizabeth? You gave Lawson permission to borrow one of the horses so he could ride to the neighboring village; otherwise, he might have missed the ceremony. He attended the wedding and then returned the next day, after spending the night with his mother. It was the family's first time together following his father's passing."

"Yes, he brought us both a piece of the bridal cake from the breakfast. I remember now that you say it. His mother insisted because of our kindness to her son." Elizabeth looked at the group, silently daring any of them to dispute what she said. "Like my husband, I am assured the 'ghost' my sister heard in her room was not Lawson. The boy's death resulted from his coming upon our intruder at an inopportune time. No one will convince me otherwise."

"Mrs. Darcy holds the theory that the boy's death was staged to appear a suicide. We are aware that Lawson could not have written the note left behind and how the windows did not lend themselves well to such a use. My wife has expressed her opinions previously to that behalf," Darcy said, summing up the discussion in his authoritative tone.

Sir Phillip judiciously moved on to another topic. "The maid— Lucinda Dodd—she had a confrontation with Mrs. Darcy's sister.

We assumed she was the one to destroy Mrs. Wickham's belongings. The question remains, why did someone kill Miss Dodd?"

"It seems logical to me, Sir Phillip," Elizabeth spoke first, "that, like Lawson, Lucinda must have surprised the intruder."

Lady Catherine snarled, "Is it not possible that Mrs. Wickham exacted her revenge on the maid? She was overheard reprimanding your servant, Darcy."

"If we accused every man or woman of murder who has spoken harshly to the help, most of English aristocracy would stand accused, including you, Aunt." Darcy defended Elizabeth more than he did Lydia Wickham. His aunt still clung to her old ways, and he feared he would once again have to sever ties with her. Besides, her defection from Georgiana brought his own personal censure.

Her Ladyship snorted her disgust, but she refused to force Darcy's hand any further.

"As Mrs. Wickham is nearly a head shorter and more than two stone lighter than the maid, it is not likely that she could first, overpower the woman, or, second, carry the body so far away from the house," Stafford pointed out.

Cathleen Donnel asked, "Is not Lucinda the maid who claimed to have had several flirtatious conversations with your unknown footman, Mr. Darcy?"

Darcy observed her evenly. "You are correct, Miss Donnel. I do not believe any of us had made that connection before now."

"Then if I understand what we have said here today," Sir Phillip made some quick scratches on the paper, "Mrs. Jenkinson's passing appears more calculated than the other two, which seem more opportunistic."

"And Harwood?" the colonel asked into the silent room.

Cathleen Donnel glanced furtively about the room. "Where is Lieutenant Harwood? I expected him to be here."

"There are a few facts about the lieutenant of which I would like each of you to be aware," Darcy took up the tale; yet, he did not answer Miss Donnel's question. "The lieutenant has misrepresented himself to my family and to me."

"How so, Mr. Darcy?" Cathleen asked innocently. Despite Adam's warning, she saw the man's goodness.

"Initially, when Harwood called at Pemberley, I expressed my surprise at his being able to travel in such inclement weather. The lieutenant assured me that Derby had received the storm's force. In reality, it was the reverse: Cheshire took the hardest hit. I am positive of my words' truth because the colonel came from Matlock today, and although the roads were muddy—"

"And miserable," Edward interjected.

"And miserable," Darcy continued, "traffic to the east has resumed. Roads headed north or west are still impassable."

Anne found her voice. "Why would Lieutenant Harwood lie?"

"Why the lieutenant offered a prevarication I will explain momentarily," he assured everyone. "When the viscount and I began our investigation, we found an unusual muddy pattern on the tree trunk closest to the tenant cottages, where my sister had seen the phantom stranger."

Lord Stafford stood to fill his glass with brandy. "It was a heel print," he said casually as he poured the golden brown liquid. "The heel's shape was irregular—not curved like those most of us wear. We discovered a similarly shaped track near Lucinda's body and again today." He returned to his seat. "When Colonel Fitzwilliam tracked in mud and snow on Pemberley's tiled foyer, we quickly noticed that the mark from the tree and from Mr. Darcy's floor compared favorably. They both came from a military-issued boot."

"That does not prove the lieutenant created the mark." Mrs. Williams appeared shaken, but she raised her chin defiantly.

Darcy smiled in perverted amusement. "You are correct, Mrs. Williams; however, Miss Darcy identified Lieutenant Harwood as being the man she had observed."

Georgiana explained, "I thought from the beginning that the lieutenant held a familiarity. He did: He wore the same style of dark cloak and hat that I have seen the colonel wear with his uniform, but there was something else. It was his blond hair tied back with the leather string that caused me to make the connection. I am sure you all noticed the lieutenant's straight blonde hair."

"The point I wish to make is that Harwood could know nothing of Cheshire's roads because he dwelled in Derby before we were beset by the storm. He has been in the area all along," said Darcy. "I checked with my groomsmen and the gatekeeper, and they report that the lieutenant has been asking questions about this household for several days. He was most interested in the Rosings Park equipage, for example."

"That scoundrel!" Lady Catherine declared.

"I imagine, Aunt, the lieutenant arrived before your journey to Pemberley. Harwood likely escaped Liverpool when you arrived to claim Anne—it is very likely the man paralleled your journey on horseback."

Mrs. Williams sniffed in disgust. "You accuse a man when he can make no defense."

"That is where you are in error, madam." Lady Catherine's autocratic tone brooked no debate. "The lieutenant practiced a deceit upon my daughter—opening my poor, dear Anne to a possible ruination—and then demanded payment for his silence." Her Ladyship's desire to keep her family's good name had gone by the wayside in her need to have the final word.

Anne felt the embarrassment of her mother's announcing her daughter's weakness to the whole room, but the shame of the incident lessened with each retelling; and in a strange way, Anne gloried in her own mistakes. They meant she had taken control of her life.

Colonel Fitzwilliam sat forward to draw the room's attention to him. "I suppose it is time that I share what I know of the lieutenant." Even Darcy turned to listen. He had his suspicions, but only his cousin knew the truth. "Lieutenant Robert Harwood accompanied me to Kent three months ago. We were to set up an exchange of information post with the British Navy. Being at Dover, it seemed only appropriate that I call upon my aunt, and I often requested Harwood's company.

"It took me little time to note the lieutenant's interest in my cousin. Thinking it but a simple flirtation, I saw nothing of which to object. In fact, observing my cousin's change of demeanor and her newfound confidence, I purposely looked the other way. Yet, something about Harwood and Anne's relationship disturbed me, and after my cousin's trusted companion, Mrs. Jenkinson, sought me out to express similar concerns, I took it upon myself to find out more of the lieutenant's background."

"And what did you discover, Colonel?" Elizabeth encouraged him.

Mrs. Williams rose quickly to her feet. "I must object, Sir Phillip, to this line of questioning. The officer is not present to defend himself against these acrid accusations. I will not allow anyone to soil the good name of an honorable officer."

She made to depart, but Sir Phillip's words stayed her leaving. "You will remain where you are, madam, or I shall have you detained by my magisterial powers."

Evelyn Williams bristled with indignation. "Am I to be another of the innocents accused without provocation?"

"You will be treated with the same civility as you treat others, madam," the baronet retorted.

After a moment's silent battle of wills, Mrs. Williams took a seat away from the others.

"Might you continue, Colonel?" Sir Phillip gestured as he accepted the lady's act of noncompliance.

"I left the lieutenant in Kent to assist Colonel Cavendish, and I returned to our unit. There, I pulled the lieutenant's official record. What I discovered nearly set me on the road again. However, when news came of Harwood's removal from Kent, I assumed all would be well. I planned to speak to Her Ladyship and Anne if the lieutenant showed himself to be my cousin's ardent pursuer."

Elizabeth slid her hand into Darcy's, sensing what they were about to hear might change everything, and she needed to hold onto the only solid thing in her life: Darcy's love. "What did you discover of the man, Colonel?"

"Lieutenant Robert Harwood's file showed the man to already be in possession of a wife." A rumble of disbelief filled the room. "A wife whom he had married some five years earlier—a woman several years his senior—a woman whose first husband had lost his life at San Domingo—a woman from Cumbria—Angel Harwood."

Lydia gasped, "Oh, my goodness!" Nearly everyone else in the room gasped also.

Cathleen looked amusedly at Adam. "Angel? It sounds like a stage name."

"I am sure it is a shortened version of Angelica, a name quite common on the Continent," the Colonel noted.

"So the miscreant already had a wife?" Worth growled. "I should have known."

Anne stammered, "Rob-Robert? Had-Had a wife? How could he offer himself to me, knowing he had given away what he so intimately professed to need?"

Elizabeth observed, "I do not understand such duplicity. His poor wife...how she must suffer."

Mrs. Williams flinched, but she again came to the officer's defense. "One can only suppose that the lieutenant had his reasons."

"But the man practiced a deceit of a most personal nature," Stafford declared.

"Exactly," Worth stated. "A proposal of marriage should not be anything less than personal."

Anne whispered, "It certainly felt personal to me."

"To you?" Mrs. Williams's composure snapped. "To you? *Nothing* is personal to you, Miss de Bourgh. You change your affections as easily as you change your gown—first your cousin Mr. Darcy— then the lieutenant—and now Mr. Worth. Do you not think that an inordinate number of *lovers* in so short a span of time, Miss de Bourgh?" Her tone slivered with contempt. "Your companion's body had not lost its heat before you turned your attention to Mr. Worth, a man whose name means nothing; for one day, he spent time with Mrs. Jenkinson and the next with Miss de Bourgh."

Worth came to Anne's defense. He worried not for his own reputation; society expected men to have an inconstant nature. "Mrs. Jenkinson spoke of Miss de Bourgh's fine qualities—the lady led me to what she saw in her charge. My true affection for Mrs. Jenkinson awakened me to the excellence of Miss de Bourgh's character."

Cathleen Donnel put into words what many others were thinking, "You defend Lieutenant Harwood's actions? His attempted seduction and ruination of a lady?" Adam took note of how her bottom lip trembled, and he realized he needed to let her go—she deserved better— deserved to return to her family a *lady,* not his mistress. He wondered if he felt the guilt that Harwood would never know.

"It would seem to me that *the lady* participated willingly. By her mother's own words, Miss de Bourgh followed Lieutenant Harwood to Liverpool. If she misjudged the man—if she knew so little of the world as to not see the man's true nature—then perhaps Miss de Bourgh learned a valuable lesson at the lieutenant's hands."

"A lesson the vulgarian hoped to make profitable," Lady Catherine hissed.

Darcy cleared his throat, silencing them all. He had been carefully observing their interactions, doing what Sir Phillip had instructed him to do—be a good listener. "Did you know Harwood previously, Mrs. Williams?"

"Why would you make such an assumption, Mr. Darcy?" She turned quickly away.

"When he first arrived, you slipped from the room before I could introduce you," Darcy thought aloud.

Mrs. Williams stood slowly, pressing her skirt's wrinkles. "As I am assured that my opinions are no longer welcome at Pemberley, I shall beg Mr. Darcy for the comfort of a coach into the village. Perhaps the lieutenant might serve as my escort. His presence, I assume, is no longer required. If the gentleman's scheme has failed, he will likely be most eager to take his leave. As I am not as naïve as many of my present company, I will have no qualms in sharing a coach for the five miles into Lambton."

"Surely, Sir Phillip, you have no intention of allowing Mrs. Williams to leave Pemberley until she truthfully answers my nephew's question," Lady Catherine declared.

"Never fear, Your Ladyship. No one will leave until both Mr. Darcy and I have the answers to many questions."

"I know my rights, Sir Phillip. You may not detain the lieutenant or me, as no crime has been committed. Intention is not action, sir," Mrs. Williams asserted.

"And what of my dear Mildred's death?" Mrs. Williams's frame overshadowed Anne's, but Darcy's cousin demanded an answer as she shot to her feet.

Mrs. Williams made a move toward the door, but Stafford blocked her retreat. "Am I accused once more?" she asked incredulously.

Worth took up the cause. "By your own words, you disapproved of Miss de Bourgh's companion and of Her Ladyship's daughter. You arranged the cups of hot cider, and I venture to say if we searched your room, we would find arsenic among your cosmetics, although I recall your most vehement denial of the traditional use of arsenic as part of a lady's beauty secrets."

Darcy noted how the lady recoiled when Worth mentioned searching her room. He instantly regretted not having searched specifically for that *beauty* item after Mrs. Jenkinson's death. Now, he clearly saw the fault in his helter-skelter efforts. Thankfully, Sir Phillip understood the intricacies of searching for the truth.

"I will allow no one access to my private quarters," the lady declared.

Darcy countered, "As this is my house, madam, I doubt you could keep me out."

"When we finish here, Darcy," the baronet summarized, "you and I will do just that. We will also search the other rooms—under my supervision, of course." His businesslike tone instilled confidence.

"Of course, Sir Phillip."

"Might we return to the issue of Robert Harwood?" Edward interjected.

Mrs. Williams's composure slipped. "What of the lieutenant?"

Sir Phillip sat straighter, aware of the importance of his announcement. "The lieutenant has lost his life."

"Oh, no!" Elizabeth gasped, turning her face into Darcy's shoulder, seeking his immediate comfort.

Every other eye in the room drifted to a discomposed Mrs. Williams. "That is impossible!" she asserted. "I spoke to him only last night."

Her admission silenced the room. "When might that have been?" Darcy's eyes eagerly assessed the crumbling aplomb of the defiant naval widow. "As I assumed last evening's meal to be the first of your acquaintance with Harwood, I would be most interested to know when you might have had the time for a private conversation."

"As would I," Sir Phillip moved up beside Mrs. Williams. "You will have a *private conversation* with me, madam." He took the lady's arm to lead her from the room.

CHAPTER 19

∼ ∼ ∼

JAMES TOOK A CHANCE by crossing the main hall of Pemberley, but his recent forays had provided no new information. He had been aware when Darcy and the others had found the maid's body—he had known of the viscount's returning to his mistress's room—he had enjoyed the play the Pemberley guests performed for their own amusement—he had observed the chaos following Mrs. Wickham's discovery of her tattered belongings and Darcy's anger when his wife had suffered an injury. What he did not know was what had occurred when Darcy's household had found the soldier's body. The lieutenant's entry into the bedchamber at the wrong moment had been a most unfortunate development.

Now, just as with Peter's "soiled" articles, they expected James to right the mistakes of his newest partner, Gregor MacIves. He could not remove the body, but he could ascertain what Darcy intended to do next. He remained in the shadows, partially hidden by the palms and the marble busts—the door to the linen closet ajar so he could hide if necessary.

Finally, the door to the blue drawing room swung open, and the guests poured forth. James turned his back and edged toward the closet, pretending to polish a nearby framed mirror. He knew the aristocracy's tendency to not actually see the household servants in attendance. He would be safe from close scrutiny. Out of the corner of his eye, he watched the usual clusters of people split to attend to their own diversions: Worth and Miss de Bourgh, the viscount and his mistress, and Darcy and his wife. But the group had added two new players.

Miss Darcy and Lady Catherine exited the drawing room on the arms of a military officer. When the trio passed him, James recognized the man immediately: He was Darcy's cousin Edward Fitzwilliam. Three years James's senior, the second son of the Earl of Matlock had never approved of James's manipulations. They had disagreed often over the years, but James had never feared the colonel. He feared Darcy, however. Although the colonel possessed fighting skills, he did not possess Darcy's quick mind. Yet, forewarned was forearmed in all matters, and James was glad to have knowledge of the officer's presence. He wanted no surprises.

The last from the room was the prudish widow, tears streaming down her face. Instinctively, James slipped through the closet door before anyone could notice, but he left it open enough to observe the final pair. The widow leaned heavily on the arm of a nobleman. Again, James knew the familiar countenance, although he had not seen the man in nearly a decade. Sir Phillip Spurlock had served the neighborhood for some twenty years as the local magistrate. James had run aground of the man as a youth for foolish pranks on two separate occasions—three, really. With the first two, old Mr. Darcy had intervened and lessened James's punishment, before anyone else became aware of his shenanigans. For the third, Darcy himself had taken the blame and suffered a beating from his father.

"Mr. Darcy." The magistrate pulled the Master of Pemberley to the side, where others could not hear—but close enough for James to listen. "Please have several of your men ready to search the Pemberley bedchambers when I have finished with Mrs. Williams."

"Yes, Sir Phillip." Darcy paused briefly. "Besides the arsenic, for what else do we search?"

Sir Phillip lowered his voice further. "For anything of significance."

When they had moved away, James eased the door open and headed toward the nearest secret passageway. He kept his head down as he passed one of the lower maids; luckily, no one else seemed about. He supposed Darcy had sent many on the magistrate's errands. "Darcy took the blame for me once, a long time ago. I wonder whether he might care to do another good turn—this time, for my friend Gregor," he murmured. He swung the door open and entered the candlelit tunnel, waiting for the obligatory click to secure his hideaway.

"Your shoes, Mrs. Williams," Sir Phillip commanded softly.

She stopped her progress into the room. "I beg your pardon, sir?"

"Your shoes, madam—remove them."

The lady looked about, confused. "Whatever for?"

"You will be detained here—in this room. I cannot secure every exit, but without your shoes, I do not believe you will have the means of an escape. The weather has improved, but a five-mile trek to Lambton is not likely without the benefit of footwear."

Incredulity set in. "You are serious, sir?"

"I am." They held each other's stares—a match of wills. Finally, Mrs. Williams stepped out of her day slippers. Sir Phillip bent to pick them up. "I will leave them with the footman outside the door. Make yourself comfortable, ma'am. I will return for you shortly." The baronet turned on his heels to make his exit.

"The lieutenant's body?" she said softly. "Is it with the others?"

Sir Phillip stared at the lady with renewed interest. "Not as yet. I wish to inspect the room once more before we move him."

Mrs. Williams did not respond in turn, but gave just a slight nod of her head. She sank, exhausted, in a nearby chair and buried her head in her hands. Silent sobs shook her shoulders. Sir Phillip waited to see if she would offer an explanation, but when none came, he left the room, instructing Darcy's man to keep the door locked unless given an order to open it by Mr. Darcy, the colonel, or himself.

James checked Mrs. Darcy's room several times through the slit to make sure no one was in the private quarters. He had done the same with Miss Darcy's room before he had made his way through the passage and across the girl's room. Now, he peered around the screen before moving to the portal. He would not be long, so he set the opening for his speedy return. Georgiana Darcy's room at the end of the hall was two doors from her brother's master suite. James opened her door enough to enter the hall, leaving the latch loosely fastened. He took a calculated risk, symbolically sending Darcy a message. The break in the weather signaled a change in the household. They must make their presence known once more and then make their escape—no more haunting Pemberley's hidden channel. They had come here for one purpose only, and tonight would be the proof of the pudding.

James quietly opened the door to the master's chamber. Decorated in rich tones of red and mahogany, the décor spoke of Fitzwilliam Darcy's tastes—never ostentatious—always refined. Even James admired the breeding and the masculinity of the man. He slid into the empty room and traversed the short distance to the master bed. Pulling back the drape, he staged the scene. "A nice touch," he muttered as he arranged a bloody towel upon which Gregor had wiped his hands and the straight razor from the lieutenant's room in the center of Darcy's bed. "Perfect." He straightened the folded cloth before letting the drape fall to its proper place. As he hurried toward the end room, he realized it might be a day or two before anyone found his clues, but it would satisfy his sense of the dramatic all the same. Darcy spent every evening in his wife's bed, so the man might not see the "masterpiece" right away, but he would find it. James had no doubts.

After slipping into the gaping opening, he turned the lever to close the wall entrance in Georgiana Darcy's room. He sought the mattress, *Sleep now*, he thought as he made his way to the antechamber. "Tonight," he grumbled. "I need some sleep before tonight."

Darcy, Stafford, Worth, the colonel, Sir Phillip, and several of the Pemberley footmen entered Cathleen Donnel's room. They agreed to start at one end of the hall and to work their way from room to room. Adam Lawrence groused about the impropriety, even though he agreed to the necessity of the search. "It just does not seem proper," he told the men as they rummaged through Cathleen's private belongings.

Sir Phillip opened the drawer holding the lady's undergarments. "Would you care to help with this one, Stafford?" He waited until Adam stepped up beside him. "It is not proper, Your Lordship; yet, I know of no other way to prove a person's innocence or his fault in such cases."

"I understand, sir." Adam held the older man's gaze for a few elongated seconds before giving in. "What must I do?"

"Check everything."

With a simple nod, Adam's hands delved into the silky items. Something hard rested on the bottom of the drawer. He withdrew it from among Cathleen's chemises and corsets.

"What have you found?" the colonel called as Adam gingerly withdrew the item.

"A book," Adam rasped out when he saw the gold-leaf pages. "I bought this for Cathleen a couple of months ago. She saw it in a window and instantly wanted it." Without thinking, his fingers traced the raised letters.

"A first edition?" Darcy asked.

Adam shook his head in the negative. "Simply a limited edition." He opened it and thumbed through the pages.

"Grimm—the brothers," Darcy peered over the viscount's shoulder. "Fanciful stories."

"Yes," Adam mumbled.

Worth picked up a small tied packet from the floor. "You dropped these." He handed the viscount a beribboned bundle.

"What have you there?" Edward Fitzwilliam asked before searching the wardrobe.

Lawrence bent the edges of the paper to take a closer look. "Letters." He fanned the stack. "From Cathleen's family and a few from me." He stared at how she had included his notes along with those from her cousins and her aunt and uncle. Cathleen cared for him—she thought of him as her family. A dried flower—a red rose—he always gave her red roses—Cathleen's favorite—rested on top. He placed the items reverently in the drawer where he had found them. Allowing Cathleen Donnel to leave him might be one of the hardest things he ever did, but it was the right thing, and Adam had no choice but to let her go—let her try to find happiness with someone who could love her the way she deserved to be loved.

"There is nothing unusual to find among Miss Donnel's things," the baronet declared.

Worth added quickly, "As we all expected."

"Who is next?" Sir Phillip asked.

"The next occupied room is that of Mrs. Williams." Darcy turned to lead the way.

Sir Phillip caught Darcy's arm to stay him. "Let us leave the good lady's room for one of the last ones. If what I suspect is there, I do not want to neglect the other rooms, and I fear the solution to one part of the mystery lies within Mr. Williams's room."

"As you wish, Sir Phillip. The private quarters, then?" Darcy waited for a moment for the man's agreement. They walked past Mrs. Williams's room and turned to the left. "This one is Lady Catherine's suite." He held the door open for the others. This time, the duty of inspecting Her Ladyship's private items fell to Darcy. "It is like touching the Holy Grail," he grumbled.

Lord Stafford chuckled. "Some pieces are probably relics in their own right." He good-naturedly patted Darcy on the back as the master of Pemberley lifted an oversized corset between his fingertips.

"I found a small portion of a chalky mixture in this jar," Worth extended the container toward Sir Phillip.

Darcy suddenly joined the others, who peered into the suspicious ingredients. He touched his finger to the powder, taking a smudge of it on the tip, and then he touched the dry mixture to his tongue's surface. "Bitter," he remarked, grimacing as his tongue spread the taste throughout his mouth. He moved to fill a glass with water to wash the acerbic grittiness away. "How can women subject themselves to such stringent measures?"

"Her Ladyship admitted to partaking of the arsenic-laced mixture upon occasion," Worth recalled from their previous meeting.

"She did," Stafford confirmed.

Sir Phillip resealed the jar. "Let us keep this as possible evidence."

In Anne's room, they found several letters from Harwood, those supposedly sent to Anne's maid as part of the lieutenant's ruse. Worth read one before the others realized the nature of the items. His expletives alerted Sir Phillip to the intimacy Harwood shared.

"Hopefully, Miss de Bourgh will not mind my commandeering these," Sir Phillip remarked as he placed the stack in the drawstring bag he carried.

Darcy glanced over his shoulder at an agitated Nigel Worth, who slammed the desk drawer closed. "I believe my cousin, as well as Mr. Worth, would happily agree to never seeing them again."

Sir Phillip smiled. "I will see what I can do." He gestured to the door. "Who is next?"

"My sister, of course. And Mrs. Darcy's and mine."

"I believe we can dispense with those rooms," Stafford remarked as they walked toward the open door.

"No…I insist," Darcy called from behind them as they exited the room. "No one should be above reproach."

In Georgiana's room, Darcy again did the honors of examining the more personal items. Not really expecting to find anything of import in the girl's room, they spent most of their time reenacting the "floating candle" of which both Miss Darcy and her brother had told the others.

"Here are some letters from you, Colonel." Worth teasingly thrust several letters into the officer's open hand. "It seems Miss Darcy prefers your correspondence to those of her other friends."

"My sister leads a quiet life," Darcy remarked. "She is a very private person; I cannot imagine Georgiana having a slew of friends to whom to write."

"Neither can I." Edward tossed the stack back onto the desk in an act of nonchalance, but a moment of tenderness tugged at his heart.

Finally, they entered the master suite, examining Elizabeth's quarters first before moving through the adjoining dressing rooms to Darcy's sitting room and bedchamber.

Edward leaned in close, where the others could not hear. "When was the last time you slept in your father's old room?" he inquired.

Darcy could feel color rushing to his face. "Of late, I seem to prefer my mother's previous room," he muttered.

Edward grinned largely. "You devil! You have finally found happiness. I envy you, Darcy."

Sir Phillip casually circled Darcy's bedchamber while Stafford and Worth examined the items on his desk and table. "I see nothing of any remark." Adam Lawrence thumbed through a stack of bills and some personal correspondence.

"Neither do I," Worth noted as he rummaged through Darcy's closet. "Other than several pairs of immaculately shined boots, there is nothing of note." All the gentlemen except Darcy snorted and chuckled.

Then the four entered the bedchamber and came up short— Edward Fitzwilliam leading the way. All eyes rested on a frowning baronet. "What is it, Sir Phillip?" the colonel asked with an air of authority.

The baronet remarked with a raised eyebrow, "You might wish to see this."

Lawrence, the colonel, Worth, and Darcy moved en masse to peer over and around the magistrate. They caught the burgundy velvet drape on either side of the posts and pulled the curtains wide to study what Sir Phillip now scrutinized.

"It appears we have found the weapon used to murder Harwood," the colonel stated. No one moved; they simply stared in disbelief at the bloody towel and straight razor.

"How in the hell did that get in here?" Worth growled. "I am very much—very tired of these games."

"Someone has been in my room," Darcy exhaled the words. "Someone is that close to my family...to my wife...to my unborn child...to my sister." His anger grew by the moment. "I want to find this man. Now!"

Adam Lawrence reached for the bloody evidence. "The man sends you a message, Darcy. He wants you to know he is still here, and he can reach you or reach those you love anytime he so chooses. If you do not stop your intruder soon, Darcy, someone you cherish will die." The viscount wrapped the blade in the towel and handed it to Sir Phillip.

A cold shiver radiated down Darcy's spine. "How do I stop him?" His eyes remained fixed on the spot, as if the blood stained the bed linens.

"Have there been any other warnings?" Sir Phillip asked as he carefully placed the items into the drawstring bag.

"None...nothing." Darcy still had not moved, but his mind now began to process the new information.

Sir Phillip looked about, a bit embarrassed. "I am chagrined to ask this, Mr. Darcy, but when did you last lie in this bed?"

Darcy laughed self-consciously. He did not mind admitting his preference for Elizabeth's bed to his cousin. After all, he and Edward had few secrets between them. It was a different story to disclose those same facts to the baronet, Stafford, and Worth. But disguise of every sort was his abhorrence. "The night my sister saw the floating light, Mrs. Darcy took Georgiana into her own bed. When my sister finally fell asleep, my wife and I retired to this bed; but I assure you, Sir Phillip, my staff cleans the room daily, whether I choose to sleep in this bed or not." He smiled slightly. "Now you all know that I am not a London nob who prefers someone other than his wife for company."

"You do not have to make excuses, Darcy, for actually loving the woman you married," Worth declared. "Were we all so lucky, society would be for the better."

Darcy heard his own words echo in his head. *You must allow me to tell you how ardently I admire and love you.* He realized that men of a certain rank, captivated by youth and beauty and that appearance of good humor, which youth and beauty generally give, might marry women whose weak understanding and illiberal minds, very early in the marriage, put an end to all real affection. Respect, esteem, and confidence would vanish forever, and all the man's views of domestic happiness would be overthrown. The gentleman would seek comfort for his disappointment, which his own imprudence had brought on, in any of those pleasures which too often consoles the unfortunate for his folly or his vice. Luckily for Darcy, he had discovered Elizabeth Bennet—her fine eyes—the liveliness of her mind—her handsome face—the depth of her passion and her loyalty—they had all captured his heart—his body and soul—and he had never looked back or questioned his decision to choose the lady as his own. He loved how she had risked everything to challenge his arrogance—how she did not accept his words unless she found true merit within them—and how Elizabeth had taken his household within her grasp and given it a great shake. "I am fortunate to have attained Mrs. Darcy's affection."

"Amen!" Edward cried. "I second Mr. Worth's avowal."

"May we return to our search?" Sir Phillip directed the conversation away from the Darcys' close association.

Darcy resolutely distracted himself from his need to find his wife and take her into his embrace—to tell her of his love and to keep her from harm. "Indeed, Sir Phillip." He glanced about the room. "Have we finished in here?"

The magistrate nodded, and the others preceded them through the chamber door. Darcy took a place by the baronet. "I appreciate your confidence in me, sir," he whispered. "You did not consider me guilty of the attack on the lieutenant."

"There *are* human contrivances in place at Pemberley, Mr. Darcy; yet, I do not consider you a man foolish enough to leave an instrument of murder haphazardly lying about and then to ask the local magistrate into your room, where he would find it." Darcy stared at the man, but Sir Phillip did not even turn his head.

"This one is mine." Adam Lawrence stepped to the side to allow the others to enter before him. "Not much in here. Neither Miss Donnel nor I planned to be away more than a week. The wardrobe is quite empty compared with those of the Darcys. Other than the books, which I have carried upstairs to while away some of the hours at Pemberley, I believe you will find nothing of report."

Again, the magistrate circled the room, lightly touching the viscount's clothes brush, his toiletries, and an empty coffee cup. "Everything seems as it should be."

Edward picked up one of the books. "What piques your interest, Stafford?" The colonel turned the book over to look at the title. "*Apotropaics*? Really, Lawrence, does that not seem a bit eccentric?"

"Darcy prefers the classics and those war journals. Finding ways to ward off demons seemed only appropriate at Pemberley." The viscount took the book from the colonel's outstretched hand. "I have always had an odd sense of humor."

Worth moved to the door. "We should probably view the rooms formerly occupied by Miss de Bourgh and her companion."

"Lead on, Worth." Sir Phillip gestured toward the connecting hall. Darcy informed the baronet that he had given orders that no one was to enter or touch the room since the evening they had moved his cousin's belongings to her new quarters. They searched the adjoining rooms thoroughly, looking for anything unusual.

"Mrs. Jenkinson owned no skin preparations that could have led to her death," Sir Phillip observed, returning the woman's toiletries to the dresser.

"Meaning that the lady's death did not come from a buildup of arsenic in her body," the colonel observed.

"Precisely," the baronet concurred. "Nor from a mistaken overage of her own making."

Worth handed the magistrate a packet of letters, smudged and crinkled with reading and rereading. "These appear to be from the lady's husband. They have been franked in different parts of the world. The late Mr. Jenkinson was a diplomat of sorts. They were probably all she had left of the man."

Sir Phillip accepted the papers and placed them in his bag. "I am sure they will lead to nothing, but I will read the letters just the same. If I can locate the woman's family, I will see they are sent on to Mrs. Jenkinson's relatives."

Worth felt the sadness of being in the room of a woman whom he sorely missed. "My chamber is two doors along the hallway. Shall we see what I have hidden away?" Worth laughed, trying to make light of what they did.

"It seems only prudent," Sir Phillip said as he led the way from Mrs. Jenkinson's former room. "What secrets do you keep, Nigel?" the magistrate remarked as they entered Worth's room.

"As a man who practices law, I have many, as you well know, Sir Phillip." Worth lit several candles, as he had earlier shut the heavy drapes to keep in the room's heat. Worth's room lacked the pristine appearance of Darcy's or Stafford's. Legal papers lay strewn upon the desk; the man evidently continued to work on his cases while at Pemberley. Several shirts and waistcoats decorated the backs of two chairs. Worth chuckled when he saw their faces. "I travel with no man of service. I must tend to my own things, and bachelors are renowned for a lack of housekeeping."

"Yet, you are a rich man, Worth," Darcy added quickly. "You can afford someone to tend to your dress."

"I have never needed to impress others with the cut of my coat. Most people who seek me out are more concerned with my ability to manipulate the law for their benefit than how fashionably dressed I am." However, their censure for his messy ways caused him to pick up some of the items scattered about the room—folding them or placing them on hangers. "I suppose I shall need to change my ways," he said sheepishly as he placed a shirt in the wardrobe, "especially if I plan to call on Miss de Bourgh. I am aware of Her Ladyship's need for all things of which society demands."

"Do not allow my vexatious aunt to change your ways to match hers," Colonel Fitzwilliam warned. "Continue to cultivate your own style." Worth listened carefully to the gentleman's unspoken words and then nodded his understanding. "If my cousin chooses you, Worth," the colonel continued, "the management of Anne's fortune and the running of Rosings Park falls under your domain. Her Ladyship will need to curry favor with you for what you will allow her as the Dowager Lady de Bourgh. Treat Lady Catherine with kindness, but also with firmness. It will increase your domestic felicity to not give Her Ladyship the upper hand."

"Thank you, Colonel."

"Worth," Lord Stafford called from behind the desk, "what are these?"

The solicitor looked a bit embarrassed, but he answered matter-of-factly. "I was making some notes for an associate in Newcastle on a case he plans to bring before the court in that jurisdiction."

"But these notes are regarding what you know of George Wickham." A touch of skepticism rang through his tone.

Worth confirmed, "They are, sir."

Darcy quietly motioned for his men to withdraw while they discussed the matter.

When the last man had closed the chamber door, the viscount asked, "Does Mrs. Wickham know?"

Before Worth could answer, Darcy took up the man's defense. "Mr. Worth prosecuted Mr. Wickham several years ago for gambling debts. Worth's former associate, Mr. O'Malley, remembered Worth's connection with Mr. Wickham. Mr. O'Malley sought a consultation with Mr. Worth. Purely by coincidence, in Nottingham, Mr. Wickham left his wife to board the same public conveyance as rode Mr. Worth."

"Has Wickham accumulated more debt?" Edward hissed. He was aware of how often Darcy had bailed out the hapless punter.

Worth rejoined the tale. "Of some quantity, if my colleague is to be believed."

Edward's protest came immediately, "Darcy, you cannot think—

Uncomfortable with the rest of the men knowing the extent of his past involvement with Wickham, Darcy interrupted his cousin's admonishment. "Mr. Wickham has placed his financial security beyond those from his family who might come to his aid." Quietly, he added, "In addition to his pecuniary problems, it appears that the gentleman sometimes lifts a hand to his wife—especially when Mrs. Wickham displays her more boisterous nature, which we all know she possesses." The other men understood the depth of Darcy's hatred for his former school chum, a man for whom Darcy's own father had tried to provide a living but who led a life of idleness and dissipation. "If Mr. O'Malley chooses to pursue this case, I will make no move to save Mrs. Wickham's husband, despite the shame it may reflect upon Mrs. Darcy or this estate."

"Is there anything else, Sir Phillip? Or may we inspect another room?" Worth inquired.

"Indeed," the gentleman replied. "Let us press on."

Worth exited, pausing briefly in the hallway to wait for the others. "Who is next? Mrs. Williams or Mrs. Wickham?"

They all waited for Sir Phillip's direction. "The admiral's widow," he commanded. The baronet turned toward the room at the top of the stairs. "I do not need to remind each of you of the importance of documenting what we find in this room." Gravely, he turned the handle to open the door.

They spread out across the room, each of them taking the responsibility of thoroughly searching a portion of the space. No one spoke, each man intent on performing his duties.

Edward opened each of the jars on the dresser. "The lady has nearly ten jars of cosmetics; yet, Mrs. Williams wore only a bit of rogue when I saw her today. I wonder whether today was an aberration." He showed them a small jar containing a blackened powder. "And what in God's name is this?"

"Belladonna. For the eyes," Stafford informed him. "The latest thing on the Continent. Gives the lady's lids a smoky quality in the dim lighting of a soiree or a dinner party."

"We should have known you would be an expert on a lady's beauty regime," Darcy smirked.

Adam made a courtly bow. "It is my lot in life—what I do best. Just ask my father, the earl. He will gladly extol my expertise in the area."

Edward examined the table. "I see nothing such as what we found in my aunt's quarters."

"Maybe Mrs. Williams did not use the poison in the same way," Sir Phillip remarked.

"I assume you mean that the lady did not consume the product; she used ointments and creams, probably because her face and skin have weathered from traveling with the admiral. But even if she did have the item, she could have disposed of the powder after Mrs. Jenkinson's passing," Stafford observed.

"I am sorry I did not think to search the bedrooms before now," Darcy said, offering an apology to the entire room.

"It is of no consequence, Mr. Darcy. Your search would not have solved your mystery." Sir Phillip gave his own form of absolution. "The lady is not your phantom, although I strongly suspect her of causing your cousin's companion to meet an untimely death."

Worth joined Darcy and the baronet. "There is nothing to directly connect the widow to Harwood," he whispered. "How will we prove her guilt?"

"I am not ready to abandon our search," the magistrate asserted. "There is something here; I feel it in my bones. Let us look closer. Does the lady have items in the bed chest? Take out the drawers of the desk. Look behind them. The same with the dressing table."

The five men plus Darcy's two footmen started to take things apart. Moving furniture and looking behind and under the room's fixtures, they studied the minutest corners with a renewed interest.

"Nothing in the chest," Worth announced as he let the lid to the storage at the foot of Mrs. Williams's bed slam shut.

"I found nothing beneath the bed either, sir." Jatson St. Denis scooted out from under the bed.

Darcy mused aloud, "If not *under* the bed, maybe *in* the bed. Possibly the lady literally slept with her secrets."

Instantly, Darcy and Sir Phillip attacked the bed simultaneously, pulling back the coverings and flipping over the pillows. Reaching for the bottom brocade pillow, Darcy's fingers brushed against something hard. "I have something." He pulled the drawstring pouch from the folds of the pillow's silken covering. "What have we here?" He loosened the golden string and dumped the contents of the bag upon the bed.

The other men now circled about. Worth expelled a low whistle when the gold coins tumbled from the black velvet bag. "Solid gold." Worth turned one of the coins over in the palm of his hand. "A small fortune."

"Where would a woman of Mrs. Williams's station get so many gold coins?" Edward questioned as he ran his fingers through them and let them plunge to the mattress.

"A man's ring," Darcy said as he cupped a jeweled band in his outstretched hand.

Sir Phillip picked up the velvet bag and turned it inside out. A folded piece of paper drifted to the floor. Carefully, the magistrate retrieved it. "Let us see what the lady conceals." Slowly, he unfolded the item, smoothing the edges as he spread it upon the bed. The men all craned their necks to understand the marriage document. Sir Phillip read the words aloud, "Robert Lewis Harwood to Evangeline Ruth Whitmore."

"Evangeline? I thought Mrs. Williams's Christian name was Evelyn," Worth thought aloud.

"Well, apparently if her name was *Whitmore* and not *Williams*, the lady might purposely call herself *Evelyn* instead of *Evangeline*," Stafford summarized.

"You are both missing the most obvious connection." Edward took the marriage certificate from where it lay on the bed. "*Angel Harwood*, as the lieutenant identified his wife, is really *Evangeline Whitmore*. The lieutenant called the lady *Angel*, short for *Evangeline*."

"If what we suspect is true," Sir Phillip started to place the items back in the bag, "the lady *is* an angel—an angel of death."

CHAPTER 20

~ ~ ~

"ELIZABETH," GEORGIANA pulled her sister into the music room, "might we talk?"

Elizabeth anticipated the nature of the 'talk,' but she readily agreed. "I am all ears, Georgiana," she responded as they took up residence before the fireplace.

Then a nervous silence followed. Elizabeth watched with amusement as Darcy's sister fidgeted. "Why do you not just tell me what is on your mind, Georgiana? I will not judge you."

The girl swallowed hard and flushed. "Could–Could you," she stammered, "could you t-tell me when you knew you loved my brother?"

Elizabeth smiled kindly. "I suspected as much." She rolled her eyes upward, trying to visualize the moment. "It would be prudent to say from the first moment he walked into the Meryton Assembly Hall, but Fitzwilliam managed to insult me with his refusal to ask me to dance, and I set myself against anything he could offer. So, from the beginning we verbally tussled for supremacy, but I suppose, in many way that was love. I hated that Fitzwilliam might find me wanting—that he might think poorly of me—might think I was lacking in some essential. Therefore, I pretended, even to myself, to despise him. I once told Jane that I knew I loved him when I realized how many depended upon him for their existence, and I realized he needed someone upon whom *he* could depend. I cannot say the exact moment; we were connected from the beginning. Your brother brought sunlight to my heart." Elizabeth nudged Georgiana's foot with her own. "Is there someone you affect, Georgiana?"

"Would it disappoint Fitzwilliam if I did not want a Season?" The girl blushed thoroughly. "I would be so out of place in a room full of strangers."

"Do you not wish to meet a young lord? Once you became familiar with Viscount Stafford, there was no awkwardness."

Georgiana looked off to the side. "Then Fitzwilliam would object? I thought as much." Her gaze fell to her hands resting in her lap. "I had simply hoped—."

"Hoped for someone more familiar?" Elizabeth understood perfectly. "Perhaps with my encroaching confinement, we should seek entertainment in Derbyshire—give you time to build a rapport with some of the local young people—give you a chance to meet someone new."

Georgiana looked devastated, but she said, "Yes, maybe that is what I need."

Elizabeth knew better—knew what stirred Georgiana's heart—what the girl truly wanted. She would see how things developed before she spoke to her husband in that regard. "Lydia loves a social gathering," she began. "Why do we not show her some of Derbyshire? Bakewell's celebration is next week. What do you say, Georgiana? Might I send for Lydia, and we can plan an excursion?"

"Why not?" Georgiana's lack of enthusiasm rang clear to her sister.

Silence filled the room as the men froze in a horrified tableau. "Can it be?" Darcy breathed the question.

Sir Phillip turned slowly toward Pemberley's master, a grim frown furrowing his forehead. "I fear we must speak to the lady immediately." He returned the coins and ring to the bag and refolded the paper. "Colonel, might you and Lord Stafford take Mr. Darcy's men and examine Mrs. Wickham's room?"

The colonel nodded.

"Mr. Darcy and I must question Mrs. Williams or Mrs. Harwood or whatever we are to call her. Worth, I want you there to ensure that the lady's rights are protected."

"As you wish, Sir Phillip," Mr. Worth said automatically. A poker face hid his complicated feelings.

"Come, gentlemen, we have a mystery to unravel."

Peter searched the antechamber for his belongings. Consumed by his frustration, he did not try to hide his anger. "I am personally exhausted by your need to control every situation. I do not know why we must take our leave so soon. I love Pemberley; it could be my home again if I could simply find a way to please my father. He wanted me here—wanted me to have the lessons of a gentleman—to take my place alongside Darcy—to have a superior life. Now, you say we must abandon the place we have established here." He slammed a stolen Pemberley book against the wall. "And do not place the blame solely upon my shoulders. I told you the woman would not allow me to leave the room. She would have sent up an alarm for the whole household. It is just as much the fault of both of you as it is mine. *You* killed the footman and *you* the lieutenant. Tell me how it is my fault! You do not own me, you know. I do not have to do what you tell me!" Peter stormed away to sulk. "I will show them," he grumbled. "They want to get Darcy's attention—make the man sorry for his former snubs—well, I know how to do that better than anyone!"

Sir Phillip led Darcy and Worth to the room holding Mrs. Harwood. "Allow me to do the talking," the magistrate warned before they entered. When the door swung open, the woman rose slowly to stand defiantly before them. "Your shoes, Mrs. Harwood." Sir Phillip extended his arm and offered her the footwear.

The lady took her slippers and stepped into them before returning to her previous stance. "So, now you know my secret," she whispered.

Darcy and Worth circled slowly to stand behind the widow. "Would you care to explain your part in the lieutenant's scheme?" Sir Phillip motioned for her to return to her chair.

A slight shake of her head said she refused his kindness. "Robert...Robert," she faltered, "was the love of my life. I married Samuel Whitmore when I was seventeen, but ours was a troubled joining. My parents thought it a brilliant match, and as they had a household of daughters, they readily gave me to the first man who offered." With her description, Darcy could not help but think of Mrs. Bennet trying to pawn Elizabeth off on Mr. Collins. "Admiral Whitmore, some twenty years my senior, wielded power aboard his ship and within his quarters. He tolerated no question of his authority. When the admiral lost his life at San Domingo, I rejoiced at being free. I spent a little over a year in mourning for a man I truly despised, and then I met Robert Harwood." The lady swayed in place, and Darcy moved forward instinctively to catch her. He gently lowered her to the seat before moving away.

"I knew Robert's failings—women always know. Society accuses us of wanting to reform a rake, but that is never our intention. We simply want to give them the love they have never known, no matter what it costs us. One night in the arms of such a man is worth all the nights of loneliness." The lady's voice trailed off in memory. She sat in silence, unmoving for several long moments. Sir Phillip took the seat beside her and quietly took Mrs. Harwood's hand in his own. He said nothing, but the gesture caused the lady to regain her confidence.

"Robert joined the Regulars in order to escape a trail of gambling debts in his home country." Darcy instantly thought of George Wickham. On three different occasions he had taken it upon himself to pay his former friend's debts. Darcy had done so around Lambton and in Cheshire prior to the costly escapade involving the man's ruination of Lydia Bennet. Mr. Wickham, at the time, was in debt to every tradesman in Meryton, and it took more than a thousand pounds to clear his expenses in Brighton.

The British military, Darcy mused, seemed the place to hide a gamester.

"My poor darling could never quit a card table while he was ahead." Mrs. Harwood shook her head in sad memory. "Then he stumbled across an opportunity two years ago, and everything changed. A gentleman's daughter outside Stratford found my Robert most attractive. My husband convinced me to remain quiet, and our first profit became a reality. The baron paid two thousand pounds for Robert to disappear from the lady's life and to secure his silence.

"Robert tasted success twice more: in Berwick and in Hull. Yet, neither was enough. The amount he won from the scam—and more—was the amount my dear husband lost at the tables. Then Colonel Fitzwilliam introduced Robert to Anne de Bourgh. When we considered the possibility, we thought ten thousand pounds was assured."

Sir Phillip asked quietly, "And your role in the lieutenant's perfidy?"

"I was to discover Miss de Bourgh in Robert's company—the outraged wife—a role I could play easily. I hated every minute Robert spent with another. Unfortunately, Mother Nature played a hand neither of us had expected. When I joined Mr. Worth on the public coach outside Nottingham, I planned to go to Liverpool. Robert had sent word that Miss de Bourgh had arrived and that he would move her to the Salty Sailor, but the storm waylaid me at Pemberley. How was I to know that Anne de Bourgh would be here also?"

Behind her, Mr. Worth asked, "When did you realize the lieutenant was in the area?"

Mrs. Harwood glanced over her shoulder at him. "When Robert walked into the morning room with Mr. Darcy. From my first introduction to the de Bourghs, I assumed that Robert nursed a bruised ego because his plan had fallen through. I had no idea he had followed the lady to Pemberley."

"Could the lieutenant have been in the house without your knowledge?" Darcy moved where she might see him.

"Do you mean could Robert be your murderer, Mr. Darcy?" Her tone became defensive again.

Darcy nodded.

"No…Robert had many faults…gambling chief among them… but except on the battlefield, Robert would never take another's life." The lady paused, looking off to the left as if seeing something only she could know. "To do so…to take another's life, one must have known pain and love and passion. Robert knew none of those. He would chase a scheme only if it had a quick ending and a decent monetary outcome. Robert never knew hard times—even in debt, he still lived as if each day belonged to him. And Robert never truly loved anyone but himself. No…no, Mr. Darcy, Robert was not your killer."

Sir Phillip gently squeezed the lady's hand; he waited patiently for her eyes to meet his. "And you, Mrs. Harwood, have you known pain and love and passion?"

The woman knew she could hide her secrets no longer. "I have, Sir Phillip," she said flatly.

"And Mrs. Jenkinson? Were you the source of the dear lady's demise?"

Silence boomed through the small room—no one breathed—no one blinked. "They all thought it was the cup of tea. The remains of the arsenic on my fingers rested on the rim of the cup, but it was really the last of the broken pieces of ice Mrs. Jenkinson consumed. I broke them from the tree and offered them to her after spreading the arsenic up and down the icy surface. The lady herself placed the flavoring over the frozen powder, thinking it was sugar. Mr. Worth was correct; the ice deadened Mrs. Jenkinson's taste. We all know the poison can be easily mixed with water, and several drops in a glass of wine or water might kill a person. So why not freeze the deadly liquid?"

"Why ever for?" Worth could not control the question. "Why Mildred Jenkinson? What did the lady do to earn such a fate?"

Mrs. Harwood still stared into Sir Phillip's eyes. "That day on the sledding hill, she thought she recognized me from Kent—asked if I had not been often at Colonel Cavendish's table. Twice, Mrs. Jenkinson had accompanied Miss de Bourgh to one of the colonel's weekly dinners. As an officer in the colonel's unit, Robert was expected to attend, and as his wife, I was part and partial to the Regulars. Of course, society never seats a man and his wife near each other, but Mrs. Jenkinson noticed me just the same. As plain as I am, I still caught the lady's eye. She asked if I had been at Dover, and even though I denied it, Mrs. Jenkinson kept staring at me. I knew it was only a matter of time before she said something to Miss de Bourgh, and then Robert's plans would be for naught. I could not let that happen; I loved Robert too much for that. I could never bear to see him disappointed. I knew from the tidbits I overheard, mostly from the servants, that Miss de Bourgh had been found by her mother in Liverpool and brought to Pemberley. Her ruination was obvious. That was why I objected to Mr. Worth's attentions to the lady. If she accepted Mr. Worth, Miss de Bourgh's reputation would no longer be an issue. Robert's big pay day and our ability to leave for Italy would be lost. You must understand; Robert and I planned to see Florence—to leave England. A person can live cheaply abroad. Mrs. Jenkinson stood in our way."

"And so you planned to eliminate the lady?" Sir Phillip asked quietly.

Evangeline Harwood looked shocked by his accusation. "Planned...planned?" she asked. "I planned nothing...truly, it was never my intention." She stared past the magistrate—through him actually. "The situation simply developed. My petticoat, you see... the lace pulled loose when we came down the hill the last time— hung below my clothing—and I asked Mrs. Darcy for help. I did not think I could reach the house without someone seeing. Mrs. Darcy suggested a nearby tool shed. While the men climbed the slope for the final ride of the day, I slipped into the building to repair my undergarment. And once I finished pulling the thread to free the lace trim, I realized what the building held—shovels and hammers and spades and other gardening tools—and of course, the fertilizers and other compounds. I wrapped the lace into a tight ball and thought to place it in my outerwear pocket, but when I tucked it away, I found a letter from Robert there, and a plan developed before my eyes. It was as if Robert told me what to do. I took the paper from my inside pelisse pocket and put some of the powder in my husband's message to me. It seemed only appropriate, after all. I did not know how I would use it, but the arsenic was there for the taking; and it was as if I could not resist it.

"Again, I thought of nothing but repairing my clothing when I entered the building. When I left the building, I thought of nothing but the poison. The opportunity seemed to present itself. When I returned to claim my spot among Mr. Darcy's party, I still held no scheme, but when Mrs. Jenkinson herself suggested the frozen sticks, everything fell into place. Providence sent me to the tool building, and Providence gave me the means by which to remove Robert's obstacle, without his approval or even his knowledge. I quite imagined my dear husband would congratulate me for my ingenuity."

"So you offered Mrs. Jenkinson the icicle that you had laced with arsenic?"

Mrs. Harwood grimaced. "The powder clung to my hands and gloves—it was very difficult to use. Later, I burned the gloves and dumped the extra powder from the packet out my window into the snow. Mr. Darcy's roses should do well in the spring." She laughed as she gazed at her hands. "No matter how often I wash them, my hands still feel gritty." She raised her hands to carefully inspect them. "Do you suppose it will ever go away, Sir Phillip?"

"I cannot say, Mrs. Harwood."

"Might I see my husband, sir?" she asked suddenly.

Sir Phillip looked about uncomfortably. "I do not think that prudent, madam. The scene is not fit for a lady's eyes."

"I must say farewell—I never knew where Samuel Whitmore found his grave—buried at sea in the West Indies, but I can offer Robert my final prayers and see to his burial."

The magistrate reluctantly nodded his agreement. He stood and offered the lady his arm. Motioning for Darcy and Worth to lead the way, he squired the two-time widow from the room.

Sir Phillip motioned for the footman to unlock the door. The magistrate caught the lady's hand before they entered. "I must caution you against this once more, Mrs. Harwood. The lieutenant's condition is quite repugnant."

"I understand your concern, Sir Phillip, but I must see Robert for myself." She seemed unusually composed.

Resigned, Sir Phillip reached for the door handle. He swung the door wide and stepped inside. Reaching back, he caught Mrs. Harwood's arm at the elbow to support her weight, expecting the woman to collapse as soon as she saw her husband's bloody body.

Instead, Evangeline Harwood calmly entered the room, her eyes resting on the lieutenant, fixing a glassy stare on the bloody wound—no longer red, turning black in the stifling air. Her husband's body had begun to stiffen—the skin hardening and becoming inflexible—but she knelt beside it and took his pale fingers in her warm hands. Emotion choked her. Evangeline had known Robert Harwood for five years—he barely past his majority when they had met and her a widow of six and twenty. Her knees had trembled when he touched her hand the first time, and Evangeline had known that she would give him whatever he wanted. She supposed it was why he had chosen her: She had allowed him a certain freedom to flirt with other women as long as he returned to her. She had given Robert Harwood her heart, but he had never reciprocated. Evangeline had never understood why he married her—maybe he had thought her widow's pension would see them through the worst of those early days of their relationship.

His handsome face had often unnerved her, but now dried blood framed it, and a grimace of pain held the muscles taut. Evangeline's fingers touched the furrowed lines. She would have liked to smooth the expression, but his skin's hardness prevented that act of compassion. "I am sorry, my Love," she whispered as she traced his bottom lip. "You deserved better than this."

She rested Harwood's hand across his waist before rising to her feet. "I thank you, Sir Phillip," she murmured, "for allowing me this moment."

"Of course, Mrs. Harwood." The woman's strength amazed him—he admired her courage, although the magistrate was now aware of the extent of her participation in the scheme the lieutenant had practiced on the de Bourghs. She had certainly planned to advance the claim he made and to create the image of ruination. Add to that perfidy a crime far worse—the death of an innocent—and he should find it impossible to offer the lady admiration, but he did. She had survived an abusive husband and a philandering one, and despite the evil she had brought to Darcy's house, Spurlock saw the woman her late husband had described. Sir Phillip saw an angel. Not an angel of death, as he had once assumed, but an angel of love—twisted though it might be—one of love.

"Come," he said softly as he placed the woman's hand on his arm once more. Darcy and Worth waited barely inside the door, but they stepped aside to allow Sir Phillip to lead the woman away. "You will be confined to your quarters," he explained as he conducted her along the corridor to her restored room. The baronet had set Darcy's staff to organizing the disarray of their earlier search of the room. "A maid will attend you as is necessary, ma'am. Your meals will be brought to you, but other than those few moments, you will remain in isolation until I can arrange your transportation. Do you understand, Mrs. Harwood?"

"As you wish, Sir Phillip." The lady turned to her jailer and offered him a polite bow of her head. "I shall await your pleasure, sir." Evangeline Harwood entered the room—never looking back.

Behind her, Sir Phillip pulled the door closed and locked it from the outside. He motioned a footman forward. "No one is to enter this room unless Mr. Darcy or I give the order to do so."

"Yes, sir."

James hated the darkened passages and the stale air and the musty smell of mold and decaying animals. He would be happy to leave Pemberley's dust-filled enclosure behind. Coming here had seemed a good idea when his friend had suggested it, but he preferred brightly lit parties with ladies in fine silks sporting low décolletages to decay and dampness. "Damn!" he cursed softly when he banged his knee against a jutting support beam, which had broken away from a cornice. "I am tired of being cold," he grumbled. "Tired of cobwebs in my hair—tired of hiding away—tired of being absolutely quiet—tired of the sound of rats in the dusky shadows."

He checked the openings to the many rooms accessible from the passageway. With the appearance of the magistrate and of Darcy's cousin this morning, the activity in the house had increased. The men searched each room, and the women clustered together in tight-lipped pockets of dread.

Shoulders rigid, he made his way to the nearest peephole, a blur of unreality resonating through his mind. A flurry of color caught his immediate attention. Lydia Wickham swirled in place. "It is the most glorious of moments, Miss Donnel," she declared boldly. "The officers choose their partners, and a kaleidoscope of colors unfolds as each lady's skirts swirl in the dance—a continual swish to the quartet."

Cathleen Donnel resisted the urge to roll her eyes. Mrs. Wickham took great pleasure in frivolity. "It sounds delightful. Now, if you will excuse me, I promised His Lordship I would begin to gather my things. He hopes to make his departure tomorrow." Cathleen curtsied and left the room.

"But I did not tell you about the promenade," Lydia called softly to Cathleen's retreating form. She collapsed dejectedly on a nearby bench. "No one seems to care." She understood how others might see her life as superficial, but it was the life she had. "I know nothing else," Lydia whispered to the empty room—the depth of her ignorance and shallowness evident. Suddenly, tears of loneliness—held in check for months—welled up in her eyes. "George," she moaned. "I wish you were here."

James watched and listened. A bitter laugh bubbled in his chest, but he pushed it away. The irony of the situation played through his head. A man of improper title might have the lovely Mrs. Wickham with a wink. The girl was so one-dimensional that she would never recognize the man's true intentions—would actually follow him without question. Noting her vulnerability, James imagined himself stalking toward her—a seductive determination his only weapon. He could easily tempt Mrs. Wickham now; she would take no care to note the difference. James would have to be willing to pay the price for interfering in his friend's affairs, but triumphing over her would give him pleasure in more than one way.

James reached for the latch, but a slight movement stayed his fingers. "Beggin' your pardon, Mrs. Wickham, but the Mistress wishes you to join her and Miss Darcy in the music room." The maid dropped a belated curtsy.

Lydia Wickham shoved lazily out of the chair. "What could Lizzy want in the music room? She certainly knows I possess no such talent."

"I no be knowin', ma'am. Mrs. Darcy just be sendin' me to find ye."

"Oh, all right. I will go."

"What do we do about Mrs. Harwood?" Darcy sat in the chair before the desk, a feeling of déjà vu returning. He had often sat there when his father still lived. At the moment, he wished for the peace he had known then even as his father had lectured him regarding his obligations. He ached to recapture those moments, but then he thought of Elizabeth—of the goodness of her heart—and of how she had made things right with Georgiana—and of how only in this time had he truly been happy. And he realized he never wanted to be anywhere but in this place—even with the evil, which surrounded him.

"When I leave, I will transport the lady to the nearest gaol." A tone of resignation coloring his words, Sir Phillip added, "It is a crying shame that a woman might love a man to such a degree of distraction that she justifies an unjustifiable act in her own mind."

"People have given themselves up to such perversions since the beginning of time—from the Bible to Shakespeare to our country's history, we observe tragedy in everything we do. Only those few moments of love allow us to travel on in life; otherwise, we would all run screaming into the nearest mire—allowing the quicksand to suckle us into its darkness."

The baronet scowled; the morass surrounding Pemberley went straight to its roots, and Sir Phillip wondered if the tree might finally be uprooted. At the moment, it appeared the Darcys were in way over their heads. The magistrate's eyes burned with curiosity. "You must know, Darcy, that Mrs. Harwood is not your Pemberley phantom. Her demented reasons for doing away with Mrs. Jenkinson have nothing to do with the murders of your staff members, nor of the lieutenant. First, those were acts of *force* and of *might*. Neither of those words describes the lady. *Pity*, maybe. *Shame*, most definitely. *Passion*, absolutely. But not *violence*. Mrs. Harwood is simply a hard survivor of a difficult life."

"Will the lady hang for this?" Darcy saw what the older man saw—a life to be pitied.

"More than likely." Sir Phillip shifted uncomfortably. "I despise this part of my duties. Give me a rousing argument between neighbors over sheep in the garden, and I go happily into the fracas, but this type of matter is not open to human reason. No logic lingers in such cases—no one can explain the enigma of murder."

Darcy pushed forward, banishing the maudlin atmosphere filling the room. "Yet, we must solve that puzzle, Sir Phillip, and we must do so before someone else in this house meets his Maker. I sent for you—for your expertise in this matter. I need your level-headed, no-nonsense reasoning to rid Pemberley of this pox."

The baronet looked about shamefacedly. "Of course, Darcy. We must put our heads together to clear your name of this blight. Let us summon the viscount and your cousin. We will need all the raison d'être and common sense to be found in this house to create understanding out of iniquity."

"If we want reason, then we should send for Mrs. Darcy also," Darcy declared.

The corner of the magistrate's mouth turned up in amusement. "You believe your wife capable of handling herself in a man's domain?"

"Mrs. Darcy has at least as fine a mind as many of the men of my acquaintance, but my wife possesses something more important. She has a strong intuition— a way of choosing the right course—except where I am concerned, that is." Darcy chuckled.

An eyebrow rose in curiosity. "Mrs. Darcy did not readily succumb to your many charms?" The baronet gestured to the room's accoutrements.

"The lady also had the acquaintance of one Lieutenant George Wickham," Darcy admitted. "It took her some months to see past the man's *natural* affability and perceive his lies for what they were."

The baronet nervously shuffled the papers he had left on Darcy's desk. "Evidently, Mrs. Darcy's sister lacks your wife's ability to see beyond a handsome countenance. I noted a bit of melancholy in the lady's demeanor."

Darcy would not share Lydia Wickham's story, but he said, "I cannot imagine living with Mr. Wickham to be an easy task for any woman, especially one of Mrs. Wickham's exuberant nature. The lady's husband, as you well know, is one of the most worthless young men in Great Britain."

"I do not believe I have heard you speak so openly of Mr. Wickham's wickedness before, Darcy. When he was a boy, I knew that he was a bad seed, although your dear father tried—supporting him at school, and afterward at Cambridge—most important assistance, as his own father, always poor from the extravagance of his wife, would have been unable to give him a gentleman's education. And the elder Mr. Wickham…he never knew how to handle the boy. Whether to use the cane or offer a pat on the back."

Darcy added to the story. "My father was not only fond of the younger Mr. Wickham's society, whose manners were always engaging; he had also the highest opinion of him, and, hoping the Church would be his profession, intended to provide for him in it."

"How might one imagine a man such as George Wickham taking to the church?" The baronet took a sip of the tepid tea he nursed.

"As for myself, it is many, many years since I first began to think of him in a very different manner. The vicious propensities, the want of principle, which Mr. Wickham was careful to guard from my father, could not escape the observations of a young man of nearly the same age with himself, and who had opportunities of seeing him in unguarded moments, which my father could not have."

"Mr. Worth seemed chagrined to have brought news of Mr. Wickham's continued debasement," Sir Phillip added cautiously.

Darcy picked at an invisible piece of lint on his sleeve. "Mr. Wickham appears determined to bring shame to his own name."

"And to yours, Darcy," his father's long-time friend cautioned.

"Elizabeth and I will distance ourselves from the connection by remaining in Derbyshire and by not acknowledging the connection unless absolutely necessary. We have discussed it and are in accord. Yet, I fear Mrs. Bennet will not be so astute. My wife's mother is singular in her devotion to her daughters, especially to Mrs. Wickham."

The baronet frowned. "And the lady's husband? What of Mr. Bennet?"

"Elizabeth's father will see the folly of supporting Mr. Wickham's reputation, but he is not likely to rein in his wife. He prefers to take refuge in his library and to allow the world to pass by unbridled."

"I pray for your wife's sake that you are wrong, sir."

Before Darcy could respond, Worth tapped on the door. "Might I rejoin you?"

Darcy motioned the man forward. "How is my cousin?" Unsurprisingly, Worth had excused himself when Sir Phillip escorted Mrs. Harwood to her chamber. He had privately asked permission to apprise Anne of the news, knowing she would need comfort when she discovered what they had all suspected.

"I left her in Miss Donnel's care. Anne took the news better than I had expected. Of course, we all knew the truth before the lady's confession. Miss de Bourgh insisted on speaking with her mother privately."

"Anne has matured from this experience although I would have her learn less harsh lessons in the future." Darcy's gaze swung back to the baronet, relief spreading across his face. "You recall, Sir Phillip, how belabored Anne was as a child."

"The girl withdrew under Her Ladyship's ministrations, very much as Sir Lewis did. If Miss de Bourgh has opened herself to a touch more of society's polish because of Lieutenant Harwood's attentions, then I will find it in my heart to forgive him some of his sins." He sighed deeply.

A quiet stillness surrounded them as the three men digested the ramifications of their discoveries. "I wish for my cousin to make a match—a love match—with a man whom she truly deserves and who truly deserves Anne. I wish her the same type of happiness I have found with Mrs. Darcy." Fitzwilliam Darcy set his shoulders with determination. "Speaking of my wife, let me send for the lady, along with the viscount and Colonel Fitzwilliam." He forced his voice to sound calm, but an agitation remained that shook him to his core.

"You sent for me, Lizzy?" Lydia Wickham breezed into the music room, bringing annoyance with her.

Elizabeth ignored her sister's petulant attitude. "Yes, Lyddie. Please come join us. Allow me to pour you tea." Elizabeth gestured toward a nearby chair and waited for her youngest sister to settle herself before she continued. "Miss Darcy and I slipped in here to be away from the baronet's investigation. Truthfully, we have been having a serious discussion, and I had hoped to recruit you to our efforts. We need desperately to return a sense of normalcy to Pemberley as soon as it is possible to do so. We have allowed the bleakness of the storm and the mystery of the deaths to blacken our days. I will not permit evil to take over my household," Elizabeth asserted. "Georgiana and I have decided to attend the Midwinter Celebration in Bakewell next week. We will make new gowns for the assembly and enjoy a day of winter crafts at the church. I know how you so love a social, and we must plan our lives after these days."

Lydia's disposition brightened immediately. "You were always one, Lizzy, to quickly revive your spirits. I remember how all the young ladies in the neighborhood were drooping apace with the removal of the regiment from Meryton. You and Jane were still able to eat, drink, and sleep, and pursue the usual course of your employments, while for us the dejection was almost universal." Elizabeth wished Lydia would speak of something besides the time when Mr. Wickham resided in Meryton, especially for Georgiana's sake, but a quick glance at Darcy's sister showed an unexpected detachment. "So very frequently Kitty and I reproached your insensibility."

Elizabeth could not repress a smile at this, but she answered only by a slight inclination of the head.

Before Lydia could take up her tale again, Georgiana interrupted. "Do you suppose, Elizabeth, that you might prevail upon our cousin Edward to stay long enough to join us at Bakewell?" The girl spoke with a calm confidence. "It would be advantageous to have an additional dance partner. Fitzwilliam does not care for my dancing with strangers."

Elizabeth watched with amusement as Georgiana manipulated the situation. Darcy's sister was taking on the hopes of every young lady. Elizabeth knew she would have to teach her formidable husband to release his tight grip on his sister's future. "I most certainly will apply to the good colonel for the pleasure of his company. Perhaps if Miss de Bourgh tarries with us, we might also encourage Mr. Worth to attend. I suspect we will see a great deal of the man if Anne remains at Pemberley."

"I think it romantic." Georgiana sighed and flushed with color.

Lydia perked up with the prospect. "As a married lady, I can avoid society's mandates for dancing with strangers."

Recalling her sister's poor behavior at the Netherfield Ball, Elizabeth cautioned, "We—none of us—will do anything that might bring shame on Pemberley or the Darcy name." She took Georgiana's hand in hers. "Yet, as your sister, I will see that you have an abundance of partners, and that your brother takes a less rigid stance."

"Thank you, Elizabeth." Georgiana squeezed her sister's hand. She looked about shyly before whispering, "I have been to only one assembly, and I danced only twice, both times with Fitzwilliam."

"Well, I promise a more pleasant evening this time. You have a big sister now, and I know what young girls like."

"Plus, as a married woman, I, too, can serve as your chaperone," Lydia offered.

"Thank you," Georgiana said, covering the shock of Lydia Wickham being *her* chaperone. "Do you think, Elizabeth, with all that has happened at Pemberley that it might be a bit presumptuous of us to attend and make merry?"

"On the contrary," Elizabeth asserted. "We will demonstrate quite impressively to Derbyshire for what Pemberley stands—for what the Darcys stand. None of what has happened here is our fault, and I will not have us hiding away as if we had guilty consciences."

"There are times, Lizzy, when you sound very much like your husband!" Lydia exclaimed.

Elizabeth smiled broadly. "I take that as the highest of compliments." She placed her teacup on a nearby plate. "Now, Georgiana, I want you to fetch those new fashion plates from your dresser. Lydia, you are to bring the color board from the bottom of your wardrobe. It is my old one; I placed it there some time ago with other mementos from Longbourn. We will meet in Miss Darcy's room in five minutes. Now, hurry, girls, we have party dresses to design."

James's fears raced as he observed the Pemberley staff hurrying about the halls, seeing to Darcy's orders. He would leave the estate tonight, under disguise of darkness. A thunderous scowl criss-crossed his face. Just like young Peter Whittington, he wanted to be a part of this world—wanted acceptance. It was truly all he had ever wanted. However, fighting the system tired him, and at moments such as these, he simply wanted to run away—to escape to his self-imposed penal compliancy.

"These passageways are not your only prison," he mumbled. "Your soul will rot in hell," he mimicked what Father Bertram had told him only a few weeks earlier. "Damned for all time." He hated the priest, but he *religiously* attended the man's mass, drawn to the belief of redemption, but never finding it.

He chastised himself for the blind rage that often controlled his actions—the beast he could not tame. *They* brought it out in him—his mother—her extravagant ways—his father—a weak man. People, especially those at the university who thought him an abomination—the joke of his graduating class—some thought him a rich man's bastard. He had tried to keep Peter from the same stigma, but the boy insisted upon pomposity to still the unspoken threats; yet, all Peter's indulgent ways did was to irritate respectable society.

Because of the intended and the unintended snubs, James had developed his own defenses, so in many ways he understood the boy's manipulations. He supposed his hardness and his foul temper were no more effective. He bit back an oath as he considered the futility of coming to Pemberley.

The sound of the turning latch set his pulse pounding. He stepped behind the screen as the door swung open. Georgiana Darcy crossed to her dresser and pulled open a drawer. She removed a large book and then stopped to look into the mirror.

"You!" she gasped before springing for the door.

James remained frozen, praying she would not see him, but as she stood, he knew the moment that Miss Darcy obviously recognized him. In the reflection of the mirror, the girl could see him standing not ten feet behind her.

Fear and panic followed the recognition, and she bolted to escape; but he reached her before she could signal the others. He caught her possessively around the waist, clamping his free hand over her mouth to squelch her scream. "Lovely Georgiana," he whispered huskily into her hair as she squirmed against him to set herself free. "You are coming with me, my Dear."

His words sent her into stupefied terror; she kicked and twisted and pushed with all her might, but James easily handled her alarm with brute force. "Play nicely, Georgiana," he hissed roughly in her ear. "Do not make me do something we will both regret."

James began to drag the girl toward the secret opening. Using his weight to press her against the wall, he quickly released her mouth long enough to flick the U-shaped lever locking the passageway.

Yet, before he could catch her mouth again, the room's door flew open, and he knew he was in trouble.

CHAPTER 21

~ ~ ~

USING GEORGIANA'S LITHE body as a shield, James spun around to face the intruder, his grip tightening around the girl's waist and his right, gloved hand recapturing her mouth. He plastered her back to his chest, jerking her head to the side so he might see over her shoulder. A split second later, Georgiana's visitor stepped around the screen and came into full view.

Lydia Wickham's normally large, wide-set eyes grew even larger—shock and confusion playing across her face. "What-what are you doing here?" she stammered breathlessly.

Pulling Georgiana tighter to him to lessen her struggle, James gave Lydia the perfect *smile*. "I came to find you, Sweetest," he said calmly.

"Find me?" She stood transfixed, trying to make sense of the scene playing out before her. "Why did you need to find me?"

"I missed you, of course, Darling. I always miss you when you are not around."

A long heartbeat kept Lydia from responding, but finally she managed to ask the right questions. "What are you doing in Miss Darcy's room? Surely, you did not expect to find me here?" Her hands fisted on her hips as she allowed the color board to slip to the floor.

James's smile purposely grew larger. "You know how *they* are, Darling. Darcy's men would not let me through the front door: I am not good enough for the great Fitzwilliam Darcy to entertain."

He gestured with a nod of his head to the dark opening standing ajar. "But I know this house. I had my ways of finding you."

"You…you came through there?" Lydia pointed to the gaping darkness.

"Of course, Darling. No one can keep us apart, especially not the Darcys." He edged Georgiana backward one step. "Now, Sweetheart, we must leave. Come along."

"What are you doing to Miss Darcy?" Some of Lydia's limited wits had returned.

James took another step toward his necessary escape. "She found me before I found you. She started to scream for help, but I could not let her set up an alarm. Not until we were safely away." His voice held a practiced smoothness although he still wrestled with Georgiana physically.

"Truly?" Lydia whispered. "You came for me?" Her hands opened like a flower seeking the sun, and she reached for him.

"You know in your heart that I speak the truth." Lydia stared mutely at him, weighing his words. "We must leave, Sweetest," he said with some urgency.

"What about my things?" She asked tentatively, turning instinctively toward her room to retrieve them.

"There is not time," he insisted. "We must leave now. Take Miss Darcy's cloak, and we will send for the rest. You are aware that Darcy must not find me here. He will have me arrested for trespassing."

Lydia looked closely at the obviously frightened Georgiana. "What of her?"

"I will tie Miss Darcy to the chair." He pushed Darcy's sister toward a straight-backed chair. "We will leave her for her brother to find."

Lydia's stubbornness took hold. "But what of Lizzy? I cannot just leave without saying farewell. And we planned to attend an assembly next week. We were to have new dresses made, and I promised to help chaperone Miss Darcy. Could we not just stay at Pemberley for a few days? I am sure I can convince Lizzy," she whined.

James's patience snapped. "You crazy chit! Darcy is never going to accept me in his house. He always hated me—the women preferred me to him—even with all his money and connections!" He spit out the words. "Now, do as I tell you and go through that door, or you will pay dearly for disobeying me!"

Lydia's head dropped in immediate submission. "I did not mean to anger you," she mumbled. "I just thought Mr. Darcy might agree to help us again. That is why I came to see Lizzy. If Mr. Darcy saw fit to help us, we could start over."

Edward Fitzwilliam burst through the study door, followed closely by Viscount Stafford. "Darcy, look at this!" The colonel shoved a small portrait at Darcy.

The master of Pemberley fought the inclination to yank the offending item from his cousin's hand. Despite his apparent outer calm, his body recoiled in disgust. "I am well aware of the picture, Edward. It spent many years suspended among several other miniatures over the mantelpiece in my father's favorite drawing room. At Elizabeth's insistence, I placed it in storage with other mementos in the room currently occupied by Mrs. Darcy's sister. In fact, Elizabeth and I agreed recently that the lady might take it with her when she leaves Pemberley." Darcy stood and walked away, unable to look at the image of his former friend without feeling contempt course through his veins.

Edward followed closely, shadowing Darcy's steps. "That explains why we found it on the table next to Mrs. Wickham's bed, but that is not what makes this miniature important."

Darcy turned angrily on his cousin—the reminder of Mr. Wickham angering him even more during this difficult time. "What is it, Edward? Why is this bloody portrait suddenly so paramount in importance?" He grabbed the picture from Edward's outstretched palm and threw it against the wall, watching with pleasure as the small frame splintered into a dozen pieces.

Edward caught Darcy by both shoulders, forcing his cousin to listen to him. Eye to eye, Edward held Darcy's shoulders in a vise-like grip. "Jatson—the footman," he began, pronouncing the words slowly—ensuring that Darcy understood. "Mr. St. Denis swears the man in the portrait is the man with whom he fought outside the east wing chambers—the man who tried to kill him."

Elizabeth stuck her head in Lydia's room, but seeing no one about, she hurried along the hallway to Georgiana's chamber. She had re-trieved some lace and muslin swatches from her own sitting room before heading upstairs to join her sisters. Breezing into her new sister's chambers in anticipation, Elizabeth came up short—her heart lurching in her chest. Coming through the bedroom door instead of the dressing room, she had no time to prepare herself for the terrible tableau performing there. Apprehension ricocheted down her spine. "What in God's name are you doing here?" she demanded. Georgiana whimpered, but Elizabeth did not allow her-self to look at Darcy's sister. Instead, she made eye contact with the girl's captor, daring him to make a false move. "You are not welcome in this house, sir. I suggest you take your leave before my husband finds out. Mr. Darcy will take a whip to you for touching his sister."

James's eyes sparked in sarcastic amusement. "Well, well, Mrs. Darcy. It has been a long time since we have seen each other. Actu-ally, that is not exactly true." He smiled greedily at her. "I have been watching you for nearly a week now. You and my old friend are quite bold in the privacy of your bedchamber. If I had known you to possess such wantonness, I might have paid you more attention."

Lydia looked at him in confusion. "You have been here a week? Since the beginning of the storm? I thought you came today."

James glared at her menacingly. "Did I not tell you before that you are not to speak unless I give you permission to do so?"

Elizabeth noted how her sister retreated with the man's words, and then her eyes darted to the open passageway—the cold of the darkness filling the room with its damp chill, as well as its evil. A full blush spread up her chest and neck with the realization that their intruder likely spoke the truth. He had watched Darcy and her in the act of love—had observed their intimacies. Despite that, Elizabeth swallowed her shame; she needed to free Georgiana and needed to set them all free of the man she now hated as much as her husband did. She had never regretted as much as she did at that moment the disgrace her family had brought to Darcy's doorstep.

She had no fear of shameful gossip spreading farther through Darcy's means; there were few people on whose secrecy she would have more confidently depended; but at the same time there was no one from whom knowledge of a sister's frailty she more wanted to conceal. Had Wickham and Lydia's interactions been conducted on the most honorable terms after their marriage, Darcy might have been able to forgive the couple. But this! Quite understand-ably, Darcy would not forgive Wickham his invasion of Darcy's home. Even more certainly, Darcy would not forgive Wickham for an attempt to kidnap his sister. And Darcy's anger would not stop there. He would be furious with Lydia, young and silly Lydia. And he would be livid with her, Elizabeth. Thanks to his marriage to Elizabeth, he had an alliance and relationship of the nearest kind with a man whom he so justly scorned. From such a connection she could not wonder that he would shrink at the outset. Now, there was a new and much more terrible transgression. She could not in rational expectation think that her marriage would survive such a blow.

"I will ask you again, sir, to kindly take your leave of Pemberley." She nodded toward the open passageway, never removing her eyes from his.

"Not without Lydia," he retorted. "She is the reason I came in the first place."

Elizabeth reached out to capture her sister's hand. "Lydia stays with me." She raised her chin in defiance.

The man weighed her words—a battle of wills played before them. Finally, he spoke—a soft growl of warning. "Which sister do you choose, Mrs. Darcy? The one of your own blood or the one of your husband's?" He tightened his hold on Georgiana. "I mean to take one of them to hold off Darcy's vengeance. I would think the lovely Miss Darcy might serve me better." He purposely nuzzled the side of Georgiana's head to emphasize his meaning.

"I will go," Lydia asserted as she stepped forward. "After all, he came for me. That is what you said; was it not?" She broke Elizabeth's hold and moved with dignity toward the opening, picking up Georgiana's cloak from where it laid across a chair and wrapping it about her shoulders. With a deep sigh, she stepped through the opening. "Come. Let Miss Darcy go," she called from the darkness.

James's smile returned, capturing the memory of his warm lips kissing the back of Elizabeth's hand. Now, Darcy's wife felt discomposed by his skillful ploy. "I believe I might take both sisters, after all. Darcy is likely to come after me with only Lydia for my company, but he will think twice if Miss Darcy is my traveling companion."

He began to drag a squirming Georgiana with him. "No!" Elizabeth reached out to him. "Take me instead. Leave Georgiana; she is not to your tastes." She began to think of ways to save Darcy's sister. She must save Georgiana from this man! "Would you not like to know me better? You said so only moments ago. You have no need of an innocent; you need a woman of experience." Drawing on her intuition, she blurted out, "Besides, I can offer you something Georgiana cannot. Mr. Darcy will protect me because I carry his heir. He will want nothing to happen to me."

James Withey's expression hardened, his eyes vibrant with anticipation. "You would go with me—willingly? You would leave this behind?" He gestured with his head to the elegant furnishings.

Elizabeth abruptly straightened before shooting him a fierce look. "I suspect when my husband realizes I have brought danger to his household, Mr. Darcy will gladly spurn my connections." Her eyes took note of the military uniform he wore—of the boots—the same as Lieutenant Harwood and Edward. The deaths—the boot prints—came back as a nightmarish phantom. The man Georgiana had seen was Harwood—but the man she had observed in the open field that first day stood before her. Elizabeth suddenly felt the chill of the darkened hole. Sternly suppressing her apprehension, she lifted her skirt and declared, "Leave Miss Darcy here; I will go without a fight."

James skeptically studied the emotions dancing across her face. Then he said suddenly, "The former Bennet sisters will do." He released Georgiana's mouth and gestured to the opening. "After you, Mrs. Darcy."

Georgiana whispered huskily, "No, Elizabeth."

"I will be fine, Georgiana." She caressed the girl's cheek with the back of her palm before stepping though the narrow opening.

James deliberately crushed the memory of Darcy's betrayal—of the damnable need to be something he was not. "I am afraid I must stop you from sounding the alarm so soon, my Dear." He spun the girl away from him before striking her across the back of the head with the gun he carried in his waistband. Georgiana swayed in place for a few long seconds, but then she crumbled in an unconscious heap to the floor.

Stepping through the opening, James reached for the familiar lever to close off the passage. He heard Elizabeth Darcy gasp at the sight of Georgiana's body lying motionless on the floor as the wall sconce swung into place. "Mr. Darcy's sister will have a headache, but that will be the worst of it," he asserted. He stared at her mockingly. He reached for the shuttered lantern he had left in the wall's recessed niche. Opening the light, he ordered, "This way, ladies." He began to traverse a narrow, damp corridor. He did not look back to see if they followed; James realized they had no idea where they were—a fact he would use to his advantage.

"George Wickham," Darcy mumbled with recognition. "In my house—in Pemberley?" His eyes darted about the room in terror. "The deaths? Wickham caused the deaths." The words *Georgiana—lovely Georgiana* echoed in his memory, and suddenly pure panic shook him. "Georgiana." He grabbed Edward's hand as he started toward the door. "He has been in Georgiana's room!"

Darcy took off at a run, mounting the steps to the private quarters two at a time—Colonel Fitzwilliam and the viscount closely on his heels. He caught the arm of the footman standing post in the hallway. "My sister?" he pleaded.

"Her room, sir," the man called to Darcy's retreating form. "With Mrs. Darcy and the mistress's sister."

Darcy did not knock before entering the room; he would apologize later if he was wrong. Coming to a sudden halt, taking stock of the room, the other two men flanking him. Darcy felt a prick of alarm. "Georgiana!" he called, but was greeted only with silence. "Georgiana!" He clenched his lips together, trying not to draw conclusions.

"The footman said she was here, as were Mrs. Darcy and Mrs. Wickham." Adam Lawrence started toward the open sitting room door.

Edward walked slowly in the direction of the screen, carefully surveying every corner of the room. The eerie silence made him think of the absolute quiet before a battle, and the thought nearly shook his resolve. Finally, a low moan signaled his find. "Here!" he called as he knelt to Georgiana's side. "Easy, Sweetling." He turned her carefully in his embrace, not wishing to injure her further. "Easy," he cautioned again as he cradled Georgiana's head in his lap.

Darcy was immediately beside him—on his knees checking for other injuries besides the gaping gash behind her ear. He handed Edward his handkerchief to stop the blood. "Stafford, send a man for Mrs. Reynolds," he snapped. He ran his hands quickly up and down his sister's arms and legs, searching for other wounds. Other than a few obvious bruises he saw nothing else.

"Here." Stafford thrust a glass of water into Edward's hands.

The colonel took it, placing only a few drops on Georgiana's swollen lip. "She is coming around." Edward carefully pushed Georgiana's tresses from her face. "I have you," he whispered huskily. "Do not try to move."

"Georgie." Darcy caught her hand. "Can you hear us?"

Georgiana stirred again—her eyes fluttering open and then closing slowly as she fought her way to consciousness. "Fitzwilliam?" she whispered.

"I am here." He squeezed his sister's hand. "As is Edward."

Georgiana's eyes opened—searching her cousin's face for familiarity. Her hand lifted for his mouth. "Edward," she murmured.

"We are all here, Love," he whispered as he caressed her jaw.

"Georgie," Darcy's anxious voice pleaded, "where is Elizabeth?"

His sister fought for lucidity. "Elizabeth?" She took a steadying breath.

"Yes, Sweetheart," Darcy coaxed. "Where is Elizabeth?"

Turning her head too quickly, Georgiana cringed with pain. "She left with Mr. Wickham."

"What do you mean?" Pure panic set Darcy ablaze. "Left *where?*"

"Through the wall." Georgiana tried desperately to explain. "He was…he was in my room. I tried…tried to get away…caught me…Mrs. Wickham came…then Elizabeth…his wife agreed to go with him…said he came for her…wanted to take me, but Elizabeth…she said she would go instead…said you would not forgive her for the deaths. You will, Fitzwilliam…you will forgive her, will you not? You must bring Elizabeth back to us."

"Tell me where!" he demanded. "I must stop him!"

"Through the wall." Her left hand gestured toward the wall sconce. "They walked through the wall." Georgiana pushed her way to a seated position. "Somehow through there. The wall shifts open…it is dark and cold."

Darcy was on his feet immediately, pushing against plaster and wood, trying to move the immovable.

"There must be a secret handle or latch." Stafford's fingers ran along the baseboard trim and other fixtures.

Without thinking, Darcy followed the viscount's example, searching frantically with his fingers in every crack and crevice. Deep in thought—thoughts of his brave wife and of what revenge he would exact on George Wickham—Darcy nearly missed the metal tip of the latch. "Found it!" He fumbled with the U-shaped hook, sliding his finger under it to lift it perpendicular to the wall. Then he took a step back as the brick and mortar shifted, spinning in on itself.

"Lord!" he gasped as he gaped into the blackness. "We need lanterns and men."

"Right." Stafford rushed out of the room as Mrs. Reynolds rushed in.

Edward lifted Georgiana from the floor. "Bring her this way, Colonel." Mrs. Reynolds cleared a path to the adjoining room.

"Wait!" Georgiana called as her cousin caught her to him. "Fitz-william." She reached for her brother.

Darcy came to her side. "What is it, Georgie?"

"He has been watching us," Georgiana whispered. "Watched you and Elizabeth . . . alone." Her ears pinked in discomfiture. . . .

Darcy recognized the meaning of her embarrassed words. "I understand."

"No, you do not. He wants her. . . wants Elizabeth. . . to take revenge on you. She went with him to ensure my safety."

"I will get her back, Georgiana. Never fear. Today will be the last day George Wickham haunts our lives."

She dropped the first of the swatches from her pocket when the movable door closed on Georgiana, hoping to help Darcy find them. Now, Elizabeth clung to her youngest sister. They followed the pale light as it made its way along the damp corridor. "Where are we going?" she demanded of their captor.

"You will see, Mrs. Darcy," he mocked over his shoulder, refusing to slow down, often leaving them stumbling through the shadows. Yet, finally, he paused and waited on the women. "This way." He gestured to the left.

Elizabeth planted her feet and caught Lydia's arm. "We go nowhere until you tell us where we are."

"You forget, Mrs. Darcy; I am not enthralled with you. I am not that wisp of a husband you took to your bed," he asserted.

"Then tell your wife of our destination," Elizabeth ordered. She shoved Lydia forward.

"My wife?" he incredulously stormed. "You think this tart is my wife?" He knocked Lydia out of his way as he closed the distance between himself and Elizabeth. "I have known Mrs. Wickham in the Biblical sense of the word, but I am most certainly not this woman's husband." He caught Lydia's wrist and bent it backward. "I would suggest that you clarify the difference for your sister, Mrs. Wickham."

Lydia winced from the pain he inflicted. "James is not my husband."

Elizabeth physically pried his fingers from her sister's arm. "Leave her alone, you brute!" she warned.

"Or what, Mrs. Darcy? What will you threaten? Will you banish me from Pemberley as your husband once did, or will you have me whipped before the stable hands as my dear father once saw fit to do?"

Elizabeth stood straight and defiant. "I agreed to come with you only on the premise that you would not hurt an innocent, Mr. Wickham."

"As I just told you, I am not that wheyface George Wickham." He hovered over her, using his size to try to intimidate her.

Elizabeth rolled her eyes in exasperation. "Then tell me, kind sir, who are you?" she said sarcastically.

"I am an associate of Mr. Wickham. James Withey. At your service, madam." He mockingly offered Elizabeth a low bow. However, as he rose, he pointed a gun at her forehead, and he cocked it. "I would strongly suggest, Mrs. Darcy, you ask no more questions and simply move along the passage. I have killed one man already; they can hang me only once for the offense."

Lydia caught Elizabeth's arm. "Come, Lizzy." She lowered her eyes to James's glare. "I know what is best with Mr. Withey."

"Lydia, you cannot be serious?" Elizabeth looked from one to the other. "He is Mr. Wickham."

"No…no, he is not." Lydia tugged on her sister's hand.

Reluctantly, Elizabeth allowed her younger sister to pull her along the gloomy channel. A second swatch of delicate lace drifted to the shadowy floor.

Edward gently placed Georgiana on Anne's bed. "Here, Sweetling." He caressed her cheek. "Mrs. Reynolds will tend to you, Love."

Her eyes grew wide, and she grabbed his hand. "You will go with Fitzwilliam? You will safeguard him?"

"Do not worry, Darling. I will let nothing happen to that brother of yours." He squeezed her hand and started to take his leave.

"I want nothing to happen to you either." She caught his hand in her two smaller ones. Edward noticed the elegant, long fingers as they wrapped around his. Georgiana interlaced their hands. "Come back to me."

A realization struck him—recognition of what he had said when he had seen her earlier that day. His cousin's gangly girlishness no longer existed: He supposed he had seen her with a guardian's eye before. Yet, even at Elizabeth and Darcy's wedding, though she had been little more than sixteen, her figure was formed, and her appearance womanly and graceful, and although he inherently knew those facts, until that moment, Edward had not truly seen Georgiana—not looked at her as a man does a woman.

"I will be back." He squeezed her hand. "Listen to Mrs. Reynolds. I want you up and ready for a game of lottery tickets when I return." He brought the back of Georgiana's hand to his lips. Something magical shot through him. Edward forced himself away from the image of Georgiana lying in bed and looking a bit disheveled.

Georgiana's eyes followed his form as he disappeared through the dressing room connection. She scanned his back with pleasure. "My cousin is a handsome man," she remarked as Mrs. Reynolds took a clean cloth and water to the blood matted in her hair.

The housekeeper glanced over her shoulder, but she did not see what the girl saw. "The colonel is of the finest cut; you are fortunate, Miss, to have him as one of your guardians."

Georgiana closed her eyes to keep an image of him in her memory. "I suppose…suppose you are correct, as usual, Mrs. Reynolds." *My cousin is not for me.*

"Murray!" Darcy called from his sister's bedroom door. "Bring Mr. Steventon here at once."

"Right away, Mr. Darcy." The footman took off at a run.

Darcy returned to stare into the gaping hole. "My God, Edward. How did I not know about this?" He gestured toward the blackness.

Edward Fitzwilliam tried to keep his focus, but his cousin's words echoed through his mind: *Come back to me.* When had Georgiana turned into a woman? And why had he not seen it before? He purposely gave his head a good shake to clear his thinking. "We need to send some men to search for the other openings. Where might they be?"

Darcy looked anxiously toward the emptiness, wanting to take action—fearing the worst for Elizabeth—but knowing he needed weapons and lights before he and the others plunged into the darkness. He prayed for Elizabeth's safety and that of their child. His impetuous wife had placed herself in danger to save his sister. "I cannot lose her," he whispered as he stared into the murky darkness. Elizabeth had taken matters into her own hands, as she often did.

"You will not," Edward's hand grasped his shoulder. "Help me find Mrs. Darcy. Tell me where you have seen or have suspected your intruder to be."

Darcy shot a quick glance toward the open bedroom door, expecting the others to appear any second. "I cannot think straight, Edward," he muttered. "What if he has hurt her?"

"Listen to me, Darcy. Wickham needs Mrs. Darcy if he expects to get away from here. He will intimidate her, but he will not hurt her. What we need now is a plan. I suggest we send Stafford and

Worth with some men to find the other openings and to enter the tunnels at those points. You and I will take weapons and follow this trail. The man will not get away with this. Murder is quite different from womanizing and gambling."

"Can she be well? I mean, in there with him?" Darcy chastised himself for allowing Elizabeth to be in danger. "I should have realized…"

"Mrs. Darcy is a resourceful woman. A scoundrel such as George Wickham will not defeat her."

"Come along," the man Elizabeth knew as George Wickham squeaked like an adolescent schoolboy. "James wants the two of you by the forest opening."

"It is cold in here," Lydia whimpered, "and my slippers are getting wet."

Peter whipped around to face her. "Are you complaining again? Nothing is ever good enough for you." He raised his hand to strike her, but Elizabeth's reprimand brought him up short. "Stop!"

Peter turned on her. "Who do you think you are to give me orders, madam?" His voice popped and cracked as if he was a boy of fourteen or fifteen. "My father taught me how to treat those below me, and Mrs. Wickham needs a lesson or two on gratitude and condescension."

Elizabeth looked at the young man, confusion lacing her voice. "Mr. Withey?"

The boy snarled his nose in disgust. "Withey will return. He always returns at the least opportune time. He asked me to escort you to the forest."

Elizabeth spoke softly, edging closer to Lydia. "May I ask your name, sir?" Elizabeth noted the open area—an antechamber of sorts, containing the missing bedding and candelabra.

The young man pompously strode across the room. "I am surprised you do not recognize me."

Elizabeth gestured to the unlit candleholder. "It must be the poor lighting." Her eyes followed him as he paced the area. "Your name, please, so I might address you properly."

"Peter Whittington, son of Lord and Lady Whitlock."

Elizabeth tried to purposely catch him off guard—a minor victory, but one nevertheless. "Then it is Sir Peter or Sir Whitlock? I am afraid I remain unaware of your family seat. I hail from Hertfordshire originally, you see." Unlike James Whitey, the young man did not heed the warning voice in his head, a fact Elizabeth would use to her advantage.

"My older brother is to inherit," he said, his hauteur even more evident than before. "I am simply a 'Mister,'" he informed her as he tossed a blanket across the overflowing chamber pot in an attempt to quell the smell.

Spotting another blanket crumpled on the mattress, Elizabeth controlled the tone of her voice. "Mr. Whittington, would you mind if I have use of the other blanket?" She gestured to the dark brown cloth. "I have no cloak, and I am quite chilled."

He examined her closely, his dark brows narrowing; she had surprised him again. "I see no reason to deny you." He flicked his wrist magnanimously in the direction of the mattress. "Gregor will have no need of it now."

Elizabeth bent tentatively to reach the bound wool cloth. "This is most kind of you, Mr. Whittington." She kept her voice neutral as she folded the wool and wrapped it around her shoulders, seeking the warmth. "Would it be too much to know, Mr. Whittington, who Gregor might be?"

"Believe me, Mrs. Darcy," the modulating voice continued, "you do not wish to meet Gregor MacIves. He is the worst of us. He is the one who took the lieutenant's life, and James sent him away for awhile."

Behind him, Elizabeth saw Lydia shrug her shoulders to indicate her own lack of knowledge of the man. "Well, then, I shall be happy for your company, Mr. Whittington." She realized she must be aware of the different stories Mr. Wickham now told in order to deal with the man. "Are there others, Mr. Whittington? Others traveling with Mr. Wickham?"

Peter offered her a measuring stare, but then he smiled non-committally. "Mr. Wickham is rarely with us these days," he declared mockingly. "Actually, as I come from the only titled family among us, I suppose the others travel with me."

Elizabeth remembered once thinking Mr. Wickham's smile one of the most compelling she had ever seen; now, she saw it for the evil behind it. Reluctantly, she nodded her head in understanding. "Then there are just the four of you?" She tried to wordlessly encourage her sister to help her, but Lydia remained compliant and silent.

Peter Whittington, or whatever he called himself, made no response to her question, but a soft, malevolent chuckle sent a shiver down her spine and her heart pounding in her throat. "I suggest ye be takin' yourself along," he growled threateningly in a Scottish brogue. "I not be a bleeding book of answers."

Wickham's bleary gaze made Elizabeth think he was suddenly very drunk. "I am prepared to go with you, Mr. Wickham." She kept her voice low, hoping he would find no offense. His behavior baffled her, and Elizabeth did not know how best to react to this singular game he practiced.

"Ye be thinkin' I be that bloody braggart? Nay, I didnae think ye would offer me a dagger to the heart, lass—ye would not curse me as such." He threw items into a cloth bag. "Didnae ye think to bring us some food? Or something we ken be selling?"

"I am afraid, sir, that we had no time to pack properly." Elizabeth nervously gestured to the blanket she wore about her shoulders. "Mr. Whittington kindly loaned me this wool cloth for warmth. However, if you wish, my sister and I could return and find you the gold and silver in Mr. Darcy's house." She did not know why Mr. Wickham chose to act out these scenes, but his portrayals made her more determined to find a way out on her own or to stall until Darcy came for her.

"A mon cannae send a lass to do his work," he asserted, standing before tossing the bag over his shoulder. "I be havin' me revenge on the mister soon enough."

"Do you understand what I want you to do?" Edward Fitzwilliam quickly organized the search. "Sir Phillip and Mr. Baldwin will stay with the ladies. Mr. Baldwin, I want no one below stairs. It is too dangerous. Collect Mrs. Harwood and place her with the rest of the women in the blue room. No one comes in or out except those of us in this room."

"Yes, Colonel."

"Worth, you will take men through the cold cellar entrance." Each man simply nodded his agreement. "Stafford, you will go through Harwood's room. Murray, you and St. Denis will come through the east wing. The latch in each room must be the same. Take lanterns and weapons, and do not hesitate to use your gun if you can get a clean shot at Mr. Wickham." No one answered him, but the intensity on each man's face told the tale. "Are you ready, Darcy?" Edward placed a gun in his waistband, another in a holster under his arm, and sheathed his rapier.

Similarly outfitted, Darcy rolled the map he had been inspecting with Mr. Steventon. "There is an exit to the wooded area behind the stables, one closer to White Peak, and one leading to the waterfall toward the turnpike road."

"I am betting on the stables. Wickham needs a fast exit, and horses are the only solution in this weather."

"Hurry, Edward. Elizabeth cannot leave this estate with that madman."

CHAPTER 22

~ ~ ~

ELIZABETH SUPPORTED Lydia's sagging body as they followed Wickham through the shadowy twists and turns. She would run for safety if she could simply make Lydia respond, but Elizabeth would not leave her younger sister behind. For some unexplained reason, Lydia was cowed by Wickham's playacting. Elizabeth sometimes wondered how she and Lydia could be children of the same parents.

"Is this normal for Mr. Wickham?" she whispered close to Lydia's ear. Lydia frowned for a moment and then nodded. "Does your husband make you call him by these silly names?"

Lydia shot a frightened glance at her husband, obviously praying he did not hear them. "You do not understand, Lizzy." She hesitated, keeping her eyes locked on Wickham's back. "He is not playacting. Mr. Wickham is each of those men, and you had best remember that."

Darcy and Edward led a handful of Pemberley's best men into the depths of the darkness. "My God," Darcy moaned, "who would have thought?" He raised the lantern to get his bearings. "The corridors must follow the house—the T shape of the sleeping quarters. There is nothing behind us. We know from what Wickham said to Miss Darcy that some rooms provided him only a way of spying on us. Others have openings such as this one. Stay sharp—the man is dangerous—has killed three people already. I do not want Mrs. Darcy to be his next victim."

"Slowly," Edward cautioned. "Mr. Wickham knows these passages; we do not. Remain alert to all possibilities."

Despite wanting to rush through the water-soaked enclosure, Darcy listened to his cousin's advice and moved cautiously along behind Edward—his eyes and ears straining for a glimpse or a sound somewhere ahead of him. When they reached the intersecting halls, they spread out.

"Which way?" Lucas asked as he turned in circles. "Up or down?"

"God! I do not know!" Darcy ran a hand through his hair.

"Down," Edward stated flatly. "Has to be down." He led the way as the corridor took a sharp descent between the house's flooring. "Be careful," he called over his shoulder. "The steps are narrow and moldy. If your foot slips, you are dropping into the darkness."

Darcy shadowed his cousin, unable to think for himself. Not since Elizabeth's initial refusal had he felt such anguish—such disorientation. If he lost her now, he did not think he could survive. His eyes searched for any sign of her—and then he saw it. "Edward, look!" He pushed past his cousin to snatch up the scrap of material. "It is Elizabeth's—from the lace on her wedding gown. See."

"At least, we know we are going the right way. Stay close. It appears Mrs. Darcy is leaving us a trail."

"Do you suppose?" Darcy gripped his cousin's arm.

"Absolutely." The colonel smiled. "You have always spoken highly of Mrs. Darcy's intelligence—her good sense. Your wife leaves you a message, Darcy. Can you not join her in finding a way to defeat Wickham? Use your connection to the lady to find her. The two of you together can be a most powerful force."

Darcy swallowed hard and took a few deep breaths to calm his nerves. Edward was right. He was not helping Elizabeth with his panic.

"'Tis as dark as a coffin," Lucas said from somewhere behind them.

"But it is not *our* coffin," Darcy growled, "not today, not ever. This is my house, and Mr. Wickham has taken my wife. If anyone is to die in this hole, it shall be he." Darcy nodded to his cousin. "I am with you, Edward. No more fear of losing Elizabeth. Neither she nor I will allow our separation."

"Then let us find your lady." Edward lifted the lantern again to take the lead. The colonel thought of what Darcy had with Elizabeth, and he nearly moaned in despair. He had spent enough years alone and enough years establishing his own good name to consider finding a wife and happiness at last. Then the image of a slender, golden-haired beauty planted itself firmly in his memory. *Come back to me.*

"'Tis dangerous to spe'k when ye should be verra quiet." Wickham pulled up short, and Elizabeth staggered to keep from slamming into his backside. He caught Lydia brusquely by the arm. "Dinnae James teach ye when ye ken and cannae spe'k?"

"It is my fault." Elizabeth tried to insinuate herself between her sister and Mr. Wickham. "I am a bit confused and asked my sister what she knew of you." She eased his grip from Lydia's arm.

"Ye cannae conceive of such a mon? That be it, Lass?" He actually reached out gently to caress Elizabeth's cheek. "Ye be the smart one; I remember." Then he caught her chin and turned it brashly to him. "I believe ye be a passionate woman, Eliza: I see it in ye eyes, and I will revel in havin' ye." He smashed his mouth hard against hers, kissing Elizabeth roughly. As quickly as he took her mouth, Wickham released her. Turning his back on them again, he grabbed Lydia to his side. "Come along," he said in the voice Elizabeth now recognized as James Withey.

Without another word, she fell into step behind the couple. Surreptitiously, she used the back of her hand to wipe away Wickham's taste from her mouth. She wondered how she could ever have preferred George Wickham to Darcy. She now fully understood, along with her Aunt Gardiner, that Darcy's real defect of character was his obstinacy. He had been accused of many faults at different times—she had been among his greatest critics—but obstinacy was his one true one. With Wickham and Lydia, Darcy had followed them purposely to town; he had taken on himself all the trouble and mortification attendant on such a research. He had frequently met with, reasoned with, persuaded, and finally bribed the man whom he always most wished to avoid and whose very name it was punishment to him to pronounce—the man who had invaded their home.

For herself, she was humbled; but she was proud of him—proud that in a cause of compassion and honor, Darcy had been able to get the better of himself. Now Wickham repaid her husband's compassion by bringing death to Darcy's doorstep. Somehow, she would stop him—she would free Darcy of George Wickham's malice, and she would free Lydia of her husband's libertine ways.

When the footman stepped on the flooring of the landing, no one at first knew what happened until it happened. The wooden planks gave way under the man's weight, and he plunged into the dry well.

"Redman!" Darcy called as he peered into the blackness. "Redman, can you hear me?"

A groan and a muffled curse told him the man lived.

"Redman!"

"Here, Mr. Darcy," a breath-deprived voice returned Darcy's plea.

"Can you move?" Edward knelt beside Darcy, holding a lantern over the hole, trying to determine the situation. "Looks as if he is on that shelf." He indicated a small ledge about ten to twelve feet below them.

A scratching sound followed by another curse answered the question. "It's me leg, Colonel."

"Great." Darcy ran his fingers through his hair. "Now, what do we do? I am not even sure where we might be in the house."

"We will have to send Lucas for help." Edward assessed the situation quickly.

Darcy nodded his agreement, but before any of them could move, light bathed the space as a wall shifted, and Lord Stafford's head appeared in the opening.

"Thank God!" The colonel exhaled the words. "Stafford, we need your help."

Adam Lawrence squeezed through the opening, followed by two footmen. Immediately, he and the others stood beside Darcy and the colonel. "What happened?" He held the lantern aloft.

"Redman fell in," Darcy informed him. "We need him out, and I need to find Elizabeth."

"We have it," Stafford took control. "Darcy, you and the colonel go after Mrs. Darcy and Mrs. Wickham." He motioned to one of the Pemberley staffers to go after a rope. "We can handle your man below."

Edward grasped Stafford's shoulder. "Thanks, Lawrence." He took up the lantern. "Come along, Darcy."

Darcy squeezed past the men. "Send one of the men to Lambton for the surgeon," he spoke softly to Stafford. "We may need him for more than Redman."

"I will see to it."

Elizabeth dropped the last of her swatches when they entered the tunnel, leaving the house itself. The tunnel reminded her of a coal mine outside Scarborough she had seen as a child. The walls were shored up with large timbers, as was the ceiling, which was barely five feet high. They all walked hunched over as they made their way toward the outside. Elizabeth's feet were as cold as she could ever remember their being—the dampness soaked her day slippers through. The melting snow trickled down the walls, heading toward an underground stream they crossed at the juncture of the house and the outside tunnel. As she blindly followed her sister, Elizabeth silently prayed Darcy would recognize the trail she had left behind. But the fact was that he had not caught up to them yet—and she was losing hope. Possibly, he had not even found Georgiana as yet. He might not know she was missing or where to find her and Wickham.

She had no idea how she might escape Mr. Wickham's clutches on her own. Elizabeth supposed she might just run and pray the man would not shoot her from behind, but she could not assign good odds to the likelihood of the "others" not attacking. When she had left with her sister, Elizabeth assumed she could talk sense to George Wickham, and if nothing else, she could bribe her sister's husband to go away and to leave Lydia behind. The scandal would not die easily, but somehow she would keep Lydia from her persecutory husband. However, Mr. Wickham's counterfeit made that more difficult. She expected the man would claim some sort of lunacy as his defense if caught, so Elizabeth now needed a solid plan to protect those she loved.

"Which way?" Darcy and Edward found the antechamber and searched for the most likely way out.

Edward quietly examined the marks along the wall. "Wickham has come in and out of here quite often. Look at the muddy boot tracks." He pointed to the dusty smears on the wooden flooring. "I suspect we will need to split up. You take the passage on the left. I will take the one on the right." Darcy nodded his agreement. "Be careful, Darcy. We must be getting close."

"You too, Cousin." Darcy rolled his shoulders to release the tension. Taking the gun from his waist placket, he allowed the weapon to lead the way. They both recognized Wickham's likely treachery, and they needed to be prepared.

Although the tunnel continued onward into the blackness, James shoved open a wooden door leading to the outside. The backside of it was covered with ivy and vines and made it easier to conceal. "Hurry!" he barked as he shoved Lydia into the open and reached for Elizabeth. "You, too, Mrs. Darcy," he growled, throwing her forward. Elizabeth landed unceremoniously in a snow bank, which quickly soaked her gown and the blanket she clutched about her. She blinked several times—the late afternoon sun reflecting off the snow blinding her after being in the tunnels for so long.

"Get up!" he ordered as he tramped toward her. He jerked Elizabeth to her feet. "There!" he pointed to the nearby stables, thrusting her forward. He caught Lydia to him, dragging her beside him as he marched toward the structure. When she stumbled, he hissed at his wife, "Walk, bitch, or I will leave you here to freeze to death." He pushed Elizabeth again when she stepped out of her slipper and paused to retrieve it. "Keep moving!" he propelled her forward with a powerful heave.

"Damn!" Darcy grumbled when the passage he had followed suddenly come to a dead end. He knocked the spider webs from his hair and shoulders before he began to retrace his steps to the open chamber where Wickham had spent his days and nights. He had come across the remains of a dog or a cat, the skeleton too decomposed to tell which, and of several birds. He imagined the darkened corridors held rats and mice. When he finished this death hunt, he would seal everything in—seal the latches and the spy holes. No one would use this space ever again.

If Darcy had had time, he would have reprimanded Mr. Steventon for not apprising him of the passageways. The man knew of the openings but had said nothing while they searched for their phantom. He wondered, as he worked his way through the closed passages, why his father had never made him aware of these sealed corridors. He knew his ancestors had built Pemberley upon the site of a ruined castle, something built in the time of William Peveril, but it had never occurred to him that secret channels paralleled the rooms of his everyday life. Likely, Mr. Wickham had become aware of the shrouded rooms through his father, who had once served as the steward for Darcy's father.

Working his way cautiously forward, as he stepped into the opening anteroom, Darcy heard it—the reverberation of a gun, followed closely by another and another.

Somehow, they made it to the stables and, as cold as it was inside the barns, being out of the still foot-high snowdrifts was heaven. Elizabeth's teeth chattered uncontrollably, and she could not stop the shivers coursing down her spine. The frozen landscape had relentlessly soaked her gown and hose and shoes, as well as her under things. The combination of the sweat from their hurried exit, the dampness of the tunnel, and the trek through the snow thoroughly drenched Elizabeth's clothes.

"What now?" she asked through a shudder.

James threw Lydia into an empty stall and then looked around nearly in a panic. The absence of Pemberley workers bothered him. Darcy evidently wanted none of his people hurt, and he had pulled them all away. "Hopefully, you can ride astride, Mrs. Darcy," he grumbled as he slung a saddle over the back of Demon, Darcy's own horse.

"You cannot expect to escape with both of us." Elizabeth determinedly challenged the man. "Let Lydia stay here."

"I need her to keep you in line." James put the bit in Demon's mouth and looped the harness over the horse's head. "Which one is your horse?" When she did not answer, he stormed toward her, pinning Elizabeth against the wall. "I asked you a question, Mrs. Darcy," he threatened. "I am not a man accustomed to having my will denied."

Anger filled Elizabeth, but she needed to stall until Darcy came—or, at least, until all hope of that had ended. "Are you the one who hurt Lydia?"

He lowered his head so that they were nose to nose. Elizabeth could smell the traces of stale cheese and bread on his breath. "So, she told you," he growled. "But it is not my domain to manhandle Wickham's wife. My domain is to make her feel the passion of the marriage bed. Any wrongdoing the lady suffers comes at the hands of our young lordship." He brought one hand to her breast and cupped it. "Very nice, Mrs. Darcy."

"If you think to frighten me, Mr. Withey, you must do better than that."

"Oh, I will, Mrs. Darcy. I most certainly will." He pressed against Elizabeth and made her aware of his masculinity. "Now, Mrs. Darcy, you must tell me which horse is yours."

She gritted her teeth and nodded her head to a nearby stall. "Pandora is mine."

"Very good, my lady." James broke away and went about putting a regular saddle on Pandora. Within minutes, the horses were ready to leave. "Come!" He grabbed a nearly comatose Lydia from where he had left her. "You, my Dear, will ride with me."

"Why cannot Lydia ride behind me?" Elizabeth charged.

"As I said before, Mrs. Wickham stays with me until we get away from Pemberley."

Elizabeth shot a quick glance at her sister. "Then what? When we escape Pemberley? What of Lydia then?"

"Then I will have no more need of Wickham's wife."

Edward Fitzwilliam emerged into the daylight. He had purposely sent Darcy the wrong way: He had seen the trail Elizabeth had left and sent his cousin on a false fox hunt. He would save his cousin from harm by apprehending Wickham himself. Darcy had a wife and family on the way; Edward would not allow his cousin to lose it all. It took him but seconds to acclimate to the cold and the light and the snow and to follow the three crosscuts leading to the stables. He set off at a near run, pulling the gun from the holster under his jacket.

Wickham rewarded his efforts. Just as he reached the fence leading to the main barns, the door swung wide, and Wickham exited with two horses. He dragged Lydia Wickham beside him, and Elizabeth hurried along in their wake.

Edward hunched down, trying not to signal his presence, moving as close as he dared without endangering the ladies. When Wickham reached to lift his wife to Demon's back, Edward knew he could wait no longer. "Wickham!" He stepped from behind the gate and into the open. "Step away from the horses."

Elizabeth wanted to warn him—tell Edward that Mr. Withey was no gentleman—he was the despicable, corrupt part of George Wickham. No field of honor existed here. But it was too late. James grabbed Lydia around the neck, using her as a human shield, and fired on the colonel. As if in slow motion, Elizabeth saw it all—saw the bullet leave the gun—saw it travel the short distance to where her husband's cousin stood ready to fire his own weapon—saw it hit his hand—saw the colonel's gun explode with a puff of smoke—saw Lydia slid from James Withey's arms—saw Withey lift the second gun from his waist and aim—saw Edward's chest explode with the impact and Darcy's cousin sink to his knees in the snow. A muffled cry cut the frozen air.

In no more than ten seconds, two people lay in the snow. "No!" she screamed as she tried to reach them, but Withey caught her about the waist, dragged her into the stable, and slammed the door behind him.

Adam Lawrence heard the shots and froze in anxiety. "We have him, Your Lordship," Lucas grunted as he strained to pull Redman's weight to the top of the well. "Mr. Darcy needs you, sir." Another heartbeat passed before Lawrence was on the move, skidding through the shadowy passages, looking for the obvious.

It took Nigel Worth longer to find the secret passage associated with the cold cellar than he had expected. Originally, he and Darcy's staff had moved items in the storage to look for the lock behind or under the food items. Finally, it had dawned on them to search behind and along the shelving itself. Once in the tunnels, they had followed the one, which led them to the area where they recently found Lucinda Dodd's body. They exited the tunnel behind a frozen waterfall, fed by the river close to the house, and came out along the same row of hedges and the copse of trees.

Instead of trying to find their return through the tunnels, Worth and Darcy's men agreed to walk the half mile to the main house via the entrance drive. As they approached the front steps of Pemberley, a shot rang out clearly from behind the house, followed by another and another. The noise set them momentarily on alert, but then the three men were on the run, Darcy's men leading the way along the road, which circled behind the stables.

Darcy took the low-ceilinged tunnel that his cousin had used only minutes earlier, running bent over and preparing for the worst as the daylight became apparent at last. Dropping the lantern he carried into the snow, Darcy shaded his eyes from the sting of the sunlight on the frozen landscape. He did not wait to confirm the tracks ahead of him belonged to his wife and cousin—it only made sense for Wickham to seek an escape on horseback.

Taking the road leading to the forested area that surrounded his estate, Darcy circled the back of the stables—the fenced area where they trained his cattle and sheared his sheep. Following the fence line, he crept carefully along the blocked slats, seeking cover in case of an attack, but nothing before the barns and stables moved. All he observed was Demon and Pandora, standing side by side, as if waiting for Elizabeth and him to mount.

Then he saw them— his cousin and Lydia Wickham lying some fifteen feet apart, both covered in blood. Darcy's breath caught in his chest as he hunched at the end of the fence line and surveyed the area, looking for Wickham and Elizabeth. Seeing neither, he ran to the colonel's side, keeping the horses between him and the stable door.

"Edward." He gently touched his cousin's shoulder. "Edward, please." A moan answered Darcy's prayer. He rolled the colonel to his back and began to check for wounds. "Where?" he asked as he took a second handkerchief from his pocket and pressed it to the chest wound after opening his cousin's jacket.

Edward Fitzwilliam opened his eyes tentatively and stared deep into Darcy's. "Wickham fired…before…before I could get…get a clean shot."

"It is well. I will take care of it. Did you see Elizabeth?" Darcy pulled a handkerchief from Edward's own pocket and wrapped it tightly around his cousin's wrist.

"Mrs. Darcy...behind him...in the stable." Darcy's eyes lifted to the building, searching for some sign of Elizabeth. "I shot...I shot Mrs. Wickham...gun went off...did not mean to."

The sound of running feet, crunching on the icy snow, brought Darcy's attention to the connecting roads from the main house. Darcy raised his gun, but quickly lowered it again when he saw Worth and the Pemberley livery. He motioned to them to come closer, but to keep low.

The solicitor crawled to reach him. "My God, Darcy!"

"I need your help, Worth. Elizabeth is in the stable with Wickham, and I need to see my cousin to the house."

"I will tend the colonel. Go after your wife." He took over the pressure that Darcy had held on the wound. "What about Mrs. Wickham?" He gestured with his head toward where the lady lay beside the horses.

Darcy's eyes followed the man's gaze. "I do not know. I am not sure how many or what kind of weapons Wickham has, and his wife rests close to the door. I will try, but at the moment, my first concern is with my own wife and child."

Again, a sound coming from the direction of the tunnel opening brought all their watchfulness to the back of the building, and then Stafford appeared before them. As he hurried to where they analyzed their next move, Darcy decided on his point of attack.

"I see from where the noise came." Stafford noted the colonel and the immobile Lydia Wickham. "What do we do now?"

"Worth and my men will take Edward to the house. I am going into the back of the stable. Once I have engaged Wickham's attention, would you go for Mrs. Wickham? I am not sure whether the lady lives or not."

Stafford looked carefully to where Lydia lay on her side in the snow. "It appears she breathes. See...Mrs. Wickham's chest rises and falls."

Darcy tried to see what the viscount noted, but his anxiety for Elizabeth blinded him to everything else. "I believe what you say."

He looked again at the forbidding building. "Give me a few minutes to take a position, and then everyone move at once."

"We have it," Stafford assured him. "Concentrate all your energies on saving Mrs. Darcy."

Darcy took a determined, stabilizing breath, and then—suddenly unable to any longer control the fierce anger building inside him—he stood. Cocking the gun he carried, he moved toward the back of the building

The muffled sound of the guns stilled the two rooms holding Pemberley's occupants: the small drawing room occupied by the house's current residents and the ballroom with the Pemberley staff inside.

"What was that?" Despite her aunt's and Mrs. Reynolds's objections, Georgiana Darcy was on her feet pacing the room. She followed Anne to a nearby window to look out.

Sir Phillip ushered them away. "It is too dangerous. Please move to a safer part of the room." The fact that he, too, carried a gun did not ease their apprehension.

"The noise, Sir Phillip?" Anne pleaded. "Was it a gun?"

He purposely ignored her question. Instead, he slid a casual arm around her waist and guided Anne to a nearby chair. "The noise came from outside the house. It could be a tenant chasing a rabbit or even a poacher, especially after so many days of cold weather. Do not become alarmed over every sound."

"But what if it was one of them?" Anne steadfastly insisted.

"We will know soon enough."

A knock at the door interrupted their thoughts. Mr. Baldwin called before he entered, "Mrs. Reynolds, we need you." The man looked grave.

"What happened?" Georgiana demanded, on her feet again.

Mr. Baldwin patiently acknowledged the girl's anxiety. "It is Redman, Miss. He broke his leg. There was a dry well of some kind, probably from the old ruins. At your brother's suggestion, I have sent Timmons to Lambton for the surgeon."

"Do we know any more about my brother or sister or the colonel?"

"No, Miss Darcy. Lucas says Lord Stafford helped with Redman and then followed the Master and the colonel into the tunnels. That is all we know at this time."

"Thank you, Mr. Baldwin." Sir Phillip excused the man to his duties as Mrs. Reynolds rushed to the footman's side.

Darcy lifted up on the small door used for supplies to ease the hinges and to silently enter the stables. Surrounded by tack and leather, he hunched behind the last stall and listened.

"Mr. Withey, you cannot hope to escape now." The sound of Elizabeth's voice calmed Darcy's racing pulse. She was alive, and that was what was important.

"I still have you," the man threatened.

Darcy recognized the voice, but something about it lacked a familiarity. It was as if he listened to a man with whom he had once shared intimacies, but also to a man of whom he had no knowledge. Shaking off the uncanny feeling this created in him, Darcy once again studied the area. He needed to know where Elizabeth stood in relation to Wickham—he could not let what had happened with Mrs. Wickham happen to her. As quietly as possible, he edged forward to the stall's end, where he could see the elongated shadows cast by the two lanterns hanging on either side of the door. Wickham and Elizabeth stood several feet apart. At least, he had that.

Darcy silently sucked in another stilling breath and moved around the corner of the last stall, hoping to come as close to Wickham as possible before the man saw him. He made it past three stalls before Elizabeth's eyes grew in recognition and past another two before Wickham turned from the door where he peered out onto the emptiness of the stable yard and brought Darcy up short. Without even looking at her, Wickham cocked his gun and pointed it at Elizabeth's temple.

Viscount Stafford waited the required three minutes upon which they had agreed before he made his move. The colonel managed by pure will to rise first to his knees and then to his own feet. Then, with the help of Murray and St. Denis, who had managed to exit through the east wing, the Pemberley footmen partially carried and partially walked the colonel toward the servants' entrance. Worth remained behind to help with Lydia Wickham.

"Are you a good shot?" Stafford asked as he sized up the situation.

Worth followed the viscount's line of sight. "Fair...better than most."

Adam Lawrence took a quick assessment of Mr. Worth's physical strength. "Fair or not, you had best cover the door. I will retrieve Mrs. Wickham. Are you ready?" Worth swallowed nervously, but he nodded his affirmation. "We move on two. One...two."

"Miss Darcy!" Murray tapped frantically on the drawing room door.

Sir Phillip jerked the door open, blocking the footman's entrance to the room. "What is it, Murray?" he demanded.

The man pulled at his forelock. "Excuse me, sir. I came for Miss Darcy and Mrs. Reynolds. The colonel, sir...the colonel has been shot."

A gasp told Sir Phillip that Georgiana stood close behind him. "How bad?" the baronet urged.

"Cannot tell, sir, but he walked part of the way to the house. We brought the colonel through the kitchen. He is on the trundle bed off the main room. He is asking for Miss Darcy."

"I am going." Georgiana pushed past the baronet.

"Go with her, Murray," the magistrate called from the doorway. "I will send Mrs. Reynolds immediately."

Georgiana rushed through the main foyer headed toward the servants' entrance, her thoughts consumed by the possibility of losing her cousin.

Murray's long gait caught up with her as she strode along. "The colonel, Miss—he will be fine. Trust me," he said as he rushed forward to swing open the kitchen door. "In here, Miss Darcy." He held a second door. "The colonel is in here." He remained at the opening, watching over the master's sister.

"Edward?" Immediately at his side, Georgiana knelt beside the low makeshift bed. "Edward, I am here." Alarm coursed through her.

Slowly, the colonel opened his eyes. The weariness present there frightened her, but Georgiana caught his hand in hers and squeezed, and, thankfully, he wrapped the tips of his fingers around hers. "Closer," he whispered.

Georgiana took a cloth from a nearby table and wet the corner and touched it to his lips. "I will take care of you." She wet the cloth again and wiped his face clean.

Edward gave her a crooked smile and tightened his hold, giving a little tug to pull her to him. A small grimace indicated the pain coursing through him, but determination outweighed everything else. "Georgie…come closer."

The girl surveyed his wounds before leaning across his chest. "What do you need? Just tell me, and it is yours. Anything, Edward."

"You, Georgie…I need you," he gasped out. Tears filled her eyes, and she did not even breathe. Her heart burst with happiness. "Tell me…it is…what…what you need, too."

"You came back to me," she whispered.

His grin grew, turning up the corners of his mouth. "Yes, Sweetest…I came for you." The colonel closed his eyes, consumed by the pain, but the smile did not fade.

Unaware of the physical chemistry stirring their hearts, Mrs. Reynolds rushed into the room and took Georgiana's shoulders and replaced the girl with her own body. "Let me have a look, Colonel," she said, all business. She gently removed the blood-soaked handkerchief to examine the wound. Finally taking note of the girl, she ordered, "Miss Darcy, you should not be here."

"I am staying," Georgiana declared, moving to the other side of the bed.

A raised eyebrow spoke volumes. Mrs. Reynolds took a closer look at how the girl she had helped to raise suddenly stared at her cousin with different eyes—the eyes not of a girl, but of a woman. "Then see about cleaning the colonel's wrist wound. It is likely that he has a fractured bone, so be careful. It will help Doctor Miller if we clean everything for him."

Timidly, Georgiana asked, "How long before the surgeon arrives?" She untied the knot her brother had tied earlier and began to gently wash the area.

"Not long now. Within the hour, I imagine." Mrs. Reynolds pressed another bandage to the chest wound. "This one is barely bleeding. It does not look too bad—appears the colonel's military regalia deflected the bullet. I do not think he has more than some fragments in the wound." She wrapped a cloth across Edward's shoulder. "I suppose I might count on you to tend your cousin's wounds?" she asked suspiciously.

"I would happily tend the colonel," Georgiana declared, coming to sit by the bed.

Mrs. Reynolds took a closer look at the girl's face, especially examining the clarity of her eyes. "Do not overdo it," the housekeeper warned. "You took quite a blow to your head only a bit ago."

"I will rest easier if I know my cousin is not in danger." Georgiana moved her chair closer, where she might touch him.

Mrs. Reynolds smiled faintly. "Then I will check on Redman again." She moved to take her leave. "I am placing Murray here in case either you or Colonel Fitzwilliam needs him. Make sure your patient does not move about."

"Yes, ma'am."

CHAPTER 23

~ ~ ~

STAFFORD AND WORTH scrambled toward where Lydia Wickham lay on the frozen ground before the stables. They bowed low to avoid detection. Worth squatted beside the enclosure, gun aimed at the stable door, using his left forearm to set his sight line and to steady the weapon. Stafford, on the other hand, scurried to the lady's side. He turned her over gently to determine her wounds. Seeing only one obvious injury, Stafford waited no more than two heartbeats before he scooped her to him and ran in the opposite direction.

Seeing the viscount's retreat, Worth backed carefully away, a bit shaken by the experience.

Stafford handed Lydia off to Lucas before saying to Worth, "We should stay close in case Darcy needs us." He cocked his gun and turned again toward the structure.

"I agree." Worth followed the viscount, but his nerves still showed.

"Hopefully, Darcy will sew things up soon." Stafford knelt along the fence line, where he might observe when the door opened but not be in an immediate line of fire. "Wickham cannot think to escape."

Worth knelt behind the viscount. "I do not believe Mr. Wickham capable of making such logical decisions. He will risk everything."

"Then Darcy will have to kill the man to free his wife?" Stafford took in Worth's inscrutable expression.

"I have no doubt of it."

"We have another one for you," Lucas called as he carried Lydia Wickham into the drawing room. Mrs. Reynolds followed the footman.

Cathleen scrambled up from the chaise upon which she sat to allow the man to place Mrs. Wickham down in her place. "Do you need help, Mrs. Reynolds?"

"I can always use an extra set of hands." The woman took a pair of scissors from her box and cut away part of Lydia's sleeve. "Let us examine the wound first, and then we will use some smelling salts to wake Mrs. Wickham. Why do you not step into the hallway and grab a few cloaks from the clothes tree. We need to warm her arms and legs so she does not suffer from the cold."

"Certainly." Cathleen hurried to do the woman's bidding. When she returned with three cloaks, she asked, "Do we know what is going on?" Cathleen adjusted the outerwear over Lydia's legs.

Mrs. Reynolds whispered softly, "Lucas says Lord Stafford and Mr. Worth rescued Mrs. Wickham from where her husband had left her. Reportedly, Mr. Wickham used his wife as protection against Colonel Fitzwilliam."

"And my cousin?" Cathleen folded a new bandage for the gunshot wound.

Mrs. Reynolds glanced quickly around the room to ensure privacy. "Lord Stafford and Mr. Worth stand guard before the stables. Mr. Darcy went in to rescue his wife, whom Mr. Wickham holds prisoner."

"Will Mr. Darcy prevail?"

"Yes, or die trying. The Master will safeguard Mrs. Darcy's life with his own."

"Let her go, Wickham." Darcy stood and stepped into the open. "It is I on whom you seek revenge."

"I do seek revenge on you, Darcy, but I am not that milquetoast George Wickham."

Confused by the man's words, Darcy's eyes locked on Elizabeth and saw that she spoke to him of the unknown—of a message she tried to relay. "I am afraid, sir, I do not know the rules of the game you play." Keeping his gun loosely by his side, Darcy infused his words with calmness as he edged forward—only inches, but forward just the same.

"'Tis no game," James Withey declared. "Ask your wife if you doubt my sincerity."

This, then, was what she wanted to tell him. Elizabeth's eyes revealed that her mind raced through a series of facts she needed to share. "Mrs. Darcy?" he spoke softly and edged still closer.

With the gun only inches from her head, Elizabeth should have been having a fit of the vapors; instead, she gave Darcy a mischievous grin before saying, "It is true, Fitzwilliam," she asserted. "This is Mr. Withey—James Withey. It is my understanding that you have met Mr. Withey previously."

Mystified, Darcy eyed Elizabeth. *Why does she agree with the man?* Darcy intuited that Elizabeth wanted to prove something to him. "I am at a loss, my Dear," he said in an intimate tone. "I do not believe I have made Mr. Withey's acquaintance previously."

Elizabeth arched one eyebrow, which said, *Listen to what I do not say in my words,* and Darcy allowed himself to relax into a serene alertness. "I am sure, my Husband, that you have simply forgotten your interactions with Mr. Withey because of your numerous responsibilities to Pemberley, and, in reality, it has been several years since you have seen each other."

"As you are an excellent example of reason and common sense, I suspect you are correct." Again, he surreptitiously moved another two inches closer to Wickham and to the gun the man held on Elizabeth.

"Might we cut through all the niceties?" Withey growled.

Elizabeth swallowed hard but controlled her countenance. Any sense of self-preservation disappeared with her need to warn

Darcy. "I shall speak forthrightly, my Husband. Unlike the affable Mr. Wickham, Mr. Withey prefers the reputation of a rakehell."

Her captor interrupted, "Tell him how he paid my gambling debts three times. Remind your husband how he took the punishment when I broke the balcony window playing cricket." Withey waved the gun about as he spoke, and Darcy considered the opening, but Elizabeth remained in danger, so he squelched his desire to strike.

With great effort, Darcy held his anger in check. "I apologize for my forgetfulness."

Elizabeth noted the beginning of understanding in Darcy, so she tried a brazen experiment. "Mr. Withey, might I ask to speak to the gentleman with the Scottish brogue whom I met earlier?"

"MacIves?" James Withey asked disdainfully.

She prayed she had not made a mistake. Darcy crept closer and closer, and Elizabeth needed to keep Withey occupied until her husband could act. "I do not believe I caught the gentleman's name," she offered.

With no more than a clenching of his jaw muscles, Withey became Gregor MacIves. Before Darcy's eyes, the man's bearing, his natural gait and movements, his gestures, and his vocal quality transformed. "Ye missed me, Lass?" The man caught Elizabeth about the waist and pulled her against his body.

Darcy's hands fisted at his side, but he maintained a strained control for Elizabeth's safety.

His wife eased herself out of the man's grasp. "Mr. MacIves." She purposely smiled at the man, "Might I introduce my husband, Mr. Darcy."

"I didnae realize ye had a mon, Lass." He brought the gun to point at Darcy. "I ken relieve ye of the burden; I will kill him for ye. Tis a mon's duty to protect his womon."

Elizabeth gasped when he made Darcy his target, but her husband appreciated the change in the situation. It kept her safe, and that was what mattered to him.

"No, I could not ask that of you," she insisted emphatically. A fresh chill of dread went through her as she watched Darcy stand tall, making himself a larger target. Before MacIves could follow through on his threat, Elizabeth asked, "Why do you not send Mr. Whittington to speak to us?" She had gambled before and made headway with Darcy's understanding, so she kept to her plan to show him what he faced. Darcy still looked a bit confused; yet, she knew she had piqued his curiosity. The sharp twist of his mouth said he had what he wanted: His enemy's attention had fallen on him. However, she wished Darcy to truly see the evil he fought.

MacIves pressed his lips together in a grim line. "Ye be 'nouncing His Young Lordship to ye husband, Lass?"

"It is what a lady does." She bestowed a polite smile on him.

As before, a change ensued; MacIves squeezed his eyes shut. When he opened them seconds later, he held himself in the stature of a young nobleman. The boy known as Peter Whittington looked down in surprise at Elizabeth. "Mrs. Darcy, you have need of me?"

"Yes, Mr. Whittington. I believe you are acquainted with my husband." She gestured toward Darcy.

Even though he maintained his stance, everything else about Wickham changed. No longer the rough Scottish lord of a previous century, the man standing before them was an immature aristocrat. "Of course. It has been some time since I have seen you, Darcy. Not since our first year at Eton."

Finally, what Elizabeth wanted him to know stood blaringly clear before him. Each of these "characters" was Wickham at a pivotal moment in the man's life. Darcy nodded his understanding, seeing how he might now get close enough to disarm his former friend. "Mr. Whittington, is it?" Darcy said, seemingly unruffled. "I nearly forgot that year was a complicated one for you. If I recall correctly, your father became quite livid regarding your responsibilities, often preferring the cane to emphasize his point. When your grades suffered, your father took it quite personally."

Whittington muttered, "Thank you for reminding me of my shortcomings, Darcy."

Darcy nodded. "You had some difficulty, as I recall, identifying your place. When word reached the school of my father's furnishing your education, many thought you his by-blow, rather than his godson."

"You turned from me that year," Whittington accused.

"My mother took ill…there were other forces of concern in my life."

Whittington recoiled with Darcy's words. "I was your friend," he insisted. "When you said nothing, they all believed the worst."

Darcy said with as much contrition as he could muster, "I was young and a bit jealous of your easiness, but I never meant for you to suffer."

Whittington bragged, "I did have an easier time with women."

Darcy made himself offer a compliment. "Women always took to you."

"All of them except my mother," Whittington snarled. "She thought me too much like my father." He looked off in sad remembrance, and Darcy moved again, but this time he silently told Elizabeth to do the same.

"Your father suffered much to please her."

"Women are the shallow sex."

Darcy eased closer. "Then it was you who punished Mrs. Wickham by destroying her room? She was too extravagant, I suppose? And what of the maid?"

Whittington puffed up with autocratic importance. "Mrs. Wickham is very much like my mother, Lady Whitlock, always insisting that her husband spend more than he has. My friend should have left the lady long ago, as my father should leave Her Ladyship."

"And Lucinda Dodd, the maid?" Darcy insisted.

Whittington frowned. "She would not let me leave. Those born to serve should never reprimand their betters."

Darcy watched as Elizabeth brushed a tear away. For himself, he made no comment. Instead, he called to mind what he knew of Wickham's childhood and of the man's years at school and university. "May I ask, Mr. Whittington, if MacIves is one of the Scottish relatives that you found when you sought proof of your ancestral connections?"

Peter Whittington became immediately angry. "You may trace your family to the Matlocks and the Attingboroughs and the D'Arcys and to the Saxon founders of this area, and all I could claim was a minor Scottish border lord who raided England for sheep and cattle and women to maintain his Highland keep. You have bloodlines dating back to the British nobility; my ancestors were nothing more than glorified thieves."

"No family tree grows perfectly straight," Darcy remarked dispassionately.

"Nay, we dinnae look so verra noble now, did we?" The Scot returned without their request and in the middle of the conversation, and for a moment, even Elizabeth appeared surprised, but she recovered quickly. "Yet I will not be shunned by a bloody prima donna lord. If'n he belies me family a'gin, he will receive whate'er I choose to mete out."

Elizabeth whispered softly, "Too many sins and too little patience."

"The borders, Lass, they be rough—it takes those who love the law and those who hate it to survive there—the clans, they know their own justice and their own loves—a hardened lot of murderers and thieves I call family."

Although the man continued to point the gun in Darcy's direction, he saw only Elizabeth, and as the Scot spoke, Darcy moved quickly to a point of advantage. Bringing his own weapon level with the man's chest, he ordered, "I will have your gun, Mr. Wickham."

A flutter of the man's eyes was all the warning they received; instantly, everything changed. The man, known as Gregor MacIves, swung his gun in Elizabeth's direction—and pulled the trigger.

"No!" Darcy leapt at the man, catching MacIves's arm and sending them both crashing to the packed dirt. Holding on with all his might, he pinned the Scot's wrist to the ground, wrenched the gun from the man, and tossed it to the side. Arms and legs flailing and twisting, they began a struggle for control—a dance of ignoble frenzy. A crushing fist to the jaw. A punch to the kidneys. A knee to the groin. Fingers opened—grappling—a barely contained fury spilling forth. A lifetime of trust betrayed—of volition violated—a voracious vortex of evil sucking them both in—taking their restraint.

Each loathed for what the other stood—the odious paranoia of allowing hate full reign—they fought relentlessly. Sweat slicked Darcy's face, but he battled on until MacIves pulled a dagger from his boot, and with one sweeping arc brought it down to pierce Darcy's back. For a split second, Darcy clung to his opponent's shoulders, and then he opened his hands and slid to his knees, a grimace of defeat flooding his face.

Triumphantly, the Scot stepped over the crouched master of Pemberley. Leaning down, he caught the knife's handle, giving it a hurried lift to do more damage, before withdrawing it from the wound. "I told the lass I would kill ye for her," he growled in Darcy's ear. "I be raising yer bairn as me own," he taunted. "We have played our game, Darcy, and I take the winning hand." And just like that, in a twinkling of the eye, James Withey returned.

James stepped away from Fitzwilliam Darcy's slumped-over form. Leaning against a wooden panel, he caught his breath while he watched with amusement as Elizabeth Darcy crawled on hands and knees toward her husband.

The sound of the gun exploding so close to her head sent Elizabeth diving for cover. Then the sting of the grazing wound caught her breath in her throat, and, for a moment, Elizabeth expected to open her eyes and see heaven; but the stream of blood running down her head said she lived. Behind her, a battle raged; bodies fell against each other as she tried to right herself and go to Darcy's aid. The blood—her blood—ran into her eye, and Elizabeth swiped at it with the sleeve of her gown—the blanket long gone. Fingers groping for a hold against the stall's wooden slats, Elizabeth caught the second rail and, with determination, pulled herself to her knees. Then she heard the gasp, and through streaks of sweat and blood, she saw the man she loved more than life crumble to the floor, a dagger thrust deep into his back.

"Fitzwilliam!" she exclaimed, needing to be by his side. Crawling across the hay-covered earth, she fought to reach him—fought to touch him.

Yet, as she made contact, a force compelled her backward. James Withey caught her hair, snapping her head around and forcing Elizabeth to her feet. "No," he hissed. "No one helps Darcy. We let him die."

Elizabeth battled the tears bubbling in her eyes as the red lines blurred her vision. "What do you want?" she demanded; her bottom lip trembled in panic. "You won! Just get out! Leave Pemberley!"

"Not without you," he declared, grabbing Elizabeth's arm and pulling her toward the door.

She contested his efforts with all her might, but when she turned her head to wipe the blood from her face against her sleeve, James used the momentary slack of her momentum to pull Elizabeth forward—catching her to his side and lifting her where he might carry her, skimming across the frozen ground. Frantically, she caught at everything to stop their progress, but nothing held, and then Elizabeth grabbed the broken handle of an ax and clasped it to her.

James pressed his shoulder to the stable door, sending it swinging open with a bang. Dragging Elizabeth toward the horses, he did not see her take a firm hold of the broken handle; but as he slowed, preparing to mount, he loosened his grip, and she spun away from him, arcing the stick upward, striking Withey firmly under the chin and dazing him long enough for her to turn toward the stable and Darcy.

Yet, the sound of a gun cocking behind her brought Elizabeth up short of the door. Anger's color ebbed with the realization. Somehow, James Withey had prevailed. She froze as her bloodied face took in his rictal grin.

When the stable door slammed open, Stafford and Worth expected Darcy to exit with his wife. Instead, the real-life Pemberley phantom carried a bloody Elizabeth Darcy toward the waiting horses.

"Hold for the clean shot," Stafford ordered as they both took aim at the abductor, but with his back to the horses, he offered no easy shot; and both men hesitated.

In amazement, they watched as Elizabeth executed an escape attempt that would knock a normal man unconscious, but left her captor only momentarily stunned before he took aim with a carefully concealed pocket pistol; and before they could react, James Withey took dominion of Darcy's wife again.

"Nice try, Mrs. Darcy," he mocked as he pulled her into his body, Elizabeth's back tight against his chest. "Before I set you free, you will pay for such impudence." He purposely cupped her breast in intimidation and squeezed it possessively.

Elizabeth clenched her fists at her sides, but she did not fight him. Her thoughts remained on Darcy. If she left with Withey, the others could help her husband. That was her mission: saving Darcy's life. "I will not fight you," she declared.

"Order Darcy's friends away." Withey pulled her closer to him, expecting Stafford and Worth to attack.

Elizabeth nodded her agreement. Taking a deep breath, she called out, "Lord Stafford, please take Mr. Worth and move away. Mr. Withey has a gun to my head and will not hesitate to shoot."

"Tell them to put their weapons down," he ordered softly.

"Please lay down your guns," she added.

Worth and Lawrence assessed the situation. "Where is Darcy?" Stafford asked as he bent to place his gun in a nearby snowdrift.

Elizabeth could not suppress the sobs waiting to escape. "Help him!" she managed to say before James pushed her toward Pandora.

Nigel Worth followed Stafford's example and lowered his gun. "She does this for her husband," he whispered to the viscount.

Withey gave her a leg up as Elizabeth rucked up her skirts to sit astride Pandora's back. "Do not try anything adventurous, Mrs. Darcy," he warned as he mounted Darcy's favorite stallion.

Elizabeth, needing to maneuver Withey away from Pemberley so the others could tend to Darcy's wounds, nodded her affirmation. Misery scraped at the back of her throat as she accepted her fate.

"Stand back!" Withey ordered as he kicked Demon's flanks and took up the leading line on Pandora's harness. Without further ado, he led Elizabeth toward the forest road.

Stafford and Worth stared in admiration as the blood-encrusted face of Elizabeth Darcy passed them. Sitting on Pandora's back, she shot a pleading look and a nod of her head toward the open stable door. Withey kept her horse abreast of his and the gun pointed directly at her, but she told them what to do without words. As soon as she and her captor passed them, Stafford and Worth ran to the stable. They hit the door and skidded to a stop when they found a bloody Fitzwilliam Darcy trying to open a nearby stall.

"Darcy?" Stafford caught him under the arm and lifted his friend, supporting Darcy's sagging weight. "Let me get you into the house."

"No!" Darcy gritted his teeth. "Saddle the horse." Pain sheared through him.

"You cannot—" Worth began, A contemptuous glare from Darcy stopped him midsentence.

Barely moving his lips, Darcy summarized the situation. "Elizabeth is my wife."

Stafford nodded his agreement. "Saddle the horse, Worth. Let me see what I can do for Darcy."

The solicitor agreed reluctantly, but he did what the viscount said. Meanwhile, Stafford wrestled Darcy free of his jacket. "Wickham may have hit a lung," Stafford whispered as he used rags he found in a nearby bucket to bind Darcy's wound.

"And he may not have," Darcy observed.

Lawrence leaned closer. "Mrs. Darcy struck Wickham with a blow that would have brought another man to his knees, but it barely stunned him. You cannot fight him, Darcy. You must kill him—without reservation—if you expect to stop him. If he gets a chance, he will rape your wife. He touched Mrs. Darcy quite inappropriately as a show of power."

"He seeks revenge." Darcy exhaled the words.

"I will follow you," Stafford asserted. "I will finish it if you cannot."

"Thank you, Stafford."

Within five minutes, Darcy sat upon Vulcan's back. It took all his determination to simply pull himself into the saddle. Stafford placed a horse blanket about Darcy's shoulders—neither of them considering his return to the tight-fitting jacket. "I will bring your coat for Mrs. Darcy," he said as he handed Darcy a gun. "Be careful, my friend."

With a nod of his head, Darcy kicked Vulcan's sides and sent the gelding in an easy gallop toward the forest road.

"They will follow," Elizabeth said quietly as they turned toward the road leading to Kympton. The horses suffered with the frozen tundra and with having stood outside in the cold so long, but Withey took no note of the conditions. He simply pressed Demon a bit harder. After that, they rode in silence for nearly a half hour, keeping to the more treacherous back roads.

Elizabeth shivered from the cold and from the panic gripping her heart. She worried for Darcy and for the colonel and for Lydia. Her family lay dead or dying, and she rode away with the man who had brought devastation to her home. "I cannot go on," she said from the depths of her resolve. "I will let you take me no farther, Mr. Withey."

"What will you do, Mrs. Darcy?" James Withey snarled. "Will you have me shoot you? Right here? Right now?"

Elizabeth did not look at him, but she answered just the same. "If that is my only choice."

Her captor ignored her verbal challenge; instead, Withey turned the horses toward a nearby church. "Let us see what God has to offer us today. Maybe something left over from the collection plate."

He slid from Demon's back and reached up to help Elizabeth from the saddle. She let her eyes fall on the small whitewashed building, and an errant thought struck her.

"Mr. Withey, might I speak to Mr. Wickham?"

"Why?" Her request shocked him. "Why him and why now?"

"I wish to speak to Mr. Wickham," she insisted.

He held her gaze for a heartbeat before a squeeze of his eyes brought the man she knew. "Miss Elizabeth, may I help you dismount?"

"Yes, Mr. Wickham, but it is Mrs. Darcy now. Remember." She gently placed her hands on his shoulders and allowed him to lift her. "We are brother and sister," she added quietly.

"So we are," he noted as he placed her hand on his arm to lead Elizabeth toward the building. "Mr. Withey was most displeased with your asking for me," he noted as they walked along.

"I had not seen you since you left for Newcastle. Of course, I was curious." When they reached the church steps, Elizabeth purposely smiled at him, trying to continue her part in this charade. "Look where we are, Mr. Wickham." She gestured with her free hand to the church steps upon which they stood. "It is the sanctuary at Kympton, the one you so coveted for years."

Wickham looked around with an assessing eye. "It is, at that, Mrs. Darcy. It is a shame your husband denied me the living once promised by his father."

Elizabeth forced evenness into her voice despite the fact that she stood in a frozen landscape, wearing a simple day dress, with blood caked about her eyes and in her hair and spoke to a madman. "It must be Providence which has brought us here today, Mr. Wickham. I am sure Mr. Darcy said the living was to come available in the late spring. Perhaps something could still be secured. Mr. Darcy will do anything to keep my regard."

"The man is not likely to change his mind, Miss Elizabeth."

She did not correct him this time. Instead, Elizabeth looked steadily at the church. "It is rather inviting. Might we take a look inside? I find it quite cold here in the open."

"Of course. How callous of me." Wickham reached for the door and opened it for her. "After you."

Darcy knew he could be no more than ten minutes behind Wickham and Elizabeth. He slumped over Vulcan's neck, clinging to the animal, making himself stay in the saddle—to find Elizabeth before Wickham violated her as revenge for past sins. He had witnessed the lunacy for himself and knew he had no choice, but it grieved him to have things come to this. Although he inherently knew he was not to blame for George Wickham's descent into hell, part of him wondered what he might have done differently. When he had first taken the blame for Mr. Wickham's transgressions, Darcy had done so out of friendship. Later, he had done it to protect the Pemberley name from scandal. Now, he realized that all he had managed to do was to give Wickham permission to continue his wayward ways—to reinforce all the wrongs the man perpetrated.

Then, as the late afternoon light began to fade, he, finally, saw them. Demon and Pandora stood before the Kympton village church. Somehow, Fate, probably with a bit of Elizabeth's manipulations, had brought them all to this place at this time. Planning his attack as he approached, Darcy rode to the cemetery beside the church. He painfully slid from the saddle. Using Vulcan as a brace, Darcy pulled himself to stand straight. He took the gun from his waistband, cocked it, and started for the church's side door.

"It is a most delightful place! Excellent parsonage house!" Wickham stared out the window. "It would have suited me in every respect."

"How should you have liked making sermons?" Elizabeth asked, trying to keep him talking. She had decided if she could get away and hide long enough to make it to the nearby village, then she just possibly might find help for herself and her husband.

"Exceedingly well." He turned back to face her. "I should have considered it as part of my duty, and the exertions would soon have been nothing. One ought not to repine; but, to be sure, it would have been such a thing for me! The quiet, the retirement of such a life would have answered all my ideas of happiness. But it was not to be."

While he spoke dreamily, Elizabeth slowly edged toward the side door of the church. "I have heard from authority that the living was left you conditionally only, and at the will of the present patron—at my husband's will." Elizabeth realized she provoked him, but it was a calculated risk. She leaned away from him; breathing heavily, the weight of her dilemma dawned fully. For the sake of the distraction, she needed to keep Wickham talking.

"You have? Yes, there was something in that; I told you so from the first, you may remember." Having been caught in the lie he so often repeated, Wickham became more agitated, pacing the length of the vestibule.

Elizabeth eased closer to her goal. She prayed that, as with the front door, the side one would be unlocked. "I did hear, too, that there was a time when sermon-making was not so palatable to you as it seems to be at present; that you actually declared your resolution of never taking orders, and that the business had been compromised accordingly—and that Mr. Darcy provided you with three thousand pounds as compensation."

Wickham's eyes flickered, and she saw James Withey for a split second, but Wickham remained in control. "You did? And it was not wholly without foundation. You may remember what I told you on that point when first we talked."

Elizabeth cautiously reached behind her and felt for the door handle. Finding it, she breathed easier. It was now or never. "Come, Mr. Wickham, we are brother and sister, you know. Do not let us quarrel about the past. In the future, I hope we shall always be of one mind." She saw the flicker again, and James Withey's rage take over.

His mouth twisted in contempt. "You had to mention that bitch and the marriage!" He stormed across the church at her, knocking over benches set for the parishioners, but Elizabeth did not wait to hear the end of his rant. She ran through the opened door to the cemetery—from a living nightmare—and into the waiting arms of her husband.

Withey stormed across the church trying to reach the woman. Wickham had not been aware of Elizabeth Darcy's scheming mind, and now James would have to find her and silence her before she sent up a general alarm in the neighborhood. "Damn!" He raced after her, out the church's side door, but a specter he had thought he left behind stood solidly among the tombstones, and James found himself on the short end of a gun.

"Step behind me, Elizabeth." Darcy moved her to relative safety as he kept his gaze on their interloper. She stilled against him, terror tightening her fingers on his arm.

"I thought you dead," Withey snarled.

A sarcastic smile graced Darcy's face. "As usual, you were in error."

"Well, Darcy, we are at an impasse. Our battle is to end this day, with only one claiming victory." Falsely, James took a small step backward. "It is my belief that you are too honorable to kill a man in cold blood, and you are in too much pain to come for me," he added brashly. With that, James dived through the open doorway, gunfire chasing him into the dusky shadows.

The gunshot surprised her, but Elizabeth did not scream. Instead, she prayed that Darcy had not killed Wickham. The man was correct; it would haunt her husband terribly, so despite what he had put them through, she wished Wickham to live. The sound of the front door banging open told her that God had answered that prayer.

"Help me," Darcy ordered as he lurched toward the noise.

She clung to her husband. "Let him go, Fitzwilliam," she begged. "I will not have you labeled a murderer."

Darcy pulled up. Looking down at her bruised and bloody face, he said, "He did this to you." He reached to caress her cheek.

"And to you." She braced his shoulder with her hands. "Let this be the worst of it."

The sound of hoof beats said Withey had made his escape, and for a moment, they thought it finished, but suddenly Demon bore down on them; and James Withey wielded a sword, slicing the frozen air.

Darcy pulled Elizabeth behind a burial crypt at the last second, but Withey circled the horse and came at them again. Everything moved in shadows: the crazed face of George Wickham yelling a curse filled with years of hate and a proud and a principled Fitzwilliam Darcy standing tall to rebuke the attack. And then Darcy reacted by instinct: He whistled to the horse—his horse—to Demon, and the stallion reared up, pawing the air with violent strikes.

James Withey barely held the reins as he charged Darcy for the second time, concentrating purely on making contact with his enemy, so when Darcy emitted a shrill whistle, at first he did not understand the man's intentions; but then the horse rose on its back legs to defend itself from an unknown attack, and James felt himself sliding from the saddle. And then a grim silence.

"My God, Fitzwilliam!" Elizabeth rushed around her husband as he calmed his favorite horse. George Wickham lay, arms and legs akimbo, on a nearby grave, his head split open and a grayish blood seeping into the frozen ground. "He hit the tombstone," she whispered to the stillness, as she reached out tentatively to touch her sister's husband. However, the man no longer moved.

Darcy stood beside her. Lifting her gently to her feet, he pulled Elizabeth against his chest, allowing his wife's grief to begin. "It is over, Sweetheart." He held her to him. "Mr. Wickham can hurt us no more."

The sound of fresh horses brought his head up, but only Stafford and Worth appeared. In silence, both men dismounted and joined them in the cemetery's middle. Surrounded by marble and wood, dismay at what they had all suffered permeated the winter's quiet. With a nod of his head, Darcy indicated for them to check the body. Worth did the honors while Stafford entered the church to set things aright. No one spoke. They had been through so much together in the past week that none of them needed words to know what to do.

"Are we taking Wickham back to Pemberley?" Stafford said at last.

Darcy still held Elizabeth in his embrace. "It is what Mrs. Darcy would want for her sister."

Worth brought Vulcan alongside of the grave, so he and Stafford could load the body across the saddle. "Did you notice the epitaph?" the solicitor asked as they clumsily lifted Wickham to the horse. "'Tis fate that flings the dice, and as she flings, of kings makes peasants, and of peasants kings."

"Wickham proved the folly of keeping bad company." Stafford shot a quick glance at the Darcys. "As Ovid said, 'The vulgar estimate friends by the advantage to be derived from them.'"

"Can you ride, Darcy?" Worth asked as he brought Demon forward.

Darcy bent his head to speak to Elizabeth. "May I take you up with me, my Dear?"

Elizabeth raised her head to look at him carefully. "Will it not hurt you?"

"It will hurt me more to have you out of the safety of my arms."

Stafford suggested, "We should leave before the village comes to see what is going on. We are lucky no one seems to be home at the parsonage. I think we will need to construct a new truth out of this."

"I suspect you are correct, Your Lordship. Now, if you and Worth will give me a leg up, we will take the back roads to Pemberley."

"As you wish, Darcy."

When Elizabeth had settled herself across Darcy's lap, Stafford handed up his coat. "This may smell a bit better than the blanket your husband wears, Mrs. Darcy."

"Thank you, Lord Stafford, but I find the odor of horse flesh quite alluring." She turned into Darcy's warmth as he draped the coat around her.

Stafford chuckled. "If I ever find a woman with your mettle, Mrs. Darcy, I will be on one knee in a heartbeat."

"I shall happily celebrate that day, Your Lordship."

EPILOGUE

~ ~ ~

TWO DAYS LATER, THE Pemberley family and trusted guests sat together in the same blue drawing room they had shared for the preceding fortnight. Of the havoc George Wickham had wreaked, Lydia suffered the most serious injuries—the bullet from the colonel's gun going completely through her left shoulder, leaving a gaping wound in her back. However, in Elizabeth's opinion, Lydia's most difficult injury to heal would be her sister's emotional state. Months of dealing with Wickham's mental decline had left Lydia vulnerable.

Georgiana needed only a few well-placed stitches. Mrs. Reynolds's diagnosis of Colonel Fitzwilliam proved correct. Doctor Miller removed the fragments of the bullet and of one of the colonel's many medals and casted the colonel's broken wrist. Elizabeth suffered only a grazing wound close to her temple, while Darcy had some muscle damage across his shoulder blade and along his spine. An elaborate bandage crisscrossed his back and chest, restricting his movement, which totally frustrated a man known to take pride in the actual running of his estate.

"Sir Phillip returns today?" Worth asked as he sipped a cup of tea.

Darcy replied, "The baronet will take Mrs. Harwood to Derby first, but he and I have decided to send her to a *friend* in Antigua with the stipulation that the lady never returns to England. There is a facility nearby, where she will be expected to serve her sentence helping some of the island's many orphans."

Worth's contempt for the idea showed. "For the heinous crime she committed, it is more than the lady deserves."

"We have been through this several times, Worth," Edward warded off the solicitor's objections. "It is the only way we can reduce the scandal."

"I understand," Worth grumbled, "but I do not have to like it."

Elizabeth reached out and patted Worth's arm. "We appreciate your and Miss de Bourgh's approval of this plan. We comprehend the depth of your disdain for this alternative, but we need to protect Mrs. Wickham."

"Of course, Mrs. Darcy. I did not mean to criticize. Miss de Bourgh simply loved her long-time companion dearly."

"As I love my sister," Elizabeth said quietly.

Worth verbalized no further objections on the subject. Everyone assumed he would soon declare himself for Anne de Bourgh, and when she accepted him, he would become head of that branch of the family. His counsel had become valuable to them as they decided how to handle the outrage associated with Wickham's intrusion.

"It still galls me that Mr. Steventon knew of the passages and never disclosed the information to me, especially as we searched for an unknown intruder," Darcy grumbled.

Edward inquired, "What did the man say when you questioned him on it?"

"He thought me to be aware of the ruins. Said because Mr. Wickham's father served my own for so long that he assumed me familiar with the layout. It seems my great-great grandfather saw a need for escape if the estate was attacked. In the 1600s, it would make sense. I must take the blame, I suppose, for not familiarizing myself with the house's history. I thought I knew it, however."

"Wickham must have known of the passageways because of his father?" Stafford thought aloud.

"One can only guess." Darcy still showed signs of irritation. "His secrets died with him."

"And what of your sister, Elizabeth?" Edward changed the subject. He sat beside Georgiana on a nearby settee—their fingers barely touching on the cushion between them.

Elizabeth watched with some amusement as Darcy eyed his cousin's forwardness and his sister's acceptance. It had taken her several hours the previous evening after Edward presented himself to Darcy to even consider a union of the two.

"Georgiana is not ready," he insisted.

Elizabeth laughed softly. "Of course, our sister is ready. Women are born ready to marry."

"You were not," he accused.

Elizabeth snuggled into his right side. "I was born to marry the most honorable man to grace this earth. It was not my fault he came to me disguised as a pompous prig." She stroked along his chin line as she spoke.

Darcy chuckled. "He was testing you, my Dear." He lightly kissed her fingers. "Trying to see if you would recognize Love when it called upon you."

"I was quite blind to what he offered, and I regret the time we wasted coming to an understanding." She turned his palm over and kissed it.

"Do you really believe this is what Georgiana wishes?"

Elizabeth kissed his cheek. "Your sister has spoken of no one else for months. Have you not seen it? Have you not heard it? At Christmas, Georgiana bought Edward a gold-tipped walking stick with his initials engraved on the handle—quite a personal and expensive gift for a man she sees only every couple of months. Besides, would you wish someone less respectable for Georgiana?"

"I would wish her a Season in London as my parents planned."

Elizabeth sat up straight, where she might meet his eyes. "I love Georgiana, but a Season would be a daunting experience for her. She is too unassuming, and despite her handsome appearance and her generous dowry, can you honestly believe that Georgiana could find a more suitable match in disposition? Edward would protect her and love her. It that not what you wish for our sister?"

"He is nearly fourteen years her senior," he objected.

"You are eight years older than I."

He sighed in exasperation. "What shall I tell them?"

Elizabeth knew Darcy would put Georgiana's happiness above his own misgivings. "I suggest a compromise of sorts. Accept an understanding between our sister and Edward, but deny them an official announcement until her next birthday, at the end of the summer. In the meantime, we expose Georgiana to other young people in the neighborhood to see if any other young men pique her interest. If not, then you will know her constancy and can accept their union with a glad heart."

"How did you become so wise?"

"Remember...I married that honorable man. I have learned empathy and compassion from him." She settled back into his embrace.

Darcy closed his eyes and thought of the exquisite happiness he held and how he had come so close to losing her. "And you have taught me about loving completely. Compared with you, I am a mere novice."

Darcy's voice brought Elizabeth from her musings. "There is no way to hide Mr. Wickham's attacks on this house, for too many people have knowledge of it. Yet, Sir Phillip has graciously allowed the Darcy family to put its own *twist* on the events. As the baronet said, it would serve no purpose to ruin the good names of everyone involved. So, for the record, Mr. Wickham invaded my home with the purpose of ridding himself of his wife. There is truth in the tale. Besides finding the letter I wrote to Mr. Laurie regarding Harwood and Wickham, we discovered a journal of sorts in the antechamber, which was kept by the one known as Peter Whittington." Darcy still could not reconcile how one man could actually be four. "It chronicles his attack on Lucinda Dodd, Gregor MacIves's fight with Lieutenant Harwood, and James Withey's discovery by young Lawson. It also describes in some detail George Wickham's contempt for Mrs. Wickham's spending habits, his growing gambling debts, their lack of financial soundness, and his plan to free himself of his wife and blame it on Pemberley. It appears that Mr. Wickham used the letter to imitate my handwriting—planned to use the forgery somehow to better his scheme."

"We have not discussed Mr. Wickham's treachery with my sister," Elizabeth barely whispered. "It will break Lyddie's heart when she knows the truth."

Darcy squeezed her hand, telling Elizabeth they would see this through together. "I have written to Mr. Bennet," he continued the tale. "I have told him the truth, but have asked him to conceal it from the rest of the family. He will propose a trip to Pemberley under the guise of celebrating Elizabeth's upcoming confinement. When the Bennets arrive, we will explain the events to everyone. Mrs. Wickham will benefit from her mother's ministrations, and it will allow the news to trickle into Meryton and not be bemoaned loudly by Mrs. Bennet's *nervous* nature. As Mr. Wickham has a less-than-stellar reputation among Meryton's residents, few in Hertfordshire will find our explanation lacking. In fact, many will expect some such perfidy. I have no fear of the locals learning of the whole truth by their usual methods of Mr. and Mrs. Collins and the Lucases. Lady Catherine will repeat what I tell her because Anne's reputation is intrinsically entangled in Wickham's story."

"How do we explain Harwood?" Worth asked. "Can we leave Miss de Bourgh's ruination out of the story?"

Darcy recognized the man's concern: Worth would make Anne his wife, and a man protects his family. "It will be quite an exaggeration, but we shall say that both Lawson and Lucinda discovered Wickham disguised in the Pemberley livery, and he killed them so that he would not be found out. Unfortunately, with Harwood, a complete prevarication will be necessary. We have stated that, as a friend of my cousin, Harwood saw Anne and Mrs. Jenkinson to Pemberley when he realized that the storm delayed Mr. Worth. Like the others, Harwood discovered Wickham in the house, and he lost his life defending our home against an unknown intruder."

"You are making the man into a glorified hero!" Stafford remarked.

"It was part of our agreement with the lieutenant's wife. Mrs. Harwood will go to the West Indies if her husband's name is not defamed by his involvement in this matter. Plus, it will save Anne's reputation, making my aunt more willing to repeat our version of the truth."

"Mr. Darcy has made arrangements to send Lydia to his cousin Wilhelmina outside Edinburgh to spend her time in mourning. It is very kind of Fitzwilliam to shield Lydia from the brouhaha surrounding her husband's duplicity." Elizabeth looked lovingly at Darcy. Despite being in company, she caressed his cheek.

Darcy continued, "I have sent for my friend Charles Bingley. He and Mrs. Bingley can accompany Mrs. Wickham north. I hate to ask them to travel in winter, but I will not hear of Elizabeth journeying so far in her condition."

"As Mr. Bingley is one of the most amiable men I know, I doubt he will refuse your request, Fitzwilliam," Georgiana offered.

"And my sister Jane can attend to Lydia upon the journey," Elizabeth added. "If Lydia is far away from the gossipmongers, she can return to England a grieving widow of a man who did not deserve her. Maybe if we are fortunate, Lydia will become more aware of her obligations to her family."

Darcy thought Elizabeth wished for the world. In reality, he hoped his wife's youngest sister would choose to stay in Scotland and would find herself a man to keep her in line and out of his sight for a very long time. "I have to ask, Stafford, if we can count on Miss Donnel to keep our confidences?" Darcy hated to broach the subject, but as the lady prepared to leave Pemberley the next day, he needed to know. Miss Donnel had no vested interest in the situation. Neither did Stafford, for that matter, but he had proved himself a true friend.

Cathleen's leaving still bothered Adam profoundly, although he fundamentally knew that she was not the woman for him. With the Darcys, he had observed perfection in a marriage, and he did not think he could settle for simply a physical attraction. He desired Cathleen, but they had little in common beyond that: She did not challenge him intellectually, nor did she demand that he be a better person. Cathleen accepted his foibles, and that was not what he required in a wife. He needed a woman more in Mrs. Darcy's mode—a woman who would, through determination and her own independence, make their dreams come true. "Miss Donnel is very discreet. Not a word of this will escape her lips." He turned to Worth. "I have asked Nigel to squire Cathleen to her uncle's home and to oversee her welfare for the next couple of months—until she is settled."

"We will leave tomorrow after Mrs. Jenkinson's service. Mr. Darcy has graciously offered us the use of his small coach and a competent driver. I cannot neglect my practice any longer, and I have other legal matters I need to address." They all assumed Worth meant his own fortune. Having it defined exactly would make his request of Lady Catherine for Anne's hand more likely to be received positively by Her Ladyship.

Edward stood to end the conversation. "I, too, must return home and offer my parents an explanation of what has happened here. It might be best, Darcy, if I see Her Ladyship and Anne to Matlock while the Bennets are at Pemberley. It will give Lady Catherine time to *perfect* her story before she returns to Kent and the very nosy Mr. Collins."

"Send word if Anne wishes to spend the spring at Pemberley, and I shall have one of my maids travel with her," Darcy said.

"I am sure the earl can manage a carriage and a chaperone when my cousin is ready to return." Edward straightened his jacket. "Would you care to spend a few days with us, Lord Stafford? I imagine my brother Charles would enjoy your company."

Stafford laughed lightly. "And I can corroborate your story."

"Exactly." Edward bowed to the room. "Georgiana, might you join me in the music room. It has been too long since I have heard you play." He reached out his hand to her.

Darcy winced when his sister placed her hand in his, but he said nothing, silently accepting what he could not change.

"I have matters to settle with Cathleen." Stafford no longer concealed their relationship.

Elizabeth nodded her understanding. "It has been an honor to have Miss Donnel among us, Your Lordship. You will tell her so for me."

"Cathleen will be pleased to hear it. Now, if you will excuse me, Mrs. Darcy." He stood and offered a bow. "I will see you at supper."

Nigel Worth followed suit. "I suppose that is my cue as well. I wish to spend some time with Miss de Bourgh. She is upset with the prospect of saying her farewells to Mrs. Jenkinson on the morrow."

Darcy accepted Worth's excuse with graciousness. "Of course, Worth."

Within moments, only he and Elizabeth remained in the room. A long sigh escaped as soon as the silence hit them. "We survived," he said softly.

"More than survived, my Husband. We prevailed." Elizabeth placed her head on his shoulder and rested against his warmth. "Fitzwilliam," she whispered. "I am so sorry to have brought such devastation to Pemberley. If you wish me to leave with my parents, I will understand."

Darcy placed his good arm about her shoulder. "Elizabeth, if you ever leave me, I would finance an army and come after you."

She smiled secretly. "You would have no need of an army, Fitzwilliam. Simply tell me I am forgiven."

"You have no need of my absolution, my Dear. It was my association with Mr. Wickham which provoked his descent. And it was my interference which aligned your family with him. *I* should seek *your* forgiveness."

"Then we are bound to each other by necessity," she teased.

"By love," he corrected. Darcy lifted her chin with his fingertips and kissed her intimately.

Elizabeth turned into his embrace, losing herself in his kiss. She lingered only inches from his lips. "And Doctor Miller said what about your recovery?" she murmured breathily.

"Not a word about that." He smiled. "Of course, I did not specifically ask." His own voice took on husky overtones. "Miller might have forbidden us, and I would not have it."

"Should we retire to our rooms for a rest?" Elizabeth boldly offered.

Darcy kissed the tip of her upturned nose. "I can think of nothing I need more."

They rose together and headed for the main staircase, arms shamelessly wrapped around each other's waists.

"Fitzwilliam," she asked as they climbed the steps together, "would you mind if I asked Kitty to stay with us when my parents return to Hertfordshire? I find I miss my family dearly, and Jane and I agree that in society superior to what she has generally known we can assure Kitty's improvement. She is not of so ungovernable a temper as Lydia, and with proper attention and management, Kitty might thrive. I could use her help during my confinement, and she might be company for Georgiana's forays into local society."

"All are legitimate reasons for bringing your sister to stay with us," he teased, "but would you like to tell me what other contrivances you have in mind? I really despise being omitted from your machinations."

"Fitzwilliam Darcy," she tried to sound offended, but Elizabeth's mischievous smile spoke volumes. "You judge me harshly, sir."

A feigned look of chastisement crossed his face. "Do I now?"

She paused on the steps, trying to look in his eyes without bursting into laughter, but her control suffered when he waggled his eyebrows in a purposeful tease. "Oh, you win." Elizabeth sighed in exasperation. "I noted how you sent the new vicar at Kympton a generous, although anonymous, donation to cover the recent damages to his church." She caught his arm to continue their climb. "And I was thinking that Mr. Spencer is a promising member of the Pemberley family and——."

"And Mr. Spencer is unmarried." Darcy finished the sentence for her.

Elizabeth presented him with a brilliant smile. "And Mr. Spencer is unmarried. Do you not think Kitty might suit him?"

Darcy laughed—a deep baritone rumbling. "We will introduce your sister to Mr. Spencer and see what happens, but we will put no pressure on the man. I would not wish for him to think his wooing your sister was part of the agreement resulting in the living I recently bestowed upon the man."

"Of course not." Elizabeth opened the door and pulled on Darcy's hand to follow. "I would never put Mr. Spencer or Kitty in such a position."

"Mrs. Darcy," he let her lead him to the bed, "I would place a bet at White's that you have already planned your sister's wedding right down to the dress and flowers."

Elizabeth began to unbutton Darcy's jacket and waistcoat. "You know me too well, my Husband." She giggled as she released the knot of his cravat. "In fact, I planned everyone's wedding but my own."

"Yet, yours was the most important, my Love."

She slipped her fingers under his shirt and stroked his chest. "It was, for it gave me pure happiness. I am truly the happiest creature in the world." She went on tiptoes to kiss him enticingly. "Perhaps other people have said so before, but not one with such justice. I am happier even than Jane; she only smiles. I laugh."

Within moments they were in the throes of intimacy, wrapped in the pleasures of love. "Will they?" Elizabeth asked as she settled in his arms. "Will people believe our version of what happened at Pemberley?"

Darcy adjusted his arm around her, trying not to make any move that would tear open the stitches across his back. "I hope any doubts others might have will go away in time," he said, trying to sound confident.

"And if they do not? What if the rumors linger?"

"Then I suppose we will go down in local lore: Bungay has its Black Shuck; Cornwall, the Well of St. Keyne; Somerset, the Witch of Wookey; and Cheshire, The Red Rider of Bramhall Hall. We will be known for the house populated by shadow people—the home of the Phantom of Pemberley."

Author's Note

~ ~ ~

WHAT THE MAJORITY OF the world once called "multiple personalities" is now known as Dissociative Identity Disorder (DID), a complicated and sometimes difficult to diagnose psychological illness. The second half of the 20th century saw public attention cast upon the disease through books and movies: *The Three Faces of Eve* and *Sybil*. But, in reality, DID has been documented for over 200 years. The American Psychiatric Association in *The Diagnostic and Statistical Manual of Mental Disorders* (or DSM-III, 1980) defines multiple personality disorder as "the existence within the individual of two or more distinct personalities, each of which is dominant at a particular time. The personality that is dominant at any particular time determines the individual's behaviors. Each individual personality is complex and integrated with its own unique behavior patterns and social relationships."

Case studies vary greatly. Some DID patients possess personalities of a different sex, race, or age. One might find the "multiple" speaking in a different accent or language, writing with a different hand, or possessing different mannerisms and ways of walking. There is the "host" identity, the one who generally seeks help for the problem, and then there are the personalities, which have specific and limited roles depending on the individual's past experiences. Most experts believe the severity and the chronic effects of the trauma the person experienced determines how many personalities appear. Also, the individual's age and degree of vulnerability at the time of the trauma show in the "alter egos" created. It is assumed by many in the field that there are five basic alters: the host who denies the existence of the other personalities; the defenseless child; the one who blames everyone else for the pain he has suffered; the strong, angry defender; and the amicable, pleasant personality. However, there can be infinite variations of these "characters."

Besides defining these types, medical experts agree that how the personalities function falls in the realm of certain behavior patterns: those which express painful emotions, those which desire skills they lack, and those with "unspoken" sexual needs. Sometimes, the personality makes only a single appearance, and sometimes he/she can be the dominant force, taking over the individual's consciousness. Generally, the "alters" are not aware of one another, but it is not uncommon for the multiples to possess a co-consciousness—an acquaintance, of sorts. In such cases, the personalities are integrated and fused into a single being.

Evidence of multiple personalities has a long history. Cases of demonic possessions and shaman images can more easily be explained if one considers the possibility of multiple personalities as a reality. In the early 1500s, Paracelsus (Auroleus Phillipus Theostratus Bombastus von Hoheheim), a Renaissance physician, alchemist, and botanist, documented an account of a woman whose "alter" stole her money. However, in the 18th century, DID, as a mental condition, was recorded in more detailed accounts. In 1791, Eberhardt Gmeline wrote of a twenty-year-old woman in Stuttgart, Germany, who became a French aristocrat as her alter. As the "French woman," the girl spoke perfect French and remembered everything the "German woman" said or did. However, as the "German," the girl remembered nothing of her "French" personality.

Benjamin Rush, who is considered the "Father of American Psychiatry," documented many early cases. Incidentally, Rush, the chief surgeon of the Continental Army, was the only man to sign both the Declaration of Independence and the United States Constitution. Rush believed there was a disconnect between the two hemispheres of the brain, causing the "doubles."

The most influential of the cases of the time period of this book is that of Mary Reynolds. Dr. Samuel Latham Mitchel first published his findings on Mary's case in *Medical Repository* in 1816. Reynolds is believed to be the first person officially diagnosed (1810) with multiple personalities. Mitchel took much of his information for the case from Mary and her relatives, the Reverend Dr. John V. Reynolds and his brother William Reynolds.

Born in England in 1785, Mary moved to Meadville, Pennsylvania, when she was four years of age. Reportedly, she came from a strongly religious family, and she was often described as melancholy and shy. No incidents occurred until Mary turned nineteen. Then, for six weeks, she became deaf and blind. Three months later, she awoke from an extended overnight sleep (some eighteen to twenty hours) to know nothing of her surroundings or her previous life. However, within a few weeks, she could again read, do calculations, and write, although it was said that her penmanship had changed dramatically. This "new Mary" was described as "boisterous" and "fond of company," as well as being a "nature lover." After five weeks of this alter, she took another long sleep, awakening to her former self and possessing no knowledge of the person she had been. This altering back and forth between the melancholy Mary and the mirthful Mary continued until Reynolds was in her mid thirties. Then, the alterations stopped, and Reynolds became the "alter" personality until her death at age sixty-one.

DID is sometimes referred to as "a child's post-traumatic stress syndrome." Severe discipline, sexual abuse, or traumatic confrontations with death or the unexplained can manifest itself into individuals who retreat into an "alter personality," one who can either absorb or deal with the trauma.

Hopefully, with better screening and diagnostic instruments, the future will bring continued growth and understanding to the treatment of this disorder. DSM-III's creation of a separate category for the dissociative disorders gave legitimacy for the condition. A number of landmark publications in the 1980s devoted special issues to a discussion of multiple personalities. In 1994, DSM-IV set a primary criterion, which a patient must meet to be diagnosed with DID. Increased interest in the field remains strong, and distinguishing DID from other psychological illnesses remains the goal.

OTHER ULYSSES PRESS BOOKS

**Darcy's Passions: Pride and Prejudice
Retold Through His Eyes**
Regina Jeffers, $14.95
This novel captures the style and humor of Jane
Austen's novel while turning the entire story
upside down. It presents Darcy as a man in
turmoil. His duty to his family and estate demand
he choose a woman of high social standing. But
what his mind tells him to do and what his heart
knows to be true are two different things. After
rejecting Elizabeth, he soon discovers he's in love
with her. But the independent Elizabeth rejects
his marriage proposal. Devastated, he must search
his soul and transform himself into the man she
can love and respect.

**Darcy's Temptation: A Sequel to Jane
Austen's Pride & Prejudice**
Regina Jeffers, $14.95
By changing the narrator to Mr. Darcy, *Darcy's
Temptation* presents new plot twists and fresh
insights into the characters' personalities
and motivations. Four months into the new
marriage, all seems well when Elizabeth
discovers she's pregnant. However, a family
conflict that requires Darcy's personal attention
arises because of Georgiana's involvement with
an activist abolitionist. On his return journey
from a meeting to address this issue, a much
greater danger arises. Darcy is attacked on the
road and, when left helpless from his injuries,
he finds himself in the care of another woman.

Mr. Darcy Presents His Bride: A Sequel to Jane Austen's Pride & Prejudice
Helen Halstead, $14.95

When Elizabeth Bennet marries Mr. Darcy, she's thrown into the exciting world of London society. Elizabeth is drawn into a powerful clique for which intrigue is the stuff of life and rivalry the motive. Her success, it seems, can only come at the expense of good relations with her husband.

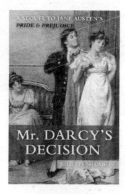

Mr. Darcy's Decision: A Sequel to Jane Austen's Pride & Prejudice
Juliette Shapiro $14.95

Mr. and Mrs. Fitzwilliam Darcy begin their married life blissfully, but it is not long before their tranquility is undermined by social enemies. Concern mounts with the sudden return of Elizabeth's sister Lydia. Alarming reports of seduction, blackmail and attempts to keep secret the news of another's confinement dampens even Elizabeth's high spirits.

Captain Wentworth's Persuasion: Jane Austen's Classic Retold Through His Eyes
Regina Jeffers, $14.95

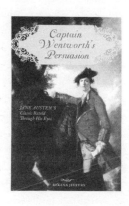

Insightful and dramatic, this novel re-creates the original style, themes, and sardonic humor of Jane Austen's novel while turning the entire tale on its head in a most engaging fashion. Readers hear Captain Wentworth's side of this tangled story in the revelation of his thoughts and emotions.

To order these books call 800-377-2542 or 510-601-8301, fax 510-601-8307, e-mail ulysses@ulyssespress.com, or write to Ulysses Press, P.O. Box 3440, Berkeley, CA 94703. All retail orders are shipped free of charge. California residents must include sales tax. Allow two to three weeks for delivery.

ABOUT THE AUTHOR

≈ ≈ ≈

REGINA JEFFERS, an English teacher for thirty-nine years, considers herself a Jane Austen enthusiast. She is the author of several novels, including *Darcy's Passsions*, *Darcy's Temptation*, *Captain Wentworth's Persuasion,* and *Vampire Darcy's Desire*. A Time Warner Star Teacher and Martha Holden Jennings Scholar, Jeffers often serves as a consultant in language arts and media literacy. Currently living outside Charlotte, North Carolina, she spends her time with her writing.